I Got Stinky Feet
Volume Two

Fools, Losers and Idiots

By Dennis Domrzalski

ISBN 978-0-9817869-0-2

Library of Congress Control Number: 2008905221

Illustrations by Dan Florentino

This book is printed on acid free paper

LOGAN SQUARE PRESS
ALBUQUERQUE, NM
U.S.A.

Also by Dennis Domrzalski

Strange Happenings

I Got Stinky Feet, Volume One

Praise for Volume One of *I Got Stinky Feet*

"The kind of book Mark Twain would have written if he had had a motorcycle. A sustained and hilarious assault on everything that is cheesy, cheap, fake, phony, pretentious and politically correct in the U.S."
—Mark Sienkiewicz, Metz, France

"Deadly funny! Domrzalski made me laugh out loud with this amazing tale. This is not just a very funny book; it is larded with many deadly truths."
—Maurice Possley, author of Everybody Pays

"Gut-busting, hilarious, a breezy read, no holds-barred story telling. Just about everyone you can think of gets reamed in these pages. A wild ride from start to finish."
—Weekly Alibi

"An adventure story that contains wit and oddball wisdom."
—Albuquerque Journal

"I had that Hunter S. Thompsonesque experience that usually only reading Hunter S. Thompson provides. Not the druggy Thompson, but the road-trip, hypocrisy-exposing, bombast male writer take-America-by-the-balls writing. Domrzalski's language is vivid, his experiences rendered in great detail with personal observations about where he's come from—and where he's going—that propel the reader to want an adventure of his—or her—own."
—Julia Goldberg, Santa Fe Reporter

"Gut-busting funny. An adventure story of the first order, one that doesn't let reality or logic get in the way."
—Ben Ikenson

"I laughed so hard I choked. This book is killing me. The funniest book I've ever read."
—Mike Gallegos

To my brother Steve and the boys on the corner and all the fun we had.

In Volume One

They would save the wicked from the pious, the rich from the poor, torch the rain forests, scar the tundra, eat their shoes and die a thousand times over if necessary. Yes, Dennis and his pal Dave are off on the nuttiest adventure of all time: a cross-country motorcycle trip begun from the frozen Midwest on the first day of winter. Along the way they've waged desperate battles against humanity's most dangerous enemies: poets, wine connoisseurs, shoe sniffers, creative writers and square dancers. And they've unraveled some of life's greatest mysteries, like why old people walk so slow. For blowhard Dave it's been a way to awe a grateful world with his supreme boldness; for his loyal companion Dennis, a chance to recover from being dumped by the peerless Shirley Kozlowski.

In Volume One these two dug up graves, escaped from car-trunk brain surgeons, slaughtered deserving idiots, met every crazy imaginable, ruined countless lives and wreaked physical and emotional havoc on a nationwide scale.

In Volume Two the guys do battle with more fools, losers and idiots: newspaper editors, sleazy lawyers, dimwitted frat boys, stingy barkeepers, fat people, Missourians, love-sick loners and demented gardeners. And they come up against the sickest, most twisted and unsanitary group of people the world has ever known.

How do they make out? Join us for the continuing adventures of Dennis and Dave.

CONTENTS

The object of life is not to be on the side of the majority, but to escape finding oneself in the ranks of the insane.

—Marcus Aurelius

Chapter 1

A Ranger Abused

Refreshed and relaxed after a couple of weeks rest, we moved on. Since we were in Arizona, we decided to visit the Grand Canyon.

There are some fools, who, in feeble attempts to be witty and clever, will say that the greatest natural wonder in the world is nothing more than a big ditch. But I won't do that. Others who see the canyon will bore you with their inept attempts to describe this monster. I won't do that either. Any attempt to describe the canyon always fails to relate its true majesty.

I will say this: The haze that hangs over the canyon and the distances involved—it's three hundred miles long and at least a mile wide—in the scene serve to soften, dull and blur every edge and crag so that you get the impression that you're looking at a painting by an artist who forgot his eyeglasses the day he painted it, or that you yourself need glasses. I squinted my eyes to sharpen my view, but it didn't work. The whole scene looked fuzzy. And there is a stillness and quiet at the canyon that is maddening. I expected such a scene of natural violence and destruction to be loud with the sounds of rushing water and crashing boulders and the earth being torn apart, but there was nothing but quiet and stillness.

There's another thing. The canyon's reddish-brown rock walls are all chipped and crumbled and gouged and tunneled and wrecked so that they look like giant redwood stairs that have suffered enormous termite and rot damage.

There is no sense in walking down to the floor of the canyon when you can stand on the rim and get a bigger and better view without working up a sweat. But I was lured into the walk down the narrow trails by the idea that I'd be descending a mile and two billion years into the earth's history. Although the walk down was fun and scenic—especially when we tried to hit people on the canyon floor with rocks—I was disappointed at its end. For there I was two billion years back into history and yet I saw no old buildings or old people or

1

rusted cars or rusted beer cans or odd-looking animals or dinosaurs or anything. From what I could tell it was still the same day as when we had started the walk down, except that it was a couple of hours later. I found a rock that I thought had writing on it that said: "Igor: I will pay you wild boar's head if you vote me be Big Man of Cave. Igana, she has nice hairy bottom. Excite me. Yours, Rock." That's what I thought it said, but Dave said I was crazy and it wasn't so. And after studying the rock for an hour or so I realized that the writing was something out of my imagination. So for me, the idea of being able to travel back two billion years into history was a fraud.

Bored and disappointed with the old rocks, I let my eyes wander up to the sky, where, zigzagging and circling against its dark-blue backdrop, were black dots about the size of a period. Actually, they were birds—eagles, I figured. I had always dreamed about being a bird; about being able to fly free and easy and drift on the winds and go anywhere I wanted without restriction, and about being able to crap on people's heads and fly away. After a while, one of the eagles took a sudden plunge and separated from the others. It was diving for food, I figured, for a rat or a mouse or a deer or some other unfortunate prey that would soon be hooked in its talons, splattered against a rock and picked to death by its sharp beak. I waited for the eagle to catch its prey and to level off, but it didn't. It kept diving. Suddenly I was scared.

"We probably look like mice to that eagle, and it's coming after us. We've got to run and hide!" I screamed to Dave.

"Nonsense," he said. "I am a man, not a mouse. The eagle can see that I am a bold man and that I'll devour it before it can get me. I am not afraid."

I was scared, though, and nervously watched as the speck of eagle kept diving and growing larger. It grew from a dot to a large blob the size of a garbage can lid. As it got closer it gained a fuzzy outline and I was able to make out two wings. It kept coming and soon I saw two more wings.

"It's a mutated eagle!" I shouted. "With four wings it's got to be the fastest flying eagle around!"

"Idiot!" Dave shot back. "Those aren't wings. They're arms and legs! That's not an eagle. It's a human! A man! He's falling!"

The man landed about forty yards away. We ran to him. I nearly threw up. Drop a ripe tomato onto a sidewalk from a second-story window and you'll get an idea of what he looked like. He was a forest ranger—that we could tell by his green uniform. We could also tell that he was dead. Dave took off the light jacket he was wearing and covered the ranger's face with it. Then we both knelt beside the guy and began to pray. About half way through the prayer, the ranger moaned. He was alive!

"It's amazing how God answered my prayer," Dave said. "I prayed for him to come back to life. The prayers of a bold man are always answered."

He took the jacket off the ranger's face, crumpled it into a ball and put it under his head as a pillow. I opened my canteen and moistened the ranger's lips and forehead with water poured onto a handkerchief. The guy moaned again.

"Don't worry," I said. "The handkerchief hasn't been used. There's no snot on it." He groaned some more, and I, sensing he was in enormous pain, tried to comfort him.

"It hurts, I know, but don't worry, kind and good man. The pain will end soon because pretty soon you'll be dead. You can't possibly survive a fall like this." He moaned again. I was getting impatient.

"Is it the prayers you don't like? Not suitable to your denomination? We'll say any prayer you like—Protestant, Catholic, Moslem, anything. Unless, of course, you're an atheist. And if that's the case we'll take our prayers back and you'll go back to being dead. Because there's no sense in wasting a prayer on an atheist. So be careful about what you ask for. And don't be picky either, because there isn't a lot we can do for you."

He moaned some more and tried to speak, but I begged him not to. There was no sense in him wasting the little strength that he had, I told him. But he persisted. His voice was weak, no louder than a whisper, and his speech was slurred. He eventually mumbled out something that we could understand.

"M... Mi... Missssouri," he said.

"Don't worry, friend," I said, "we'll make sure that you're buried there. It won't be long now, anyway, you're going fast."

Amazingly, he had the strength to be terrified at those words. His eyes bulged out; he raised his head slightly, shook it from side to side and stuttered out:

"Nnnn, noooo Missouri. Haaate that state." His head dropped and his eyes closed and I thought he was dead for sure. But suddenly his eyes opened again and he started talking. Again I pleaded for him not to speak, but the plea was ignored. There was something eerie about the situation. The ranger should have been dead, and here he was talking. It seemed to me that some force, perhaps God, was making him speak. I was convinced that he wouldn't die until he told his story or made his last confession. His voice, strangely enough, had changed. It was louder, clearer and stronger than before, and we could easily understand him. But still, the voice had a painful, moaning quality to it that made me cry. We knew he didn't have much time left so we let him talk and never interrupted once. He said:

"My name is Joe, Joe Atkinson. I'm a ranger and I give tours up on the rim. Been doing it for twenty-five years now, since I was twenty-five years old, and never until today have I wished for another job. When I got to the ranger station this morning there was a group of people standing outside waiting for a tour. There was about thirty of 'em or so—men, women, children, babies—all kinds. I figured that they were from Missouri—ohhh."

The ranger paused and let out a moan filled with so much horror that I wanted to run and hide when I heard it. In a minute or two, he continued his story:

"I figured they were from Missouri because they were all wearing t-shirts that said, 'I'm from Missouri. Show me!' written across the fronts and backs. Well, I walked right past 'em and went into the office and checked in with my supervisor, and then I went back out and looked them people over for a while. I always do that when I've got a large group. You've got to. You never know who you might run across these days. There are so many crazies out there. And I just like to get a feeling for the people, you know, gauge 'em, so I can decide how to conduct the tour. Some people are real nature experts and history buffs and want a long, detailed tour, and some just want to look at the scenery and take it all in. No two groups are alike, and you've just got to gauge 'em before you go out.

"Well those people looked real friendly and nice. They were all laughing and smiling and talking, and so I just got their attention and introduced myself. I didn't tell 'em anything fancy—it was real simple. I just told 'em, 'Good morning folks and welcome to the Grand Canyon. My name is Joe Atkinson and I'll be your tour guide today.'

"But I'll tell you, for some reason that wiped the smiles off of their faces. They just stood there with these dumb, quizzical looks and stared at me. After a while, this big fat man they called Bismarck—ohhhhh." He paused again as if sickened by the word, moaned, closed his eyes and squirmed in pain. It was more than a minute before he calmed down enough to continue:

"Well, Bismarck walked up to me and said, 'Can you prove that?' I had no idea what he was talking about and so I asked him, 'Prove what?' And then he said, 'That you're Joe Atkinson.' I thought he was kidding, you know, being from Missouri, they have odd senses of humor and all, and I figured it was a practical joke and so I laughed. I wanted to let them know that I was one of them, that I could laugh at their jokes. But I shouldn't a done that. The fat man got real mad—I mean real mad—and he pointed his finger in my face and said, 'No joke Jackson. Can you prove that?' And then I said, 'Prove it, why?'

"That got him even madder. His face got all red—I thought he was going to explode—and he shouted at me, 'Why? Why I'll give you why.' And then he stomped on my feet and shouted, 'Because we're from Missouri! Don't you know our state motto, you buffoon?' When I told him 'no,' the whole group started coming at me. They looked mean, like I had insulted them. Fat Bismarck grabbed my shirt with his stubby fingers and started counting. I thought he was going to smash me in the face with his fist. When Bismarck counted to three the crowd stopped cold, and all at once, in unison, like they were a choir, they screamed as loud as they could, 'Frothy eloquence will neither convince nor satisfy us; we're from Missouri. You'll have to show us! We're from the Show Me state! You'll have to show us!'

"When they finished, Bismarck was grinding his teeth and snorting like a pig, and he put his face right up close to mine and he said real loud, 'That's why, now let's see some IDs Yogi!' I was going to argue with him but that crowd wouldn't let me. As soon as Bismarck stopped, they all started in, and just like before, they shouted all at once, 'If you don't show us some IDs Yogi, we will break your neck. We're from Missouri. You'll have to show us!'

"I'll tell you, that convinced me to run. I had the feeling that these people were screwy. Who ever heard of asking someone to prove that he is who he says he is? Bismarck still had my shirt so I kicked him in the leg, and when he let go, I ran into the office and locked the door. I mean, I wasn't going to give a tour to a bunch of lunatics like that. My supervisor was sleeping, like he always does, and so I woke him up and told him what had happened and asked him to kick those people out of the park. But he wouldn't do it. No. He told me that they were the public, the taxpayers, and that they signed my paycheck and that I had to do what they wanted. And then he said, and I remember these words exactly, he said, 'Joe, if you don't, they'll complain to Washington and you'll lose your job.'

"Lose my job! I didn't want that to happen. I love this job. It's the only one I ever wanted. I worked hard to get it. I went to college for six years and I worked nights seven days a week to pay off my tuition and my congressman for pulling strings and putting me on the list ahead of other applicants and getting me the job. I jumped ahead of thousands of people on the list. That cost a lot of money and a good chunk of dignity. Ever since then I've had to tell the congressman that his ideas are brilliant. No, I didn't want to lose my job. And I'm close to getting a supervisor's position, too, and I don't want to lose that. I want to be able to come in to work and sleep too. So anyway, I went out and showed them my IDs—showed them every one I had, too. I showed them my driver's license, Social Security card, my old draft card, voter's registration card, my college ID, my old military ID. I even showed them my birth certificate. But they weren't satisfied. No. They wanted to talk to the doctor who delivered me! Can you believe that? The doctor who delivered me! He's been dead for ten years. When I told them that they got mad. They didn't believe me, and they wanted me to prove that too. I don't even know where the man is buried. I just know he's dead.

Show Us, Yogi!

"Well, I don't know how, but I satisfied them and we started the tour. The first thing I showed them was a Ponderosa Pine. It's a special tree, the largest of

5

its kind in the area. And, there's a family of Bald Eagles nesting on top of it. Well, I told them all about the tree. I told them how old it was, how much water it expires a day, how much it probably weighs, and then I pointed to the top and said, 'Folks, way up there on top where you can't see, there's a family of Bald Eagles nesting.'

"I thought they'd be impressed, but they weren't. They didn't get excited and look up and strain their eyes and necks like most people do. They just stood there and stared at me with those stupid, quizzical looks on their faces. Finally, Bismarck walked up to me and said, 'That won't wash Ferguson. We're from Missouri. You'll have to show us.'

"Show 'em? Can you believe that? They wanted me to climb up the tree and bring down the eagles and the nest and, oh, I'll tell you that I was mad. I wanted to tell them people off, and I would have, too, but I knew that if I did they'd complain to Washington and I'd lose my job. So I climbed the tree. It was terrible. The tree had such a large circumference that I could barely get my arms around it. I kept slipping and sliding down it, and I ripped my clothes on the bark and scraped and scratched my arms until they were bleeding. But I got that eagle down. And when I showed it to them I got angry. Oh boy, did I ever! They stood there and stared at it—it was a baby eagle—and they looked as stupid as they did before. They didn't say anything. Bismarck was the only one who spoke. He called me Byron and asked if the eagle was real. I couldn't believe that! I mean, the thing was chirping and struggling all the time to get away. Anybody with half a brain could see that it was real. I was disgusted. I mean, how do you please people like that? I just handed the bird to them and told them to see for themselves. You should have seen that crowd then! All those hands started feeling the eagle and poking at its eyes and pulling its beak and legs and yanking out its feathers, and ohhh, it made me so sick that I grabbed the eagle back from them because they would have killed it. I took it and climbed up the tree and put that poor creature back in its nest.

"And I'll tell you, I wish now that I would have stayed up there with it. And I wanted to, too. But I knew that if I didn't come down they'd complain to Washington. Well, it went like that for a while. Every time I told them an interesting fact about something, they'd stand there and look stupid and scratch their heads, and Bismarck would call me Yogi or Walsh or Nelson or Matthew or Bedford or something—he even called me Bathsheba—and tell me that they were from Missouri and that I'd have to show them and prove whatever I just told them. They had me doing everything—climbing more trees, sticking my head in bears' mouths, eating lizards and roots and berries, hollowing out logs and tree trunks, racing deer, starting rock slides and building log cabins. They even made me eat my shoes because I told them that some pioneers had once beat starvation by eating theirs. I told them that Congress was a worthwhile institution that benefited the nation, and they asked me to prove that too. But they gave me a break on that one because even they realized that it was an unprovable statement.

6

"But about halfway through the tour I learned my lesson. I shut up and didn't give them any facts that they could use against me. If I saw an unusual tree or something I pointed to it and said, 'That's a tree,' or 'That's a bush.' I didn't tell them what the Indians and pioneers used it for or made out of it or what it's used for today or how it got its name or anything. I gave e'em plain, simple facts. It worked, too. I didn't have to show them anything special after that. But I'll tell you, keeping my mouth shut was the hardest thing I've ever done. I mean, giving details and facts and explaining things—giving life to a tour and making it interesting and fun—is natural for me. That's what I live for. And not giving facts and details was like holding my breath. I can only do it for so long before my body's natural mechanisms take over and start me doing it. To hold my tongue and give a dull, lifeless tour took all the strength I had. But I had to do it because I knew that they were just waiting for me to screw up so they could order me to show them something and prove something.

"And let me tell you this: The longer I went without giving them a fact, the madder they got. It was as if they were alcoholics and I was withholding liquor from them. It was frightening. They became irritable and started swearing at me and throwing rocks at my head and at animals. After a while, they tried to trick me into giving them facts. Every time they saw something unusual they started asking all kinds of questions. Ohhh. I can still hear those dumb, stupid voices. 'How many trees are there in this forest, Yogi? Say Bedford, how much does that boulder that's the size of a house weigh? Do trees taste good? Is your boss a transvestite?'

"They had me so confused. A couple of times I slipped and started giving them facts, but I always caught myself just in time and stopped before I said anything that would get me in trouble. It made them angrier and angrier. And I'll tell you, it was a losing battle for me. My strength was going. I knew that I couldn't hold out much longer and that if the tour lasted as long as it should have that I'd break down and give 'em a fact and be a sorry man. I was scared, but I smartened up, used my head, and rushed up the tour. I cut back on my talking and quickened the pace of our walk. Then I got us jogging, and then I shut up completely and speeded up the jog until we were sprinting through the woods. We rushed by everything, and finally, when we broke through the trees and got to the rim of the canyon, I just pointed out at the canyon and said, 'There's the canyon, folks.' I didn't tell 'em how deep it was or how many different kinds of rocks they could see or how long the Colorado River has been eroding the rock or anything. I didn't give them anything that they could use against me, just 'There's the canyon, folks,' and *that* they could see for themselves.

"I'll tell you, right then I was the happiest man alive because that was the end of the tour! I was exhausted. My willpower and strength for withholding facts was nearly gone. Just a little longer and I would have broken down and gushed out a million facts. I was so happy. We stood there and stared out at the canyon for a while. Nobody spoke for a few minutes. Finally, Bismarck asked me in a real mean voice, 'Is that about it, Milford? Is that the tour?' When I said that it was, he kicked me in the leg and started to turn away. But there was a mean, sneaky look in his eyes, and suddenly he shouted to the crowd to get ready to return to the ranger station and leave the canyon. And then he spit. It was a signal! Because when the saliva hit the ground all thirty of those people turned around and started shouting questions at me again. They were screaming out the questions, all thirty of them at once. They were trying one last time to get facts out of me.

"'Yogi, what is this? What is that? How many teeth do bears have? How many needles are on that tree?' It was terrible. I fell to my knees, put my hands over my ears, shook my head and started shouting out don't knows. 'Don't know, don't know, don't know' is all I said. I was sick to my stomach. I didn't have much strength left. I knew they were going to break me. I started crying. They were acting like maniacs, jumping up and down and stomping their feet and shaking their fists at me and pounding their fists on the ground. Their faces were all red and they were foaming at the mouth and they were all screaming questions at me—question after question after question. I uncovered my ear to scratch my nose and I heard a question, 'Say Hodgkins, what is the temperature of the sun's surface?' God help me, I pleaded to myself, because I needed help right there. I knew the answer to that last question. I knew that the temperature of the sun's surface is about ten thousand degrees Fahrenheit, and I knew that if I told them that they'd make me go to the sun and prove it, and my god, I don't have enough vacation or sick time built up for a trip like that. The answer started coming up out of the back of my throat. I could feel it, actually feel it! And then it got up on the back of my tongue and moved to the middle and then to the tip and I started opening my mouth and forming a word—the word ten—with my lips and I knew I was doomed, and then they stopped. No more questions! They gave up. They didn't know that they had broken me; they were making so much noise. It was a miracle.

"But I'll tell you, those people were mean, angry and full of hate. They were glaring at me, and their hands were clenched into fists, and their noses were crinkled up, and their eyes were squinted, and their teeth were showing and they were growling at me just like mad dogs. Then Bismarck swore at me and called me an idiot, and then he yelled and swore at the others and told them to start back to the ranger station, and they started back and I was happier than ever. But just as they started walking back, a couple of the kids started pushing each other, you know, horse playing. Well, one of them fell into me and I was standing right on the edge of the canyon and I lost my balance and almost fell off the edge. They almost killed me! My nerves were so shot by then that I just blew up and lost my temper and yelled at the children. I was screaming at them. I told them that if I had been pushed a little harder I would have fallen over the edge of the canyon and plunged one mile to my death.

"Oh. Before I knew what I was saying, the words were out! I had given them a fact! I never felt so sick in my life, not even now. I was hoping and praying

They Made Him Jump

that they hadn't heard it, but when I looked up I saw what I had feared. They had formed a semi-circle around me and surrounded me on three sides, with my only route of escape out over the rim. They stared at me with those dumb looks, but I could see that they were gleeful and gloating. Bismarck, smiling like a fool, walked up to me and said, 'Fall over and die, huh Yogi? Well.' And then he raised his arm and started counting, and when he hit three, he and the rest of the group shouted: 'We're from Missouri, you'll have to show us!' Then Bismarck called the two kids forward and ordered them to push each other into me. They did, but I was able to brace myself, and they weren't strong enough to knock me over the rim. I could have stayed there all day, and I would have, too, but I knew that if I did they'd complain to Washington. So the next time one of them fell into me I jumped. They'll be down in a few hours to see for themselves if I died or not."

The ranger paused here. By his face I could see that he was realizing the implications of what he had said. When he fully comprehended the situation he let out the sorriest, most pathetic and sickening moan I have ever heard, and said:

"I hope I die before they get here." He paused again and shook and trembled violently and shot me the horrified, panicky and doomed look of a man who finally realizes that the only reason he is married is because he himself uttered the words "I do," and continued:

"Because if I don't, I'll—I'll lose my job."

Those were the last clear words he spoke. He weakened and his voice trailed off into a whispered slur, and in a minute or two his eyes closed for good.

"I will avenge your death kind and good ranger," Dave said solemnly as he shook a fist at the sky. "Fat Bismarck and his vile friends will suffer a bazillion times more than you did. A bold man says so. When I'm finished the world will know that the state motto of Missouri is the stupidest around and that those who use it are idiots. But good ranger, why you jumped and believed those absurdities about losing your job is a mystery. Everyone knows that any attempt to fire you based on the Missourians' complaints would have been tied up for years by your federal employee union."

CHAPTER 2

Confronting The Missourians

After praying over his body for a few minutes, we wrapped the ranger in our jackets, for we didn't want his insides to spill out, and picked up his body—I the legs and Dave the arms—and began the long walk up the trail to the rim, where we intended to report his murder. Three hours later and near the rim, we came across a group of overweight people who were on their way down to the canyon floor. The fattest one had a large, flat nose. We knew immediately who they were: Fat Bismarck and the Missourians.

Bismarck saw the body and wailed:

"Poor man! Blessed, confused creature, why is it, why oh why did you jump and commit suicide? Life was not as bad as you imagined. We tried to counsel this lost soul, this tired man who saw bleakness where we saw hope, and sadness where we saw laughter. He told us of his plans for suicide and we tried unsuccessfully to change his mind. On your knees everybody and pray for his soul. Pray for his deliverance. Ask the Almighty to forgive him his sin."

Before the first knee touched the ground, Dave barked out a different command.

"Up, you vile, despicable hypocrites! You cowardly murderers! Liars! Reptiles! We know what happened! The ranger told us his story! We will avenge his murder! You people will pay the most terrible price," he said in the most hate-filled voice I had ever heard. He glared with a demonic intensity at the

Fat Bismarck

SHOW ME
I'M FROM MIZZURA

11

crowd, and they looked scared. Bismarck tried to bluster his way out of the predicament.

"My friend, you appear to be intelligent, and I'm sure that you are, but you must consult your dictionary and look up the difference between murder and suicide," he said with a forced laugh and a wave of his arm. "For it would be dreadful to have two mistakes made in one day. We pity this good man as do you."

"I ain't your friend. Get it straight. Listen closely. I'll talk slow so you understand. We know what happened. Or maybe you'll understand this: We know the truth."

Whether it was Dave's hatred, or that final word, but something affected them, even Bismarck. They stared silently at each other with worried and desperate faces that acknowledged the need for a plan of attack or escape. After glaring at them a few minutes longer, Dave snarled:

"We're going now to report this man's murder and the fact that you witless pigs killed him. Mark the words of a bold man: The truth always wins. Youse will pay. And the world will know just how stupid your state motto is."

The Missourians followed as we tramped to the park headquarters where a small crowd of officials and the ranger's wife had gathered, for Bismarck had reported a suicide after the ranger had jumped. We placed the body on a large, wooden table in the middle of a meeting room. At our request more officials were called, including state, federal and local law enforcement authorities. The dead man's wife, a ranger herself with red hair and a figure that Dave said was incredible considering that she was almost fifty, sobbed and watered her husband's hand with tears as she clutched it protectively in hers and held it to her face and gently kissed it and rubbed it across her cheeks and caressed it with her slender fingers. She kissed that hand so lovingly and so often that I feared she was going to eat it.

"I realize that she liked the guy, but if she eats his hand, who knows what she'll do with the rest of him. We could lose a lot of evidence," I whispered to Dave. "Maybe we should point that out to the medical examiner."

"Good idea. *You* tell him. And I'll back you up seven hundred and forty-three percent as I ride the hell out of here. Stop thinking so much. It's hurting my head."

I took the answer to mean that my theory was slightly flawed. But I still wanted to give it a shot, and was about to say something, when the wife, while watering her husband's hand with her tears, shrieked:

"Why? Why? I thought we had heaven here on earth! Why did you not tell me of your internal demons? Why did you commit suicide?"

"Because, and I say this with an unbearable sadness, he hated all of your guts," Bismarck said as he tucked his t-shirt into the waistband of his dirty white shorts. "By your faces and your aggressive motions, I can see that you are offended, insulted and angry at those words. But please, remember that I am only the unfortunate messenger. I merely relate the sad, dreadful, insulting and hurtful thoughts that were concocted by the mind of another. To be brutally truthful, Ranger Joe was a troubled man—troubled in the worst way. He considered all of you in this room—his friends, associates, colleagues, supervisors and all of you law enforcement people—to be corrupt, inept, unimaginative and lazy. Bribe-takers and racketeers are the terms he used. He said that everyone in the National Park Service was corrupt and lazy. He said we had more to fear from law enforcement authorities than we did from all the crooks and murderers out there. He went on and on about how he tried to report all of you to the FBI and about how the FBI was itself corrupt. If there are any judges in the room, I must report that he considered you bribe-takers too. He said it was his goal to have you all convicted and imprisoned. He said he hated his co-workers.

"I myself bounded to your defense. I sat this confused and troubled man down and explained to him the errors of his thoughts. I told him what kind, good, wonderful, honest and talented people you all were. I suspect that it was his own inadequacies and his unwillingness to admit to his own glaring faults that led him to lash out at you and to try to try destroy your lives and careers. He hated himself. But rather than work to change and fix those things in himself that he hated and despised, rather than work to overcome his own faults, he decided to try to bring down others, to bring down you good folk. Why? Because it takes hard work to change yourself and overcome your weaknesses. Hard work. And, my friends, he recoiled from that hard work. He wanted to do it the easy way, the cheap way; the way that says, 'If I'm in a mud pit, rather than dragging myself out and cleaning off, I'll drag others down here with me so that they can keep me company in my wretched vileness.'

"We prayed as a group for him. We begged him to see that he, too, could find a decent way in life if only he took that first step. We begged him to see sunshine instead of darkness, love instead of hate, and honesty instead of corruption. We told him he could beat the depression that was suffocating his natural good will and his faith in his colleagues. We said that he could change his life and be happy, that he could love, live and prosper, and that there is always something good in life to be thankful for and always something to celebrate.

"We worked ourselves into a health-threatening exhaustion by pleading with him to change his attitude. We petitioned the Almighty to show mercy and forgiveness toward this man and to change his outlook and to save his life. But our humble supplications went unanswered, which must tell you something about the character of the ranger. If the all-forgiving Almighty saw no hope in him, saw no reason to cleanse his soiled soul, what were we as mere mortals to do? Our final benediction to heaven on his behalf, offered with tearful sincerity by us, was rejected as well. And when we finished that final prayer he jumped off the edge and plunged to his death. And I mean he jumped. He took a fifty-yard running start and nearly flew over the edge, shouting as he fell: 'Everyone I know is corrupt and dangerous!' We, of course, reported the incident immediately and started down to the canyon floor, hoping that he would have survived. But alas, it was not to be, and we believe that this tortured soul will find rest and comfort in the hereafter. We offer our condolences to the widow, along with our pledge to pray daily for his troubled spirit. That is our story. I am told that these two gentlemen have a different version of events. I certainly want to hear it."

Before Dave could begin, the widow wailed: "Liar! Liar! How can you say such vile things? Especially about bounding to our defense! You're too fat to bound half an inch, let alone to someone's defense. Joseph loved and respected and admired his colleagues. He tried to emulate so many of you, saying always that he was blessed to be in such talented, exceptional and esteemed company, while he himself was so ordinary. He was lovingly optimistic, not morbidly depressed, and respectful of your talent and honesty. He did not make false accusations as this man asserts. He did not think you were corrupt. We were married for twenty-three years. Never once in that time did he speak disparagingly of any of you. I believed in Joseph for twenty-three years, and I believe in him now. I will stand by him. Nothing—nothing— can shake my faith, trust and belief in him. I will defend him until I die."

Throw Him To The Jackals!

"Kind and good woman, I mean not to hurt by relating these stinging comments. But they are true. And even you, who loved Joseph for all those years, did not escape his poisonous accusations. He said you were a lousy forest ranger who didn't know the difference between a Silver Maple and an Arizona Sycamore, or between a Balsam and Lombardy Poplar. He said your tours were dull and boring and that your degree of knowledge about forestry qualified you to work in a toothpick factory, not a forest or a national park. He—"

"Beast! And pig! I'd kill you if you weren't already dead," she screamed as she frantically beat the ranger's corpse with her fists.

"Throw this pig's body to the jackals! That is, if we have any jackals out here. By the way, does anybody know what a jackal is?"

She had to be pulled of the body and dragged out of the room. When she was gone, Bismarck told everybody that we had our version of events. Dave told the ranger's story with authority, passion, power and eloquence, and when he finished, we were laughed out of the room and told to never return.

CHAPTER 3

Served And Sued

W e found a campsite nearby and drank heavily and brooded. But a couple of hours and two whiskey bottles later we turned to the idea of revenge to boost our spirits, and spent the rest of the night dreaming up ways to torture the Missourians. The talk so buoyed our spirits that we didn't care any more that no one believed our story, and we went to sleep happy in knowing that we had beaten depression.

The stabbing headache I had the next morning wasn't made any better by the loud, shrill voice that was shouting our names in front of our tent. I crawled out into the bright sun, rubbed my eyes and demanded of the young guy in the dark-blue suit, blazing white shirt and blue tie who was shouting that he stop and explain himself.

"I'm here to serve you," he said cheerfully as he dug into a brown leather briefcase he held in one hand, and as Dave crawled out of the tent.

"Serve us?" I asked, "Forget it. We don't need liquor right now. We had enough last night. We could use some food, though. But it doesn't look like you have any. And seriously, I think you're overdressed for the job."

"Fool," he said with a giant grin, "I'm here to serve you with papers. You have been sued—named as defendants in a lawsuit—and I am here to give you a copy of the lawsuit and assure that you have been properly served."

"Who's suing us?" Dave demanded.

"A Mister Bismarck."

"What's he suing us for?"

"Defamation and slander."

"Say what?"

"Say defamation and slander. He is seeking huge monetary damages from you two. He alleges that you have falsely accused him of murder and of being an obnoxious jerk. The lawsuit says that by relating Ranger Atkinson's story to a group of people yesterday you slandered him and caused severe and irreparable damage to his reputation in the community."

"But wait a minute," Dave said, "That story is true. He knows it's true. What kind of a jerk is he?"

15

"A big one," said the server. "Of course he knows the story is true, and that's why he's suing you. He wouldn't be a jerk if he sued you over something that wasn't true. That's what jerks do."

"Well then we'll take it to court and win. Justice will prevail," I said with a righteous indignation. "Right?"

"Wrong. The courts are no place for justice. You'll lose. Courts are not places were justice is meted out; they're places where disputes are resolved. Half the judges are on the take, so you can't expect justice from them. The other half are either on drugs or booze or some screwed up, misguided personal agenda that blinds them to reality and the law. Most of them are political hacks who will 'split the baby,' that is, who will give something to each party regardless of who is right or wrong. That means that even if you're wrong you get something from them, and if you're right you don't get all that you deserve. Everything is backwards in court. Black is white and white is black. Truth is bad and lies are good. You naive fools. Just, truthful and proper actions are condemned and punished, while unjust and improper actions and lies are applauded and rewarded.

"Let me give you a little quiz to show you how things work and prepare you for this sorrowful event. Say you take a large, heavy, metal hammer and deliberately smash yourself in the head with it and give yourself brain damage, whose fault is it?"

"Mine!" I shouted. "I did it to myself."

"Wrong. You go to court and collect damages from the hammer manufacturer for making a dangerous product and for failing to put a warning on it that says if you smash yourself in the head with a hammer you could hurt yourself. It's the manufacturer's fault. Here's another one. Say you take that same hammer and smash in an old lady's head with it and kill her? Whose fault is it and who goes to prison?"

"The hammer manufacturer!" I answered.

"Wrong again. It's the old lady's fault, and if she were still alive she should go to prison. Why? Because she should have known to get out of your way. Simply by being in your way or in your neighborhood, she provoked you into abnormal, hateful, murderous behavior.

"Here's another twist on murder. Say you just start killing people because you don't like them, whose fault is it and who goes to prison?"

This one I was ready for. "Adam and Eve!" I shouted.

"Close, but wrong."

"Then God's, because he made Adam and Eve and he made us all," I shot back.

"An excellent answer, but not the right one in this case. And the only reason for that is that no one can find God to serve him, but believe me, the lawyers are working on it. And they're also trying to figure out ways to collect damages from God. The theory on that one is, if you can get the guy into court and find him liable, you can probably get a judge to order him to poof you up a diamond or a gold mine or bundles of money, or at least a few thousand fish. The problem is, it's hard to track down an invisible guy. So, since he's not available, who do you sue for turning you into a murderer?"

"Cain," I said. "He's the first killer, the first murderer. I learned to kill from my distant brother or cousin or uncle or great uncle or whatever."

"Wrong and right. You're getting there. He would be another excellent choice, but he's dead and unavailable, and it's doubtful that he left an estate that you can raid for damages."

"I could sue everybody else on the planet because they're all relatives of his."

"Good thinking, but an impractical choice. Can't fit several billion people into a courtroom."

"I give up. Who do we sue in this case?"

"Publishers. The people who print bibles. The story of Cain and Able is in the Bible. You learned to murder from Cain. By publishing the Bible, they subjected you to immoral and murderous ideas that caused you great psychological damage and caused you to kill. Publishers have billions of dollars. You can collect big-time from them.

"Here's another one. Say you boil water for tea or hot chocolate, and in the process of pouring it into a cup or mug, you spill it onto yourself and burn yourself? What do you do?"

"Race to the hospital?" I asked.

"No. You race to a lawyer's office and then to the courthouse and you sue. But who do you sue?"

"Yourself for being a careless, clumsy, irresponsible jerk?"

"Wrong. There's no such thing as personal responsibility in the courts. So, who do you sue when you've burned yourself with hot water?"

"The people who made the stove that heated up the water?"

"A pretty good choice, but not the right one. You sue the water company for delivering to your house a product that could be made dangerous—a product that could be heated up and made to burn you alive. They should be putting out a warning that says water can be heated and potentially burn you. Now, here's a twist on that case. Say you go into a restaurant and order hot coffee and then spill it on yourself and burn yourself. What do you do?"

"Scream 'Ouch!' or, 'Holy Jesus, I've burned myself, it hurts!'"

"No. Once again you sue. You sue the restaurant for failing to tell you that the hot stuff you ordered is hot, and that hot stuff can burn you if you spill it on yourself."

"But that seems like common sense. Everybody should know that."

"Ah, there's your mistake, relying on common sense. There is none anymore. It's an archaic, obsolete, discredited notion. Why should you rely on common sense or personal responsibility when you can blame someone else? Common sense is a dirty word in the legal system. If you ever use it in court you'll most likely be held in contempt and tossed into prison.

"Now here's the situation with your case. Even if everybody conceded that the story was true, you'd lose. Because, if it is true, you'd be showing Bismarck

17

to be the jerk, liar, cheat, murderer and sleazeball that he truly is. And if you do that, all the people out there who didn't know that about him, who thought he was a halfway decent guy, will now know that he's a sleaze and a cheat and they'll think less of him than they did before, and his reputation will have been damaged. He's probably worked hard to keep people from knowing that he's a jerk. So you two will lose."

"We're doomed!" I cried. "We're involved in litigation! We'll lose everything, even if we win! The lawyers will take all of our money. Our reputations will be ruined. I don't want to lose."

"Don't worry. We won't. How do you win court cases in Chicago?" Dave asked.

"Well, I—"

"You bribe the judge. It's simple. We'll bribe the judge and everything will be okay."

"Can't do that," said the server.

"Why not?" Dave asked.

"Because Bismarck has already bribed him."

"We'll spread around more money than he can. We'll out-bribe him. There ain't a judge or public official around who can't be bought. We'll give the black-robe money so he can buy cheap jewelry for his mistress. No big deal. We'll cut a better deal with him."

"No you won't. The judges out here are not like those in Chicago. These judges are honorable; they stick to their bribes. Once they're bought, they stay bought. Once they're bribed, they don't go and look for a bigger bribe from another party. That's dishonorable."

"Well, no matter, we'll fight this and get it over with."

"Good day and good luck," said the server.

Demanding To Serve God

Chapter 4

A Despicable Lawyer

We decided to represent ourselves, and filed our response to the lawsuit the next day. Our request for a quick proceeding was granted. The day after that we were in the office of Bismarck's attorney, a skinny, childish man in his forties who tilted his head when asking questions, and who, I later learned, had successfully sued his elderly mother to stop her from buying medication to control her high blood pressure because the spending emptied her bank account, which he was in line to inherit.

His office was in an old, stately, ten-room Victorian house that he had seized from clients—an elderly, blind, crippled couple who had lived there all fifty years of their marriage while raising their family—after they had failed to make the final, fifteen-dollar payment on a one-hundred-and-twelve-dollar legal fee they owed him. He had evicted the couple a few weeks earlier and they were living in a gravel parking lot in a shelter made out of sticks and cardboard boxes.

Unfortunately for the couple, the parking lot was owned by one of the lawyer's friends. The lawyer was preparing to sue them for trespass. He was also preparing to go to court to demand that the couple's seeing-eye dog be killed. He was angry because the dog had led the couple across a street he had been driving on, and since they walked slowly, he had been delayed by several seconds in getting to a meeting where he was to take all seventeen dollars and three cents from the bank account of a seven-year-old girl with leukemia he had sued. He was angry because the girl had left a few seconds before he arrived, and even though he gotten her money, the delay had cost him the opportunity to see the child cry.

The couple was without their dog for the time being because the lawyer had convinced authorities to seize it on grounds that the oldsters had been cruel to it. It was being kept in a private pound where the charges for its room and board were accumulating daily, and growing well beyond the couple's means to pay.

The lawyer was also preparing a lawsuit against his unborn daughter, hoping to recover future earnings from her as damages for his loss of sleep caused by his wife's complaining at night about the discomfort of being pregnant. But he decided to delay the action, figuring he had a better chance of recovering money from his wife, and so he sued her. He had a habit of pinching and rubbing the seat of his pants with his thumb and index finger and then sticking the fingers underneath his nose and sniffing heartily. The habit appeared to give him immense satisfaction and pleasure, because the only time he smiled was when he sniffed his fingers.

We were there so he could take our depositions, or question us about the facts of the case. It was to be a quick, pleasant and simple exercise in truth finding, he said to me as I sat in a chair directly across a large wooden table from him.

"We're looking only for the truth," he told me. I was ready, for what could be more fun than the truth, I thought to myself as I waited for his first question. He began:

"Exactly when was it, five, ten or fifteen years ago that you began hating my client and meticulously plotting to destroy his reputation and ruin his life by slandering and defaming him?"

"I, uh, uh. Jeez. I, I can't answer that."

"You can't answer it? You mean you don't remember when you started hating my client and plotting to ruin him?"

"Uh, uh. I, uh. No."

"So you do remember? Why don't you tell us when?"

"Uh, no!"

"No! Are you refusing to answer questions? Because if that's the case I will move for sanctions against you."

"No! I, uh. I can't answer it because I didn't know your client until a few days ago. I didn't know him five or ten or fifteen years ago."

"So you hated him and set out to destroy his reputation when you didn't even know him? You hated and ruined him from afar? Do you always try to destroy people you don't know?"

"No. Uh. I—"

"No what?"

"No, I don't always try to destroy people that I don't know."

"So you try to destroy just some of them?"

"No!"

"So you try to destroy all of them?"

"No!"

"Let's get this straight. You don't destroy all of them and you don't destroy some of them, right?"

"Right!"

"So the only stranger you've tried to slander and destroy is my client, right?"

"No!"

"Then there are others?"

"No!"

"Let me go back to an earlier question. You didn't even know my client and you hated him and you tried to destroy his career from afar, is that correct?"

"No. It is not correct."

"What is not correct?"

"That I tried to destroy your client from afar?"

"Okay. So you tried to destroy him from close up?"

"No!"

"I don't get it. First you say that you didn't try to destroy him from afar, and now you say you didn't try to destroy him from close up. Are you lying to me?"

"No!"

"Then why the discrepancy?"

"I didn't try to destroy your client!"

"So you ruined his reputation by accident?"

"No!"

"Okay. I think I've got it. You didn't *try* to destroy my client, and you didn't do it by accident, so what you're telling me is that this was

He Sued A Seven-Year-Old With Leukemia

something that came so naturally and easily to you that you didn't have to put a lot of effort into it. Is that correct?"

"No!"

"No what?"

"It was not something that was effortless."

"Well then, how much effort did it require on your part to destroy him?"

"None!"

"So it *was* effortless?"

"No!"

"Well, did it require a medium amount of effort to slander him?"

"No!"

"A little amount?"

"No!"

"Do you even remember how much effort it required?"

"No!"

"Is it because you don't care that you ruined my client?"

"No."

"So you do care?"

"Yes!"

"If you care, then why did you slander him?"

"I didn't!"

"You didn't care?"

"No!"

"That's what I thought. You just didn't care, did you?"

"No!"

"Are you having trouble here today? Trouble with these questions?"

"Yes."

"Is that because you slandered my client and are ashamed of it?"

"No!"

"You're not ashamed of having slandered an innocent man?"

"No!"

"Good god! Then you're proud of the fact that you ruined his reputation?"

"No!"

"Then you do feel remorse?"

"No!"

"I didn't think so!"

"Look, I can tell this is getting rough for you. You're sweating and twitching and looking desperately at your partner for help. But I have only a few more questions, so hang in there, okay?"

"Sure."

"Is my client a sleazy, despicable, vile, filthy liar who should be hanged from a tree by his tongue?"

"I, uh. I, uh. I—"

"Just answer yes or no and stop trying to delay this deposition."

"I, uh—"

"Yes or no?"

"No!"

"Would you agree that if someone's not a liar then they must be telling the truth?"

"Sure."

"And if my client says you defamed him, and you say you didn't, then who's the liar?"

"I, I—"

"You or him?"

"You!"

"Me! You're calling me a liar? You don't care who you defame, do you?"

"No! I mean—"

"You mean you will lie about anybody, anyplace, anytime. Right?"

"Wrong!"

"Please, I don't want to defame *you*. Tell me what I've got wrong."

"I will not lie about anybody, anyplace, anytime."

"I believe you."

"Good. Glad we straightened that out."

"Let's straighten it out further. Since you don't lie about anybody, anyplace, anytime, the only person you lie about is my client, right? You've saved it all for him, haven't you?"

The questioning went on like that for several more hours. When it ended, I could barely find my way out of the room, had developed an immense dislike for this alleged truth seeker, and had the sick feeling that I hadn't helped our case too much.

We deposed Bismarck the next day. Dave asked the questions:

"Is your name Bismarck?"

"No."

"Are you overweight?"

"No."

"How old are you?"

"I don't recall."

"Are you from Missouri?"

"I would think that since you profess to know so much about me you would know where I'm from."

"You *are* from Missouri."

"I don't hear a question."

"What were you doing at the Grand Canyon?"

"I have never been to the Grand Canyon."

"That's a lie! We saw you there—on the trail—with our own eyes!"

"Your partner there wears glasses, which means his vision is flawed. If you believe that you saw me at the Grand Canyon then you're lying."

"Why did you kill Ranger Atkinson?"

"I don't know a Ranger Atkinson."

"Why did you kill the ranger?"

"I have not killed a ranger."

"But he jumped off the edge and plunged to his death!"

"If a ranger jumped off the edge of the Grand Canyon, I would think that would be an act of suicide."

"Why are you so fat, you human pig?"

"If you want to know anything about my physical condition, I would think you would consult a physician."

"What color are your eyes?"

"You're sitting across the table from me. If you want to know the color of my eyes, why don't you look at them?"

"They're black. Black as sin! Do you admit that your eyes are black?"

24

"Since my eyes are stuck in my head, I can't look at them to see what color they are, so 1 cannot admit that my eyes are black. Maybe you're capable of looking at your own eyes, but I'm not."

"How many hands do you have?"

"As many as God gave me."

Bismarck lied for seven straight hours, leaving us drained and depressed.

The trial began a week later. Bismarck and his attorney presented their case first, and then Dave recited the ranger's story verbatim. When Dave finished and declared us innocent of the charges, the judge leaned over the bench, glared at him and asked in the sternest of voices:

"Mister defendant, this wild and bizarre tale you have just unleashed upon this court, I have only one question for you about it, and the answer could either win or lose the case for you. The question is this: Can you prove it?"

Dave's face turned white, and he trembled and stammered out: "But, but, but the ranger is dead!"

"Can you prove the story?" shouted the judge.

"No."

"Then I rule in favor of the plaintiff and will assess damages and penalties forthwith," the judge boomed as he slammed his wooden gavel on the bench.

Bismarck, his attorney and the other Missourians laughed. Realizing that we had nothing but our motorcycles to give up for damages, we ran out of the courtroom, hopped on the bikes and raced away.

Out Of There!

CHAPTER 5

Out For Babes

We fled south on the highway at top speed, racing the bikes so hard that their engines screamed and seemed ready to explode. I drove faster than Dave, that's how scared I was. It wasn't the possibility of having to turn over the bikes to the Missourians that I feared, or even Bismarck. I was afraid that if we were caught, the judge would order me into deposition again with that lawyer.

So when we suddenly, on Dave's lead, veered off the highway and speeded into the city of Flagstaff in the mountains of northern Arizona, I was furious.

"We've got plenty of gas, we're not hungry, the roads are clear, there's lots of daylight left. We're being chased. We fled from a formal court proceeding, which is a serious offense that we can be jailed for. We don't need to be stopping!" I screamed through my helmet after we had stopped in a gravel parking lot. "Why are we stopping?"

"Calm down and stop whining," Dave said while leaning up against his bike and undoing his helmet's chin strap. "Millions of people break the law every day. There are thousands of swindlers, murderers, rapists, liars, thieves, deadbeats and fashion designers roaming the country at any given moment. All have done things worse than we have. So relax.

"Besides, they're not chasing us. Bismarck was happy to see us go. Now he can harass everyone else up there without bother from us. He just wanted us out of the way."

Flagstaff was the location of a mid-sized state university. It was a small city, consisting mostly of gas stations and restaurants. It had a museum, too, but I thought it second-rate because most of the stuff in it was old.

"You know what a college campus means?" Dave asked.

"Mindless conversation? A contempt for common sense? An infatuation with discredited and failed political and social ideologies? A fear of the real world? People wearing berets?"

"Jesus Christ, no. You really do need to lighten up. It means coeds—women—smooth-thighed, firm-assed, willing women, and if you don't screw things up like you normally do, dates for us."

We got a motel room, showered, ate, and in the afternoon, walked toward the campus while Dave explained how we were going to going to get dates:

"All we need do is walk around the campus and look tough, confident and manly. Women like guys who are decisive and who carry themselves well. And despite what all the experts and shrinks say, women don't want wimps. They like strength."

"So what exactly do we do to act manly and strong?"

"Put on the most hateful glares possible. We don't want that kind of vacant, mindless hatred that you see in bikers, the kind that says you have no idea what it is you hate. Only nuts do that. Be specific. Focus on the person who's walking toward you and look like you hate them and are ready to bite off their face. Do that and the women won't be able to resist us, or at least me, and we'll have more partners in one night than most people have in a lifetime."

"You're crazy. That's one of the stupidest things I've ever heard. Why don't we just go up to some women, and in a nice way, introduce ourselves, tell them that we're on a trip, that we're lonely and could use some company tonight. Why don't we just be nice to them and treat them like human beings?"

"Because that'll never work. All the books say that we're supposed to be nice and civil to each other, but the truth is, men and women are just animals who size each other up on the basis of sexual appeal. Women want guys who will give them healthy kids and who will protect them from wild animals. It's caveman stuff. We're born like that. And to women, strength equals sex appeal. They want real men, not sissified wimps. Since most of the guys on college campuses are wimps, we'll be doing the women here a favor by making ourselves available to them.

"All we gotta do is walk and glare and look real intense, and there's a good chance that they'll rip off their clothes right in front of us. It's not only possible, it's probable."

It was a perfect day for walking: freezing cold, with snow from previous storms still on the ground, and a dense, grey cloud cover that not one ray of sunlight could penetrate. We glared, looked intense and walked around, through and across the campus three times and passed scores of women, none of whom ripped their clothes off and demanded that we use our manly attributes to bring them to ecstasy.

"This isn't working," I told Dave, "and I know why."

"Why, big brain?"

"There's only one possible reason that they're not attracted to us. They're all lesbians! They don't like men! Why else would a woman not be attracted to us?"

"That's ridiculous. It's the stupidest, most offensive and obnoxious thing I've ever heard. Don't you ever stop to think how unrealistic and insulting your theories are? This one makes no sense because even if they were lesbos they'd still have an uncontrollable desire to smother me, the world's boldest man, with their glistening bodies. No brag, just fact. That's how strong my sexual magnetism is. I can cure any lesbian of her lesbianism.

"I can walk into a room where naked, oiled up lesbians are groping each other and sliding around and having the wildest, most intense time, and I can be bundled up head to toe in winter clothing, and they'll take one look at their

27

naked, glistening, panting partners, and one look at me in long underwear and it'll be all over. They'll renounce their lesbianism and beg me to get naked with them. It is another god-given gift that I have."

"You're kidding! How many lesbians have you cured so far? Hundreds? Thousands? Millions?"

"I haven't cured any yet because I haven't tried. There's been no time. Besides, I keep thinking about how unfair that would be to all of the heterosexual women in the world who want me. If I cure lesbos, that's less time in life that I have with other women. I have ethical problems with that."

"If the women here aren't all lesbians, why is it they haven't demanded that we have sex with them, and how come we don't have dates yet?"

"It's because they're scared. They're afraid that they might not live up to my high standards; that they might not please me. They figure that their only decent shot in life, their only chance to break out of their bleak existences, the only thing that will give them a reason to live, is to satisfy me. So they all have this one dream, this one ace that they can play in life. That's where the problem is. If they please me, they go on to a fulfilling and happy life. But if they fail, the only dream, hope and chance for a happy life that they've ever had is shattered. They're crushed. They mope and waste away physically and emotionally and become useless, unproductive citizens who are a burden to the rest of us.

"Now, if they never try for me they are never rejected, and they can cling to the idea that if they had tried they would have pleased me. That gives them hope, something to live for, and an eagerness to go on with their bleak lives. They face the possibility of total personal destruction if they fail to achieve a dream they've pursued. So what's better, to have people live hopeless, unproductive lives because they chased a dream and failed, or to have them live productive lives because they cling to a dream never pursued? I sympathize with them. They might find other men, but none as good as me. That would be like being exiled and having to live in Milwaukee or New York instead of Chicago. Death would be better."

"Well, what would you do if you were in their position? Would you have sex with you?"

"I've told you before that I don't like your trick questions. So stop it."

"Well, what do we do now?"

"Our job now is to help them overcome their fears. There is no sadder, more pathetic thing in life than fear. And there is no greater service to mankind than helping someone overcome fear. We must make ourselves even more attractive and manly than we are now. We must make ourselves, and remember this word, *irresistible*. These women want real men. We'll show them real men."

With that we threw off our coats and walked around the campus, flexing our muscles, stomping our feet, glaring and swearing loudly.

"Swearing is cool," Dave said. "There ain't a babe on earth who isn't impressed by it."

We stomped around the campus several more times, but remained dateless.

"We're going to have to do even more," Dave said. "Give even more of ourselves to help these women. We've got to act even manlier."

"If it's manly things we need to do, maybe we should climb mountains or lift weights, or do carpentry, or fix things. Maybe we could even read poetry. Some men read poetry," I said.

"Wimps read poetry. And those other things ain't manly enough."

"So what do we do?"

"That's easy. Act even manlier. We start drinking," Dave said as he pulled a quart of whiskey out of a motorcycle bag he was carrying. "Tough men can hold their liquor. And babes are impressed with that. Drink up!"

We stomped around the campus glaring, smoking, drinking, stomping our feet and flexing our muscles. After eight more circuits, we were drunk and still dateless.

Even more manly action was needed, Dave said, so we began spitting whiskey at people.

"Spitting whiskey on someone," he explained, "is an act of defiance, confidence, manly irreverence and true boldness that all women admire. Who wouldn't admire it?"

We stumbled through a few more trips around campus, and apparently the word was out on us by then, because everyone who saw us coming, fled. I pointed out to Dave that people were running away from us, but he wasn't concerned, at least not in the way I figured he would be.

"They're running away, not because they're scared of us, but because we embarrass them," he explained. "We're the ultimate men, and all these people know that they will never be able to reach the level of existence that we're at right now. They feel inferior."

As the afternoon wore on we resorted to other manly activities, things like burping loudly, kicking dogs and other small animals and ridiculing everyone we saw. After seventy-three circuits around the campus, we were tired, drunk, sick, cold, hoarse, sore-footed and dateless. I was depressed, but Dave remained optimistic.

"These women are worse than I thought," he said. "The ultimate manly action is now called for. Follow me."

Soon we were crouched behind a large boulder from where we spied a dozen men and women who were building snowmen, laughing and having snowball fights.

"There's what I mean," Dave said. "Those women aren't having fun. A woman doesn't want a man who will build a snowman. They don't respect or desire those men."

"But they're laughing and kind of wrestling with each other," I said. "They seem happy."

"They're not."

"How can you tell?"

"Because they're smiling. No one who smiles is happy. Only people who are pretending they're happy smile."

"So what do we do now?"

"Engage in the ultimate manly act."

"Which is?"

"Violent behavior. Women want badasses, men who will fight. They want men who will defend them, the children, the house, the pets and the pots and pans. Let's give them what they want!"

We shed our shirts, and bare-chested, charged out from behind the boulder, throwing punches and shouting: "The badasses are here to fight!" We waded into the group and punched and kicked our way through the men, who, in a few minutes, were beaten and fleeing.

Some of the women fled too. Those who remained screamed at us to go away. But we didn't. Instead, Dave leaped on a boulder, pounded his chest with his fists and shouted:

"My partner and I here are badasses who fight. We'll kick the living crap out of any of these wimpy guys on campus, including your boyfriends, husbands, brothers, sons, fathers, uncles, cousins and grandfathers. All we do is fight. We fight when we get up, fight all morning long, fight during lunch, fight all afternoon, fight during supper, fight after supper, fight all night long and sleep a little and then get up and fight some more. We love fighting so much that we've both changed our names. Mine is Fight A. Fight, and his is Fight N. Fight. All we do is fight. That makes us big and real men, and makes all of you eager to have sex with us. We understand your needs, and we are filled with compassion. And so, in order to avoid confusion and jealousy amongst yourselves, we have a sign-up sheet so you women can make appointments with us. It's first-come, first-serve, so sign up fast. We'll only be in town a couple of days."

"Vile, filthy, sickening pigs!" one woman screamed, while the others bombarded us with iceballs and shouted for someone to call the cops. "Take your violence-mongering and your anti-feminist poison out of here. Practice your violence elsewhere."

Most of the iceballs hit, and they were serious about calling the cops, so we had to retreat. We sprinted away and hid behind bushes, between buildings, behind boulders, on top of roofs and underneath parked cars until we were sure that the women had stopped chasing us. Then we ducked inside a building and a bathroom to discuss the situation.

"These women are shyer than I thought," Dave said. "We'll have to increase the intensity of our efforts. We need to give them more to go on."

"But I'm tired, sick and dizzy," I said. "Why can't we just go back to the motel and sleep?"

"If we did that we would be letting these women down. I'm not going to do that. We have a responsibility to help them fulfill their womanly desires. We must never give up."

Our Seventy-Third Circuit

We didn't. Our next stop was the athletic building, where we, still shirtless, stood, strutted, flexed our muscles, glared and swore outside of the exit to the women's locker room.

"Do what I do," Dave instructed as he clenched his hands into the kind of semi-fist that's used to give a thumbs-up signal. Only he turned his hands in a thumbs-down manner and held them about waist-high in front of his body so that his thumbs were pointing to his crotch.

"You're pointing directly and deliberately at your crotch," I said. "That's sick. Why are you doing that?"

"It's not sick; it's body language, and I'm doing it to pick up babes. I read about this in one of those best-selling books on body language. The book told about this guy who was standing in a room by a fireplace, and all the women in the room were approaching him and cooing and wanting him. And why him and not the other guys? Because he had his hands in his front pants pockets with his thumbs sticking out and pointing to his crotch. He wasn't pointing on purpose, but no matter, the effect of it was to communicate to the women that he was a big man and ready.

"And the women were attracted to the guy simply because he was pointing to his crotch with his thumbs. So if he got all the women in the room by unintentionally pointing to his package, imagine how many women we'll pick up if we point on purpose. Now stick out your thumbs and hold them out in front of you and point them at the center of your manliness."

I did as ordered. We stood four feet apart at opposite sides of the exit door and scowled while pointing our thumbs at our crotches. Some women who came out gasped when they saw us, others looked scared, some averted their eyes, and all raced for the exit door. Soon, women were peeking their heads out of the locker room door, apparently to gaze at us. They all pulled their heads back inside, though. After a while, we noticed that no more women were leaving the locker room or even peeking out the door. I was concerned and asked Dave about it.

"They're just scared," he said, "Shy. But we'll get some bold and aggressive ones pretty soon. Don't worry. We'll get some who want to attack us."

He was right. We were attacked the moment he finished talking, but it wasn't what we were hoping for. A brigade of angry women who were dressed in baggy, black martial arts robes began kicking and chopping at us with their feet and half-clenched fists. They hit us at least a dozen times, and we were forced to retreat into a corner where they surrounded us.

They were a dozen strong, healthy, powerful looking and angry. They were members of a campus female watchdog attack group, they told us, who escorted women around campus in order to protect them from muggers, rapists, fiends, murderers, jealous ex-boyfriends, and glad-handing politicians.

"So why are you attacking us?" Dave asked. "We ain't any of those. We're just trying to get dates for tonight. I realize that you all might not approve of the idea of women dating men, but that's your problem until I can find time to cure you all. Now leave us alone so we can attract some hot babes—"

Whoosh! The wind from a flying, twirling kick launched by an attractive blonde who was the brigade's leader slammed me into the wall and snapped Dave's head back. Had the kick connected, his head would have flown off.

"Get it straight pigs," the blonde said as she coiled for another kick, "we love to lock our muscular, twitching, and oh so sweaty thighs, around men— real and deserving men—not pigs like you two. The men we delight experience our womanhood in provocative and fantastic ways that you two human pimples could never imagine and will never experience.

"And just so you two pathetic creeps know, we like men who are so secure and confident in their manhood and sexuality that they don't need to fight or strut or glare or stand half-naked outside of a women's locker room pointing to their crotches. And our men don't need liquor either to make them strong. They have inner strength, real strength. They don't have to pretend like you two do. Our men are strong enough to admit that they're weak. Our men know how to cry. We want men who start discussions, not fights. We date men who know that the greatest achievement in life, the noblest action, is to walk away from a fight or an argument. You know what real strength is? Love, compassion and sensitivity. And you know what fear and cowardice and weakness is? Hatred, bluster, bitterness, anger and aggression."

"Then you're a coward," Dave told the blonde, "and weak too."

"How do you figure that?" she demanded.

"Because my sense is that right now, you're angry at us. And we know that anger is cowardice."

Whoosh! She and her partners unloaded more kicks. They missed, but the wind slammed both of us into and partially through the wall. I fell to the ground.

"You two morons are phonies," the blonde snarled. "You're weak, pathetic cowards. If you want dates, why don't you just try introducing yourself in a nice way to women? Why don't you just say that you're in town, are lonely and are looking for pleasant company? That would work a billion times better than the idiotic games you two are playing. You two are not men."

"And we're not mice, either," Dave shouted as he suddenly began convulsing and weeping. Within minutes there was a huge puddle of tears on the floor at his feet.

Whoosh!

"Why are you crying?" the blonde demanded.

"Because I'm sensitive. I know how to cry. Now will you date me?"

They all kicked again, and this time the wind nearly knocked us entirely through the wall.

They advanced on us as we picked ourselves out of the rubble. I could see in their eyes that this time they meant business.

"Hold on," Dave pleaded as he brushed plaster and dust off himself. "You've got me wrong. I am strong in my manhood and sexual identity. Hear this: I am a homosexual. I say that with pride, not fear or shame."

"Where did that come from?" the blonde demanded.

"From you. I am so secure in my sexual identity that I can say that."

They coiled again and were about to kick us through the wall when I spoke:

"Stop! We're not the misfits that you think we are. We're just two lonely goofs trying to get some dates. I'm Dennis. He's Dave. We're on a long motorcycle trip, and all we're looking for is some company. So don't kill us. We're kind of nice guys. If you're not doing anything tonight, give us the chance to prove it."

Amazingly, she and another brigade member agreed, and Dave and I had dates for the night. They introduced themselves. The blonde's name was Kathy. Her brunette companion was Cindy.

CHAPTER 6

Dates And Self-Doubt

There is no more magical feeling in the world than walking down a street all bundled up on a cold winter's night knowing that you have a date with a member of the opposite sex, and that for at least one night you're better off than the millions of lonely, depressed people in the world who are sitting by themselves in dimly lit, sparsely furnished apartments drinking heavily and wondering if they'll ever find someone who will love them.

We were walking back across campus to Kathy and Cindy's dormitory room after having stopped at the motel room to rest, clean and sober up. The wind that had picked up was bending tree branches, causing power lines to sway like jump ropes, blowing over garbage cans and helping make the early evening walk the finest moment of my life up until then.

The energy of storms had always unleashed an optimism in me that blunted my depression and filled me with the idea that I would succeed in life. This storm was no different. But now, I was filled with the knowledge that I was fulfilling a dream that after the disastrous experience with Shirley I thought would never be: I had another date! I felt like sprinting to the dormitory. Dave was happy for me.

"You know what this means for you, getting a date again?" he said with a giant grin on his red, shivering face.

"What?" I blurted out giddily, hoping he would say that it would mean sex at the end of the night.

"It means that you're not a homosexual."

"I'm not?"

"Well, I hope not. What do you think?"

"How am I supposed to know?"

"You'll know by the end of the night. If you have sex tonight—and I mean sex with one of these women—then you're okay. If not, I think it's time to worry."

While we walked, Dave lectured me on dating etiquette.

"There are a zillion things that you need to know for a successful date," he said. "Don't act like a jerk or look like one or insult a woman too much or spend all her money or let it seem like she's smarter than you. No woman likes being smarter than a man. Don't step on her feet. That means you're clumsy.

They translate that into being awkward in bed. Don't eye other women while she's watching. Don't *ever* eye other men. Buy her at least a six-pack. Never ask to wear her underwear, at least not on the first date. And, this is the single most important key to a successful date: If you ask to take her underwear home with you to wash it, don't let her catch you smelling it in the john. Men blow more dates by being caught snorting underwear than by any other reason. And pretending that the undies are a substitute for your lost handkerchief doesn't work. I've tried."

I happily absorbed the advice, and Dave eagerly gave it until just before we knocked on the door to women's room. They greeted us with smiles. Once inside, Dave and I smiled, for Kathy and Cindy had changed from baggy sweat clothes into tight-fitting jeans and body-clinging sweaters.

It was a typical dormitory room: small, with a hard, tile floor, cinderblock walls that were painted a dingy cream and that were cluttered with posters containing inspirational messages, as well as with posters of female athletes. There were two plain, book-cluttered wooden desks set near two windows that offered a view of the lighted courtyard, and on either side of the room, up against the walls, were two small beds.

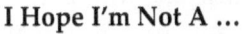

I Hope I'm Not A ...

They offered us wine that had been chilled in a small refrigerator, and we sat on the edge of the beds and drank. Dave, in his ebullient, aggressive way, spoke first.

"Nice beds," he said with a big smile. "It feels like they get lots of use."

"They do," Kathy said. "We use them every night."

"You seem like the types who would," Dave said with a leer.

"We use them every night because we sleep in them," Kathy replied.

Dave, Kathy and Cindy talked and laughed while I sat there silently, feeling awkward and stupid. Cindy, who was my date, sensed my uneasiness, held my hand in a comforting manner and asked if I was thinking about anything.

"Yes!" I blurted out. "I keep thinking that everybody in this room is going to die. Someday we will all be dead. And I'm wondering why you decided to go out with us. We don't have much to offer. I don't even think I'm interesting."

They laughed. I blushed.

"The truth is," Cindy said, "You two seem more pathetic than dangerous, and we wanted to talk to you and try to change your attitudes. We feel we'll do womanhood and humanity a favor if we can get men to realize that they don't have to fight or act tough in order to impress women. And we feel that if we can get all people to see the value of respect, love, self-restraint, and common human decency, we'll all be better off. True strength is being able to walk away from a fight and to turn the other cheek. We like men who are brimming with compassion and sensitivity. And honestly, you two aren't too bad looking, and we do get horny. Who knows, if you guys change your attitudes, you can never tell what'll happen. Sleeping is not the *only* thing we do on these beds."

I eventually gained confidence and joined the conversation, although once I began, the talk was one-sided because the others weren't as knowledgeable as I was about coffins and funeral homes. We made plans to go ice-skating, have a nice dinner and then go to a bar for a few drinks. We left the room, and during the walk to the ice rink, Kathy talked more about her idea of what men should be.

"Men are big jerks," she said. "They're always challenging each other and being territorial. And they're so jealous. I once dated a guy who started a fight because some guy looked at me. You think that he would have been proud to be with a woman who was so attractive that other men looked at her. You think he would have said, 'Everybody is looking at her and she's with me!' But no, he was so insecure that he started a fight. The sick thing is, he started it with me. He accused me of doing something wrong, of dressing too nice and of looking too good. I never saw *him* again. Men must learn that violence is wrong. Men must learn that women will not tolerate or reward their anti-social behavior. They need to understand that to women, a man who diffuses a tense situation or walks away from a fight is attractive, and that one who brawls isn't. Men need to know that it is *always* wrong to fight."

The conversation continued, for it was a long walk, and after a while, Dave offered this:

"I know you are going to think that I'm saying this just to get down your pants, and believe me, I'd like to, but I agree with you. Always have. If only all women thought like you do! I would love to be myself and to not have to put on an act. I'm a bold man, true, but I would love to walk away from jerks who are harassing me or my date, or from drunks in bars who challenge me. That would give me more time to be with women. But I've always been told that— and it always seems like—women want and expect men to defend their honor and to fight and stuff like that. So all this time I've just been acting the way I've thought that women want and expect me to act. I hate having to play games. I'll say this: It's over. I'm changing now."

I exclaimed that fighting was useless because we would all die anyway. We both got big hugs and long kisses!

"I have a feeling," Kathy said with a coy smile, "that this evening is going to last a lot longer than any of us first imagined."

"Me too," said Cindy as she tossed her head back and laughed. "And I think we're going to enjoy ourselves in ways we might not have considered this afternoon. But you know what, we've got to get rid of these misconceptions that we have about each other. I know that men think that women want them to act tough, but that's not true. I wish I knew where men got such nutty ideas."

"So do I," said Dave. "And when we find out, we should denounce them as enemies of the human race."

"Hallelujah!" Kathy shouted.

CHAPTER 7

Obnoxious Frat Boys

We took our place at the end of a long ticket line in front of the skating rink and continued our conversation. Soon, five drunken guys showed up and lined up behind us. They had six-packs of beer and half-pints of whiskey under their parkas, and they were rowdy, noisy, obnoxious and constantly shouting the name of their fraternity. Before long, they were pushing and shoving each other and spilling beer and liquor. Eventually, they began staggering into me and Dave.

And pretty soon, they were spilling beer and liquor on us. I was furious. They were disturbing our peace and interrupting my first date in four years. Plus, they were taller than we were, appeared to be more muscular, and were better groomed and better looking. I feared our dates would be attracted to them, and I suggested to Dave that we leave.

"No. These guys are going to get us laid," he told me quietly when the women were talking to each other. "You have to learn to play life like an instrument. Try to turn every situation to your advantage. The more we stand here and silently take this crap from these guys, the more impressed the women will be. And you know what that means for us? If these fools don't start a fight with us, I'm going to cleverly provoke them into one. That can only be good for us."

The frat boys continued their obnoxious behavior.

"What fine, sweet, delectable babes we have here," one said to the women. The others asked for the women's names, made a variety of lewd remarks, whistled and jeered, grabbed the women in ways that amounted to sexual assault, and finally, one spit out this remark: "We're looking for a couple of ladies named Pussy. Any Pussies here?"

Dave and I held our tempers, although just barely, and I took a try at settling the frat boys down and diffusing the situation.

"You guys have a good eye for the ladies," I said nervously. "And you're right, these two women are exceptional. We agree with you. And if they weren't with us, who knows, they might be with you. But they *are* with us and they'd appreciate it if you would settle down. Real men give ladies what they want. And I know you guys are real men."

Before I could congratulate myself for making such a clever speech, the frat boys attacked us. They tackled us to the ground and landed several punches and kicks before we worked ourselves free and scrambled to our feet. I was poised to start swinging back, but Dave stopped me.

"Remember," he said, "the women believe that it is always wrong to fight. And remember, turn the other cheek. Do what I do and I guarantee that we won't even have to take them skating or to dinner to get sex."

Following Dave's lead, I stood straight as a statue with my arms folded across my chest and faced the five. One frat boy slugged me square in the middle of the forehead. Another crunched my nose.

"I'm depressed," I mumbled to Dave as I took a blow to the center of the mouth.

"Why?"

"Because they keep hitting me in the middle of my face. I can't turn the other cheek if they don't hit me on either side of my face. The women will think poorly of me."

"God, you're stupid," he mumbled back. "Since they're hitting you in the middle of your face, just turn around and offer them the back of your head."

"Good idea."

They clobbered the back of my head, and when I faced the frats again, they landed sharp punches to both sides of my face, which allowed me to—constantly—turn the other cheek.

Dave was beaten worse than I was, and we were both drenched with beer. One vicious blow busted Dave's bottom lip open. The frats laughed.

"Laugh if you must, cowards," Dave said, "Violence is wrong. It is a sign of weakness. Peace be with you. I offer you my other cheek."

Several minutes of absorbing blows from close range left our heads bruised, bloody, badly swollen and us barely conscious. The frats berated us as cowards and ridiculed the women for dating wimps who wouldn't fight.

"At least we wouldn't stand there and let you two be harassed," a frat who had short brown hair and who wore one leather glove told the women. "At least we'd protect you. We'd be real men. We wouldn't let ourselves be beaten. Now, we're going to count to three, and if when I finish you babes aren't out here with us, we're going to come and take you. And it'll be painful and ugly. We're going to hurt your sissy dates a lot worse than we've already hurt them. Sexy, horny babes belong with us. We know what you babes want, and we know how to give it to you."

The frats then tore off their coats and shirts and stood bare-chested in the cold, braying and pounding their chests with their fists. Dave laughed.

"Why the laugh?" I asked. "Is it because you see the sweet irony in this? You see that just this afternoon we were acting as idiotic as they are?"

"No. They just checkmated themselves. This goof just placed an insurmountable obstacle in their paths that makes it impossible for them to come after the women."

"What is it?"

"Think. Concentrate on the fact that they're frat boys."

"I got that, but what's the insurmountable obstacle?"

"Counting to three. They can't do it."

"One!" shouted the frat.

"Let's hold hands," Dave told us, "and not worry. We'll get through this."

"Two!"

"Hold steady, and remember that love is stronger than hatred, and gentleness more powerful than violence."

"Four!"

"What did I tell you? We might be here for years."

"Two and uh, uh."

"Wait a minute! This is ridiculous!" Kathy shouted to the frats. "We'll come with you guys willingly and eagerly. These guys are wimps! They won't even fight even to defend our honor or our lives or anything. Sissies! No woman likes a wimp who refuses to defend her. At least if you guys were in the same situation, you would fight for us. And they're all bloody. Yeech! They're weird. Where did they ever such nutty ideas?"

With that, Kathy and Cindy raced to the frats. They leaped atop two parka-clad shoulders, squeezed their thighs around two sets of frat ears, grabbed some beers, tossed their heads back, laughed, encouraged and guided the hands that were groping their bodies, and shouted as they raced away:

"Two of you will be winners tonight!"

Angered by it all, I pleaded with Dave that we follow and drive the women insane.

"We can't make them crazy," he said.

"Why not?" I demanded.

"Because they already are."

The Frat Boys Win

CHAPTER 8

Past Life Regressions

I t's difficult to lapse into a coma while standing, but I nearly did after my anger subsided and the consequences of our being dumped hit me.

"It's not that bad," Dave offered as we stood outside the skating rink.

"You're pale. You're trembling violently. You're sobbing and are staring blankly into space. You're cold to the touch. You look like your life has just ended. It's not that big of a deal."

"I want to die."

"Knock off the self-pitying crap. No woman is worth destroying yourself over. The stupidest thing humans do is mope over lost loves. It's pathetic to depend on others for your happiness. Depend on yourself."

"It's not that. It's what this means."

"And that is?"

"That I'm a homo. You said so yourself."

"No. All I said is that you might have to start worrying about it. Now calm down and just worry about it."

I did, and soon my color was back and we were trying again—since it was a Friday night and still relatively early—to find women who would go out with us.

Unfortunately for us, the campus weight-loss and mental health clinics were closed, and so we resigned ourselves to a dateless night.

But we soon found entertainment. An advertisement plastered on a campus kiosk told us to "Dare To Discover Your Link To The Past! Learn About Your Previous Life! Experience The Awesome Power Of Hypnosis In A Fascinating Evening Of Past Life Regressions With The Nation's Foremost Hypnotist, The Great Doctor Erno Bernard!"

"Past life regressions," Dave explained as we walked to the campus auditorium where the show was to be held, "are where people get hypnotized and revert to their previous lives, back into the people they were before they were themselves, and sometimes that could mean going back centuries."

"People have lived previous lives? Is this stuff real?"

"It's a theory. Some people believe in it, and some say it's nonsense and all a big hoax."

"What do you think?"

"Don't know. But I do think that I've lived before."

"Why's that?"

"Because I'm so smart and so bold. No one, not even me, can accumulate this much knowledge and boldness in just one lifetime. So I had to have lived before. And there's another reason I know it's true. I used to have a rock collection, meaning I used to like rocks. How would I have come to like rocks if I hadn't lived before as a caveman?"

We entered the large auditorium and had to stand in an aisle against a wall up near the stage because every seat had been taken. Dr. Bernard was obviously popular, for hundreds—young college students and older townspeople—had turned out for the show.

DAVEMAN

It was easy to see why he was popular. The head of silvery gray hair combed straight back lent an authoritative and distinguished look to his stocky frame. His white shirt seemed to glow, and even though he worked coatless with his shirt sleeves rolled up and wore red suspenders, he radiated an air of professionalism and a thorough, but relaxed, competence. For twenty minutes he gracefully walked the stage, microphone in hand, and lectured us about the wonder and safety of hypnosis and the marvels of past life regressions. He told astonishing stories of how ordinary people had "regressed" into famous figures, and assured us that there were probably many in the audience who had lived before and who had lived interesting lives. He cautioned that not everyone could be hypnotized, and that not everyone had lived previously, but urged us all to find out whether we had had past lives.

"Don't be afraid of the past!" he shouted. "What fear is there in knowing that you might have been Abe Lincoln or King Arthur or Cleopatra or Mary, Mother of Jesus? I need volunteers!"

More than a dozen people rushed to the stage. Dr. Bernard advised patience and asked them to wait in line because he worked best hypnotizing one person at a time.

The first subject was a young man named Bob, a stoop-shouldered dental student who, under questioning from Dr. Bernard, told the audience that he earned average grades, had no job, few friends, no social life, no dates and was attending school courtesy of his parents' money.

"Sometimes I just don't know why I'm here," Bob said with an overpowering depression. "Sometimes I just want to die. I've got nothing going for me."

"Ah, but you have everything going for you, my young friend," chirped Dr. Bernard in his hearty, optimistic voice. "All problems are surmountable. You have everything going for you because ahead of you is life. My friend, life is the greatest gift of all. But you might also have life in back of you. Who and what you were before may provide you answers for the future and bring you happiness. Let us start you on your journey!"

The student sat on a brown couch in the middle of the stage. Dr. Bernard swung a watch in front of his face, told him he was getting weary, then sleepy, and then, in less than two minutes, Bob was snoring. Dr. Bernard spoke softly, but deliberately, and commanded Bob to take himself back into time.

Bob slowly curled into fetal position on the couch while telling us he was a baby in a womb. Then suddenly he straightened out, screamed, and as far as I was concerned, began babbling.

"You're speaking Italian!" Dr. Bernard shouted with a pleased look on his face. "Where are you?"

Bob babbled some more and the doctor interpreted:

"Ah, so you say you are in Venice! What year is it? Seventeen-fifty-eight, you say! Splendid! You say you are entangled in affairs with several women? You will have to leave town on the threat of death from jealous rivals? Amazing! You have a marriage proposal, no several, on the table! Oh my! All the men of Venice are envious of you? Who are you? What is your name? No! Unbelievable! Just plain astonishing! Welcome my friend, Giovanni Casanova, the greatest of romantic lovers!"

All in the audience, with the exception of Dave, burst into wild applause and approving cheers. Bob—I mean Giovanni Casanova—sat on stage and rambled on in alleged Italian. Dr. Bernard translated and told us of Giovanni's many romantic entanglements with women and of his romantic exploits.

Dave was angry. "This is a fraud," he said. "I can see right through it. This ain't real."

"That's what I'm thinking, too," I said. "I mean, the doctor is doing the translating? How do we know that he even knows Italian? And if he does, how can we trust his translation? Is that why you think this is a fraud?"

"No. That's got nothing to do with it. I know that that mope could not have been Casanova."

"Why not?"

"Because if anyone was Casanova, it's me, not some hunchbacked geek."

Dr. Bernard snapped Bob out of the hypnotic spell, and all cheered wildly again. Bob excitedly asked what had happened and if he had been someone in a past life. When told by the doctor that he had once been Giovanni Casanova, the world's greatest lover, Bob leaped into the air, punched a fist at the air and shouted, "All right!"

The crowd screamed approvingly again, and Dr. Bernard exclaimed: "I knew it just by looking at you son!"

Bob walked off the stage in a cocky, confident strut. Several women in the audience chased him to his seat and tried to sit on his lap.

Next on stage was Betty, a fat, unmarried, forty-three-year-old woman who worked as a waitress in town and whose face looked as if it had been splattered with mud because of all of the moles on it. She had been divorced twice, had served three years in prison on a robbery charge, had three children who had been taken from her by the state and placed in foster homes because she was a bad mother, and was now trying to live a good life. But that effort was faltering because two weeks earlier she had been evicted from her apartment for failing to pay the rent.

"I knows I ain't never been this bad or so low," Betty said while on the verge of tears. "I feel that somewhere before things was better for me and that I was a good person, maybe even pretty."

"You are as pretty as a rose and as desirable as every new day!" snapped Dr. Bernard.

"Do you really think so?" Betty sniffled as she wiped tears from her eyes with her ham-like fists.

"I know so my dear. Now let us begin your journey!"

Betty awoke from her trance speaking what sounded like English, but not the English we spoke. She seemed to be carrying on a conversation with somebody:

"Ah, my lady, thou art more precious than yonder knights who ride passingly poorer than wouldst she whose beauty far exceeds the nourishment thy receiveth from a pig and the merriment thy gaineth from ever so generous partakings of the bladder of wine."

"My Lord, weary thy no more with compliments and praise so noble. Thou words about thy beauty are spoketh with an eloquence fat with truth that all of history shall knoweth: That thy's beauty and grace exceedeth that of all others. Words pregnant with such truth cannot beeth made more truthful by repetition. Sayeth once only what thou believeth.

"Nay, for a crime against the gods would beest a single recitation of thou's beauty. For here rideth the fairest lady of all creation."

Dr. Bernard broke in: "My lady. Where art thou?"

"In forest madeth dark in day byeth trees that grow rich."

"Does thou walk?"

"Nay. It beeth on the back of the beast by which thy passeth ground."

"Who beeth with thou?"

"Thou's head must beeth small. For thy rideth with Arthur and Launcelot."

"No! You must be—"

"Guinevere."

"Queen Guinevere! Queen Guinevere of King Arthur's time and the Knights of the Round Table!"

"It beeth so and spoketh now thrice."

The audience went wilder than before. People stood on their seats and cheered and clapped and howled and whistled. Dr. Bernard beamed.

The cheers continued as Dr. Bernard snapped Betty out of her trance. She seemed scared, but pleased by the ovation, and eager to know who she had been. And when Dr. Bernard, with a great flourish, shouted, "Queen Guinevere of King Arthur's Court! The fairest lady of all creation!" Betty slumped to the floor and began sobbing. Through her tears she mumbled, "I knew it! I knew it!"

"We all know it!" Dr. Bernard shouted with a great smile. "It *beeth* so!"

The cheering intensified, and Betty walked off the stage crying, smiling and waving to men in the audience.

Next up was Sharon, a woman in her early thirties who worked as a clerk in a curio shop and studied healing with crystals by night.

"Crystals can heal every ill," she said with a rigid smile that bore none of the elasticity and suppleness of true enthusiasm. "They can wipe out cancer, heart disease, gout, depression, warts, athletes foot, negative thoughts and even acne. I am working to become the world's greatest crystal healer."

When Dr. Bernard put her under, we discovered that Sharon had lived as Marie Curie, the great French physicist who won two Nobel Prizes and who was famed for her research on radioactivity. The audience again erupted into applause. The cheering intensified when Curie told us that she intended to live her second, third and fourth lives as a crystal healer.

A plumber named Bill followed Sharon. He, it turned out, had lived as King Henry VIII. Others followed. Stan, an architecture student with failing grades, had lived before as one who designed the Cathedral of Notre Dame. Buddy, who had been dishonorably discharged from the army, had been the great Napoleon. Anne, a frumpy social worker, had been the great woman's suffrage advocate, Susan B. Anthony.

Dr. Bernard was now being mobbed by audience members who demanded to be hypnotized. He began hypnotizing groups of twenty and thirty people at a time. Everyone had lived as someone else, and always as some great figure in history. Dave was not impressed.

"This is crap," he said. "You see what's going on? All these people who are misfits and worthless nobodies in their real lives suddenly have lived before as great and famous people. It's pathetic. They're trying to deny the fact that they're nothings. And they're trying to become important, not by hard work, study, ambition and intelligence, but by fraud. If a leech attaches itself to a whale, that doesn't make the leech a whale. But these bums think it's so. They're worthless, nothing leeches who are attaching themselves to famous people in the hopes that they too will become important and influential. This is a sham. If anybody has lived before, you can bet it's been me, a bold man. I'll show these idiots."

By the time that Dave strode with an angry confidence onto the stage, all in the audience had been hypnotized but us. The crowd, though abuzz, was nearly spent from the emotional journey it had been on, and seemed to have exhausted its ability to cheer.

Once on stage, Dave turned to the audience and announced: "I will show you what true greatness is. For before you stands a bold man. Doctor Bernard, take me to my past."

The doctor obliged, and soon Dave was reciting the Gettysburg Address.

"I," he told the crowd, "am Abe Lincoln, the freer of slaves and the conqueror of hillbillies; the great man who called this great nation the last best hope for the human race. And yes, I have a terrible headache. Getting shot in the head really hurts."

The crowd, summoning its last bits of emotion, let out the wildest and most prolonged cheer of the evening. When it had subsided, Dr. Bernard tried to bring Dave out of the trance.

"No," Dave—I mean Abe—said.

"Why? Have you more to say?" asked Dr. Bernard, who by now was sweating, and whose once crisp white shirt was wrinkled, damp and rising out of his pant waist.

"No," Abe replied. "I have lived other lives, all of which must be explored."

The crowd and Dr. Bernard gasped. "Other lives!" he exclaimed. "I've never experienced this. It is unprecedented."

"Unprecedented indeed," said Abe.

"Who else have you lived as?"

"We the people of the United States, in order to form a more perfect union."

"You are?" asked Dr. Bernard.

"Thomas Jefferson!"

The cheering grew wilder.

"Excellent," said Dr. Bernard. "Now let's go."

"No. There are other lives I have lived."

"It can't be so!"

"It is! I am also George Washington, Patrick Henry and Benjamin Franklin." The crowd went crazier.

"It can't be so!" shouted Dr. Bernard. "They lived at the same time. You can't be three people at once."

"I was and am! And there are others."

"Who?"

"Squanto the Indian, Peter the Great, Genghis Khan, General George Patton, Ulysses S. Grant, George Washington Carver, Martin Luther King Junior, Count Casmier Pulaski, Thaddeus Kosciusko, General Zhukov, J.P. Morgan, Andrew Carnigee, Henry Ford and Thomas Edison."

"It can't be! You can't be Pole and Russian and white and black!"

"Yes I can. And there are others."

"Come now. Who else have you lived as?"

"Moses!"

The crowd dissolved into delirium. Hundreds rushed the stage and tried to touch Dave, treating him with a reverence that said he was the world's one true deity. Others, overcome with emotion, slammed themselves into walls. Dozens wept. Some screamed, "Bless him! Bless him!" Others were paralyzed with awe.

Dave had lived other lives as well—the Three Wise Men, Mark Anthony, Sitting Bull, Geronimo, Lewis and Clark and Plato. He spent twenty minutes naming his different lives, and when he had finished, a single, adoring, deafening chant of "Hero! Hero!" rose up from the exhausted, delirious crowd. As he glided off the stage with a look of supreme satisfaction, Dave bent over, and like a miracle-performing god placing hands on the infirm, gently patted the heads of those who had mobbed the edges of the stage.

Not to be ignored or overshadowed by Dave's heroics, I stepped on stage,

Dave's Past Lives

determined to show that I too had seen previous greatness. Dr. Bernard, now barely able to stand, began swinging his watch.

I remember only waking up to resounding jeers and derisive shouts from the audience. People were throwing shoes, vegetables, wads of paper, seat cushions and other junk at me. I was stunned. I had expected the same wild ovations that Dave had received. Before the hypnosis, I had thought—hoped—that I might have been Mark Twain or Edgar Allan Poe or some other great author. But instead, I left the stage wondering who I had been to so offend the crowd.

"Was I Hitler or Stalin or some evil menace?" I demanded of Dave as I met him in the aisle. "Or General Custer or some other pathetic figure in history?"

"No," he said in an embarrassed voice. "You weren't a person."

"Good God!" I screamed in terror as I clutched his arms and shook him. "Was I the devil or—"

"No. You were an animal."

"A mighty, majestic buffalo perhaps? A soaring bald eagle? Or a fierce and fearless grizzly bear?"

"No!"

"What was I then? Why are these people laughing at me?"

"Because in your past life you lived as an earthworm—a slimy, stinking worm."

Even I saw the ignominy in that, and as we left the auditorium, I picked up a rotten tomato from the floor and smashed it on top of my head.

CHAPTER 9

A Whiny Crybaby

The Worm

"**D**on't you feel too bad about having lived as a worm," Dave told me as we walked out of the auditorium and back into the frigid night down a narrow, tree-lined campus path. "At least you lived as something. And being a worm is better than having been a cockroach or an ant or a maggot or a fly. At least worms eat leaves and other decent stuff, not dog crap like flies eat. And look at it this way: You got a nickname out of this: Worm. You're The Worm. From now on I'll call you that."

Before I could scream or grab Dave's neck to choke each last stinking breath of life out of him, we were interrupted by what sounded like somebody crying. We trudged off the path into an adjoining patch of woods and in the direction of the sound. After walking about thirty yards we found a boulder the size of a small truck. We walked around it and found a guy sitting in the snow crying, his back against the boulder and his head on his knees. He was a little younger than us, and aside from being hatless, appeared properly dressed for the weather, so we figured that it was something besides the cold that had triggered his crying spell. We knelt beside him and Dave questioned him:

"What's the matter, crybaby, did the girlfriend dump you? Maybe she dumped you because you're a wimp who cries too much. Are you a wimp? Buck up pal, there's other babes out there, even for goofs like you. Now shut up, because crying makes me sick."

The crier lifted his head and looked at us. His sad, red, puffy eyes made me wish that Dave hadn't been so hard on him. He wiped his eyes and runny nose with his coat sleeve, apologized for crying, thanked us for caring and said that a lost love wasn't the cause of his grief.

Dave offered him a sip from a half-pint of whiskey. The crier accepted, and through continuous tears, told us his story. His name was Louie Delgado, and he was an eighteen-year-old freshman from a small ranching and farming community in southeastern Arizona. He was crying, because to his shock and horror, he had just been expelled from school. The banishment was devastating because Louie was the first in his family to attend college, and because the expulsion appeared to have put an end to the great things that were expected of him by his family, particularly his father.

Louie's father had dropped out of high school in his junior year in order to help out his family with the ranch. It was a blow because his dream had been to go to college, study history, become a professor and write books. But the hard times that set in required sacrifices of everyone, and Louie's father accepted his hardship without a word of bitterness or anger. Eventually, work on the ranch became his passion and love, and the dream of studying history faded; however, it wasn't forgotten. The older Delgado wanted for his son the opportunity for career choice that had eluded him. He wanted Louie to have the freedom to choose a career and not have circumstances dictate one to him.

Through hard, constant work and a disciplined savings plan, Louie's father made the ranch a financial success and saved money to send his son away to school. The day of Louie's departure was one of proud accomplishment for his father. He had managed to provide his son an opportunity that he had never had. It was a sad day, too, as it is for any parent whose children leave home to strike out on their own. The realization that Louie, who just years before was a soft-skinned boy who looked to his parents for protection, shelter, food and the answer to every question in life, was on the verge of manhood and independence hit Mr. Delgado hard and caused him to cry.

Louie cried, too, for like all young people who leave home, the thrill of independence was tinged with fear and apprehension about the future. During those last tearful minutes before he boarded the bus that would take him to the university campus, Louie and his father talked. And his father, in a final burst of parental emotion, offered Louie advice on how to succeed in school.

"College is hard, my son. You will be competing against some of the finest minds in the country. You're smart, but like me, not a natural born genius, so you'll have to hit the books," Mr. Delgado said. "Hit those books constantly. Hit them day and night, every day and never stop. If others want to waste their time by drinking and smoking and carrying on all the time, that's fine. But I want you, my son, to hit the books. Your dreams depend upon it."

Louie had his own ideas about how to make it though college. Although he knew that study was important, he also wanted to meet new people, go to parties, get drunk, have fun and break away from the small-town mentality that had been so much a part of his life and that he felt had had a stifling effect on his development. But he worshiped his father, and his faith in his father's advice was absolute, and so Louie set foot on campus determined to become a top student. He approached the task with a limitless energy and an enthusiasm that no amount of hard times, misfortune or temptations to party could diminish. So compelled was Louie to succeed in college and make his father proud, that his academic career became a holy crusade.

He was at the books constantly—every day and every night—just like his father had advised. He got up early and went to bed late each day in order to put in more time with the books. He began to revolt against the concept of sleep because he knew that he had to work harder than others, and to him, sleeping was time away from his precious books.

Louie declared war on fatigue and sleep. He started drinking coffee, first one cup, then two, then three, then whole pots at a sitting in order to stay awake. He looked forward to weekends because there were no classes to steal away his time with the books. Invitations to parties and other social events came his way, but Louie declined them all, so dedicated was he to hitting the books.

At first, Louie pushed himself out of a sense of duty to his father. But pretty soon the books became Louie's passion and love. They broadened his horizons and led him into a world he had never known before. Hitting the books became an obsession, and he entered a state of bliss whenever he worked with them. Louie's love of books grew to the point that he began to feel guilty if he wasn't hitting them. And so he began to work on them everywhere—in classrooms, restaurants, washrooms, grocery stores, the cafeteria, at sporting events, while walking to and from class, and even at Sunday morning services. Every spare moment and ounce of energy he had was directed at the books. He even piled volumes next to his bed so that when, sadly, he did tire and sleep, the books would be at hand the instant he awoke.

Louie didn't know how other students hit their books, but he usually hit his with a club that he had made out of an oak tree branch. When the club wasn't handy, Louie pounded the books with his fists, bricks, large rocks, boards and metal pipes. He would also throw them against walls, stomp them with his feet and pound them against his head. He even pounded them against other peoples' heads when his was too sore and bumpy.

He was proud of himself and could say without bragging that he had hit more books during his first week of school than any other student had done during his or her previous four years. And for that, for following his father's advice and becoming a record-setting book hitter, Louie was expelled. He was bewildered and was still trying to figure out what had gone wrong.

Word spread quickly around campus about his behavior during Louie's first week of school, and when he hit his books outside, other students would gather around him and laugh. At first, Louie couldn't understand their boorish behavior. But then one day he figured it out. They were jealous! They were afraid that he would hit more books than they would and pass them up in school.

Hitting The Books

But rather than shaming or deterring him, the laughs spurred Louie to increase his book-hitting efforts. He began carrying his club around campus, and after he had finished hitting his books, he began to hunt up other students and hit their books. His efforts were not much appreciated. Students called the cops on him, and the campus daily newspaper wrote a story about him and editorialized that he was a danger and a menace to everyone. Soon, students who saw Louie walking down the paths with his club made wide detours around him or simply ran off in the opposite direction.

But Louie wasn't deterred. He adopted the tactic of surprise. He hid in bushes, behind trees and garbage cans, and when a student with an armload or backpack full of books went by, he jumped out and went to work with his club.

It was in second month of school that Louie learned that the school library had six million books, many of them rare and priceless volumes. Determined to make his father real proud, Louie picked up his club and a pipe and raced to the library, or, as he called it, the "Learning Man's Palace."

He smashed, pounded and stomped books for thirty minutes, stopping on every floor and hitting books on every subject—history, art, science, literature, you name it—before being subdued by police, handcuffed and hauled off to jail.

Louie couldn't understand what he had done to get into such trouble. Upon release from jail, he was taken into a private meeting with school officials in the university president's office. The president sternly told Louie that his behavior was far below that of a good college student and that he was being expelled from school.

Louie was hit with a crushing sorrow. He had followed his father's advice and was getting thrown out of school for it. The sorrow turned to anger when Louie, sitting alone in front of a half-dozen school officials, figured that they were condemning his father's advice and condemning his father. It was the lowest point in his life.

But Louie was also blessed with a boundless optimism and an unshakable belief that hard work could solve any problem. After all, it was his father's earnest and dedicated toil that had rescued his family from financial ruin, turned the ranch into a success and sent him to college. So right then he decided that it wasn't his father or his advice that the school officials were taking offense to, but himself! He believed that their message was that he wasn't working hard enough, that he wasn't hitting enough books!

In that instant, Louie decided to quadruple his book-hitting efforts and convince the officials then and there to reverse their decision to expel him. He sprang from the plush, leather chair, charged the office's book case, broke its glass doors with his fists, grabbed an armful of books and began beating them with a maniacal ferocity. He threw books to the floor and stomped them, flung them against walls, smashed them into his head, threw them out of windows, flung himself, books in hand, against walls; and then, in one grand, final effort to convince school officials that he was a good student, Louie picked up an unabridged dictionary and started smashing it against the president's bald head. His efforts failed to change any minds, and the expulsion order was reissued a dozen times over.

Louie was devastated by the expulsion and sickened by the fact that he had not lived up to his father's expectations. He had vowed to commit suicide that night at midnight, which was now only five minutes away. The only thing that could reverse that decision, Louie said, was our sympathy, compassion and encouraging words that his problem was solvable and that his life was worth living.

"Please, time is running out," he pleaded. "Can you say anything that will give me hope and prevent me from killing myself? *Anything?*"

We thought about it for a moment, said we had no words of kindness or support, and walked away to look for a tavern.

A Perfect Tavern

CHAPTER 10

Torture!

We speculated over beers about how Louie had killed himself, because by the time we reached the tavern he was supposed to have been dead for fifteen minutes.

"He didn't have any weapons or pills. I think he just wanted to freeze to death," I said.

"Naah. He drowned to death in his tears," Dave said. "And I'm glad, because he gave all men a bad name. Crybabies make us all look bad. A man should never cry and should never ever think that life's problems are too much to handle."

As we ordered our third beers, the tavern's front door burst open, and in walked Louie, a giant smile on his face and a beautiful woman on each arm. The women gazed lovingly at him, kissed him, playfully grabbed his butt and laughed at his jokes.

"Gents!" Louie exclaimed as he and the women swept past us on our bar stools, "an excellent day and a wonderful life it is. I have decided to live, thanks to these wonderful women."

"What happened? Why did you change your mind?" I asked.

"Right after you two left these women heard me crying. They wiped away my tears with their soft hands and kissed me."

"Why?" I asked the women.

"It was just so nice to see a man crying," said one. "I wanted to smother him with myself right there. We told him that no problem was that bad, and in the morning, after a night with both of us, he'd be much more optimistic."

"Indeed I will," said Louie with a huge smile that made it obvious what he was anticipating.

"Drink fast." Dave ordered, "This town makes me sick."

We guzzled the beers, walked quickly back to the motel, checked out, packed the bikes, and in the cold, dark morning, drove away.

It was around noon when we stopped and fell off our bikes from fatigue, just off a dirt road deep inside a national forest. The sky was cloudy, it was cold, and we were too tired put up our tents, so we wearily unrolled our sleeping bags, stuffed ourselves inside them and went to sleep.

It was dark out when I was shaken awake by Dave.

"Shhhhh," he cautioned before I could speak. "Something strange is going on. Listen."

We sat up silently in our sleeping bags and didn't move. The screams and shrieks that we heard froze me into a feeling of helplessness and terror. The sky had cleared into a picture of shimmering stars and a nearly full moon, which intensified my fear. I wanted to burrow deep into the ground. Somebody was being terrorized, tortured and murdered, and I might be next, I thought. Would it be a bullet to the head, I wondered? Or a knife to the stomach, or a long and painful torture? That the shrieks were coming from somewhere close by scared me even more.

"Somebody is getting killed or sacrificed," I whispered. "Let's get out of here."

"I don't think we can right now," Dave nervously whispered back. "If we start the bikes, whoever is out there will hear us. They'll know that they've been discovered and they'll come after us. Killers kill witnesses."

"We could walk the bikes down the road a mile or two and then start them."

"Too dangerous. There might be a lot of them. They're probably more familiar with this area than we are and they might have lookouts posted. And even if they don't, if there's a lot of them around and we happen to run into one, we're at a disadvantage in this dark."

More screams came, and then shouts and clamor as if someone was begging for their life, and then the sound that is the most terrifying of all; the sound that says there will be no way out, that there will be no mercy, that your tormentor is not a human, but a devil; the sound that indicates certain doom and pure evil: maniacal laughter.

"They could be cult members, or Satan worshipers sacrificing someone or killing someone just for the fun of it," Dave whispered. "Or druggies who are out of their minds torturing someone."

"What do we do?" I asked.

"We have to at least try to find out what's going on, and if possible take action to try to save some lives. It's our duty as humans. And no matter what we do, it's better than hiding here and being scared."

We armed ourselves with wrenches and screwdrivers from our tool kits, and with Dave in the lead, crept slowly in the direction of the screams. Eventually we reached the top of a ridge that sloped down on the far side for about thirty yards into flat ravine, which was also about thirty yards wide.

We crawled down the slope, which was thick with large trees and under-brush, until we saw a huge campfire. We edged closer, trying not to make noise, and hid ourselves behind boulders and fallen trees. Soon we were about twenty feet away from the fire and were able to clearly observe the scene.

Two men and a woman were lashed by their necks with leather strips to three separate trees. Their clothes were shredded, their faces filthy, their bodies bruised and bloody and their screams and moans constant. Before them was a short woman of slight build who was riding a black horse. She was wearing black, tight stretch pants; black, knee-high leather boots with spurs; and a black, aviator-style, waist-length leather jacket. She had short, black hair. In her right hand she carried a whip, with whose wooden handle she constantly beat her prisoners about their heads and shoulders. In her other hand she gripped a long stick, the tip of which she turned into a red hot coal by placing it in the campfire. A large knife was sheathed in her pants belt. She paced the horse furiously back and forth in front of the three while she ranted and shouted obscenities and a steady stream of hateful insults and threats at them. Suspended over the campfire by a big frame made of tree branches was a giant, black cauldron.

At one point she got off the horse, put her face just inches away from one of the men's and raged: "Are you cold?" When he failed to answer she unsheathed the knife and smashed his mouth with its wooden handle. "Are you cold?" she screamed again. When he spit out some bloody teeth and sobbed "No," she flailed him viciously with the whip. "Are you cold?" she demanded again. When he mumbled "Yes," she raged again, "I thought so. This'll warm you up," and began jabbing his body with the red-hot end of her stick and laughing. His pitiful wails fueled her anger and fury. "Stop crying you wimp! I hate noise, especially people screaming! Why are you screaming? Stop screaming!" she shouted as she stomped his bare toes with her boot heels and clubbed his face with the stick.

She moved on to the next tree and demanded to know of the hysterical woman tied to it if she was hungry. A weak answer of "No" that gurgled from the woman's throat sent the short one into a new frenzy. She pummeled the woman about the head with her fists, kicked her in the knees with the pointy toes of her boots and jumped up and down screaming, "Stop saying no!" After the anger had subsided somewhat, the short one demanded again, "Are you hungry?" An answer of "Yes" enraged her even more, and she took out the knife, sliced off a clump of the captive's hair and shoved it into her mouth. "If you're so damn hungry then eat this," she said.

She remounted the horse, walked it to the third tree and maneuvered the beast so that one of its front hoofs landed heavily on the man's bare foot. When he wailed in pain, she jumped off the horse, which she kept in position on the man's foot, and sneered in his face, "What's the matter, is twelve hundred pound horsey crushing your weak, pale foot? Have your foot bones been crushed into tiny pieces by horsey? Aww. That must hurt."

After being berated and abused some more, the whimpering man lapsed into hysteria after being told that his belly would be slit open, his intestines nailed to the tree and that he would be made to sprint in a circle until all his "slimy, gooey, messy, filthy, vile, disgusting, bloated intestines" were pulled from his body and wrapped around the tree.

As she untied the man to make good on her threat, the short one announced a change of mind. The three would be boiled alive in the cauldron of oil suspended above the fire until they were "tiny, coagulated lumps of tar." After that, she said, the lumps of tar would be beaten by diseased bums with body scabs and big hammers until they were powder. She then untied the other captives. Being exhausted, the three made no attempt to escape. They limped passively up a wooden stepladder that led to top of the cauldron. There they were ordered to pause, and there they stood to suffer one final humiliation of being yelled at and ridiculed.

As the short woman launched into another rambling tirade against the three, I risked a whisper to Dave, who was crouched next to me behind a fallen tree:

"What do you think is wrong with her?"

"Nothing. Seems like perfectly normal behavior to me."

"Really?"

"No, stupid. I think she's mad about something."

"About what, though?"

"I think they're waiters who didn't bring her food on time, or brought it

Not Exactly Normal Behavior

cold or forgot the pickle with her pastrami sandwich. Bad service really sets some people off."

"And you're calling me stupid?"

"Yeah. How the hell am I supposed to know what's wrong with her? We just got here. Now shut up and watch and stop asking stupid questions, and maybe we can figure it out."

While the short one berated the three, Dave devised a plan to free them.

"There's only one of her, and she's obviously crazy and no match for us, so here's what we do. When I give the word, we both jump out from behind this tree and start yelling to get her attention. After that I'll do all the talking."

After screaming at the three for several minutes, the woman ordered them into the cauldron. As the sorry-looking man who was to have been gutted was about to throw himself in, Dave gave the signal and we leaped out.

"Don't jump!" Dave shouted as we showed ourselves. "Stop! We're here to rescue you! Don't do it!"

The man stopped and stared stupidly at us. The woman spun around like a tornado, planted her feet stiffly, and through molten brown eyes shot us the most hateful glare I think the world will ever see. She spun around again and ordered the three to resume their death march.

"No," Dave shouted. "She's sick. She's crazy. Listen to us and you'll live."

She wheeled again and glared at us. "After I finish with them," she snarled through teeth clenched so tight that air could barely get through, "I'll kill you two. And it'll be ten times as brutal and as painful as what these idiots have gotten."

"You're crazy," Dave laughed, "and you make us laugh. You don't scare me, and you don't scare my friend here. Whatever your sick game is, it's over. You can't just murder people because you don't like them or because they don't agree with you. Only cops and real pious religious types do that. And why are you trying to kill them anyway?"

She looked hurt and bewildered by the question, but recovered and responded with the indignant tone of one who thinks that their belief constitutes the world's one great truth.

"Because they're scum," she said as if it was obvious and the world knew it.

"Scum?" Dave asked.

"Yes. They are worthless, vile scum who endanger the world. They are an affront and the greatest threat to intelligence, fairness, ambition and decency the world has ever known. They are the sickest, most despicable people ever—pure evil and pure stupidity."

"Pure evil and scum?" Dave said, "They must be college professors."

"No."

"Bartenders who never give you a free drink?"

"No."

"Then who are they?"

She spit at the three, and in a tone of undiluted hatred, snapped:

"Newspaper editors."

CHAPTER 11

Editors Must Die

The answer surprised us. We had heard similar sentiments about newspaper editors, but hadn't given much thought to them. I had always figured that newspaper people were smart. But now we were with a crazy lady who was on the verge of committing murder because of her hatred of editors. This was adventure!

We listened as the woman continued to blast editors. After thirty minutes she declared with an unshakable conviction:

"They must all die horrible, vicious, painful deaths. And these three must be the first to go."

"Sorry," said Dave. "No one is dying until we're sure they deserve it. If they do, no problem. And if the world will be a better place without newspaper editors, we'll help you. And as crazy as you are, you're short and are no match for us."

She smiled and said, "Oh, gents, don't underestimate me. Don't be that dumb," walked close to me, snarled, "You make me sick," and then began beating me with her stick.

After a short scuffle, Dave grabbed the stick and subdued her with a bearhug, releasing her only after she agreed to calm down. She told us more about her hatred of editors, and, in time, convinced us to see for ourselves what scum they were by going to a newspaper with her and getting jobs. We agreed that if she was right we'd help her kill the three and any other editors so deserving.

The sun was rising and we finalized our plan over a breakfast of bacon and eggs. The captives by this time had slumped to the ground in exhaustion. They moaned for food. The woman, whose name was Paulette, threw them the uncooked, fatty ends of her bacon strips and we all laughed as they fought each other for the tiny lumps of fat.

"The only problem with this plan," I said, "is that Dave and I have never worked for a paper. We're not reporters. We don't know the first thing about it."

"That's no problem," Paulette said. "You don't have to know anything. The stupider you are the better. Editors love people who are as dumb as they are. I'll tell you exactly what to say and how to answer questions. Follow my instructions and you'll get jobs."

We broke camp and marched the weak captives through the woods to a dirt road where Paulette had a small rusty horse trailer hooked to a red compact car. She walked her horse into the trailer, chained the captives to the back and then walked toward her car.

"What are you doing?" Dave asked her.

"I'm about to drive away. Follow me."

"But what about these three?"

"I'm going to drag these scum behind me, drag them through the woods and over asphalt until every last piece of their rotten, stinking flesh is scraped from their bodies. And then when they're bloody human sores, I'm going to coat them with salt."

"Why don't you at least put them in the trailer?"

"Because they ain't good enough to be in the same space with my horse."

After some haggling, Paulette agreed to let the three ride in the trailer. However, she refused to give them new clothes, even though the temperature was near freezing.

We found our bikes, which weren't too far down the road, and followed Paulette as she drove out of the forest and onto the highway. A few hours later we were in a fairly large city and in the office of the editor of one of the city's two newspapers.

"Goody, goody!" exclaimed the editor, a large, rounded, stoop-shouldered, rumpled, young-looking man named Jimmy who was sitting on the floor in the corner of his spacious, clean office with a pie in his lap and a slimy piece of pie filling stuck to the tip of his right thumb. "Goody! Goody! I have pulled out a plum from this pie. Bless this day and bless us all! Isn't this neat?"

"It's extra, extra neat, Jimmy. God is looking out for you today. Happy, happy," Paulette, who was unable to disguise her disgust, told him.

"Neato," Jimmy responded as he lifted his heavy body off the carpeted floor. "Let's offer a prayer of thanksgiving for this bountiful blessing."

We all knelt for a few minutes as Jimmy gave thanks for finding the plum. "Do you like me, Lord? Because I like you," he concluded. Once off his knees,

Jimmy shuffled over to us, gave each of us a double-handed handshake as well as a hug.

"Acgh!" he said sharply. "What can I do for you?"

"They want jobs as reporters," Paulette, who worked at the paper, said.

"So you do, acgh," Jimmy responded. "What can you do?"

"Pray," Dave and I said at once, just as Paulette had instructed us to.

"Acgh! Have you ever been reporters? Or have you written anything?"

"No," we both responded. "We don't know the first thing about reporting. Absolutely nothing. We can't even construct a proper sentence."

"Hmmh. Ahhh, anything else?"

"Yes. We pray all day long."

"Hey-hey. Neat. Ahhh, what do you think a newspaper should be and do?"

Dave answered: "A newspaper should make people feel happy. Everybody should be happy. We should print happy news, nothing negative, just big, juicy, feel-good, happy stories. A smile a day beats working for pay, I say. Newspapers must be mongerers of happiness."

"Acgh. What else?"

"A newspaper should never offend anyone. If the truth is negative or hurts somebody, a newspaper should ignore it. A newspaper should level

Jimmy Pulled Out A Plum

out life's valleys and mountains so that everything is smooth and bland. A newspaper must create a set of artificial morals and standards and have no tolerance for individualism or personal freedom and choices. A newspaper must be an advocate of inequality. Some people are more equal than others. And newspapers must advocate greater rights for groups and people the editors hang around with. Those rights must come at the expense of equality for everyone else. A newspaper must cave in to the slightest complaint. Newspapers must dismiss as irrelevant, silly and incorrect, political and social opinions that are the opposite of those held by reporters and editors, and, we believe firmly that a newspaper must never print stuff that readers can use; it must exist to serve the artistic yearnings of its staff. A newspaper must be driven by design and photographs, rather than content, meaning news and words. In fact, to a good newspaper, words should be irrelevant."

"Lordy, you fellows are smart, in touch and in tune. Smart enough to be my superiors, that's certain. You're hired. You start right after I make a special announcement—an announcement of happy news to the staff. For this newspaper has made another giant step toward our goal of becoming the best small newspaper in the nation. Paulette and fellas, join me out here."

We followed Jimmy as he shuffled out into the large, open newsroom that was filled with messy desks. He stood by a desk in the middle of the room, held a bell in his hand, rang it loudly so that the dozens of staffers in the room gathered around him, and proudly announced in a loud voice:

"Happy news everybody! Happy! Happy! We have just taken another giant step toward our goal of becoming the best small newspaper in the country! Yes, we are achieving excellence! The numbers are in and, hey, in the past six months our circulation has declined by ten thousand! We are selling fewer papers today than we were six months ago."

A great cheer went up from most in the room, although there were some unhappy faces in the crowd.

"Ouuuuu, Jimmy! Wooooonderful news. I am sooooo impressed. You are sooooo smart!" cooed a thin blonde with a leathery, age-worn face who wore a flowing, pink chiffon dress and who flitted around the edge of the crowd while smiling, giggling to herself, brushing up against men and batting her eyelids. She was braless, and the erect nipples of her small, sagging breasts showed prominently through the thin material of her dress. "Right on," she continued. "Let's dance. Let's paaaaarty!"

Another cheer went up from the crowd. Jimmy looked proud. "Thank you! Baba," he said in a rush. "Babawaba, you're brilliant, too. Aren't we all smart?"

"Ouuuuu! I am sooooo smaaaaart, it's truuuuue."

A man with red hair, a pear shaped body and who was munching carrots spoke next. "We're on our way to achieving design excellence too, Jimmy. We've won an award for using white space as a design technique. Bravo for us!"

"Oh, Dandy," Jimmy said. "Bravo for us indeed."

"And we've won a photo award, too," said a short fat woman with a sour-looking face. "We ran a full page photo of the sky at night. The stars wouldn't reproduce, and so it just came out black in the paper. The judges loved it. They said it was unique, dynamic and creative."

"That photo spoke to me," shouted a short brunette. "I took that photo and it's still speaking to me. In fact, I can barely hear all of you because that photo is speaking to me this very minute. Oh! It just said that I'm brilliant!"

"Dandy wandy," Jimmy said. "That photo doesn't speak; it shouts loud and clear that this is the best darned newspaper staff in the whole darned world. Next time we get a great picture like that we should run it as a two page spread. That'll win us even more awards."

There was more applause from the staff, but not from Paulette. She was angry and spoke up: "But Jimmy, our circulation is falling because no one is reading us anymore. There's nothing in this paper. If we keep losing circulation we'll go out of business. I want someone to read my stories."

"Acgh. That's ego. That's ego talking," Jimmy snarled in disgust. "You're being negative again. What's the matter, are you angry? Why are you always such a naysayer?"

"Right on, Jimmy and shame on you Paulette," said the carrot-munching Robert. "The reason those people aren't reading us is because they're not as creative or as smart as we are. They wouldn't recognize creative brilliance if it smacked them in the eyes as a full page of black ink, like our picture of the night sky. I know there are people out there who don't recognize the genius in that image. They don't understand our use of imagery. So we don't want them even buying our paper. They're just cretins. We're artistic and brilliant. They don't deserve to receive our paper or to view our great work."

Baba Sucks Up To The Boss

Paulette continued her argument: "We can't just keep printing full pages of black ink and giant pictures. We need news, hard news and more news. If the circulation keeps falling, we'll all be out of jobs."

Her argument was met by jeers from most of the staff. A short, lumpy, doughy, pale-skinned man with blonde hair and a big, round wet spot on the crotch area of his pants scolded her:

"Why is it, Paulette, that you hate this newspaper and these fine people? Hatred, envy and anger will not be tolerated in this newsroom. Hatred is counterproductive to a good working atmosphere and it stifles debate. And let me say that people who hate do so because they recognize that others are more talented than they. Hatred is jealousy, and that is negative. Let me ask you, Paulette, have you ever had a full page of black ink printed with your name on it? Don't answer because we all know the answer is 'no,' and that proves my point."

"Dale," said Paulette as she glared at the doughy man. "You might be the managing editor of this paper but that doesn't give you the right to run it into the ground and out of business."

Dale bristled, stomped his feet, clenched his fists and shouted angrily:

"Paulette, have you seen your psychiatrist today? You're angry again. Anger and hatred may be food for your dark soul, but it is out of line and intolerable in a newsroom. I'm warning you: keep on with these outbursts and we'll fire you."

"But you're angry, too," Paulette shot back. "How come you can be angry and I can't? How come you can stomp your feet and I can't? I think you're operating under a double standard, hypocrite."

"Don't change the subject. I am a manager who is trying to prevent someone from destroying this paper and from slandering good, talented people. We are not going to let one angry person, one hate monger, destroy the peace and tranquility of this newspaper. You are threatening to kill and destroy. I am trying to give life and preserve. Now, if you're jealous because everyone else is more talented than you are, admit it and move on. This meeting is over."

As the staffers made their ways back to their desks, Baba approached and brushed her breasts against one of Dave's arms.

Doughy Dale, Hypocrite

"Excuuuuuse me. You must be new here. Men are always coming on to me. I don't understand it," she cooed. "They can't keep their hands off me. You know what I do on weekends? I walk around my house buck naked all day. I love the feel of my skin against a man's."

"Well, I'd like to invite myself over and get naked with you," Dave said.

"Pig!" she shouted. "That is sexual harassment! I'm filing a sexual harassment complaint against you. Jimmyyyyy!" She followed Jimmy into his office. A few minutes later Jimmy called Dave in. I followed.

"Bad man, Davey," Jimmy said from the chair behind a wooden desk. "Sexual harassment is bad. One more instance and you're fired."

"Hey! She came on to me. She rubbed her chest against me and talked about getting naked in her house and how she liked the feel of her skin against a man's," Dave protested.

Jimmy leaned back in his brown leather swivel chair, looked at Baba while tugging at a clump of his hair, and asked:

"Baba, anything to that?"

"Jiiiimyyyyy?" she said while giggling and fluttering her eyelids, "Jiiiimy-yyyy?"

"Acgh. I didn't think so. Davey, that's bad. Do it again and you're fired."

Jimmy looked at his watch, got up from the chair and headed for the door. "Time for the news meeting."

CHAPTER 12

War Ain't A Story

Thirty-two people jammed into a small, glass-walled conference room and sat and stood around a twelve-foot-long wooden, oval table. Jimmy sat at the head position at one end. Doughy Dale sat next to him. Baba flitted in while smiling and giggling.

"Acgh. Okay. What have we got for news?" Jimmy asked.

A bald man with a potbelly and scabs on his head spoke calmly:

"The wire says that enemy airplanes with armed nuclear warheads have sneaked in under our radar and are headed for our city and our Air Force base. Our planes are up and are trying to destroy the intruders. This is war. A great lead story for Alpha One."

"Is that alllll?" Baba asked. "That is sooooo boring. I mean war, come oooooon! That is sooooo out of date. Must we?"

"But the wires have sent over great pictures of our planes trying to ram the enemy planes out of the sky," the bald man said.

"That's a picture, not an image. We use images. Photos aren't good enough for us," the red-headed man, who was the design editor, said.

The sour-looking brunette, who was the photo editor, spoke next:

"Philosophically, airplanes trying to ram one another out of the sky doesn't work for me. It speaks to people who want to know about wars. How dare we publicize war! That's counter to our mission. We should be waging peace, not promoting war. Newspapers have no business writing about war."

"But our readers want to know about this. They *need* to know about it so they can protect themselves and their families. This is *war!* Are you people crazy?" the bald man said.

"They do not need to know about war!" the photo editor huffed. "War is violence, and the people in *this* room oppose violence. We are not going to promote violence by writing about war. *We* set the agenda in this city, not the readers. *We* know better than *they* do."

"But every other media outlet will have it, and our competition will, too," the bald man, now a little agitated, countered.

"Acgh. We don't follow the pack at this newspaper. We set the agenda. I say we forget it for today. But let's start planning for a big breakout on it three weeks from now. We'll do it smarter and brighter than everyone else," Jimmy said.

The bald man slammed a sheaf of papers onto the table and attempted a sarcasm. But the defeat took the fervor and sting out of his wit. "Well, we still need a photo for Alpha One," he said.

"I've got a brilliant image," the sour woman said while making no effort to hide her contempt for the bald man and his story idea. "After all, unlike some of us here, I am trained to spot and create brilliant images. We've got an image of a painter who has a meaningful goatee and who wears a beret. And what is he doing? He's painting a portrait of me. It speaks volumes! It speaks today, and it will continue to speak centuries from now."

"Neato. Acgh. We go with that. Delightful," Jimmy said. "But we still need a page-one story. What's out there?"

"The mayor has been indicted on four hundred and fifty-three counts of bribery for taking twelve million dollars in bribes over a three-year period," Paulette said. "He's accused of taking money from the contractors who built those three bridges over the river. The indictment says he took the money in return for looking the other way when the contractors used rusty steel, broken bolts and rotted wood to build the bridges. Those bridges collapsed last week and seven thousand people died. Last year the city bought fifteen fire trucks from companies that gave bribes to the mayor. But when the trucks got to the fires they fell apart or burned up. Why? Because they were made of plastic and plywood. The mayor took the bribe money and looked the other way when his fire department got fire trucks made of wood. This is sick. It goes on. The company that supplies food to the homeless shelter bribed the mayor as well. For fifteen thousand dollars he looked the other way while the company put poison in the food. Hundreds of homeless people died. The company did it in order to cut down on the number of people they had to feed. They had a flat-fee contract that required them to feed every one who stayed at the shelter. The company executives reasoned that if they killed people they would have to feed fifty people instead of five hundred, while still getting paid for feeding five hundred. They thought they could pocket the difference. Now, the mayor is threatening to kill himself, his family and all five thousand people who work at City Hall. I think that's news. And besides, no one else knows about it and we'll have a scoop."

Another person spoke now. He was a reporter named Ned who stood over six-feet tall, had a pot belly and a face and head that, because he had almost no chin, looked like a bowling ball. Ned spoke with a methodical, machine-like, inflectionless cadence. His words were spaced evenly and exactly apart from each other, and all carried the same droning tone so that his every sentence was like a long, slow moving train with an endless string of identical, rusty cars.

"I say to you this," Ned started, "through the judicious, skillful and expert use of sources, I have uncovered the fact that the new orphanage was built by a contractor who bribed the mayor. The building, according to a top-secret and highly-guarded engineering report that was slipped to me by sources who said that if there was anyone on this paper who was brave enough to expose this wrong it was me, and if there was anyone who could write this story onto the front page it was I, was built with toothpicks, discarded wood, mud and water-soluble glue and will collapse at any minute, bringing down tons of mud and toothpicks on three thousand and twelve terrified, screaming children, sending them all to horrible, gruesome deaths. The building was supposed to be built with standard, durable construction materials, but the mayor, for a measly five thousand dollars, signed a waiver that allowed toothpicks to be used instead. And I tell you this, the engineering report, which was provided to me at the risk of death, concludes that the children should be moved out of the building immediately. But the mayor has signed an order halting the proposed evacuation because the contractor that operates the orphanage gets two hundred dollars a day for each child in the place. If the children are evacuated the contractor will get nothing. It is said contractor who bribed the mayor, I have been told by those who know. The grand jury is indicting the mayor on these charges as well. I tell you this, this I tell you, this is a natural page-one story. Give us your wise thoughts, editor."

"Acgh. Ned, any grand jury sitting for twelve months can ruin a good man's reputation just like that. Will he be found guilty of these charges?"

"That is not for me, but rather for a jury of the mayor's peers to say. I deal in facts, sir, not speculation."

"And by printing this we'll be dealing in speculation, too, won't we? I mean, Neddy, by your own admission, everything is speculation until the jury decides. By even covering the trial we'd be engaging in speculation."

"But Jimmy," pleaded Paulette, "while bad things were going on, while flimsy materials were being used to build bridges and orphanages, the mayor looked the other way! He looked the other way!"

"Acgh," Jimmy said with the dismissive wave of a hand that gave notice that he thought the charges were irrelevant. "Maybe he looked the other way because there was a better view. Or maybe there was a twitch in his neck, or maybe he saw a saint walking by. If I was looking at something bad and then saw a saint walk by I'd turn my head, too, and look at the saint. And if I did that I have no doubt that people like you would accuse me of looking the other way. There could be a logical reason that he looked the other way. Let's not be hasty and ruin someone's reputation. Besides, the mayor said he likes me."

"Must we endure more boring politics. It is sooooo dull," Baba said as she slouched in her chair and feigned sleep.

"Are there any images of the mayor actually taking the bribes?" the redhead said in a tone that suggested he was offended by the story idea.

"Are you crazy?" Paulette countered in angry disbelief. "The mayor didn't call to say, 'I'm taking a bribe today, boys. Why don't you send over a photographer.' It doesn't happen that way, stupid."

"With no image we can't run it, at least not on page one. Maybe we can run it with the obits or something. Naah. With no image it doesn't run."

"I understand and appreciate your insistence on imagery, but I ask you this," Ned deliberately chugged on. "Does not this newspaper and each of its employees have a duty and responsibility under the Constitution of the United States of America, drafted in 1787, signed September 17th of said year and placed into effect June 21st, 1788, to hold our politicians accountable and to report to the people? And by refusing to print this story are we not shirking that responsibility and thus despoiling the greatest of all human documents, the Constitution of the United States of America?"

Jimmy frowned and snapped: "But what's the Constitution, Ned, when we've ruined someone's reputation? This is a tough decision. Paulette, if we print this story will people read it?"

"Read it! They'll go crazy over it. They'll consume it. They'll buy every paper we put out."

"Acgh. Then we kill it. That would increase our circulation and be counterproductive to our goal of becoming the best small paper in the country. And besides, the company that constructed the orphanage is owned by the publisher's brother. We can't attack the publisher's brother. Now, do we have any *real* stories out there?"

Ned Deliberately Chugged On

"I do," said a high-pitched, sugary voice from the corner that sounded like it belonged to a four-year-old. It was Bess, the paper's relethicology reporter. Relethicology, we later learned, was a made-up word that was a combination of relevance, ethics and ologies. Bess's job was to report on what people might be thinking, or could be thinking, but never actually thought. Unlike the methodical Ned, her every word dripped like cuteness coated molasses, and her face was a constant smile. Bess spoke baby talk better than a baby.

"I have a pretty story about a pretty little teddy bear that was made with a smile sewn into its pretty, tiny little face. The pretty little teddy bear smiles all the day long and does not hurt anything or anyone. I have a second story about air. I have discovered that air does not think. Nor does it read or write. And,

71

boo-hoo, air does not smile. And I have an image of air to accompany the story."

"Geemanee! Neato!" Jimmy cried as he jumped out of his chair. "Show us the image, Bessiewessie."

The ever-smiling Bess held up a photo of nothing—no sky, no horizon no trees or landscape, no building or people or nothing, just blank space. Most in the room gasped.

"Bravo and stupendous! Brilliant!" exclaimed the redhead. "A great entry point into the paper!"

"This is why I say we have the most talented staff in the world," Dale, the managing editor said. "We put it on the front page and run with it."

While the others were applauding and offering Bess their congratulations, Ned cleared his throat and spoke: "I ask you this Bess: That photo that has nothing in it, that is blank, that is nothing but nothing, nothing but void and emptiness, did you take it by putting the camera inside of your head?"

Bess blinked slowly several times and smiled.

"Let's discuss Bessie's really neat stories," Jimmy said. "Any ideas?"

Baba pursed her lips, a move that made her upper, sun-damaged lip wrinkle with dozens of vertical lines and that gave her face a mummified look. Then she tossed her head back, looked somberly at the ceiling as if in deep thought, shook her head back and forth as if annoyed, and then, finally, after a minute or two, leaned forward, and with a serious and concerned look that said she had gotten an idea from heaven and was afraid that she might perish before making it public, said:

"On this story I think we need to—" She paused here, looked at the ceiling again as if asking for permission to reveal a divine secret, lowered her head, gazed solemnly at the others and blurted out, "follow the money!"

The room was again filled with gasps as well as shouts of "Great idea!"

"Baba," Jimmy said. "Every day you're sounding more like an editor. But you are one. I should have known that such a great idea would come from an editor. You are—"

Before he could finish, another editor jumped out of her chair as if she too had been struck by holy inspiration and said: "On this story we need to know how we compare with other cities! What are cities in this region doing?"

Then another editor, this one with a wild look in his eyes, shouted: "But is the teddy bear a local bear? Is he local? If not, how can we localize this?"

There was a growing frenzy of ideas in the room that seized every editor.

"But," shouted one above the excited chatter, "what about the children? How does this affect the children?"

Another, who refused to be left off the train of delirium, shouted: "But, but, but—dammit. We need to know this on this story—listen to me. We need to know: Has the system failed?"

Screamed another: "Where are the skeletons buried?"

It was all exhilaration in that room, for the most part anyway. Ned, Paulette and a few others looked depressed. Dave and I were bewildered. The meeting had already lasted an hour. Now, as it appeared to be ending, Doughy Dale began to talk and tell stories. For nearly an hour he told personal story after personal story. Baba occasionally punctuated her constant giggles with a "right on!" for Dale. Others wore looks of deep and consuming interest, while some laughed as if Dale's anecdotes were pure comedy. All of Dale's stories were as interesting and as funny as his last, which went like this:

"When I was in Washington, D.C., there was a restaurant that was a gathering place for influential and powerful politicians and business people. Every day I would walk past that restaurant and seethe over the injustice of the fact that even though it was unintentional, by catering to the wealthy, they were excluding the poor and those without influence. I would walk around that restaurant and think that if there was anyone who could break the influence barrier and bring justice—even a small piece of it—to the world, it would be me. One day I walked around the block constantly—five, six, seven, eight, who knows, maybe a dozen times. Maybe it was two-dozen times. But I walked and walked and walked, and finally, as I was about to go in and demand that one from the lower classes be seated and served, the place closed for the night. I walked home, and, because I had walked so much, dropped from fatigue and fell asleep. When I woke up the next day I realized that I probably would not have liked the place's food anyway."

Most in the room laughed as if it were the funniest thing they had ever heard. They gazed in awe at Dale as if he were an intellectual genius, and acted as if they were blessed to be in the same room with him.

"Great story, Dale. Acgh. Neat. Meeting adjourned," Jimmy said.

The meeting had lasted nearly two hours. The room was stuffy, and Dave and I headed for the door. We were the only ones who did.

CHAPTER 13

Total Insanity

"Lerps meeting. Lerps. Lerps meeting," Dale said with an enthusiasm that said this was enjoyment that was nearly sinful.

"What is lerps?" Dave asked.

"Long range planning and strategy," Dale chirped. "This is one way we set the agenda for this newspaper and for this city. This is where we plan for the future. Now, it's late January, or is it February? Who knows. Paulette, what are you going to have for us in June and September? What's going to be breaking in the summer?"

"You people are crazy. How the hell am I supposed to know what the breaking news is going to be seven months from now? You people are obnoxious, thirty-something, smug, snobbish idiots. You can't predict the news!"

"Paulette, are you refusing again to work within the system, or is this just your way of telling us that you don't have anything for September?" Dale demanded. "Because if you don't have anything and don't want to work with us, we understand. Have you taken your anti-depressant medicine today? We need to have these pages filled in advance so we can—"

"So you can sit on your fat, smelly, sweaty, pimple-studded butts and do nothing but ignore real news and put your fluff in the paper and sit around and congratulate yourselves for being artists and brilliant thinkers while all the while the circulation is crashing. You prima donnas, you self-absorbed fools."

"Paulette, who's the best reporter on this newspaper?" Dale asked.

"I am. Why?"

"Do you know how to run this paper better than we do?"

"Damn straight I do."

"You know better than everybody else in this room, right?"

"You got it, you lumpy, pale pig."

"And we don't have any daily news in this paper any more, right?"

"Right. Because you're all lazy, self-important prima donnas and leeches."

"Paulette, we don't have anyone to cover the City Council meeting tonight. Will you do it?"

"Hell no! I don't do cheap shit like that."

"Well then, cover the police beat tomorrow at six in the morning."

"Hell no again. You know the rule. I don't get up before eight-thirty in the morning."

"I have just one question: Who's the prima donna?"

Everyone laughed. Paulette fumed.

"You people are ruining this paper!" she screamed.

Jimmy was angry, and he addressed Paulette sharply:

"Paulette, I have just one question: Can you tell us what's going to be breaking in June?"

"No. I can't."

"Acgh. Well, you've failed us, and you've failed this newspaper. And we're tired of your anger. We're all trying to work as a team here, and if you're bent on destroying, instead of cooperating with us, then fine. But I think it's low and immoral for someone who can't produce to attack those who can."

"Ooooooh Jimmy. Why can't we progress?" Baba offered as she tossed back her hair with a flourish of her right hand. "I have ideas for..."

As Baba explained her ideas, Jimmy, Dale, the redhead and the sour woman swooned.

"Glory be, Baba! That's four years from now!" Jimmy exclaimed. "You're giving us a story for four years from now. Grando and neato. That's what I call planning! You're a genius! What's the story about?"

"Kind of a trend piece. It'll be a thorough, profound look at what society's morals will be in the year *six thousand*."

Everyone gasped again. Jimmy could barely speak:

"You're, you're a super-genius! Not only are you filling up the paper four years from now, but you're projecting four thousand years into the future. That's a real trend piece, Baba."

"I'll need a lot of lead time on this, and certainly I won't be able to do any daily coverage until this project is completed. And certainly I'll need some time off to clear my mind and psych myself up for this one. I know I've used all of my vacation time, but—"

"Baba, no daily news for you. Take however much time you want. I want you to be refreshed for this package. This is big. Let me ask, I know this might be unfair, since it is so far off, but how long will this piece be?"

"Perfectly fair, Jimmy. It'll be seven, maybe eight hundred words, sixteen inches of copy at the most."

"Stunning! Not only will this be an in-depth look at a complex subject, but it'll be short, friendly and compelling. Baba, you *are* God's gift to this newspaper."

Baba cooed, smiled, giggled, batted her eyelids and tried to pretend that she was embarrassed by the compliments. "Do you really think so?" she asked in mock innocence as she shrugged her shoulders.

That meeting lasted an hour. By the time it was over, editors were working up plans for stories and projects twenty years into the future.

"Meeting adjourned," Jimmy said.

Again, Dave and I were the only ones who walked toward the door.

"Next meeting," Jimmy said with a broad and enthusiastic grin, "is Baba's writers group. But before I turn it over to Baba, I've got a giant announcement. Baba has won another contest. The Society of Journalists Who Work to Impress Other Journalists this morning named Baba writer of the year!"

A mighty cheer went up. Through the noise, Jimmy continued. "Let me read to you her winning entry. Here it is:

"'Soooooooooooooooooooooooooooooooooooooooooooooooooooooooooooooo.'

"Here's what the judges said: 'The greatest one-word sentence ever written! Smooth, seamless, bold, compelling, imaginative, original, devoid of gimmickry, and, most importantly, all informative. We envy Baba!'"

"Baba isn't writer of the year!" gushed the redhead.

"Acgh. No negativity here."

"No. Really. She's the writer of the century!"

"Amen!" cried Jimmy. "Amen!"

"No, she's the writer of the millennium!" someone shouted.

"You're all wrong! All wrong!" Dale screamed as he jumped onto the table and started stomping his feet. "You're all wrong! I'm right. Baba is the writer of all history. The greatest writer of all time!"

Baba feigned annoyance at the cheers and praise, although she let the Praise Baba Fest continue for thirty minutes. Finally, she said:

"Princess Baba is, I mean, I am sooooo—" A wild cheer went up at that word. "I am sooooo happy and I sooooo deserve this! But we must never rest on our laurels. We must move on. That's why we have a writers' group meeting, so we can all create great writing. We're here to analyze each other's work and improve ourselves. I've brought in several of my poems for you all to study, appreciate and learn from. Here."

All in the room got a stack of Baba's poems. The first one read:

> The giggle-babble of the babbling brook
> Hurts my pus-filled eye.
> Above us all God is good
> In the clear blue sky.
>
> Babble-wabble, dabble-babble.
> Babble-wabble do.
> The giggle-babble of the babbling brook
> Says hello to you—Genius!

Baba's meeting lasted an hour, and when it was over, Dave and I—again— were the only ones who made for the door. Next was the paper's goals meeting. During the hour it lasted it was decided that there should be weekly meetings to decide whether the paper should have goals. Committees were organized, and they were charged with setting up meeting schedules of their own.

After the goals meeting there was a meetings meeting. This meeting was to determine whether more meetings were needed, and to plan them. Committees and subcommittees were created. During the ninety minutes that meeting lasted there was a general acknowledgement that there weren't enough meetings at the paper. The committees and subcommittees were to hold meetings to think of new ideas to have meetings about.

The next meeting—this one lasted only thirty minutes—was held to fill up extra time between the meetings meeting and the mission statement meeting. The mission statement meeting lasted forty-five minutes. Here, most agreed that there needed to be more meetings to decide whether the paper needed a mission statement. Then there was a forty-minute-long sensitivity training meeting during which everyone held hands, sobbed and told each other how brilliant they were.

It was during this meeting that Dave blundered badly. In an attempt to be sensitive, he told Baba: "I apologize for acting the way I did earlier today. I like your dress, but I think you would look better in blue."

"Personal attack! Personal attack! Personal attack!" Dale screamed. "That is a personal attack and unacceptable at this newspaper! Take your anger else-where. The rule at this newspaper is that we are *perfectly* sensitive. We don't say or write anything negative or insensitive about people. That is forbidden."

Baba dropped her head onto the table, let it rest there for a few moments, lifted it slowly as if she were weak and faint with shock and hurt, and said:

"Why Dale? Why are they so filled with hatred?"

"Because they're jealous Baba. They're jealous of your talents and of mine."

"Dale, he reminds me of others on the staff, Fred and Bill. They are vicious, vile, reckless, libelous, stinking, racist chauvinist pigs. They are sick and evil. They remind me of the governor. By the way, that jerk is cutting state govern-ment's budget. Programs will be lost. He's going to fire state workers. Ohhhhh! I'm going to write about it. I'll slam him so hard he'll never recover, so hard that he'll lose the election. He is the enemy of the people. We've got to make him lose the election."

"Amen! Babawabba."

Dave was furious:

"Wait a minute. You just said it was the rule at this paper to never say or write anything negative or insensitive about people. Your precious Babawabba just broke the rule. What—"

"No she didn't!" Dale screamed as he jumped on the table and stomped his feet. "Baba is perfectly sensitive."

"Bull!" Dave shouted as he looked around the room for help with the scared eyes of one who knows that two and two is four and who can't believe that everyone else is saying five. "She just dumped all over the governor and two of your staffers. She's as insensitive, mean and as hateful as anyone I've ever met."

"You vile, filthy animal, you! You scum of the earth! You hate monger! You enemy of sensitivity and correct behavior! You pig!" Dale screamed.

"But—"

"No buts!"

"But what about your rule?"

"The rule is that we don't write or say anything negative or insensitive about people whose political and social views the editors and most of the staffers share."

"So you're saying it's okay to write negative things about people whose political and social views you disagree with?"

"That is not negativity, Bub. That is legitimate, necessary, responsible journalism designed to protect us from insensitive, reckless, biased, hateful pigs."

"How come your political views are right and theirs are wrong?"

"Because we know better than everyone else! Meeting adjourned!"

This time we stayed in our chairs. It was a good thing, because the reorganization meeting was next. Jimmy stood and addressed the staffers as if he were a father speaking to children who needed his enlightened guidance.

"It's not that there are problems with this newsroom. There aren't. We're the best little newspaper in the country," he gushed. "But I want us to get better. So we're going to reorganize the whole staff."

"But Jimmy, we just reorganized last week," Paulette pleaded. "And before that we reorganized the month before, and before that we reorganized two weeks before and before that it was only a week between reorganizations. In the past six months we've reorganized twenty-seven times. What gives?"

"Acgh. What gives is that you're being negative again. You know my saying, 'Stand still and a meteorite might fall on your head.' No lip from you, Paulette. We reorganize. I've noticed that we have at this paper one editor for every reporter. There's something wrong with that equation; it's too much. I'm going to change that so the ratio will be more reasonable and better attuned to what this paper is about. We'll reduce the number of reporters and increase the number of editors so that we'll have three editors for every reporter. We're going to do away with regular beats. From now on, I want reporters, not in government buildings where they can walk around and talk to people and where we can't see them, but in this newsroom chained to their desks. Another rule: No reporter ever leaves the office. And from now on, we cover the city, not by beats, but by telephone numbers. Every reporter will get a set of telephone number prefixes to cover. I think that will give us substantial coverage of the city. There are some glaring holes at this paper, though. And I've decided that two things we desperately need to cover are happiness and baking soda. In fact, I'll toss it out now: Anybody have any ideas on where we should go with these stories?"

Baba pursed her lips and looked all serious again—this time as if the weight and originality of the idea she had was going to crush her—and said, "Follow the money! We need to follow the money!"

"How do we compare to other cities?" offered another editor.

"Is this local?" demanded another. "Can we localize it?"

"But, but, but what about the children?" another editor pleaded with a solemnity that suggested that every child was near pitiless death, only he knew it, and only a quick and correct answer to the question could save the helpless creatures.

"Has the system failed?" bellowed another.

"Where are the skeletons buried?" inquired another.

"Acgh. You guys are brilliant. But on with business. I was just at a management seminar and they said all businesses need to improve internal communication, and that the best way to do this is for all of us to stop speaking to each other in English. Instead, we should talk like frogs and dolphins. Rrrrrbiiit. Rrrrrbiiit. Ee, eeeee, ee. Eeeeee. Ee, ee, eeee. Ee!"

Jimmy was answered instantly with an "Eeeeeeeeeeeeeeeeeeeeeeeeee!" from Baba.

Soon, the room was a loud, disconcerting babble of people making frog and dolphin noises, and was full of the smiling faces of people who thought they had gone to heaven. They went on like that for fifteen minutes until Jimmy finally squeaked, "Meeting adjourned. Eeee, eeeee, eeeee, eeeee!"

"Design meeting!" snapped the redhead. Dave and I were nearly dead from fatigue. Each meeting sapped us of strength and enthusiasm. But it appeared that to the redhead and most of the others, the meetings were nourishment. With each one they gained strength and energy, and by now they were human dynamos and in a state of bliss.

"Acgh. What have we got for tomorrow?" Jimmy asked. He was handed some page layouts by the redhead, who was beaming at his own work. Jimmy's eyes bulged as he examined them, and he gushed, "By golly, geemanee,

We Were Dolphins And Frogs

these are award winners! Robert you *are* a genius!"

Jimmy held the layouts up for examination by all. The room erupted into applause and shouts of congratulations. Jimmy asked Dave what he thought.

"You're running all the stories and pictures sideways—"

"Exactly!" Jimmy shouted. "This will win us a design award for sure. What other newspaper in the country would do something like this? This will put us at the head of the pack."

"I hate to be contrary," Robert gushed with an ever-building enthusiasm and a sense of body-bursting triumph, "but it won't. But what we run the next day will. Look at this!"

When he held up the page layouts some in the room fainted.

Baba responded with an, "Ooooouuuuu!"

Dale cried, and Jimmy sunk to his knees in a prayer of thanksgiving. Everything in the newspaper that day was going to be run upside down!

There were five more meetings, and even after all these years my mind is still too numb to remember what they were about. When the last one ended we shuffled out of the room while struggling to remain standing. Jimmy bounced out of the room as if refreshed by a long night's sleep in cool air under heavy blankets. Dave grabbed his arm, and with a look of bewilderment, asked:

"With all of these meetings, doesn't anybody around here ever do any work?"

Jimmy answered him with the slow, lazy blink of a contentedly grazing cow.

CHAPTER 14

Another Reorganization

As we staggered out the door and to our bikes, Dave offered his impression of the paper: "These people are all crazy, just crazy."

"What gives you that impression?" I asked, receiving a glare for an answer.

"Because they act just like you. Anyway, we'll hang around here for a little while. It might be fun. And it looks like this nutty little woman might be right. Editors might deserve to die. If that's the case we'll have to help her. We've got nothing better to do, and besides, it's not every day that you run across an entire group of crazy people who ain't locked up."

We arrived at the paper the next morning fresh from a night's rest in a motel room. Jimmy had already gathered the staffers in a circle around him in the middle of the newsroom. He was making an announcement. We approached and listened:

"Out with the dolphins and frogs. I don't think that'll take us where we want to go. We reorganize today, right now. From now on we are no longer editors or reporters at this paper. We'll be yodas, free rangers, maestros, big dudes, hair pins, doors, fans, heating elements, bath tubs and closets. The big dude's job is to lift the bar. Maestros will maestro a story through from the writing—excuse me, the yodaing—to design. And we're no longer covering the city by breaking it down into telephone prefixes. We're going to cover this city in a new, exciting, enriching and compelling way that'll make the competition wonder what the heck is going on, and bring us a step closer to being the best small newspaper in the country. We're going to work smarter and harder than the competition. We're going to cover the city based on shoe sizes. Each yoda will be assigned a range of shoe sizes and will cover people in the city who wear that size. This is going to take us—"

Dave and I slipped away and out the doors with Paulette and Ned. At Paulette's insistence we headed downtown and to a small, dark, closet-like pressroom in the basement of the City Hall building. Paulette opened the door and we were met by a rank odor that was a combination of mildew, dirty clothes, unwashed flesh, stale coffee, liquor and cigarette smoke. A guy was sitting on a long, bench-like table that was secured to a wall. His fingernails were long and encrusted with dirt; his brown hair long, uncombed and oily; his reddish-brown beard long and untrimmed; his eyes, a dull, yellowish brown; his once white shirt dim, wrinkled and stained; his blue jeans shiny from dirt and wear; and his brown, waist-length leather jacket worn, cracked and dirty. He was smoking a cigarette and sitting in a contorted, twisted position that made him look like a pretzel. One hand held the cigarette and the other an aluminum soft drink can.

"Who's the stinky bum?" Dave asked. "Get the bum out of here; he smells."

Ned rolled his eyes and cast them downward as if embarrassed. At the same time he winced as if in fearful anticipation of the harsh consequences to be received for an impropriety.

"That bum," Paulette said in her high-pitched, nearly frantic, sneering, angry way, "is Fred." She leaped in the air, and as her small feet crashed onto one of Dave's boots, continued: "He's one of our reporters. He's our friend, and this is where he works. We call it the Fred Cave."

"Your friend stinks and you oughta get him out of—"

"Say mon," the pretzel said. He smiled faintly and took a long, deep drag from the smoke and a swig from the soda can simultaneously.

Covering The City By Shoe Size

"What does 'mon' mean? Doesn't this guy speak English?" Dave asked.

Paulette sneered again: "He said, 'Say, man.' Can't you understand that? Because if you can't, and if you call him a bum one more time, I'll gut you."

"Cool down, little lady, before you get burned. You're dealing with a bold man."

"Oh, someone'll get fried to a black, ugly crisp, and it won't be me, you—"

The two were on the verge of blows, when Ned interrupted:

"Fighting amongst ourselves is dangerous and plays into the hands of the powers that be. They want us to destroy each other so they can gain unopposed control of the paper and spoil the minds of those in the community. It is to our disadvantage to fight amongst ourselves. We must—it is our duty to—educate these two fine reporters as to the status of the organization."

Their anger subsided, and we sat in chairs and listened as Ned told his story:

"The first thing I must do is warn you: Leave this newspaper. It is a dangerous place, far more dangerous than you or I or anyone could have ever imagined. When I arrived here many years ago this was truly a great newspaper. I was recruited by an editor who believed that news was king and that our responsibility was to serve the public, not ourselves. I remember it vividly. He said, 'Mister Ned Vohonovich, we need a reporter who can write his or herself onto the front page of this newspaper every day without fail, morning, noon and night. I say to you, you look to me like that reporter.'

"He was right. Back then we were news commandos. We have always been outnumbered by the morning paper three or four to one. They sell one hundred and ten thousand papers every day. We used to sell forty-six thousand, but now we sell twenty-eight thousand. We worked hard, and I dare say that with Ned Vohonovich leading the charge we scored many an impressive victory. Our circulation was increasing slowly, but surely and steadily. Soon, my vast talents were recognized and I was promoted to assistant city editor, a position that, although indispensable to the paper and to the world, was not the proper vehicle with which to showcase my immense talents, and certainly a vessel so woefully short of the volume needed to hold the abilities of one as good as I, that even the gods who made it turned their heads away in shame and bothered not to seek repentance because so great was their sin that they knew none was possible.

"I skillfully commanded reporters in the city editor's absence, which was nearly always, and we captured the news hills. And even when he *was* there, his strategic and tactical plans were flawed. He would line reporters up like missiles and press buttons to fire them. But because he was journalistically challenged and knew not how to direct reporters or what was real news, his missiles landed in the desert and did no harm except to kill lizards and snakes. When I pressed those buttons, I tell you that the reporters went on stratospheric, supersonic, intercontinental flight, and they landed and blew up in cities, doing immense and terrible damage.

"I had devised a fool-proof plan to become city editor. Since he was incompetent and I was the brains of the operation, it was necessary to illuminate and magnify his incompetence so that everyone could see, none could deny, and all would be ashamed of it. I had to plan for something gigantic to break while he was on duty alone with no one—especially not me—to run the operation. I also had to be nearby and on hand so that when his incompetence was revealed I would be summoned to rally the dispirited and insubordinate troops, bring organization to chaos, charge and take the hill, be hailed as a savior and then be installed as commander-in-chief, all to the wild applause of the adoring troops. I would be like Charles de Gaulle marching back into Paris after its liberation in World War II.

"My plan was this: He usually arrived at ten o'clock in the morning, a little too late to begin directing troops for the afternoon edition of the paper. So I had to plan to get him here at eight o'clock on a day when something was happening. The fighter plane standing in the way of my bomber was his wife and children. His wife worked the graveyard shift in a funeral parlor embalming bodies, writing prayers for the deceased and adding on unnecessary 'extras' to the funeral service, thus inflating the bills for the bereaved survivors. He had to remain at home caring for their young children, ages nine, eleven and twelve, until she arrived home from work to assume that responsibility. Her quitting time was nine o'clock, and she arrived home at nine-thirty. He arrived at the newspaper at ten a.m. I needed at least three consecutive days of sustained action in order to fully show up his flaws. So, I needed three consecutive days in which his wife would be at home in the early morning so he would be free to leave and assume command. But, a minefield blocked my way. I had to be indisposed at the same time she was off and at the same time a big story was breaking.

"I could not plan this during her vacation time because they took vacations together. Getting her children sick and triggering her maternal instincts would have been fruitless because he could have cared for them while she was at work. However, I recognized that she would have to remain at home for a sustained period if her children died. Then she would be wracked with sorrow and guilt and he would be free to arrive at work at precisely eight o'clock. I set a plan in motion for the children to die. Every day I gave their father candy—chocolates, hard candy, soft candy, powdered candy, liquid candy and anything with sugar. I even gave him boxes of sugar cubes, bags of granulated sugar—white and brown—as well as crates of sugar cane. My plan was for him to give the candy and sugar to his children. Several years of candy eating would rot their teeth. I knew that. The family, being of modest income, and the cost of dentistry being high, would choose to ignore the tooth decay and delay buying the children dentures. Thus, being toothless, the children would be unable to chew food. Their food intake would drop, nutrition would suffer and they would eventually waste away until death took them from the sugary nightmare they called life. This was an iffy plan because of the length of time needed, although I had calculated that under a constant sugar bombardment the average young person's tooth would decay in six months, three days, two hours, three minutes and twelve seconds. The beauty of the plan, however, is that it had a second component, an insurance policy. With so much sugar in their systems it was a certainty that the children would be hyper. Hyperactivity in children can lead to broken bones, concussions and brain tumors. It can also lead to high blood pressure, which can lead to a fatal stroke. However, I am not one to place all of his eggs in one basket. I knew that it could possibly take years for Plan A to develop. So I devised and implemented a second strategy. A sure way of keeping the wife home in the morning would be, I reasoned, to get her fired. Then she would *have* to stay home. But here was the dilemma: She worked by herself with the corpses at night, so there was no one to watch or to determine whether she performed her job as required, or whether she blundered. And if she incorrectly embalmed the corpses or mishandled them or bruised them or hurt them or insulted them or treated them with disrespect, well, they weren't going to complain. So I needed someone I knew to die so I could monitor their treatment at the funeral home at the hands of his wife. I had sick relatives all over who would walk into traffic without looking, and one by one, I convinced them to move here so that they might die and further my plan. Several are here; none are yet dead. There is a third aspect to the plan. Since none of the relatives were close to me, it would have been implausible for me to take off work for one of their deaths. So I had to devise a plan that would ensure my innocent absence from work when his wife was off. Contracting a disease myself was a sure way, and I've been eating fatty and carcinogenic foods and drinking enormous amounts of liquor in the hopes of becoming sick. But, again, my engineering background told me to always have an alternate plan. So, if I couldn't be hospitalized or bedridden with disease when she was off, I was in need of an accident. A car crash wouldn't do because most people survive them with little injury. I needed a bigger, more plausible accident, an accident to which everyone would say, 'Ned Vohonovich is one unlucky fellow; he surely could not have planned this. No one could have.' So I planned that on the day his wife was at home either caring for their toothless, malnourished, dying children, or pitying herself for being fired from a good-paying job, I would walk out my front door and a meteorite would crash onto my head, thus disabling me. It was a perfect plan, a plan devised to appear perfectly natural and to not arouse suspicions.

"The plan developed as intended. The editor fed the candy to his mangy children. Their teeth rotted and the parents could not afford the necessary dental work or dentures. Within six months the children were all gums, and Ned Vohonovich was on his way to becoming city editor. Then some minor problems developed. The children, unable to eat, suffered from extreme malnutrition and hovered near death. The wife saw their demise as an indication that she was a failure as a parent and mother and committed suicide by drinking embalming fluid and sealing herself inside a coffin. Her death, rather than sending the children into their final death spiral, awakened their will to live, and although gumless, they began eating oatmeal, soups and yogurt. So healthy was their diet that in just three weeks they had made the astonishing transition from malnourished customers for coffins, to healthy, strapping kids who, even at their young ages, enrolled in health clubs and lifted weights. The children went on to become health freaks and have since opened up chain of health spas and started a brand of oatmeal. They're making millions of dollars each year. And the editor—"

"How long ago did all of this happen?" Dave asked.

"Half a score and two years."

"And what happened to the editor?"

"As I was about to say before I was unprofessionally interrupted, he decided to quit, do nothing and live off his children's wealth."

"How long ago did he quit?" I asked.

"In years, a quarter-score."

"What happened then?"

"Well, I had always tried to be diplomatic and win the publisher's good graces by being a team player. Whenever we had gotten a good story into the paper, I told him that it was because of the efforts of my rival. So when my rival quit to pursue a life of wealth and sloth, the publisher reasoned that I was the incompetent one and he hired someone from the outside to replace the guy. I was demoted to reporter. I know what you are thinking, and I concur. Yes, it is time for Ned Vohonovich to reassess his strategic thinking and develop another plan of bold action and success. I am planning to drive the former city editor into bankruptcy so that he will be forced to return to this newspaper. I will manage to become his assistant again, and I will show him up as the incompetent he is and take control of the newsroom myself."

"Ned, your convoluted schemes have never worked and never will work," Paulette said.

"I tell you Paulette, the reason you get nowhere at this newspaper is because you are not patient and because you do not know how to plan to beat the system. I do."

Before Paulette could respond, the telephone rang.

CHAPTER 15

The Mayor Goes Goofy

"**H**ello and good morning, this is Ned Vohonovich, senior reporter with the...Yes, I understand. We will be right there Mister Mayor. Thank you and good bye, and have a nice day sir." After he hung up the phone, Ned turned to us and said in his deliberate cadence that never had a hint of joy, anger or excitement:

"That was the mayor. He is on the roof of this twenty-story building. He has five thousand city employees lined up on the roof and in the stairwells leading to it and he has commenced throwing them off the roof to their deaths. He promises to kill them all and then fling himself off the roof so that he will splat to death on the concrete below. He will grant us an interview, as will the doomed employees. I say we go now."

We didn't merely "go," as Ned had suggested, and as he did in a slow, deliberate gait in which his stride and pace never changed. Bug-eyed and nearly delirious, Dave, I and Paulette raced out of the small, dark pressroom and nearly flew to a nearby bank of elevators. I had never seen five thousand people thrown to their deaths before, and being one who ached for adventure and an interesting life that was full of incidents that I could later tell stories about, I secretly hoped that I'd be able to toss a few of them off the roof myself.

The wailing, begging for mercy, hysterical shouting, screaming and the last-minute prayers and pleas for forgiveness from the employees on the roof touched and angered us.

"What vile human pig, what devil could put people through this?" Paulette snarled.

Ned, who had arrived on the roof several minutes after we did, expressed—what was for him—emotion: "This could be one of the darker chapters in human history. A stain, no doubt, on the canvas of human affairs."

"I can't believe how evil, sick, twisted and deranged this mayor is. I hate him. This is wrong. This is outrageous," Paulette huffed.

Not wanting to be excluded from the outrage, I said with a grave indignation that was meant to underscore their anger and confirm it as appropriate: "This *is* sick. This *is* inhumane. Only a beast, only the sickest of the sick would make people wait in line to be killed. He should be throwing them off all at once. Making them wait like this is torture."

"That is indeed a unique view of the situation," Ned said, "and undoubtedly an accurate one. However, I submit to you that killing them in the first place is wrong."

Before I could respond, the mayor shouted for us to come near. A brunette with a thin, sharp, pointy nose, that because her head was held aloofly high was always pointed skyward, and whose voice was a bark, stood at the mayor's side as he threw screaming employees to their deaths.

"Will you be able to get this in the evening edition of your paper?" the woman asked sternly.

"I say to you Karen Blake, you are an efficient mayoral flack. You will not miss an opportunity to get your boss's name in the paper. Have you people no shame?" Ned asked her.

"The only shame in this situation would be if you didn't get this story because you insulted the mayor's public relations expert," she huffed back. "You and your colleagues are the only reporters who have been allowed up here. That could change."

"Understood. Might I quiz the mayor?"

"Go ahead, Ned. I'm not offended by your cynical attitude," the mayor, a short, stocky man who wore round, gold, wire-rimmed glasses said as he cheerfully threw employees off the roof.

"I ask you this, Mister Mayor, the most important question of all, describe in excruciating detail what you had this morning for breakfast."

"Ned, what kind of an idiotic question is that? I always thought you were smarter than to ask something that dumb. That's pure stupidity. I'm flinging people to their deaths off a twenty-story building and that's all you can ask? That question is stupidity to the thousandth power."

"I thank you for the compliment about my intelligence and counter with a compliment of my own. I have always regarded you as a shrewd, intelligent, capable, productive and successful public servant, Mister Mayor. But the question is not mine; it is an editor's. That is the first question they ask on stories like these."

"Ned, I'm not going to answer that. It insults my intelligence and the intelligence of the great and intelligent people of this great city," the mayor said over the wails for mercy of a young man he cradled in his arms and tossed off the building like a sack of flour.

"Understood. Then Mister Mayor, let me ask this," Ned asked while scribbling notes with a pen on a yellow legal pad. "How is it that this could have happened here? Are you harboring some deep resentments that have grown out of an abusive childhood? Did you lack self-esteem as a child? Did your parents not nurture you? As a child were you—even once—criticized?"

"Ned, what's gotten into you? These are really dumb questions."

"I know. But they will be asked of me by my editors and I must get them out of the way."

The mayor bent down to pick up his glasses from the roof, for they had been knocked off his face by a thrashing, screaming young woman just before she was flung overboard. "Ned, I wasn't abused, neglected or unjustly criticized as a child. I'm normal."

"Throwing city employees off the roof of a twenty-story building does not seem like normal behavior, Mister Mayor. Why are you doing this?"

"Because I'm angry."

"My editors would frown upon that. They say anger is bad."

"Yes, but Ned, listen. I'm angry at myself. All the charges in the indictment are true. I committed all of those crimes and took the twelve million in bribe money. I am guilty as charged—guilty, guilty, guilty."

"I must say, Mister Mayor, I have never heard of this—never heard of a politician admitting wrongdoing like this. This is amazing. I am obligated, however, to correct you. It appears that you took twelve million and twenty thousand dollars in bribes. Despite the inaccurate accounting, your admission remains amazing."

"It *is* amazing," Karen blared, "because this is an amazing mayor. Make sure you get in your story that this is an honest mayor. The most honest mayor we've ever had. What other mayor would be so honest as to admit to this?"

"It is noted. But Mayor, what exactly is it that you are angry about?"

"That I sold myself short, Ned. Sold myself for a mere twelve million and twenty thousand dollars. That's way too cheap. And now I'll go to prison for a measly twelve million bucks. I should have held out for more."

"A startling admission, Mister Mayor."

"Startling indeed!" the public relations aide blared again. "This is a mayor who has ambition; a mayor who will push himself; a mayor who isn't satisfied with being second, third or fourth best. This is a mayor who wants to excel; who holds himself to high standards. This is a mayor our children should emulate. They should never stop trying to be the best that they can be. Get that in."

"Duly noted. But Mayor, if you are angry at yourself, why is it that you are killing innocent people?"

"Because Ned, it's human nature to blame others for your mistakes and to take your anger and frustrations out on them. It's human nature, and Ned, I'm human."

"Not only that, but he is the most human of humans," Karen shouted. "Most people take out their problems on their families or a handful of friends and acquaintances. That's predictable, understandable and very low on the scale of cruel and illogical behavior. And really, Ned, to be cruel and illogical is to be human. So the more cruel and illogical the behavior, the more human you are. Taking stuff out on relatives and friends is barely cruel and so just barely human.

This mayor is taking out his frustrations on the entire city payroll and on people he doesn't even know, let alone like or love. He is the ultimate example of cruelty, and thus the ultimate in being human. Tell your readers that."

"It is my intention to do so. Mayor, it is ten-thirty in the morning, how many people have you killed so far?"

"Seven hundred and thirty-five. And I intend to work faster and finish the job before noon, because—"

"Because he is the hardest working, most efficient mayor in the universe," Karen interrupted. "When this mayor starts a job he finishes it; he's no quitter."

"So you are vowing to kill them all?"

"Yes."

"Will you then take your own life, Mister Mayor?"

"No."

"Why not? Have you not already pledged such action? Pledged it to me just minutes ago on the telephone?"

"Ned, I was just babbling."

"And impressive babbling it was. But Mister Mayor, by not taking your own life, will you not be reneging on your own promise?"

"No. My promise was to kill all the employees, and that promise I'll keep. I merely *suggested* that I might kill myself. No pledge was made, and by living I will violate no oath. This mayor keeps his word to the public. And why, Ned, won't I kill myself? Because after I vent my anger and frustrations out on these innocent people I won't be angry any more and won't need to kill myself."

Another Employee Overboard

As the mayor merrily threw another employee overboard, four fat, angry-looking men burst through a stairwell door and onto the roof. They rushed the mayor while shaking their fists and angrily denouncing him. The angriest, a short, fat man with a face that had the sandy, dirty color and lumpy texture of a russet potato, challenged the mayor.

"Mayor! You can't keep killing these people!" he shouted. "It is a violation of—"

"Of the code of humanity? Of God's law?" Ned asked with calm, but inquiring deliberation.

"No, you fool," the man snarled contemptuously as if angered by Ned's inability to see the obvious. "It's a violation of the contract this union has with the city. Right here," he said while pulling a sheaf of papers from the back pocket of his blue coveralls, "it says in article one hundred fifty-three, section seventy-three, subsection forty-eight, paragraph nineteen: 'It shall be a violation of this contact for the mayor or any of his advisors to knowingly throw city workers to their deaths from the top of City Hall.'"

The mayor was contemptuous of the union man and wasted no time in challenging the contract: "Well then, I'll just gun them down instead. Or I'll knife them. Or we'll bury them up to their heads in sand and run lawn mowers over their heads."

"Sorry mayor," the union man shot back. "The contract says you can't ever kill a city employee unless it's for cause. It's clear that these people have done nothing to merit death. They have not defaced even one of the three thousand three hundred and forty-two large photographs of yourself that you've put up at City Hall; they've never made jokes about your weight problem; and they have never snidely suggested that your wife, and not you, runs the show here. So, as it stands now, you are in violation of the contract. And if you continue killing these people, we will—"

"Don't try and bully this mayor with your blustery, hollow threats. This mayor will not submit to ugly intimidation," the mayor huffed. "We'll take this to the media. Ned, did you hear this union representative try to bully me? Attempting to extort the mayor, that's a story, Ned."

"No. We'll take *this, your willful violation of a collective bargaining agreement,* to the press, to the media!" the union man shouted with the triumphant excitement and dance of a boxer who has just knocked down an opponent. "And that will mean—"

The mayor and Karen staggered as if hit by a horrific revelation. They turned their terror-stricken faces toward each other and finished the sentence together by shrieking simultaneously: "Negative publicity!"

"No! No, no, no," the nearly delirious Karen screamed as if begging for deliverance from a cruel fate. "This mayor holds union contracts sacred and will never knowingly violate one."

The union man showed no mercy. "Unless you stop this killing now, we will file a formal complaint with the labor board!" he shouted while shaking a fist in the mayor's now-pale face.

The mayor and his aide, stung by the bold affront, rallied and countered with a shrewd proposal.

"Back off from your threat and I'll give you a job," the mayor said, "where you don't have to do anything, where you can goof off all day and get paid big money."

"I've already got one of those. I work for the city," the union man said.

"Then I'll put you on the payroll twice."

"I laugh at you. I'm already on three times. You forget that my brother-in-law runs the Personnel Department."

"I'll get a law passed that allows you to take for your personal use, a small percentage of all union members' dues."

"Sheeeeeit. I *already* skim off a *large* percentage of their dues for my personal use. You ain't giving me nothing."

"But I'll make it legal. That way you won't have to worry about the feds trying to indict you."

"I already don't worry. I cut them in on the action and they leave me alone."

The mayor then launched a more powerful counterstroke:

"If you don't back off I'll get you dumped as union president. I'll ruin your reputation so bad. I'll turn your name into mud so quick that the union rank and file will call an immediate special election and oust you as president. Then you won't have your sweet little perks."

"The love that my men have for me and my corruption is deep, and you, you little twit, you can't do anything to shake it."

"I can and I will. I've got affidavits in my back pocket—signed affidavits— from people who once saw you, and even though it was years ago it'll still stick, from people who once saw you do some actual work. Once your members get hold of that you'll be laughed off the planet."

The union man staggered as if hit by a vicious blow. Both men eyed each other wearily and tottered with exhaustion like two boxers who had been battering each other and who no longer had the energy to throw another punch. But the union man summoned his last bits of strength:

"If you don't stop killing these union members, I vow to you that come election time this union's policy committee will not endorse you for re-election."

It appeared to be the knockout blow. The mayor went pale again and reeled backwards. He was dazed and as confused as someone trying to buy a pipe wrench in a clothing store. One more blow, even a light one, would have put him out. But the union man was spent and could muster nothing more.

The mayor slowly regained his wits and mumbled: "I still have the affidavit. I'll read it here and now to these people and you'll be shamed forever."

Then the mayor wheeled around, and in a tired voice, addressed the several hundred employees who were on the roof:

"Employees and union members," he started, "before you go to your deaths, I have something to read to you."

"Nooooo!" the union man screamed. "Not that. Let's make a deal!"

"Okay," the mayor said. "We'll each walk away from here with something. I get to kill twenty-five hundred employees, which is half of what I want, and I make no mention of the affidavit and I get your endorsement. You keep twenty-five hundred union members and you double their union dues to make up for the money you'll lose from the dead ones."

"It's a deal!"

"Mister Mayor, is this not a cave-in?" Ned asked. "Is this not blatant pandering to the union? You had promised to kill all five thousand city work-ers—"

"Don't call them that, Ned, it offends them," the mayor said.

"Don't call them what? What offends them?"

"Workers. Don't call them workers. They take offense to the title. These people haven't done any real work in years."

"Mayor, have you not broken your promise in return for a political endorsement?"

"No Ned. We have revised the promise. A promise is an evolving, shifting thing. In the world of politics it can change from one day to the next, from one hour, hell, from one minute to the next. Here's the beauty of it, Ned. When you live by evolving promises, even though your action might be in total contradiction to your original promise, you haven't broken your promise. When you live by evolving promises, you'll never break a promise again."

"A rather self-serving theory, Mister Mayor."

Before the conversation went further we were drenched from above. A sudden thunderstorm had developed. Karen Blake screamed: "I need an umbrella! Somebody get me an umbrella now! Now!"

No umbrella was forthcoming and Karen was in a panic.

"Karen Blake, it is only water. Why are you afraid of water?" Ned asked.

"Because, you idiot, my nose is permanently pointed toward the sky, and if I don't get an umbrella my nose will fill up with water and I'll drown."

"Then why don't you tilt your head forward?"

"I can't. I was born a stuck-up snob. My whole family was. My head is permanently fixed in this position."

There was a scramble for an umbrella, but it was too late. Karen Blake drowned in the thunderstorm.

We raced back down to the press room. Fred was sitting where we had left him and was still smoking. Ned picked up the phone and dialed the office. "I need an editor," he said

Drowned In A Thunderstorm

calmly. "The mayor has broken his vow to kill five-thousand city employees for a cheap political endorsement from the city employees union. He is a mayor who cannot be trusted. He has already killed seven hundred and will kill twenty-five hundred by noon. In addition, he has admitted to taking twelve-million and twenty thousand dollars in bribes. He says he is guilty. This is the story of the century. What do you mean they are in a pre-meeting meeting? You must get one out. You can't? They've left orders that they not be disturbed? Fine. Have one call me when the meeting ends."

Forty minutes later the phone rang. Jimmy was on the line for Ned, who repeated the story again and emphasized its urgency and importance. After a few minutes Ned hung up the phone, turned gloomily to us and said:

"He doesn't want the story. Says we have a giant picture of a pretty yellow flower on the front page and that he's not going to break up that package for breaking news. He says we should do a big breakout on this for next month."

Ned was dejected, but not beaten. "Listen to this," he said, as he put the telephone's speaker on so we all could hear. He dialed the office again and said: "I propose another story. A fluffy kitty cat is sitting outside City Hall and passersby are petting it. If the editors are in a meeting, tell them."

Within seconds, Jimmy and the other editors were on the speaker phone. "Great story, Neddy," Jimmy said. "We want it. We also want to advance it."

"We want to own it!" shouted another. "We will set the agenda and make it ours."

"Follow the money," said another voice.

"How do we compare with other cities?" asked a fourth.

"What about the children?" demanded a fifth.

"Has the system failed?" someone asked.

And finally, another editor shouted: "Where are the skeletons buried?"

CHAPTER 16

Being A Crime Reporter

A Strange Crime

For the next few weeks I busied myself with learning to be a police reporter. Since I was scared, shy and pretty much hated people and didn't like talking to anyone, the job was difficult. I would discourage anyone who doesn't like talking to people from being a reporter. I didn't like cops, and from what I gathered, they didn't like reporters. At first, I wasn't very aggressive about getting stories. When one cop told me that officers in his station only talked to reporters on days when the sun rose in the west, I meekly agreed to call back when that occurred and hung up the phone. When one told me that he only talked to reporters when Halley's Comet appeared in the sky, I agreed that it was a logical and necessary practice and agreed to call back when the comet arrived. When one told me that he would only speak to reporters when they developed brains, I agreed to never call him again. When several cops told me that they only spoke to reporters on their days off, I began to suspect that they were trying to avoid me and that they didn't want to talk to me.

Eventually, though, I gained confidence and managed to get some cops to say "no comment," a statement that I greatly appreciated. I got some decent stories. There were dismembered torsos, headless bodies, sex crimes where jilted lovers had directed their anger at their former lover's genitals, teenagers who sledgehammered their parents to death while they were sleeping, people

95

who killed babies for fun, sickos who raped, a teenager who fatally shot his parents because they wouldn't let him watch monster movies, a woman who gutted a pregnant woman with a car key and stole her baby, other assorted atrocities, and my favorite, a man who stole and sniffed women's shoes.

These were good and important stories, I thought, but the paper never ran them. Jimmy said they were too negative for a family newspaper. When I argued one day that these crimes represented the truth about a part of society, and that by not printing them we were withholding the truth and lying to our readers, I was dismissed by Jimmy as an "egomaniac and sick person."

"Our readers don't need to know the truth, especially when the truth is troubling," he said.

"How are they supposed to change things for the better if they don't know in the first place that things are screwed up?" I asked once. "If there's somebody out there kidnapping children and raping women, don't you think people need to know so they can protect themselves?"

"This is a family newspaper. We don't want to alarm anyone," he said.

I never really enjoyed the police reporting job, but I came to appreciate it and wallowed in the myth that I was a hard-bitten, hard-drinking crime reporter. And, like so many people in any profession, I often preferred myth and title to the hard work of real reporting. So I memorialized my brief and mediocre career as a police reporter with this poem. At least I think I memorialized it.

Crime Reporter's Poem

His Name was Dennis Domzalski.
The crime beat was his game.
He smoked cigars and drank a lot
And had a gorgeous dame.

He worked like hell to dig up crime.
A damn good job he did.
The bad guys couldn't hide from him.
He knew where they hid.

He hated crime, oh my god,
How it made him sick.
When his stories ran in print,
The criminals had their pick

Of any jail in the land
To spend their wasted lives.
And D'd walk off and drink some booze
In the local dives.

"Whiskey, straight—bring it now,
Leave the bottle Jackson.
Who's that sweet thing down the bar?
I'll betcha she wants action.

"Hey babe, come here, sit by me,
I'm a crime reporter.
Barkeep, yo, over here,
And take this sweet thing's order.

"Ya say your name is Baby Jane.
Sounds like bull to me.
You shouldn't lie you silly thing.
Let's see your ID.

"Yeah, I can check it, yes I can,
'Cause I'm a crime reporter.
My beat's this nation from its core
To its every border.

"It says your name is Sally,
Sally Cozinetti.
I used to know a bum named that.
You got a brother named Eddie?

"No? So what? Who cares?
I don't give a damn.
He's probably dead; he's probably shot.
He got it 'Bam! Bam! Bam.'

"Sal, my name is Dennis.
My name is Dennis D.
I'm rough and tough and real mean
'Cause crime's got hold of me.

She Was One Hot Babe

"I hang around police stations.
I see crime all the time.
I think about it day and night,
It's always on my mind.

"We've got to stop the bad guys.
We've got to put 'em away.
We've got to make our nation's streets
Safe for kids to play.

"I don't like kids—don't get me wrong—
I hate their little guts.
The way they giggle and laugh all day
They must all be nuts.

"But crime is bad; it hurts the nation,
And someone's got to stop it.
We've got to put the crooks away
And take away crime's profit.

"That job's part mine, Baby Sal,
'Cause I report on crime.
All the bums that I write up
Wind up doing time.

"Impressed you say? I thought you'd be.
Let's go to my apartment,
Where you and I can both remove
These stupid, silly garments."

They left the bar. He took her home.
He walked her through the alleys.
He said how tough and mean he was
And bragged to his sweet Sally.

"Don't be scared," he said to her.
"I'm here to protect you.
If bad guys try to beat us up
I'll just shoot a few."

That thrilled the daylights out of her.
She fell into his arms.
She was doomed and couldn't resist
The crime reporter's charms.

They found his joint, a boarding room,
Above an all-night diner.
He bought her chili and asked her then
If she was a minor.

She said "no." They went upstairs,
And he unlocked the door.
When the chili was all gone
He asked, "Do you want more?"

"No," she said, "it's you I want.
Please take off your shirt."
This he did and plus some more
And he removed her skirt.

They kissed it seems so passionately,
It's clear that love was there.
He removed his Ban-lon socks
And she her underwear.

Other garments went in time.
She nibbled on his ear.
He looked at her so lovingly
And held her very near.

She told him that she loved him so.
She said, "You're mine all mine."
When he asked her why, she said:
"'Cause you report on crime."

They embraced so wickedly
And fell onto the bed.
She rubbed his chest and other parts,
Good feelings filled his head.

He thought of home and dear sweet mom
And wondered what she'd say,
If she'd seen how he'd grown up
And found new ways to play.

Time went on and things got warm,
The moon was full that night.
They kissed and hugged and romped around—
Things seemed so very right.

The moment was soon approaching
When their love'd be final.
That it was there and both felt it
Of this there's no denial.

He looked at her. She looked at him.
He seemed a little frightened.
She assured him tenderly,
How his face then brightened.

He made his move to finalize
Those mutual loving feelings.
Closer still he moved to her—
And then he was sent reeling.

Ring! Ring! Ring! Dong! Dong! Dong!
He heard the sirens screaming.
Fire trucks is what they were.
He knew he was not dreaming.

He jumped up to the window
And saw the trucks go by.
"Fire! Fire! Fire!" he screamed,
"Who? What? When? Where? Why?"

He quickly dressed and looked at Sal,
Who by then was crying.
He tried right then to comfort her
And said, "Bums may be dying."

"I'm sorry, Sal," he said to her,
"It's such a crazy time.
But someone may have torched a joint
And that's a damn big crime."

He donned his hat, a gray fedora,
And slid right out the door.
He winked at Sal and said to her,
"I'll be back for more."

The blaze was cheap, really cheap.
There was nobody dead.
A mattress fire was all it was
In some old drunk bum's bed.

Dennis phoned his editor and said,
"Chief, nothing's up.
It's home I'm bound, I'll see ya 'round."
The phone he then hung up.

He stopped into a liquor store
And had a few quick shots.
He thought of Sal at home in bed
And knew he missed her lots.

Well, he rushed home to his sweet Sal,
But she had left by then.
She left a note on the table
Written with his pen.

"I loved you so you crazy man.
I had a damn good time.
But now I hate your guts, you bum,
You broke this heart of mine.

"I hope we never meet again
And that you'll learn in time,
To take your openings when they come,
'Cause love can't wait for crime.

—Bye, Sally."

CHAPTER 17

Greedy Government Employees

While I was trying to be a police reporter who never talked to anyone, Dave gabbed with everybody while he covered local government. He made friends with dozens of government workers, drank with them when they weren't working, which seemed to be every minute of their existence, and attended parties and meetings where they fraternized, plotted strategy and denounced the public.

The big issue then was how to improve the public employees' pension plan. The police, firefighters, janitors, secretaries, jail guards, bus drivers and all other city employees wanted more lucrative pension benefits. Years earlier, city employees had decided to forego large pay increases in return for pension plans that allowed them to retire with more money at an earlier age. When Dave and I became reporters, city employees could retire after thirty years on the job at sixty-five percent of their top pay as long as they were fifty-five years old.

Private-sector employees in the city, most of whom had to wait until age sixty-five to retire, and who, through their taxes, funded the public-sector pension plans, resented the fact that large parts of their wages went to fund pension plans that were more generous than theirs. The morning newspaper made some noise—barely audible squeaks—in its editorials about the unfairness of taxpayers having to support with their backs and toil, a golden throne for public employees.

Since the retirement rules for public employees were made by the state legislature, dozens of city employees decided to run that year for the legislature. Dave and I attended their first strategy session, which was held in a dark, smoky bar during the day when they were supposed to have been working. The employees took several hours taking care of meeting "preliminaries," which I observed meant that they guzzled beer after beer. Only when they could barely stand did the strategizing begin. A tall, broad, lumpy man with a huge belly, who stunk and who looked as stale and wrinkled as a pile of dirty laundry, ran the meeting. His name was Pullup. He was so named because his pants wouldn't fit around his enormous belly and kept falling down, revealing portions of his hairy ass. Because this grungy creature did have *some* dignity, he constantly pulled at his pants waist in vain attempts to yank the pants back up above his ass.

Fortunately for our optical health, Pullup wore relatively snug-fitting pants that day and tugged at them only every few minutes.

The strategy, Pullup said, would be to get city employees and union members elected to the legislature in large numbers so they could then rewrite the pension laws to give themselves cushier pension plans at taxpayers' expense. That goal, though, was to be kept secret. The official campaign strategy that would be sold to the voters was that the public was being overtaxed and that public employees would come to their rescue if elected. However, if the newspapers or public opposed the pension hikes once they were proposed, it would be slyly suggested that because the city employed women and minorities, those who opposed the pension hikes were racists and sexists, an ugly, hateful charge that made the strongest, most loving and caring people cower and apologize for being something they weren't.

Pullup At "Work"

Pullup's strategy speech lasted only ten minutes. Afterwards, the drinking, which had remained heavy during his talk, got heavier. But there were two final matters of official business that had to be taken care of before the heavier drinking could commence. The first was to reveal the design of a bronze statue that would soon grace the entrance to the public employees' union headquarters building. The bronze, Pullup said between beers and burps, was to be a massive twenty-five feet high. Without fanfare, flourish or a speech—that would have required him to put down his beer—Pullup tugged a soiled, light-blue bed sheet off a four-foot high object that had been set on top of the bar. By the way those employees brayed, screamed, cheered and carried on, I thought that another barrel of beer had been tapped. That hadn't happened—yet. The frenzied cheering was for the model of the bronze that Pullup's tug had unveiled. The statue was that of a man and woman, each cradling an infant in their arms, bent over at the waist so that their butts were in the air. The man's pants were down around his ankles and the woman's dress was lifted up. Looks of distress and terror were carved into their faces, which were turned back and up toward three men who stood behind them. The infants were sobbing. Dangling by a short chain from the couple's necks were long rectangular signs that said "The Public." The man who stood the furthest behind the couple was gleefully rifling through a purse and wallet, which obviously had been taken from the two. Two men with lustful eyes and wide smiles stood suggestively close to the couple's behinds. The men's hands were positioned as if they were pulling down their pants zippers. The three men were identified by prominent patches on their shirt sleeves that said "Public Employees." A large plaque at the base was engraved with the work's title: "Screw 'Em"

Finally the cheering diminished, the room hushed and a deep solemnity fell across the drunken employees. "Time for the oath," Pullup said gravely. Their right hands raised up and they recited the oath along with Pullup: "I swear that each and every moment of my life I will screw the public. I will ignore them and take their money. I will treat them with contempt and utter disrespect. My animosity toward them is bitter and permanent. I will never assist a member of the public. Rather, I will work to keep them in their proper and natural state of helplessness, confusion and ignorance. They exist for me to leech off of, not to serve. I take this oath in remembrance of my fallen brother Zebediah,

Screwing The Public

a hero who died at his position from overexertion after being awakened by a despised member of the public who was seeking service during normal working hours on that tragic day in the sorrowful year of six hundred and twelve B.C."

When we returned to the newspaper office, Dave wrote his story:

City Employees Are Out To Screw The Public.

The city's public employees union today launched a campaign to elect dozens of its members to the state legislature with a goal of seizing control of the lawmaking body and increasing pension benefits for city employees.

But the candidates won't ever tell that to the public. During a secret campaign strategy meeting today in a local bar, a union leader said that candidates will campaign under the guise of tax relief for city residents.

"Our mission is to deceive the public so that we can get elected," Local 2505 President Pullup Radmon said during the meeting. "We will campaign on a platform of tax relief for the public. We will say they are overtaxed and that we will come to their aid. But once we're in office, we'll turn the tables and up our pension plans and tax them like they've never been taxed before!

"We'll empty their wallets, purses and bank accounts. It'll be good for them. They won't ever have to worry again about how to spend their extra money because they won't have any. We'll take it all. And when we're done, the wage-earning public will be our slaves."

Jimmy killed the story. "Acgh, guys, that's too traumatic for our readers. It's negative, offends people—it certainly isn't happy. It's not warm and fuzzy. And who says that these public employees don't deserve good pension plans?"

Thirty-four city employees were elected to the legislature that year. They acted quickly once the sixty-day legislative session began. A bill that made employees eligible for retirement after twenty-five years of service at seventy percent of their top pay with no age requirement was quickly passed by both houses. The governor vowed to sign it.

The morning newspaper opposed the plan, saying it was a rip-off of the taxpayers. Jimmy supported it. "It'll only cost each of us a few more cents a year—joy!" he wrote in an editorial.

A week after the first bill passed, a second one was introduced and approved. It said employees could get eighty percent of their top pay after twenty years on the job, and again, with no age limitation. The morning paper howled fraud. Jimmy saw it as a "logical and fair correction" to the original bill.

Three days after that, another bill was introduced in both the House and the Senate. This one cut the time until retirement to fifteen years of service and boosted the benefit to ninety percent of pay. Protests mounted and busloads of angry citizens stormed the capitol building on the day the bill was to be heard by the finance committees of both houses. But legislative leaders canceled the hearings that day. The angry and frustrated protesters left, but vowed to return the next day and the day after, and every day, if necessary, to denounce the bill in committee. At midnight, when the protestors were at home sleeping, the finance committees were convened and the bill was heard and approved within ninety seconds. It was then sent to the floors of the respective houses where it passed instantly.

The morning paper was furious and so was the public. "This vile deception is a crime against the public!" the paper screamed in a rare, front-page editorial. Jimmy considered it a "thoughtful amendment" to the original proposal. Legislative leaders, feeling the public outrage, vowed to reconsider the plan. They did, and the next day they cut the time of service needed for retirement to five years and increased the pension benefit to one hundred percent of top pay. The morning paper called for indictments and public hangings of legislators. Radio talk show hosts called for beheadings and torture. Angry citizens stormed the capitol with pitchforks, bricks and firebombs. Jimmy counseled caution and brotherhood. "Why can't we all get along?" he pleaded in an editorial. "This negativity on the part of residents is troubling. We do not condone violence in any case, ever. Besides, the pension plan will only cost each of us a few extra dollars a year."

The next day another bill was introduced. This one said that public employees could retire with full pay on the day they were hired, and at the pay they would have received had they worked and gotten raises for forty-five years. A companion bill was introduced as well. It granted full pensions to the spouses and children of public employees—employees who could retire with a full pension without ever having even put in eight hours on the job. The two bills were merged.

The morning paper devoted all of its pages the next day to venomous and unrestrained attacks on legislators. It urged citizens to kill the lawmakers and to burn their bodies. Jimmy pleaded for restraint and understanding. "After all," he wrote, "this is only going to cost each of us three-quarters of our paychecks and our houses."

Private sector workers rioted. Legislators were dragged from their homes and beaten. The capitol was torched. Government buildings were ransacked. The National Guard was called out, but refused to muster. The governor went into hiding, and legislators were beginning to think that they had misread the public's mood. Momentum was building to repeal the bills. The governor issued a statement that he would consider a veto of any pension bill.

Then the union struck back. Its leaders leveled charges of racism and gender bias against the morning paper and everyone who opposed the final pension bill. Those who opposed the bill hated minorities, women and children, they said. Jimmy agreed with them. The morning paper backpedaled with apologies to any minorities or women it had offended. But it still opposed the new pension plans. Then the government workers struck harder. They got the state's attorney general to declare that those who fought the bill would be prosecuted on charges of conspiracy to neglect and abuse children. "All who fight this bill are guilty of genocide against children," the attorney general declared.

Most residents backed down, but the morning paper stood firm. Legislation was then passed that made operating a newspaper with opinions contrary to legislative leadership a crime. Police raided the morning paper, shut it down and arrested the owner. The morning paper's opposition to the final pension bill ceased and the measure was approved. The governor immediately signed it.

Jimmy cut the staff's wages so he could pay himself more. He needed the extra money, he said, so he could pay his increased taxes and still have money left over to buy an occasional bag of groceries.

CHAPTER 18

More Reorganizations

During those few weeks of legislative turmoil, the paper went through four more reorganizations and seven design changes. We were now covering the city based on peoples' weights—each reporter was assigned to cover people in a certain weight range—and we were running pictures diagonally. We did away with the sports section, then brought it back as the front section. We ran stories in type so large that only two or three words could fit on a page. One day we were able to fit only half a story in the entire paper. Then we reduced the type size so we could cram four thousand stories into a fifty-page paper. In one edition, all the photos in the paper were of milk cartons.

I asked Jimmy why we changed so often, and questioned whether the constant change was good for circulation. He looked at me like I was crazy and offered this explanation:

"Acgh, Denny, you don't want to let people get used to one style or design. Because when they do and you come along and change things, they get angry. By maintaining a state of constant change, the readers don't get used to any particular style, and thus they don't get angry when you do change. I developed this theory all by myself."

That was abundantly obvious, I said, and walked away. It seemed crazy and illogical to me, but who was I, a mere reporter, to question an editor and a manager?

Fred had made a trip to the office that day where he helped create a scene. He stood in the middle of the room, surrounded by Baba and five other women. I approached and listened to the conversation.

"I'll bet that your dong is sooooo long that it scrapes the floor," Baba said while the others laughed. A chubby woman with dark hair and an angry look permanently affixed to her puffy face disagreed.

"Bull. That thing's probably so small that he can't find it," she said.

"Smaller than that!" shouted another. "I'll bet it doesn't exist."

"I have no doubt that he *can't* put a cow to sleep," laughed a third.

"And how about those manly testicles, marbles, no doubt," a fourth said to more laughter.

"Peas!" Baba shouted.

"No! Grains of sand!" the puffy-faced one said angrily.

"Well, Freddie Eddie," said a woman who was an editor. "I think I want to—I want to. I want to, ouuu! all over you. And if you don't let me, you'll work the midnight shift. What do you say to that?"

Fred smiled bashfully and shuffled away toward me.

"They really piss me off," he told me. "They always do this to me."

"Every time you come up here?"

"Yeah. It's always the same."

"How often are you up here?"

"Two or three times a week."

We walked into a small, long room that contained our mail boxes—a rack of small wooden boxes nailed to a wall. We got our mail, one piece of which was a note to the staff from Jimmy.

"It has come to my attention that our female staffers are increasingly being subjected to the heinous crime of sexual harassment. This must stop," the note said. "Sexual harassment is wrong; it is a crime and it will not be tolerated in this newsroom. Any employee found guilty of sexual harassment will be terminated. So as to gauge the extent of the problem in this newsroom, I will be giving our female employees a questionnaire on this subject to complete. We want to know how often and how terribly they have been subjected to this awful, awful crime."

I was struck by the fact that only the women were to get the surveys. I had just witnessed the blatant sexual harassment of Fred.

"Why don't you ask for a survey?" I asked him. "Or why don't you ask that the men get the surveys as well?"

The poor man looked terrified. He backed away as if I were evil or poison or in some other way life-threatening. "No, no, no," he said, shaking his head in fear. "No!"

I was disgusted that men weren't getting the survey. After all, we could be subjected to sexual harassment too. I wrote a short note in the in-house newsletter saying that men too should be given the survey, and I used the example of how Fred, although I didn't name him, had been ridiculed by the women. That constituted sexual harassment, I wrote.

The reaction to my note swift and vicious. I was accused of being a pig, enemy of women, Neanderthal and a monster. The puffy-faced woman who had helped ridicule Fred, and who was the city editor's wife, was the most vicious. She taped her hand-written response to the newsroom bulletin board:

"That man is a criminal, and his chauvinistic proposal that men should get the sexual harassment survey is a crime. Sisters, hear me shout: All men are rapists! All men are pigs! Men have been subjugating women for all of history. They have enslaved us. They are all criminals. All men should be tried and executed for their crimes against women. No, forget the trials. Just execute them. And this pig should be the first to die. Shoot him in the back of the head. Cut off his things and let him bleed to death."

I responded with my own note that I wasn't a rapist:

"I have never raped anyone, and since I've only been on two dates in my whole life, I've never enslaved a woman. And I don't think that *every* man is a rapist. I would like to see some facts to back that statement up. And if it can't be backed up, I would think that the writer just defamed hundreds of millions of men across the world."

Jimmy refused to run my rebuttal in the newsletter. He called me into his office to explain why.

"Denny," he said as he tossed a copy of my reply on his desk. "This is rubbish and I'm mad at you for writing it. How dare you defend men! And how dare you write something so negative and so angry. You know that anger isn't allowed at this paper. What you wrote was a personal attack. We do not allow personal attacks at this paper."

"But Jimmy, you're a man. What—"

"Yes, I'm a man, and I'm a pig. And I apologize for it every minute of my life. You should too."

"No. I haven't done anything wrong. She's wrong and you're wrong. And I didn't like her attack. I didn't appreciate it."

"I don't care what you appreciate. You're wrong."

"No I'm not. This is America, and that's my opinion."

"This may be America, but this is also a newspaper. And at a newspaper, employees cannot, I repeat, cannot express their opinions unless they are the correct opinions."

"But what about free speech? This is a newspaper. My God. You'd think that I'd be allowed to express an opinion."

"Don't give me that free speech crap. This is a newspaper. Newspapers hide behind free speech; they don't practice it."

"How come she got to write her note and attack me? That was angry and negative. That was a personal attack if I ever saw one."

"There you go again. You're walking on thin ice, buddy."

"What do you mean?"

"I just told you that personal attacks aren't allowed at this paper, didn't I? And what do you do? You turn right around and level a personal attack against another employee."

"What are you talking about?"

"You just said that she launched a negative, angry personal attack against you. That's a personal attack against her and that's forbidden."

"How come she can call me a rapist, which I'm not, and I can't accuse her of making false accusations against me, which she has? Why is it that she can express her opinions, but I can't express mine? Sounds like a hypocritical double standard."

"You're pushing me, buddy. For your information, some opinions are more privileged than others. Some opinions are right and some are wrong. When you have the correct opinions, then you can express them. Now get out of here and stop challenging authority."

Within a few minutes I was in trouble again. The puffy-faced one had posted what was supposed to be a sarcastic note about me on the newsroom bulletin board. I took exception to it and wrote on it that I didn't think she was very funny. Jimmy saw it and summoned me into his office.

"What is the meaning of this?" he demanded.

"All I said is that I didn't think she was funny."

"That's a personal attack. How dare you make judgments about people! This is America, buddy. You can't say that! Take it back!"

"No!"

"You're on probation. Get out of here."

I goofed up again a few hours later. The puffy one put a note on the bulletin board saying that she thought orange was the most beautiful color.

I replied with a note that said: "I respect your opinion, but I like grey. I think grey is the most beautiful color." Minutes after I posted it I was in Jimmy's office again.

"I'm cutting your pay as punishment for disrupting this newsroom and for disobeying my orders."

"But you said I could express an opinion if was a correct opinion. This was subjective. All I said was that I thought that grey was the most beautiful color. How can that be an incorrect opinion?"

"Because it's not what we think! I see only two solutions to this problem. Either I fire you, or you go to newspaper management training school. Which do you want?"

Being fired would not have bothered me because we were on vacation anyway, but I chose management school. On my first day there I was given a three-thousand-page manual on how to be a successful manager. The instructor told us that the manual was the bible of management training and that we would study it until we had it memorized and its theory was second nature to us. The first page said: "To be a successful manager you must always, in each and every instance where something has gone wrong, BLAME THE EMPLOY-EES!" The second page contained only three words: "BLAME THE EM-

PLOYEES!" The third page read the same, and so did the fourth and fifth—and so did all three thousand pages! Each day we were quizzed on what we learned. The students who repeated those three words with the greatest enthusiasm were given the highest marks. We received a second manual, which said on every one of its two thousand pages: "Play favorites. Employees who never disagree with you are never wrong; reward them, and punish those who disagree with you." A third manual told us that the way to succeed in the newspaper business was to abide by the theory of "Enforced Mediocrity."

"Take no chances. Make no waves. Rock no boats. Side with the establishment. Never stick up for individual rights," it said.

I fooled the instructors into thinking that I was an honors student, and I was dismissed from the class and sent back to the paper, which was in turmoil.

Paulette had repeatedly requested time to pursue a story about how the U.S. government, in a top-secret experiment, had injected people with poisonous, radioactive materials decades earlier. The experiment was done at the dawn of the nuclear age, and the dozens of subjects were never told of the injections. And, the doctors who conducted the experiment never got permission from the subjects to fill them with poisonous substances. It was, Paulette said, a bombshell story. Paulette needed time to research the story and write it. The editors wouldn't give her the time.

"You're to cover neighborhoods and people who eat sugar-coated cereal," one editor told her. "I forbid you to work on that story."

Others at the paper ridiculed Paulette, saying her story would never go anywhere. The paper's science writer said he saw nothing wrong with the government injecting people with poison because it was done in the name of science. "If anything, we should be celebrating this experiment and calling for more just like it," he said in a note on the bulletin board. "Attaboy, scientists!"

So Paulette worked on the story on weekends, at night after work and sometimes in between other assignments. Most of the other reporters hated her and refused to help her with the story. Some editors wanted her fired for working on it during the weekends. That, they said, was insubordination.

There were other problems, as well. For a long time, Paulette, Ned and a few other reporters had been challenging the heavy use of graphics and photos, as well as the lack of hard news in the paper. Baba, most of the other reporters, and the designers and photographers composed the opposing faction. They wanted more and bigger pictures. They said news was useless. One day Paulette and her allies wrote a lengthy piece for the newsletter in which they challenged the move toward photos and graphics. The other side wrote back with a challenge of its own. The debate raged. It was called "Anger." The editors didn't like it.

Jimmy and Dale called a staff meeting. Attendance was mandatory.

"This is bad," Jimmy said as he unfolded a lengthy copy of the debate essays. "This is bad, bad. I'm ending this hateful debate now. Bad people. Anger is wrong. We are all going to get along and treat each other with civility. There will be harmony in this newsroom. Dale has a plan that will accomplish that. Dale?"

"Yes, I do have a plan. But first, let me explain why Jimmy and I have decided to kill off this ugly debate. There cannot be free speech if people are angry with each other. That means we have to limit what we say around here. From now on, there will be no angry words. We are censoring you. Only through censorship can there be free speech! From now on, to ensure harmony at this newspaper, you must say these words whenever I give an order, express an opinion or make a decision for the good of this newspaper. This one sentence will solve all of our problems and make you all model employees. Simply say to me, 'Yes, Dale, you are right.'

"Now let's practice this. Say along with me, 'Yes, Dale, you are right.' And finally, people, be happy. This is a glorious day! You are now all free to think, free to think exactly like me!"

They repeated it, even Ned and Paulette. Dave and I didn't. We couldn't stomach anything so demeaning.

"These people are sheep," Dave told me. "I'm going to say something. The truth is, newspaper editors and managers cry that journalism is legally protected by free speech laws, and then they try to stomp out free speech in their newsrooms. This is the greatest hypocrisy ever in the history of ever."

Ned, who was sitting nearby, overheard Dave and urged him to remain silent.

"I'm telling you, bad things will happen if you push them any further. I know. You have no idea how serious this is."

"I am a bold man, not a coward. I will speak the *truth*," Dave said. Ned cringed at that last word.

"Whatever you do, do not use the t-word. I tell you that you must not use it. For your own sake and well-being, heed my advice."

"Sorry pal, we are two bold men, and we will speak."

Dave stood up and spoke passionately about the employees' hypocrisy and cowardice. We both urged the employees to stand up for their free-speech rights. Dave ended by saying, "This place is an asylum, that's the truth. We speak the *truth*!"

Jimmy and Dale were livid and with trembled with rage. "What do you two speak?" they demanded.

"The *truth*!" we shouted.

"Security!" they screamed.

Dave and I were quickly surrounded by armed, uniformed guards who began beating us with night sticks. Soon, all went dark.

Security!

CHAPTER 19

Going To Die?

It was still dark when my eyes opened, but I could see a little. I was cold and damp and lying face down on a dirt floor. Dave was on the ground next to me, still passed out. I roused him with a few kicks to his shins and some elbows to his ribs. He sat up, clutched his temples with both hands, sighed and asked if I had any aspirin.

"Well then go get some," he ordered before I could even answer the question.

"I can't. I've got a headache," I said.

Even if I had been feeling well, I would not have been able to go get aspirin. We were in a dark, musty cave that stunk intensely of urine. It was maybe a hundred feet long and thirty feet wide and was lit by four small light bulbs that dangled from wires stretched across the thirty-foot-high rock ceiling. Water dripped in dozens of places from the roof and pooled on the floor, turning patches of it into mud. We got up and slowly picked our ways in the dim light to the cave's far end where we found a huge, steel door. We tried opening it, but had no luck. It was locked. We were prisoners!

"Are we going to die here?" I screamed in a total loss of composure.

"Who cares about that. My question is: Will we ever have beer or cigars again?" Dave said with a nervous laugh.

We were startled and frightened by a slow, sad, hopeless voice that came from a corner of the cave: "The answers are 'yes' and 'no.' Yes, you will die here, and no, you will never have beer or cigars again."

The voice belonged to a thin, rickety, dirty man with wild grey hair down to his shoulders, a grey moustache and beard that merged into one great mass of grey and made his head look like an orange covered with mold. He was hunched over, and even though he used a thick tree branch as a cane, he was barely able to stand. His clothes were so worn and tattered that it looked as if he were draped by a huge cobweb.

"You will never get out. You will rot here. This is the dungeon. Scores have come and have never left except by coffin," he told us.

"Whose dungeon is it, and why have we been tossed into this hole in the ground that stinks of rotting flesh?" Dave asked.

"It's an old mine of some sort and was originally turned into a dungeon by newspaper editors and managers. They later offered it to corporate managers and politicians throughout the city. In short, everyone who is a boss of some sort has the right to throw employees into this place. Why are people thrown in here to rot? For having an opinion different from bosses and for telling the truth. In this town that's a crime punishable by death. They hate the truth. It drives them crazy. There are armed guards outside the door. Our only food is stale and rotting leftovers from their managerial banquets and luncheons. They throw it down from the ceiling and laugh as we fight each other for the scraps. There are twenty more of us down here, all with sad, horrible stories to tell."

We asked the guy, whose name was Mark, his story. He said:

"'I've been down here two years. Won't last much longer. I worked for the afternoon paper. They had me covering dried flowers—not gardening or botany, just dried flowers. I couldn't write about the process of drying flowers, how large an industry it was or what types of flowers were best for drying, just dried flowers. My stories were usually something like, 'Daisies are flowers that can be dried,' or 'Dried flowers are dry.' When I wrote that dried flowers are dry, the

Mark Had Told The Truth

editors demanded to know where my information came from and that I attribute that statement to an expert. It was bizarre. Everyone knows that a dried flower is dry. Once I sneaked a line into a story that said the sun rises in the east. Again, they wanted attribution. So I looked in the encyclopedia and cited it as a reference that the sun rose in the east. They wanted more definitive attribution. One day I wrote a story that said dried flowers are dead. Not only did they want attribution, but I was buffeted with a storm of questions from editors. I remember them. 'Follow the money! How do we compare with other cities? Can this be localized? Has the system failed? How does the affect the children? Where are the skeletons buried?'

116

"I couldn't believe they would ask such stupid questions on a nothing story. I couldn't answer the questions because they weren't applicable. But in a moment of frustration and rage I screamed to them that the skeletons were buried in the cemetery. They put me on probation for that. I had had it with them and so I insisted one day that dry flowers were dry, that they were dead and that that was the truth. They seized up at that last word and had me brought down here. There are others here. You should meet them."

As we picked our way in the dim light back down the length of the cave, several hideous looking creatures—walking skeletons—stumbled out of the shadows. Mark introduced us to one who was covered with a shredded, olive green woolen army blanket.

"My, myyy, mmm, my, nnnn, nnnnaa, naaaaame is Jack," he stuttered. "I have been hhheeeere fourteen mmmm moooonths."

Jack, too, had worked for the afternoon paper. One day the paper ran only headlines on its front page. But the words were jumbled so that readers had to decipher them. For instance, "the," was spelled "het" and, "today" was spelled "ayotd." The paper's designers and graphics experts thought it was an ingenious way to draw readers to the paper. They considered it an "entry point" into the paper, Jack said. At that time the paper was selling thirty thousand copies a day. The day of the jumbled headlines, it sold only four copies.

Jack told the editors that their idea was idiotic and had cost the paper twenty-nine thousand nine hundred and ninety-six lost sales. For that they threw him into the dungeon.

Susan, an emaciated, ancient-looking thirty-year-old, had also worked for the paper. Her crime: Telling an editor that his shoe lace was untied. It *was* untied, but Susan had no business speaking the truth, and so she was tossed into the cave.

Daniel was a haggard giant who had worked in a grocery store. He told the company's managers that their idea to close the store during daylight hours and keep it open only from one to three o'clock in the morning was dumb and would cost the store business and money. The store managers stuck to their plan. Almost no one shopped between one and three in the morning and the store quickly failed. The managers gave themselves bonuses, blamed the loss of business on the employees and threw ten of them into the dungeon. Several had since died.

Kevin, who said he had only a few hours of life left, had worked in the banking business. One day he got into a dispute with a manager over the manager's height. The manager claimed he was six-foot-three. Kevin said it wasn't true, and put a tape measure to the guy. He was only four-foot-seven. The manager fumed. Kevin got the dungeon.

Grace, who even in starvation and sickness maintained a dignified poise, once entered a company-sponsored contest at her public relations firm to guess the weight of the company's founder. She guessed correctly—three hundred and fifty-three pounds. One of Grace's co-workers guessed one hundred and fifty-five pounds. The colleague was promoted to vice president and given a big raise. Grace was taken to the cave.

Eddie, a former bank teller, once caught his supervisor stealing money from a teller's drawer. Eddie reported the incident to his supervisor's supervisor and was promptly thrown into captivity.

Only Four-Foot-Seven

Joe, who got to the dungeon two days before we did, had an equally sad story. He, his co-workers and his boss played a softball game against the employees of another lawyer's office. The stakes were high. The winning team got all of the losing team's clients, which meant that the losing team would have to close. Joe's boss, a prominent lawyer, had demanded the game because he wanted to drive a rival lawyer out of business. Every time up at bat, Joe homered. In fact, he drove in all of his team's eleven runs. In each of his four times at bat, Joe's boss struck out. His final strikeout occurred in the bottom of the ninth with two outs, the bases loaded, Joe on third and the team behind by one run. The boss blamed the loss of the game and of all of the firm's clients on Joe. If Joe had only stolen home plate in that last inning, the company would have been saved, the boss said. The boss filed for bankruptcy, got to keep his 20-acre estate, and sent Joe to the dungeon.

Melanie was a beautiful black woman who had been in there only a few days. A new executive took over her calculator manufacturing company and vowed to triple the company's already substantial profits by firing employees—all of them! When Melanie told him that if all the workers were fired there would be no profits because no one would be making calculators, she was ridiculed and banished to the dungeon. We had reported on that story in the days before we were sent there. All of the employees were fired and the company collapsed. The chief executive officer had given himself a $10 million bonus just before the firings. He then blamed the collapse on the employees.

After listening to all of the sad, horrible stories, I blurted out my conclusion: "We should all be managers! That sounds like fun and pays well!" Had the inmates not been so weak they would have beaten me to death. And had we not scampered away from the water that was falling from the ceiling, they would have asked Dave to kill me, and I think he would have.

"How does it rain in a cave?" I asked as we huddled together near a dry spot.

"That's not water," Mark offered weakly. "That's urine. They're peeing on us. It happens every day, two or three times a day. Hundreds of editors and managers from throughout the city come here and urinate on us through holes that have been drilled through the roof. It's their form of recreation. On weekends they have picnics up there. They drink huge amounts of liquids and then piss on us. That's what we're here for, to be pissed on by managers. Usually we hear them laughing and carrying on. Sometimes they ridicule us and throw rocks down on us through the bigger holes. We can't get out. We're doomed."

That's Not Rain

"Only a person who believes he is defeated is in fact doomed, my friend," Dave said. "But you are fortunate that a bold man—meaning me—has been put here with you. We'll get out of here. Give me some time to think of a plan."

One plan was for Dave to dig straight down through the earth, emerge on the other side of the globe and then come back and raise an army of workers and storm the cave and rescue us. Even I knew that wouldn't work, and I said so, explaining: "You'll burn up once you get to the earth's molten core. It'll be too hot, unless, of course, you wear a fire-proof suit. But I don't see where you're going to get one in here."

Dave had additional plans. He thought of using his stinky feet to overpower the guards, of scaling the cave's walls, and of trying to dig our way out through the roof at night. That was once tried, Mark said, but failed because layers of reinforced concrete had been poured on top of the cave and covered with earth. The holes through which the managers peed on us were specially drilled, as were the openings through which they tossed rocks down on our heads. But they weren't wide enough for an adult—even a skinny, starving one—to get through. Dave eventually settled on what he called a "bold, incredibly funny" plan, and set us to work.

For several days we used rocks and whatever sticks were in the dungeon to dig, chip and grade the floor so that all the urine from the roof drained toward and pooled in front of the huge steel door at the cave's entrance. We graded it so that dry spots for us to stand on were left at the cave's edges near the door. Then Dave ordered that we bring down the wires from the ceiling. No one could climb the walls, so Dave put me on his shoulders and ordered the stronger captives to climb on top of me and on top of each other so that we formed a human ladder. It took seven of us standing on each other's shoulders to reach the ceiling. The frail Mark was the last one up, and he undid the wires and brought them down to the ground. Dave unscrewed one of the light bulbs and tossed it aside so that he had in his hand a bare, but live socket. A light switch that could turn the power on and off was embedded in the wall near the door.

"We're going to electrocute them," Dave told us. "We'll get them all down here, and when they step in this pool of piss, I'll throw the wires in, flick the switch and turn on the juice and zap! They'll be fried! It's a great plan."

"It's a great plan except for one thing," Mark said weakly. "They never come down here. They pay the guards to do their work. They want no involvement with us other than to piss on us."

"We'll get them down here, and it won't take long. We'll get them so angry, so full of rage that they'll all come storming down here wanting to break our necks themselves. If I'm right, it's a Saturday, and there should be hundreds of them up there."

We waited anxiously to make sure the managers were on the roof in force. The signal that they were came when dozens of streams of urine poured from the ceiling. Dave told us it was time to act.

"Chant along with me and as loud as you can—even the weak ones— 'Managers make bad decisions! God bless the truth! Let's go, 'MANAGERS MAKE BAD DECISIONS! GOD BLESS THE TRUTH!'"

It wasn't more than five minutes after we began chanting that the urine streams dried up. We could hear shouts and a massive shuffling of feet on the roof. In another three our four minutes there was a commotion raging outside the steel door.

"Kill 'em now!" was the general refrain we heard amid the angry shouting and demands for our lives. They began banging on the door.

Dave ordered us to the dry sides of the cave near the door and to keep on chanting. In a few more moments the door burst open and a mob of managers rushed in. The urine puddle was five feet wide and twenty feet long. When they were all inside, Dave threw the light socket into the puddle and flicked on the switch. A massive scream went up and then all was quiet except for a few moans. Dave turned the switch off and we walked over the bodies to freedom.

"Let this be a lesson," Dave said after we had gotten some fresh air and as we gazed upon the three hundred and seventeen corpses lying in the pool of urine. "When you piss on people, you get wet too."

CHAPTER 20

Revolt!

After long showers, hearty meals and parties with our fellow former captives, Dave and I returned to the paper. Unfortunately, none of the paper's editors had gone to the cave that weekend, and they were alive.

There was a great commotion in Jimmy's office. Reporters from TV stations and newspapers throughout the state were questioning him. Baba, Dale and the other editors surrounded Jimmy. They were laughing and congratulating each other.

"You must feel proud that Paulette has won the Pulitzer, journalism's highest award, for exposing the fact that the government injected unwitting Americans with poison during this reckless, dangerous and secret experiment?" one reporter asked. "She is one hell of a reporter, isn't she?"

"Paulette is, without question," Jimmy said with a child-like smile, "mentally retarded and useless as a reporter. This Pulitzer was a team effort on the part of all these editors. *We* did this story and *we* won this award. Paulette didn't want to do anything with this story. Sometimes she begged for help. Often, when she didn't want to do anything with it we had to force her to. Eventually, she refused to work on it. That was in the story's early stages, and that's when this team took over. I'm proud as heck of these people. I'm proud as heck of me."

Paulette, who was in a corner listening, trembled violently at Jimmy's remarks. She was speechless. One TV reporter shoved a microphone in her face and asked: "My, my, Paulette. Is it true that you are mentally retarded? And do you feel ashamed of yourself for trying to claim this Pulitzer that these editors won?"

Paulette burst into tears, convulsed violently and slumped to the floor.

"Well, there you have it folks," the reporter said into the microphone. "She *must* be retarded. Now Jimmy, tell us about all of the amazing work *you* did on this prize-winning story."

Jimmy held court with the reporters for several hours. In the meantime, we had carried Paulette to her desk and put her in her chair where she sat speechless and dazed. After the reporters packed up and left, Jimmy, followed by Dale and the others, pranced to the middle of the newsroom. Jimmy addressed the staffers who had gathered around him:

"I have two grand announcements, people. Two announcements that will take us where we want to go as a newspaper, where we deserve to go, where we rightfully belong. After today, the competition—nay, the world—will wonder what the heck we're doing here. First, there are still bad words, insensitive words, being spoken in this newsroom. Just the other day I heard someone say that they didn't like one of Baba's stories. That is intolerable. So, in order to be a perfect newsroom, a newsroom where never again an insensitive, negative, hurtful, troubling, disrespectful, injudicious or incorrect word or opinion is spoken, I have decreed that beginning later today, at two o'clock, no one in this newsroom will ever again speak to each other! We won't write to each other or in any way communicate. This will guarantee that no offensive words will ever be spoken again. And don't *think* anything offensive or negative either, because we'll find a way to stop you.

"Secondly, and finally, I am announcing that with today's edition we guarantee ourselves the distinction of being the best small newspaper in the world. Today, we have achieved design perfection—the ultimate, the absolute pinnacle of achievement. We will win every design award here and forever more. My friends, starting today, this is our design." With that, Jimmy held up a copy of the paper and began opening the pages. All were blank!

"But Jimmy!" screamed Paulette, who had recovered from her daze. "You're telling us that we're going to be printing nothing but white space, nothing but blank pages?"

"Yes! Isn't it grand? This is the ultimate use of white space as a design technique."

A wild shriek pierced the air, and Paulette, Ned, Fred, Dave, I and a few other reporters attacked Jimmy and the other editors. Within minutes we had tied them up and marched them outside to the parking lot, where, ever since we had arrived at the paper months earlier, Paulette had had a cauldron of boiling oil set up. The three editors she had caged in her horse trailer had long ago died because she had forgotten about them. Jimmy, Dale, Baba and the others were marched up the steps of the wooden platform next to the cauldron. They pleaded and begged for their lives and sobbed and shrieked and prayed and begged some more. Dale was thrown in first. His cries of pain and the stench from his boiling body sickened me. Baba was next. Others went in time, and soon the cauldron was overflowing with tar-boiled flesh. Finally, it was Jimmy's turn. He wailed a hundred times louder than the others. Up on the platform, Paulette dipped large metal ladle into the cauldron and pulled it out. It contained at least a quart of boiling oil.

"Consumed with hatred?" she screamed at Jimmy. "Whose Pulitzer prize is it? Whose is it? Is it the team's, or is it Paulette's?"

"It's Paulette's," Jimmy gurgled back. "It's yours."

"Why didn't you tell that to the reporters? You lying shit," Paulette screamed as she plunked one of Jimmy's hands into the ladle." He screamed. She laughed.

"Am I mentally retarded?" she demanded.

"No," he replied.

"Then why did you tell them that?"

"Because I wasn't thinking straight or seeing things clearly. I—"

"We'll fix that!"

Paulette yanked Jimmy's head back, ordered one of the reporters to hold his eyelids open and poured boiling oil into his eyes. She then scooped another ladle out of the cauldron and poured boiling oil into Jimmy's ears. His screams were hideous. Finally, Paulette ended the torture and dumped the blinded Jimmy into the cauldron. The rest of us gleefully scavenged for wood to keep the fire under the cauldron burning intensely. After a few hours the editors had, like Paulette wanted, boiled down to a lump of tar the size of a baseball. Since there were no diseased men around to pound the lump into powder, Paulette and the employees kicked it and spit on it and then took turns driving over it with their cars and trucks, and they eventually ground it into powder. It was a liberating experience for them. Paulette, for the first time since we had known her, laughed and joked. Like a carefree child, she nimbly performed cartwheels, and happily vowed to help old people cross streets. The others raced back into the newsroom with the happy sense of relief and deliverance of a boozer who has finally found an open tavern.

Paulette bounded to the top of a desk in the center of the newsroom. The others crowded around and listened as she said through tears of happiness:

"The revolution has begun and ended. We are now free from the mediocrity, the mendacity, the stupidity and the favoritism of Jimmy and his band of ugly, despicable shitheads. We are free to turn this back into a real newspaper. I'm the editor and I will lead you to this new day. We are turning back the clock. We are a newspaper like those that existed in the good old days, like what existed before Jimmy and his sick crowd took over and ruined this business with their shallow and authoritarian ideas. Bless this day, because you are now all free! Free to think exactly like me!"

They Deserved It

CHAPTER 21

Back On The Road

Paulette was hurt and angry that we chose not to stay and think exactly as she did. As we got on our bikes to drive out of town, she huffily ordered us to stay. Dave smiled benignly upon her as if she were a hurt child, patted her gently on the head, and said in his most comforting tone, "Don't go too crazy, it'll stunt your growth." Then we drove off.

It was a blessing to be back on the road in the fresh air and out of the suffocating newsroom. It was late spring, the air was warming and becoming sweet with the smell of blooming flowers, budding trees and greening grass. We were in heaven and acted like it. For days we did nothing but ride for the sake of riding and enjoying the warm weather and the sun.

There's nothing—not drinking beer, not money, not anything, well, maybe brooding—that can match the exhilaration of riding a motorcycle on a warm, sunny day down a lonely country road with the wind in your face; your arms, legs and chest tingling from the hurricane-like massage they're getting; your hair flying back, clothes flapping furiously in the wind as you race your shadow down the open road while feeling cleansed of all despair, depression and doubt, and overwhelmed with feelings of absolute clarity of purpose, confidence of success, total freedom, the idea that everything is possible, that you *will* succeed in life and find love, wealth and happiness; and that of all the things that a human can do in life, this is the best!

That's what Dave said it feels like. I was worried that I'd be beheaded by a flying, shredded truck tire, or that my tires would blow out, the bike go down and that I'd be dragged and scraped across the highway and turned into a giant wound that would never heal. I was also worried that the bike would break down and that I'd be stuck without transportation in the middle of nowhere and subsequently be robbed, beaten and murdered.

Dave sensed my stress and suggested that we stop in a bar in the nearest town to drink beer and calm my nerves. We stopped in a Colorado town of two thousand people and two intersecting main streets that were loaded with storefront businesses. One main street ran parallel to railroad tracks.

The train station at the south end of town had seen better days. It was a wooden, two-story structure that had been bleached gray by the sun. Several windows were broken, the wood-shingled roof looked bone-dry, and a long, wooden, shed building at its southern end had a roof that bowed in the middle like an old horse's back. The railroad tracks forked around the station, the front side of which was used for passenger business, while the backside was for freight. Hand-pulled wooden luggage and cargo carts with rusting, steel-spoked and rimmed wheels sat resting and unused in shoulder-high weeds.

Dominating the town's southern end were three tall, wooden grain elevators that were as worn and gloomy as the train station. Much of the town looked broken-down and dirty, but it was still a working town, meaning it was an agricultural center for the surrounding countryside and a place where people worked hard and scratched out meager livings.

We found a tavern. It was dark inside and had a long wooden bar, wooden stools, mounted fish on wooden plaques behind the bar, photos on the walls of people with the fish they had caught and the deer and elk they had shot while hunting, and a decent-sized crowd, mostly of men, at lunch time. We found two empty stools at the bar, sat down and ordered beer. During the course of drinking them and ordering several more, Dave struck up conversations with others at the bar, including the bartender, a young, lanky dark-haired guy about our age who went about his work competently, but without enthusiasm. His face was tinged with sadness. His eyes seemed always to look through and beyond us as if searching for some unobtainable prize. And although they searched, their youthful sparkle was dulled by a sense of hopelessness.

Dave figured the guy had been dumped by a woman and that he was depressed over his lost love. We were determined to discover the cause of his sadness.

"You never know," Dave said, "he might commit suicide. He might be the saddest person on Earth besides you, the gloomiest of the gloomy and even gloomier than that. His story might be interesting. We need to find out what's bugging him."

I agreed, and the next time he came by to fill our glasses, I, in my enthusiasm to be the first to get his story, blurted out: "So, pal, tell us why you're so depressed. Give us your life story. Have you gotten dumped by some broad?"

He jerked back his head as if dodging a punch, slammed our beers down and hurried away to serve other customers.

"You idiot," Dave said. "You don't get people to talk by confronting them. That scares them. You've got to approach this gently and slowly. You're like a sledgehammer. To get people to talk you've got to draw them out gradually so they don't become defensive and think that you're trying to get something out of them."

Even after our beers were drained, the bartender was reluctant to come back and fill them. But eventually he did. I had been ordered to say nothing. Dave was silent as well. The bartender was a little less scared of us on the next round, and by the time he brought the one after that he had lost the defensiveness and fear that my outburst had caused. When he put down another round, Dave opened up slowly:

"Nice place you guys got here. You must really enjoy working here."

If ever a question had opened someone up, that was it. The bartender ignored the other customers and began pouring out his heart to us. His name was Paul. He was almost twenty years old, and he hated the town and his job. He was the bar owner's son, and had been working at the place since he was seven. He dropped out of high school to work full-time at the bar, and although he initially enjoyed the work, he had since come to regret that decision. He felt stifled by the small town and wanted something different. He dreamed of going to college—at least to the community college in the bigger town one hundred and twenty miles away—so he could study and see what there was to life other than working in a dark bar in a small town. Paul's interests were wide and varied. He talked about studying art, finance, history, architecture, literature, music, physics, metallurgy, medicine, law enforcement—anything and everything. He just didn't know exactly what. And even if it was his fate to work the bar, he'd be more willing to spend his time there if he had at least tried, as he said, "to touch the stars."

That he had dropped out of high school was a problem for Paul, but a solvable one. He had read and studied a lot on his own, for he had an active and inquisitive mind, and he easily passed an exam and earned the equivalent of a high school diploma. The other problem was more difficult. Paul's father, Jack, was nearing sixty-five, and he wanted to retire and have Paul take over the bar. Jack was reluctant to see his son go to college, and certainly he wasn't going to help with any kind of financial support. Eventually, however, Jack, seeing how miserable Paul was, agreed to stay on at the bar and to help him with money for college.

Now there was another problem. Because Paul didn't have a real high school diploma, the college admissions officials wanted a letter of recommendation attesting to his good moral character, high values, loyalty, honesty, abilities, love of knowledge, desire to work and good citizenship. The letter had to be written by someone other than a family member, for school officials wanted an unbiased opinion from a party with nothing to gain or lose from Paul's admission to college. Dave and I figured that bar patrons, many of whom were business owners and leaders of the community, would be willing to write him a letter. But it wasn't so. In the previous two years, as Paul had become increasingly despondent about his lot in life, his behavior at the bar and treatment of customers degenerated correspondingly.

Paul was so angry that when patrons sat down to have drinks and talk about their troubles, he would openly ridicule them and suggest that they were losers. That the customers could accept, for they understood the frustration of being trapped, and they sympathized with Paul's desire to leave. But Paul had scores of times in those two years committed the bartender's unforgivable sin, a sin for which he was now thoroughly hated: He had refused to give out free drinks. There were no rounds on the house from that angry, frustrated, young bartender.

And so the few people he had asked to write him a letter of recommendation had flatly and angrily refused to do so. Others had threatened

A Stingy Barkeep Has No Friends

to reveal his bartending sin to school officials and to post flyers around the state detailing and remarking negatively on his refusal to buy rounds on the house. That threat depressed Paul even more than not being able to go to college. Because a bartender who refuses to buy drinks is universally despised and truly walks alone in life. And so without that letter, Paul was stuck in the bar, forever losing the chance to try to touch the stars for which he so desperately longed.

"Worry no more," Dave proclaimed after Paul had tearfully finished his story. "I've written dozens of letters of recommendation. I'll write one for you right now. You drive it to the school tomorrow. I'll pretend to be a big shot businessman in this town. We'll get a hotel room with a phone number in case they call to verify that I exist. And once they do, you're home free and in college. Get me a pen, some paper and an envelope."

Dave spent forty-five minutes writing. He folded the letter when he finished, put it in the envelope, licked the glue, sealed it and handed it to Paul with a smile.

"You're in college now, pal," he said.

CHAPTER 22

A Real Jerk

Paul was giddy as he took the envelope from Dave's hand, and he almost accepted Dave's suggestion that he buy the house, or at least us, a round of drinks.

"It's a good idea, but it'll be even a better idea when I get accepted into college. I'll be back in a couple of days, and when I return, I'll buy rounds all day, and we'll have the biggest party ever," Paul exclaimed as he tore off his white apron, threw it on the floor behind the bar and raced out the front door. "This is the greatest day of my life! Thank you! You're a saint! I'm in college now! I owe you everything!"

After finishing our final beers, Dave and I left the bar and started walking to a hotel that had been recommended by Paul's dad. It was away from the main street just near one of the better residential areas in town. It was an old, but comfortable place, and the rates were reasonable, we were told.

We headed down a residential street lined with trees and old, two and three-story wooden homes that were stately even at their age. Down toward the end of the block we noticed a large crowd and a couple of police cars. Hurrying along, we got closer and saw that sheriff's deputies and movers were taking furniture from a house and piling it on the street.

It was the nicest house on the block—a three-story, white, wooden clapboard affair with an open porch that wrapped around the entire building. A white picket fence surrounded a large front yard with a lush, green lawn and bright flowers along the borders. The house was freshly painted and in excellent repair.

Many in the crowd surrounding the house were shaking their heads as if in disbelief. Some were gently wiping tears from their eyes. Most were speaking in hushed, sad tones. It was an eviction, we were told. What shocked and saddened those in the crowd was that it was the town's first eviction in more than twenty-five years. It wasn't a flashy or wealthy town, but the people there worked hard, saved money, paid their bills and helped each other out, and so it was particularly sad to see a neighbor go under.

It was even sadder to see who was being evicted: A woman in her mid-thirties and four crying children—two girls and two boys from about four to ten years old—who were clinging to her dress and sobbing in a corner of the yard.

It was a pity and a cruel, heartless disgrace, I thought, that a widow and her four children were being tossed out onto the street.

Even more heart-rending was that the nation had just gone through a severe recession where unemployment had reached staggering rates and inflation had skyrocketed. But we had come through it, and the economy was beginning to show signs of recovery. Unemployment was high, but improving rapidly; interest rates were falling; inflation remained low and capital was becoming readily available. It was a shame, I thought, that the woman and her children had managed to hang on during a severe recession only to lose their grip when things were starting to get better.

It was a disgusting scene in another way. While everybody around the house—even the sheriff's deputies who were removing the furniture—looked sad and depressed, there was a lone soul who was smiling. He was a guy in his thirties who was wearing a dark, three-piece suit, fancy, shiny leather shoes and sunglasses. A white silk handkerchief was neatly folded and placed into his suit coat's breast pocket, and he wore a white silk scarf around his neck even though it was a comfortable, late spring day and everybody else was coatless. He stood in the front yard with his arms folded across his chest and smiled broadly as the deputies and movers carried furniture out of the house. He was unconcerned and unmoved by the sobs of the woman and her children.

Knowing that only three types of people find joy in other people's misery, I figured he was a banker, lawyer or a reporter who needed suffering people to write a prize-winning story about. The sight of him standing there smiling made me sick. Emboldened by the alcohol, I decided to follow him to his home or office and smash out his teeth. I picked up a decent-sized rock and threw it at him, but it missed. A couple of times the jerk actually started giggling. Apparently it was big joke to him to see a widow and her children being evicted. When he giggled a third time, the alcohol took over completely and I lost all fear and stormed over to the fence where he was standing. Dave followed. I was going to punch the guy's face in, but held back at the last minute, and instead glared at him and snarled:

"How would you like to be evicted from this planet, goof?"

He apparently didn't hear and asked that I repeat myself.

"How would you like it if you were being evicted?"

"Oh, I don't mind. It's really not that bad."

"I don't think you understand, slime. How would you like it if *you* were being evicted?"

"I just told you, I don't mind," he said with that sickening smile. "It's not that bad. I'm the one who's being evicted. That's my wife. Those are my kids, and that used to be my house."

I was stunned, and wondered how someone could be happy about being evicted. I tried to make sense of it and asked him if the house was overrun by rats or termites, or if it was haunted or ready to collapse.

"No," he answered. "It's a great house. It's in wonderful condition; it's solid, sound and sturdy."

"Then how come you're so happy? What's the story?"

"I'm not what you would call thrilled about the situation. It's just that I'm not sad or depressed. How can I be? This is going to be good for the country, for the good old U.S. of A. It has already been good for the country."

I had no idea what he meant, and by that time I didn't really want to know. Nonetheless, I continued to question him:

"How did you lose this house? What went wrong?"

"I couldn't make the mortgage payments and the bank foreclosed. That's all there is to it."

"How could you not make the mortgage payments? You don't look poor. What do you do for a living?"

"I'm an engineer."

"You've got to be making pretty good money, then, right?"

"Absolutely. Although I'm based in this small town, I have a nationwide business and have been doing quite well. I make a lot of money."

"Then how could you be losing your house? How can you not make the payments? What did you do with all of your money?"

"I spent it."

"On what?"

He paused a moment here, inhaled deeply, puffed out his chest, put on a proud look and answered: "Durable goods."

"What are durable goods?"

"Washing machines, dryers, ovens, refrigerators, TV sets, microwave ovens, dishwashers and other appliances."

I had no idea what he was talking about or where he was going, but I was intrigued. I asked why he purchased durable goods, and got this answer:

"To help the economy. What do you think?"

"I don't know what I think. Why don't you explain?"

"The economy has been foundering, and that's been hurting the nation, which I just can't stomach. I'm not going to watch the greatest economic power in history go down the tubes and not do anything about it. No, I wanted to do my part. I wanted to be a loyal American and to help out. I didn't want to see this nation turned into a second-rate economic power. So when all the economists said that the only thing that would pull us out of this recession was a consumer-led recovery—an upturn in consumer spending and increased sales of durable goods—I went out and spent. I wanted to show that there was one consumer who had confidence in the economy. I mean, increased sales lead to reductions in inventories. That leads to increased production to build the inventories up again. That means more jobs, a decrease in the unemployment rate, increased tax revenues and a healthier economy and nation. More tax dollars means that we can spend more on defense and scare the hell out of our enemies."

Astonished by his reasoning, I asked the guy how he could possibly think that his buying a refrigerator, washer, dryer, TV, oven, other appliances and furniture would have an impact on the economy.

"Are you crazy?" he laughed. "Only a traitor would buy one of each. "I bought twenty-seven washing machines, seventeen ovens, thirteen dryers, thirty-three TV sets, sixteen refrigerators, seven sofas, two dozen microwaves and forty electric can openers. Do you realize that if everybody spent like I did, the economy would be flying? There'd be no such thing as unemployment, and we'd all be rich. Follow me."

He grabbed our arms and led us down to the basement where he stored all the stuff he had bought. It looked like an appliance warehouse. When I expressed shock that one person could buy so much, his eyes lit up with pride. He hurried us from room to room, excitedly blurting out the numbers of things he had bought and how much they cost. Each sentence was spoken faster than the previous one, and he was working himself into a frenzy. We asked if he had set up funds for his children's education that he could have borrowed from for the mortgage.

"Sure. And I *did* dip into them. In fact, I depleted them completely. Spent all of the money, but not on the mortgage!"

"Then on what?" we asked. By now he was giddy and nearly incoherent. He began dancing a little jig and blurted out:

"I placed some machine tool orders. The machine tool industry is the backbone of our economy. I couldn't dare go without pumping some revenue into that industry. We need a broad-based economic recovery, you know."

By this time we knew were dealing with a lunatic. We figured it would be dangerous to stay in a confined area alone with him and so we walked up the stairs and out into the backyard where we were met by another incredible sight. Parked side-by-side in the spacious yard were four huge, brand new tractors, a reaper, two hay balers, a combine and a big plow.

"What is this stuff?" I asked.

The guy could no longer contain his sense of pride and accomplishment. He started singing "God Bless America" and the national anthem. When he finished he said he had taken out a seven-figure loan to buy the farm machinery.

"We've got to support our domestic companies in this area," he gushed. "If we don't, they'll go under and our farmers will have to buy equipment from foreign companies, and those people across the sea will have us at their mercy. That would amount to a loss of sovereignty. I couldn't let that happen."

When I asked if he was sorry for having bought all the stuff and having lost his house, he became angry.

"Are you an American or not?" he shouted. "Are you some kind of a nut? Of course I'm not sorry. How could I be? Haven't you seen the latest statistics? All of the leading economic indicators are up. Inflation is down, interest rates are falling, the unemployment rate fell by two-tenths of a percent last month, factory orders are up, retail sales are up, housing starts are up and things are looking good. We've got a recovery going, and I can proudly say that I'm partly responsible for it.

A Consuming Ass

"Consumer confidence in the economy is growing. People are buying more products. Pretty soon companies will have to start calling back laid-off workers to meet increased demand. Increased supply means that prices will drop and people will buy even more. Companies will have to hire new workers. That translates into a greater tax base and increased revenues, which will lead to a tax cut, especially for capital gains. That'll provide the incentive for business expansion, and companies will hire even more people. Pretty soon everybody's going to be working. Our economy is going to be booming. We'll be out-producing the rest of the world combined. We'll flood the market with so many electric tooth brushes and microwaves that the Japanese and everybody else won't know what hit them. We'll be the kings again!

"And as far as the house goes, look at it this way. I'll be able to buy it back. Buying something twice, now that is patriotic! I'll be pumping twice as much money into the economy as I would have if I hadn't lost it. That's good for the nation. This is a great occasion. Sometimes I wonder, though, what's wrong with my wife. She's opposed my every move in this economy-rescuing venture. I get the feeling that she's a foreign sympathizer, you know, un-American. Let me tell you, fellas, shopping is *the* American thing to do. Yes sir, people who don't shop are traitors. I say give me shopping or give me death!"

We felt bad for the guy's wife and kids. But even so, we were so disgusted by his attitude that we spent the next few hours helping the deputies move furniture out of the house.

CHAPTER 23

A Haunted Hotel

Our hotel had been built one hundred and five years earlier as a large farm house. It was converted into a hotel after the town had grown and swallowed up nearby farmland. Even though the rooms were small, it was comfortable and quaint. The rooms had bathtubs, not showers. The floors were wood and not carpeted, and they creaked constantly when walked on. Each room had a small fireplace. The drapes were thick as quilts and dusty. The walls were covered with flower-patterned wallpaper that had long ago grown dingy, and they were decorated with various paintings, some of people, some of cowboys and cattle roundups, and some of nature scenes, such as mountains and streams and valleys. We got two rooms. Both had paintings of a sad-eyed Guernsey cow hanging crookedly from the wall above the beds. And the beds, unlike the low-to-the-floor, streamlined models that you find in modern hotels and motels, were large, bulky affairs with massive wood and post frames whose mattresses were a good four feet off the ground. The hotel kept a ladder in stock for midgets to use to climb into bed, although we were told that not a single midget had ever stayed there. And, unlike the stiff, almost board-like mattresses in modern motels, ours were large, almost pillow-like things that nearly swallowed us. They were incredibly comfortable. To say that being on one was like sleeping in a cloud would not be an exaggeration. And if anyone thinks that nothing can beat riding a motorcycle down a lonely country road on a warm summer day, they ought to try jumping onto a soft mattress in a dark room and covering themselves head to toe with a warm, fluffy quilt.

The price of a room was indeed cheap because few people stayed at the place on account of it supposedly being haunted. Those who did stay usually left early because they heard ghosts and were frightened nearly to death. At least that's what the stooped, brittle, bald old man who owned the place and showed us to our rooms said. Of course, this was a time when the nation was in a haunted house craze and when every person who owned an old, decrepit building, especially in small towns that no one ever visited on purpose, tried to cash in on the craze by claiming their place was haunted. We dismissed his claim with laughs.

135

We told the old man about our need to masquerade as big shots for a day or two if college officials telephoned so that Paul could get into school. He agreed to go along and to refer to us as pillars of the community and with appropriate reverence and awe. He also agreed to track us down at the bar should the officials call when we were enjoying refreshments.

It was early evening by the time we had gotten the bikes, unpacked, settled in, taken baths, put on fresh clothes and were ready for a leisurely stroll through town and for dinner. For me there is no greater pleasure in life than being on vacation and looking for a place to eat in a small town. The pace is unhurried. There's no worry about tomorrow's work, and in towns with two main streets, a

restaurant is always easy to find. We settled on a restaurant and bar where the steaks were as delicious as advertised, and the beer cold and inexpensive. After dinner we sat at the bar and listened as patrons talked about how stupid and dangerous it was for us to stay at the haunted hotel.

"Nobody ever stays there, at least those who know better," the bartender told us. "The place *is* haunted. Nearly everybody in town has heard the ghosts, and it's scary as hell. We had one couple come through, maybe seven years ago, who stayed there. They left screaming about three o'clock in the morning and drove away faster than you two drink beers. Later that morning, the state police found them about fifty miles outside of town screaming hysterically along the side of the road. They were taken to a mental hospital and given the best help available, but nothing could snap them out of their shock. They've been in an asylum ever since.

"The old man who runs the place is crazy. He bought it forty years ago on a dare—had some family money, still has, apparently, 'cause that's all he's done is run the place, and he gets very little business—and set out to prove that there was no such thing as ghosts. But, the story goes, within the first few months of him running the place, his hair turned white and he turned into a recluse.

"The people who owned it before him tried everything make the ghosts go away. They remodeled, put up fresh, bright wallpaper, sprinkled the rooms with holy water, said prayers for those poor souls who had been slaughtered there, and had a priest come and bless the place. But they couldn't make a go of it.

And, sadly, two of their children had to be put into an asylum because they were so scared. That caused the man who owned it to commit suicide—he was sickened by what he had put his children through. His wife gave it up and sold it. She also went insane, again, apparently out of guilt over what she had put her kids through. A lady died there one night by falling down the stairs and breaking her neck. She was running away from the ghosts.

"Everybody in this town is afraid of the place. Police won't go there. Kids avoid it. When adults drive by it they turn away their eyes. I know it sounds crazy and ridiculous, but it *is* haunted, and it's scary as hell."

Others at the bar pitched in what they knew about the hotel and urged us with the deepest sincerity to stay somewhere else. The story that emerged about the place was this:

One hundred and five years earlier, one Mr. Joseph Gates, twenty-one, of New York City, and his bride Maria, eighteen, arrived to take charge of a five-thousand-acre ranch/farm that his family had purchased for him. Gates, who suffered from asthma, poor eyesight, gout and arthritis, had since he was a youth growing up in a two-room, sooty apartment, dreamed about leaving the cramped, dirty streets of New York for the vast, clean expanses of the West. His father, a successful tailor, had hoped his son would follow him into that business. But as it became clear that young Joseph's health would fail in that congested city, the older Gates put aside money to help his son buy a large piece of land.

Gates and his bride were full of boundless enthusiasm when they first arrived. They were starting a new and gloriously free life together in the West. Their plan was to operate a ranch and dairy farm. The nearby town astride the railroad tracks would provide, not only a ready market for milk and beef, but also an outlet to other, larger markets, should Gates expand his operation, which he had every intention of doing. Their plans were optimistic and grand. They would start big and get bigger. The first order of business was to build house worthy of their grand plans. Money from his father's tailoring business secured the house, a three-story structure with gables, an attic, basement and fifteen rooms, most of them bedrooms, for the couple planned a large family.

Seeds, equipment and livestock were secured, and Gates, asthma and all, went to work. The first few years were a modest success. Gates managed to sell his milk and beef in town, and the couple had two children. The following years brought three more children and continued success in the local market. Gates' beef was praised as the most delicious around, and his milk the creamiest. He was now poised for expansion into other markets, which to him meant great wealth. Gates bought up surrounding ranches and soon amassed an empire of ninety thousand acres. He filled the land with cattle, and was ready to start, as he often joked, watching railroad cars filled with his money roll into town.

But then, as it often does, life intervened in a harsh way. Being around hay, manure and flies had done nothing for Gate's asthma except make it worse. It had been in remission for a while, but now returned with full fury. Many days he was bedridden because he couldn't breathe. On the days he could breathe, which were usually cold winter ones, his arthritis nearly crippled him. His eyesight deteriorated as well. Even glasses couldn't help, and poor Gates was bumping into walls, trees, fences and cattle. He broke a leg and badly bruised a hip when he fell out of the hayloft one day. Soon, he couldn't work the ranch. Maria couldn't do it by herself, and the children, although physically capable, didn't want to. They wanted to go live in New York City!

Gates' empire, real and imagined, began to shrink. He had to sell off pieces of his land and cattle herd cheap in order to support his family. His dreams of empire, wealth and status shattered, Gates turned to the ruin of all men: the bottle. He drank more and more as the ranch shrank, and he became more abusive toward his family with each bottle he emptied. Soon he was beating Maria and the children—when he could catch them. Luckily for them, he could barely see, walk or breathe, and so dodging him was easy.

That frustrated Gates even more and made him angrier and more abusive. Unable to beat his wife and children, Gates unleashed his sick behavior on the family's herd of Guernsey dairy cows. Filled with liquor and his sick anger, Gates would beat the cows with sticks, rocks, metal bars and anything else he could find. He was vicious, and bloodied and killed many an animal. Those that remained alive didn't give milk because they were so scared of Gates' behavior. That made him angrier and even more vicious. It was particularly hard on the cows in the winter when they were confined in the dairy barn. In time, Gates had killed twenty cows, including one called Bossy, who

Crazy Gates

had been named by one of his daughters and who was her favorite.

Sickened by Gates' behavior, Maria and the children reported his murderous ways to authorities. He was charged with cruelty to animals and was scheduled to go on trial. But a few weeks before the trial, Gates set a trap for his family.

138

He locked them in the basement and kept them there for several days without food. When he felt they were sufficiently weakened, he went down and tied them up. Then, in front of the children, he hacked Maria to pieces with a hatchet. He did the same to four of the children. One daughter, however, freed herself, got out of the basement and raced on a horse into town to report her father, and Gates was arrested. Upon returning to the house, the girl was overwhelmed with grief and hanged herself.

The ghosts in the hotel moaned constantly at night, and although no one had ever seen them, they were believed to be Maria and her five children. And there was proof they existed. The attic once had been used as a store room, being stocked with flour and oats and other grains for cooking. But every so often, the bags were ripped open and the grains strewn about and eaten. And it wasn't mice or rats that did it. The rips in the burlap sacks were large, as if made by human hands or hatchets. Every time new bags were put in, they were ripped open within days. The shuffling and pounding of feet could be heard in the attic. And not just two feet or four feet, but several, like a whole family! It was said that the ghosts had it out for all people, especially men who drank heavily. It was their goal, legend had it, to drive such men to suicide.

After hearing the stories, I wanted no part of the hotel, and recommended that we check out immediately, before it got dark and the ghosts came out. Dave, of course, would have none of that. If there were ghosts we would find and confront them. And if we went crazy in the process or committed suicide or otherwise got killed, so be it. This was adventure!

CHAPTER 24

Ghosts!

I t was clear and dark and the stars were out in force as I walked with great trepidation with Dave back to the hotel. I didn't want to die, knew I didn't have to, at least not at that point in time, but yet was walking voluntarily

toward, if not certain death, permanent insanity. It occurred to me that maybe I should trust my own instincts, make my own judgments and stand up for myself.

The old man was still up at the front desk when we returned. He wished us a good night, told us again the place was haunted, and suggested that we be careful and that we pray to protect ourselves.

I wasted no time in locking my door, jumping into bed, pulling the covers over my head and trying to curl up into a little ball. I also tried not to breathe, figuring that if I did breathe, the ghosts would hear me, but gave that up after the first try. From then on I tried to breathe as quietly as possible. I also tried to not swallow, figuring swallowing would also make noise and give me away to the ghosts. I lay there perfectly still and breathing as quietly as possible, when there was a knock at my door.

Good god! The ghosts were at my door already! I remained silent and still. Maybe, I thought, if no one answered, the ghosts would move on to the next room. Then there was another knock—three soft raps—on the door and an "ouuhhhh" coming from outside. God! I thought, if I answer the door they'll chop my head off. If I don't, they'll get angry and walk through the door and walls and chop me up while I'm here in bed. This is a losing proposition.

Then there were another three soft raps and another "ouuhhhhh," followed by "Come ouuuuut so we can kill you."

If ever someone was about to explode, it was me. My heart was pounding and I was sweating. But I remained silent and still, and in a few minutes—it seemed like a lifetime—I heard footsteps moving away from my door. After another few minutes I slowly and silently pulled off the covers, got out of bed and tiptoed towards the door. Hearing nothing, I slumped in exhaustive relief into a sitting position against the wall next to the door. And then the doorknob jangled, the knocks came again and the voice said, "We'll kill yooooou no matter what. Open uuuup." Then there was laughter, and I knew then that Dave had been playing a joke on me that I didn't appreciate.

"Open up," he whispered from behind the door. "Open the damn door!"

I opened the door and yelled at him for the bad joke.

"Relax," he whispered, waving a flashlight that pierced the dark of my room. "Have some fun, some sense of adventure. We're going to get to the bottom of this. Now my hunch is this: If there have been ghost-like noises, it's probably been the old man down there making them. Not only does he seem a little weird, but he needs some publicity for this place, and if he can conjure up a ghost, people will eventually come and pay big money for the thrill and for the adventure. But mostly, I think he's just a sick, perverted guy who gets his jollies by scaring people. And if there are ghosts, don't worry, they can't physically hurt you. All they can do is try to scare you. It's up to you to keep your wits. Now get a flashlight and let's go ghost hunting."

The two flashlights guided us through the dark, narrow hallways. No one else was staying in the hotel, so we checked all the rooms on our floor. They were all open and all neatly made up as if waiting for guests. Like our rooms, they all had paintings of a cow on the wall above the beds.

Next we checked the rooms on the second floor, and then those on the first floor. They were empty. Then, acting on Dave's suspicion that the old man was the one making ghost noises, we checked in on him. He was behind the desk, asleep in a padded rocking chair. We walked down another set of stairs to the basement. By this time I was sick with nervousness and fear. When Dave tried to open the basement door, I grabbed his arm.

"This is where they were killed; where they were hacked to pieces," I whispered. "We can't go in there."

"That's exactly why we're going to go in there," he whispered back. "If there are ghosts anywhere in this house, they're going to be at the scene of the murder. Let's go."

The door was open and we inched our way forward trying not to bang into anything or make noise. But clumsy me bumped into an old wooden box in the middle of the floor. We pointed the lights at it. Inside was an old, wooden-handled hatchet!

"The murder weapon!" Dave quietly exclaimed. "This is spooky."

Inside the box and underneath the hatchet was a brown paper bag. It was stuffed full and tied with old, yellow twine.

"We should leave now," I insisted. "This just isn't right."

"No. We stay. Untie and open up that bag."

My hands trembled uncontrollably as I undid the bag. Even Dave was trembling. I could tell that because the light from the flashlight he shown on the box bag zigzagged all over. I put my hand in the bag and pulled out a stack of old, yellowed, brittle newspapers. They were dated ninety-two years earlier and one of them, called the Gazette, had this headline: "CRAZED, DRUNKEN GATES HATCHETS FAMILY TO DEATH! COW KILLER MURDERS WIFE AND FOUR CHILDREN!"

The stories detailed the murders and the sorry plight of Maria and the five children. They contained graphic descriptions of the crime scene, including the fact that all of the victims had been beheaded. And the stories comported to what we had been told about the hotel and Gates in the bar. The papers had stories about the sad suicide of the daughter who survived the murders, and contained editorials demanding Gates' immediate execution. Other papers had stories about Gates' trial, conviction and eventual hanging.

"Well, we know that story wasn't bullshit," Dave said.

"True," I said. "But why is this stuff down here? I can see somebody saving it, but why here?"

"Maybe it's not somebody, maybe it's the work of the ghosts."

That thought scared the hell out of me, but not as much as the low, faint groaning noises we heard drifting through the hotel. We both made for the door as fast as our fear would take us. We checked the front desk and found that the old man was still snoring in his rocker. The rooms on the second floor revealed no ghosts, neither did those on the third floor. While we were on the third floor, however, the groaning became louder and the sound of stomping and shuffling feet carried through from the ceiling above.

We made our way slowly up the stairway to the attic. Old burlap sacks that had clearly been ripped and clawed open were strewn on the floor outside the attic's main door. Corn kernels, oats and barley were also strewn on the floor. We said nothing, but trembled in the darkness and put our ears to the door. The moaning was clear and distinct, and there were multiple sets of footsteps.

"Well, we go in. Let's go," I said with a reckless bravado that masked my overwhelming fear and approaching insanity. But this time it was Dave who was wavering.

"Maybe it's best if we just leave this alone," he said. "We're messing with the supernatural, and to be honest, that's wrong *and* dangerous. Troubled spirits don't need us to further add to their misery. Let's go."

But we couldn't go. The main door to the attic door started opening. We shut off our lights, and with a perverse instinct driving us, slowly pushed the door open the rest of the way. All was dark except for wisps of light floating and dancing and darting around the room. Some were tiny flashes, but others were larger, like tosses of stardust or miniature comet tails. We crept forward, saying nothing, and eventually crouched behind an old door that had been stored on its side.

The light show continued and grew more intense. The flashes of light danced everywhere, making it seem like the room was filled with hundreds of humming birds with lights on their bodies. The low moans started up again and so did the footsteps. The light activity grew even more frenzied, intense and compact, as if individual pieces were coming together to form the whole. It seemed that images were forming before our eyes. And they were! First I made out what appeared to be a skinny leg, and then another. Then I saw a body, and then Dave shouted that he saw a tail! Yes a tail! The vision formed before us: a herd of Guernsey cows!

They pawed at the floor, kicked around the empty burlap sacks with their hoofs, stretched their hairy necks forward, pointed their chins upward and mooed. They were cow ghosts! The poor things were hungry. We stood up from behind the door and introduced ourselves, but it was obvious that they couldn't comprehend, although when I called out, "Here Bossy. Come Bossy," a sad-eyed beauty ambled forward and stared at me with her giant, round, brown eyes. It was the same cow in the paintings above the beds! They wanted us to pet them, and we tried, but you just can't pet a ghost.

We instructed the cows to stay there, picked up several of the empty sacks and raced out of the hotel to the railroad station where we picked weeds and other greens and grasses for the brown and white spotted beasts. We returned to the attic, dumped the grasses on the floor and watched as the cows ate eagerly and gratefully.

CHAPTER 25

Attacked!

The cows ate until sunrise, when they disappeared—to go to sleep, I figured, or whatever it is that ghosts do during the day.

"You tell no one that we found cow ghosts here," Dave sternly warned me. "No one will ever believe it and they'll think we're crazy. If we keep the secret, we can come back here some day and buy the place and advertise it as a haunted house and make millions from gullible people who want the experience of being scared out of their wits. No need to mention that the ghosts are harmless dairy cows."

"And besides," I interrupted with great excitement, "we'll always have free milk and butter. Why would we want to share a windfall like that with anyone?"

Dave had no answer to that question, and so we walked back down the stairs to our rooms and went to sleep.

It was early afternoon by the time we were awake, dressed and ready for more adventure. Our stomachs were growling, and so filling them with food was our first priority. At the front desk, the old man was surprised that we were in such good spirits and was shocked when we paid for another night's stay. He asked whether we had heard the ghosts. We said we had, that we found their racket to be charming and pleasant—not scary at all—and just the thing to lull a body to sleep.

"Not an ounce of excitement at all. Nothing," Dave told him. "If they're ghosts, then they must the friendly kind, or very tired ghosts." We then asked if the college officials had called for us, and were told they hadn't.

"That letter was so good, so classy, so thoroughly convincing that they probably won't call," Dave said cheerfully as we walked out the door and headed toward the main street. "Some people are so inherently good and trustworthy that their word is beyond question. That's me. You know, they probably saw that letter and decided to let Paul in right then and there without waiting for the new semester to start."

Steak and eggs, fried potatoes with onions, steaming coffee and cold juice will start off any morning right; they start off an afternoon even better. Having stuffed ourselves at a cafe, we headed to Paul's tavern. Jack was tending bar, but hadn't heard yet from his son. We settled in at the bar, ordered several ice-cold beers, and started to enjoy the afternoon. It was during the fourth round that we heard a commotion outside.

There were loud shrieks punctuated with obscenities and interrupted with proclamations of hatred and vows of revenge. We heard cars being kicked and windows being smashed. An older man ran into the tavern to tell us that a madman was loose and headed our way. The madman was breaking windows, knocking over trash cans, shoving old people, women and children, and punching out car windows. The police had been called, but hadn't yet arrived.

"Better run," the old man advised us as he hobbled out the back door. A few patrons left and followed the oldster. Jack pulled a rifle out from behind the bar, unlocked the safety and held it ready. He was about to head out the front door to protect his large glass windows from the lunatic when the front door burst open and the madman shrieked:

"You goddamn freak! You ass! You! I'll kill you! I'll break every bone in your body! Yooooou!"

It was Paul! His eyes were wide with rage, and his hair was actually standing on end. I had read in books about that happening, but figured it was just a literary device and not something that occurred in real life. His body was tensed, the veins in his neck and head bulged out, his fists were clenched, his face was red, his ears were red, even his eyelashes were red—he seemed on the verge of exploding—and he charged at Dave, wildly throwing punches. Dave jumped off his barstool and easily dodged Paul. The young bartender charged time and time again, but Dave was always able to avoid him. After several failed charges, Paul slumped to the wooden floor and sobbed. When his rage was finally spent, he stood up, pulled a letter out of his back pants pocket, slammed it onto the bar, and in a defeated, heartbroken voice, asked Dave:

"How could you have done this to me? Destroyed me like this? I never did anything to you. I didn't even ask for your help. What kind of person are you to have done something like this? What kind of a letter of recommendation is this?"

Jack picked the letter up off the bar, unfolded it and started reading:

"To whom it may concern: I am writing this letter of recommendation on behalf of Paul Henry Webster, a truly remarkable human being. He wants to enroll in your college, but needs a letter attesting to his general character before he can be admitted. This is that letter. I can attest to his honesty, citizenship, thirst for knowledge, moral character and reliability.

Paul's Head Nearly Exploded

"I have known Paul for all of his twenty years and have watched him grow and develop. As a baby he whined and spit up on his parents' clothes. As a four-year-old he threw violent temper tantrums. As a seven-year-old he defied authority and dismissed his school work as unimportant. At age ten he started shoplifting. At thirteen he was smoking cigarettes and lying to his parents about it. In the seventh grade he and some of his classmates constantly disrupted class and tormented a seventy-year-old nun with insults and constant disrespect. At age fourteen he was laying big rocks on train tracks in the hopes of derailing a train—passenger or freight. At age fifteen he was wildly rebellious. Around that time he began drinking alcohol and experimenting with dangerous, mind-altering drugs. As a teenager he shunned sports, preferring instead to hang out on street corners with his friends and smoke cigarettes. Now, at age twenty, he stands before you, the culmination of those years of development.

"I can attest to these things about my relationship with Paul: *I* have never bailed him out of jail. He has never once come to me for counseling about homosexuality, drug addictions, habitual lying, compulsive stealing, uncontrollable anger, arsonist tendencies, hatred of blacks and other minorities, laziness, paranoia, alcoholism and addiction to pornography. He has never missed a day of work because of any of these problems.

"As far as his honesty goes, *I* have yet to catch Paul lying, and he has never stolen anything from *me*.

"In terms of his love of family, Paul has never verbally or physically abused his parents or grandparents in public. And when it comes to citizenship, I say that Paul has never in my presence bitterly denounced this country and advocated for the assassination of its leaders.

"Paul is also an avid and enthusiastic hunter. He'll shoot anything that's alive—raccoons, skunks, chickens, sparrows, cows, you name it—and often is so carried away by his zeal that he hunts without a license and out of season.

"Paul is currently employed as a bartender in his father's tavern. So far, the elder Webster has yet to report missing funds to the police and has yet to file an insurance claim for losses of large amounts of liquor inappropriately consumed on the job.

"As this is a letter of recommendation, it is decidedly tilted in favor of Mr. Webster and meant to highlight the positive. To be sure, Paul is human and has flaws—some of them glaring and dangerous—and for the sake of a well-rounded, balanced picture of the man, you might want to know of some of them. My integrity is absolute, and as a humble servant of the truth, I feel duty-bound to at least make you aware of the fact that Paul is far from perfect. Should you wish to inquire about his many faults call me at the above number and I will be delighted to provide whatever negatives about Paul that you might want or need. Call early, for it will require several hours.

"I am, your very obedient servant,

"David 'Captain of Industry' Nadolski.

"P.S. Undoubtedly, your college has an Economics Department. I am a businessman with an expertise in creating monopolies. Should you at any time require an instructor or speaker to detail to your young, impressionable students exactly how to crush competitors, establish monopolies and then gouge helpless customers, call on me and I will be more than happy to oblige. I do not believe that knowledge should be hoarded. I believe it should be shared so that from it all of mankind can benefit."

Not a soul in that bar—and there were plenty of them, and plenty of drunk ones, too—was happy with us after the letter was read. In fact, they wanted to kill us for libeling Paul and for killing his chance to escape the bar and the town. And no matter how Dave tried to explain that the letter was highly flattering to Paul and made him look like a saint, no one bought it. We were forced to make a tactical retreat from the bar. Our tactic was simple. We jumped off bar stools and sprinted out the door just steps ahead of the mob of angry drunks who chased us. We reached the hotel just as they were about to pounce on us.

CHAPTER 26

A Nutty Escape

We were safe in the hotel. The mob, like everybody else in town, believed the building was haunted, and so they refused to walk up its front steps, let alone go in and drag us out and beat us with the sticks and empty beer bottles they carried. But they surrounded the place and settled in for a siege.

Kegs of beer, barbecue grills, lawn chairs and TVs and radios were brought in for the mob by other townsfolk, and they all had a party while waiting for us to come out.

I was scared. Each new shout from those beer-drinking lunatics for us to surrender and be killed left me wishing that I never left the grocery store job. That was a miserable, hopeless, dead-end existence, but it was better than being holed up in a hotel that was haunted by cows, and better than waiting to be killed.

And we *were* waiting to be killed. At least two hundred people had surrounded the hotel. They were armed with guns, rifles, baseball bats, tree branches, steel pipes, hammers, screwdrivers, beer bottles, pitchforks, crowbars, old shoes, dirty underwear—you name it, they had it. By late afternoon they had made two hangman's nooses out of ropes and thrown them over thick tree branches. All afternoon they shouted for us to come out and be hanged. The situation was hopeless, I thought, because even if we could have gotten out of the hotel unseen, we could have never gotten to our bikes and made an escape because the bikes were parked right in front of the place. We'd never get past that mob!

Dave was calm. His serenity affected me and I slowly became less despairing and more confident, and I started thinking of plans for bold action.

"We'll use the Chicago thing on them!" I shouted. "We'll drive them crazy!"

"No. It's not necessary," Dave said. "You only use the amount of force necessary to achieve your goal. These people are harmless. Using Chicago on them would be like using a sledgehammer to kill an ant. It would be a waste of resources."

"Then we'll dig our way out of the basement with nails and pieces of broken glass. It might take weeks or months, but we'll do it."

"Naah. Too much work."

"Why don't we just call the cops and demand a police escort out of here?"

"That would make us look like sissies. Besides, I think the police chief is one of those out there who's calling for us to be hanged."

"So what do we do?"

"We relax, drink beer and wait for night, when we will carry out my simple, but effective plan."

We couldn't relax, though, because we had no beer. And the old man at the desk refused to go out and get some. Since the only beer around was in the kegs that the mob had, we had to put Dave's plan into effect early. He tore the white bed sheets off two beds, cut eye, nose and mouth holes in them with a pair of scissors, and threw one over me and the other over himself.

"We're gonna be ghosts," he said cheerfully. "They think this place is haunted. They're afraid of ghosts. We'll scare the hell out of them."

"This is way too stupid," I said. "This is too stupid even for us, and even for this trip. They ain't going to believe that we're ghosts. These sheets aren't long enough. You can see our boots and pants. They'll see that, too, and figure out right away that we aren't ghosts. This kind of thing works in cartoons and in comic books, not in real life."

"Shut up and stop being so damn literal. Have some fun. Just follow me and do what I do."

Draped in our white sheets, we stepped onto the front porch, screamed a few "boos!" at the mob and then ran at them. They scurried away in panic like a swarm of ants that's been stepped on, and then huddled in fear across the street when they saw that we had halted at an abandoned beer keg. We lounged for a while and drank several beers on the sidewalk, scared the mob with more "boos," and then dragged the keg back into the hotel. After we closed the front door behind us, the mob flooded back across the street and again surrounded the hotel.

Around midnight, we went up to the attic, said good-bye to the cows, gave a huge hug to Bossy, promised them we would return some day, put on our sheets, walked out the front door, scared the mob away again with some "boos," loaded two small beer kegs onto our bikes and played a final joke on the mobsters. Dave wrote a note and taped it to one of the hangman's nooses. It read:

"Hi. We're a couple of the hundreds of ghosts who live in this house. We've been kind of bored for the past 50 years. It's fun to scare people, but hardly anybody stays here anymore. So we're going to ride these motorcycles for a while. We're stealing them from those two idiots. They're still inside and they're afraid of you. The loud one says he's going to write letters of recommendation about all of you and mail them all over the country.

"Be Wary Travelers! But don't give up. They can't hold out forever. But don't you go in there because the ghosts will get real mad and they will scare the hell out of you. Just wait for the two to come out, because they eventually will. And when they do you can hang them. Your beer is cold and delicious. Thanks. Remember: The answer is eternal vigilance. Wait them out and avenge their insults no matter how long it takes!

"Bye, Ned and Fred, two of the ghosts."

Still draped in our white sheets, we got on the bikes, started them up, slammed them into gear and drove away. As we sped away through the chilly night, I looked back and saw the mob surge back across the street and resume its siege position.

CHAPTER 27

A Likeable Fat Man

There are many lucky souls in the world. Some people can drink heavily all their lives without ever getting liver disease. Others can eat bacon every day and never suffer a clogged artery. Still others live to see their worst enemies die.

Among the luckiest people, though, are those who can help a friend in need and who can help restore a damaged reputation.

I am one such lucky person.

A few days after the ghost caper we wound up in a small town in western Colorado where we met Fat Myron, a school teacher on disability retirement who was also the town's mayor. Myron was more than fat. He was huge. And like so many fat people, he was the subject of vicious, hateful, libelous stories about his eating habits. Such stories, with their cruel exaggerations, serve only to ridicule and humiliate fat people. They are told by losers who are so insecure and worthless that they promote themselves, not by hard work, solid accomplishment and vigorous, but fair, competition, but by tearing down and destroying others. If someone runs faster than these gossip-mongering misfits, they don't concede the race and congratulate the opponent for having longer and faster legs; they try to chop those legs off.

Although Myron had laughed off thousands of fat person stories, he was shattered by a particularly cruel story that was circulating at the time about his eating practices. He appealed to us then, and we pledged to him years ago in that small town, that we would debunk the story at every opportunity. Dave and I have told hundreds of people the true story, and I feel that as a decent human being I am morally obligated to refute the ugly lie here so that Myron's reputation will be permanently restored and that all of history will know the truth about how much this good man eats.

We liked Myron the instant we met him. Nearly six feet tall, he was in his forties, gray-haired and balding, incredibly fat, and walked around town neatly dressed in huge green work pants and solid-colored flannel shirts. He drank huge amounts of wine and got tipsy, but never sloppy or drunk, told wonderful stories about old mining towns, laughed like a demon, and most importantly, shared bottle after bottle of wine with us.

We spent several days in town eating and drinking with Myron. We listened to his stories and got to know him well. The vicious lie that humiliated Myron began when some sick soul who was undoubtedly looking for a cheap, easy laugh at someone else's expense maliciously changed a true story about one of Myron's daily walks along the country roads outside of town.

The story began when Myron was strolling the countryside one day minding his own business and enjoying the sunshine and fresh air. He was bothering nothing except the unfortunate ants and bugs who happened to be sleeping or looking for food in the same spot that he decided to place his size fourteen feet. He was on a gravel road, and after a couple of hours, his shoes were filled with stones. It was an uncomfortable situation, so Myron plopped himself down in the middle of the road and took off his shoes.

Along, though, came an elderly rancher on horseback who was driving a large herd of cattle to a railroad spur where they could be loaded on to railroad cars and shipped to market for slaughter. The cattle, unaware of their impending doom, were moving along briskly. But when they came upon Myron they stopped. The steers were scared and wouldn't move or go around the considerable obstruction that Myron was to them, and so they just milled around and mooed and kicked up dust.

This perplexed the rancher. He rode to the front of the herd to see what was delaying the cattle. There he found Myron sitting in the middle of the road casually flicking stones out of his shoes one at a time. The rancher dismounted, walked up to Myron, tipped his white cowboy hat in a sign of greeting and respect, and in a polite, country manner, explained that he needed to get the herd to the rail spur by nightfall or lose a big sale and a big chunk of money that was necessary to keep the ranch operating for another year. The rancher said that Myron's discomfort, although unfortunate and something worthy of attention, was delaying the cattle drive. He asked Myron if he could dump the stones out of his shoes all at once instead of one at a time.

Myron was a jolly fat man, but he was a stubborn one as well. When he became fixed on a certain course of action, nothing could dissuade him from it.

"Good sir," Myron told the rancher in an annoyed tone, "these stones entered my shoes one at a time, and that is how they shall leave."

"I understand your position," the rancher replied in a conciliatory, but urgent voice, "and if it were my shoes that were loaded up with stones, I'd try to dump 'em out in the exact order they come in. But for the sake of saving a family ranch and of supplying the nation with beef, can't you please make an exception and dump 'em all out at once?"

Myron was deaf to the rancher's plea and stayed in the middle of the road taking stones out of his shoes one at a time.

The rancher, now a little angered, asked Myron if he would be kind enough to move off the road and into a field from where he could continue taking the stones out of his shoes one at a time. Myron refused. He told the rancher that as a Colorado citizen he had as much right to the road as anyone else. And now a little agitated himself, Myron told the rancher that his cattle looked sick and that he should have been ashamed for trying to sell diseased meat to the public.

That enraged the rancher. He let out a shriek so fierce and so loud that it shattered Myron's eyeglasses. Myron assumed a disaffected air and calmly told the rancher that he would have to pay for the glasses or be a sorry man.

The old man snapped and started throwing rocks at Myron. But Myron ignored the assault and laughed loudly when some of the rocks bounced off his belly and into his shoes. Myron's indifference added to the rancher's frustration. The old man started swearing and screaming and pounding his fists on the gravel road.

Myron's stubborn streak now began to

Fat Myron

displace the more moderate and compassionate aspects of his personality. He took joy in seeing the rancher lose his temper. In an effort to anger the rancher even more, Myron began flicking stones at him.

That was about all the guy could take. He punched the air with his fists, gritted his teeth and let lose with such a flurry of fat man insults that even his cattle turned their heads in shame and disgust.

Myron was angry. His belly trembled, but he kept control of himself and dispassionately took stones out of his shoes one at a time while ignoring the rancher. Then the rancher struck again, this time viciously and unfairly. He put his angry face right up to Myron's and snarled that he had seen bigger bellies on women, and that Myron's girth could easily be gauged with a standard tape measure.

That infuriated Myron. He jumped to his feet. His face was red. His belly shook and his fists were clenched. He wanted to punch the oldster, but he was a Christian who shunned violence, and thus refrained from throwing the blow. But revenge is revenge, and Myron wanted to hurt the old man. If he couldn't do it physically, he would do it financially. So Myron lumbered over to the herd of cattle, picked out the largest one, and in full view of the old man and other cattle, ate it!

It is hateful stories like this that ruin people and lead to so much anger and violence in the world. This story is not true. I know that to be the case because Dave and I hunted down the rancher and got the truth from him.

One Hungry Fat Man

Myron was furious about the story. It ruined his reputation in that town, where every time he was seen in public he was laughed at and ridiculed, even by children, old people, cripples and members of the clergy. He was embarrassed and furious that even people he knew well and who purported to be his friends believed it. And it wasn't his own reputation that concerned him. No, Myron was not selfish. His concern was that overweight people not be subjected to the heartless, stereotypical caricatures that make light of their eating habits and that so thoroughly denigrate an entire class of people, and he asked us always to tell the truth about the incident. Tell it I must. Myron did not eat one cow; he ate the whole herd. And he would be proud to tell you that too.

CHAPTER 28

Disturbing Thoughts

We had been on the road for several months now, and although I was gaining confidence and growing intellectually; and had already learned more than I had ever thought possible, gained a degree of poise and experienced more adventures than most people did in a lifetime; and although Shirley would have never recognized the new me; even though I *knew* she would love my new sense of self-worth and want me back, there was still something missing. There was a huge void, a sick feeling that I might never experience one of the things that had sparked me to dream the impossible, and that had enslaved my imagination ever since Dave had first suggested that I would experience it on this, the greatest adventure ever in the history of ever. So while we were eating lunch and smoking cigars on the side of a road one day, I told Dave about my worry. He asked what I thought I was missing and not experiencing.

"We've been on the road for several months," I said, trying to temper my disappointment so as not to seem ungrateful for all of the adventures we had already had, "and we haven't eaten anybody yet. We have yet to engage in cannibalism."

His silence, which lasted a good twenty seconds, told me that he too was feeling empty about the promise that he had made that summer day when he first proposed that I buy the bike and take the trip. His words, though, told me something different.

"Why do you want to eat somebody? First you want to dig up graves, and now you want to eat people. They could put you away for stuff like this."

"But you promised. You said we'd eat shoes and rats and drink oil and gnaw down trees with our teeth. Ever since I was a kid and read about cannibals, I've wondered what it would be like to eat somebody. Haven't you thought about it?"

"Actually, I have. I probably shouldn't say this, but I used to wonder what it would be like to eat certain parts of people, especially women, you know, stuff that you probably shouldn't admit, stuff that could make people think you're a pervert."

"You mean like toes and ears?"

"No. I mean like—"

155

"Not those and that!"

"Yeah, I mean those and that."

"Wow. You're sicker than I thought. You're as bad as I am," I said in disbelief.

"You've thought about the same thing?" Dave asked.

"Yeah. Are we sick? I mean, thinking about eating somebody is one thing, but thinking of eating their private parts, that seems kind of sick. Are we bound for an asylum?"

"No," Dave said as he popped a can of beer and tossed a second one to me. "Well, yeah. We are sick. But so is everybody else. Everyone has thoughts like that. Most people are afraid to admit it. There's a pervert in all of us. Most of us never act on the weird things we think about. But people do think about things like this. I mean, people did actually used to eat each other. I don't know why, but they did. Some Indians used to slice open the chests of their opponents and rip out their hearts and take huge bites out of them while their victim was on the ground and still alive. That's pretty sick, but they did it. I think it goes back to these primitive urges we all have. When it comes down to it, we're just animals. And even though we like to think that we're super intelligent beings, we're just animals."

I popped the beer, drank it as fast as I could, and leaned over and got another out of a brown paper bag. "Why are people afraid to admit that they think weird stuff like this?" I asked.

"Because they're afraid that if they admit even having such thoughts that they'll actually do the stuff. They're afraid to admit that there's a dark side to all of us, a dark side that we have to fight from coming out. And again, thinking those things doesn't make you a pervert. There are all kinds of babes who wonder what it would be like to cook a guy and eat his parts. That's just the way we are. The thing is, we're at least willing to admit to thinking crazy stuff like this. There's no shame in that. Remember, pretending that bad things don't exist won't make them go away. And remember that a bold man never apologizes for who and what he is. Those who admit to such things are a billion times stronger and a bazillion times more confident than those sissified wimps who are afraid of their feelings. Don't be a sissy. And remember this, babes don't like wimps; they like guys who are strong, confident and self-assured."

"Are you saying that if I want to show a babe how confident I am I should tell her I want to barbeque her and eat her private parts?"

"Yes, that's exactly what I'm saying, you big goof. Do that and you'll have babes galore. What do you think?"

"I don't know, but I'll remember that. But damn, what do you think it'd be like to eat somebody? Would they taste good? Would they be greasy? Would blacks taste different than whites or Chinese? Does one race have tougher meat than the other? Would we be better barbecued or broiled? Do Catholics taste different than Protestants? What would be the best part? What do boobs and asses taste like? How much meat is there on us? Seriously, is there enough meat on a human? Would we become addicted to eating people? Would we taste better than snakes and rats? Would we—"

A Sick Thought

"You've spent a lot of time thinking about this, huh? A little too much, I think."

I had thought about it. In study classes in high school I would fold my arms across the tops of the wooden desks, lay my head on them, close my eyes and daydream and put myself in situations that I thought I would never be in. In those dreams I always found love. Never was I shy. And never was I at the back of the line taking orders from everybody else because I was afraid to assert myself. No, in those dreams I had taken over the world and I was the one giving the orders. And I had always wondered what it would be like to eat people. I had been ashamed of some of my thoughts, but no more. Travel had changed me. I was no longer going to apologize for my intellectual curiosity and for wanting to be a cannibal.

"No, not *too* much, not *enough*," I said. "You can never go wrong in thinking too much. You've said so yourself. If we ate somebody we could write about it. I think people would be curious. We'd be adding to the world's body of knowledge. What greater contribution to life could we make?"

"I'll tell you what greater contribution we can make. If we could invent powdered alcohol, or freeze-dried alcohol, you know, so you could carry around little packets of it and just add water to it and have beer and mixed drinks just like that, we'd make an incredible contribution—the greatest contribution of all time, of ever. Then we wouldn't need to lug beer and whiskey around in bottles and cans. That would decrease the amount of garbage going to the garbage dumps, and the world would use several billion fewer bottles a year. That would free up more sand for beaches and kids' sandboxes. Wouldn't it be great? You just open a little foil packet, pour it in a glass or canteen, shake it up, and presto, you've got booze and are getting drunk. Now that would be a contribution to society that would top even the toilet and linoleum. But anyway, I've never eaten anybody. It would obviously be scary. I mean, to eat a person you'd have to kill someone. That's pretty serious stuff. And as bold as I am, I'm not so sure we should do that, unless we come across drug dealers, peacenicks or people who do yoga."

"Well, do you think we'll eat somebody on this trip? It would be different."

"Where we gonna get the body? You gonna kill somebody?"

"No, but maybe we could raid some funeral homes and get a few stiffs there."

"Can't. They embalm the bodies and put chemicals in them. They'd be inedible."

We spent a while more discussing cannibalism, drinking beer, smoking, eating and wondering what it would be like to eat a human. When we finished I had the feeling that we never would eat anybody on the trip and that if I were ever to do so I'd have to do it on my own. But I intended to keep my eyes open for yoga places.

"Dave," I asked as we prepared to leave and picked up our empty beer cans from the ground so we could throw them in a garbage can later on, "do you think that on this trip we'll meet any women who think about eating guys' parts?"

He looked up at me, shuddered and said:

"Let's hope not."

CHAPTER 29

A New Companion

As we picked up the last few cans, someone started shouting at us:

"Trow dem cans back on da ground! Trow 'em down! Trow dem cans back on da ground you goofs! Ya ain't gonna be hauling garbage around witcha. Trow 'em down I said!"

It was Phil, the produce clerk we had met in the grocery store in Arkansas, the guy who had conned us into working for him one Saturday while he boozed at the tavern across from the store's parking lot! Unbelievably, he was on a motorcycle. He had pulled up a few minutes earlier on the gravel road behind us. We had been vaguely aware that someone was behind us, but we really had taken no notice of him because our minds were so intensely focused on the subject of cannibalism.

"Trow dem cans back on da ground 'n leave 'em dare!" Phil barked as he walked across the road while pointing a crooked right index finger at us.

I was scared. He was walking fast and was nearly across the road. His black hair was a wild mess and his face was contorted into a look that was one-quarter anger and three parts hatred. His facial contortions and a really scraggly black moustache added to his demented look and convinced me that we were dealing with a crackpot. I threw the three cans I had in my hands to the ground.

"Pick those cans up and pick them up now," Dave ordered. Then he turned to Phil, stood straight and silent and glared. I was hoping that Dave would drive Phil crazy with frightening words and a scary routine, although I figured it wouldn't have mattered much because Phil seemed crazy already.

When Dave spoke it was straightforward and simple:

"Screw you, jerk."

That stopped Phil cold, and he and Dave stood and glared at each other. I hurriedly picked up the cans and watched.

"We're picking up these cans because we're not slobs, we're not vile, stinking, useless litterbugs," Dave said. "Only an ass, only a total jerk leaves crap on the road. Are you telling us you're a total jerk? And by the way, why don't you lose those lazy speech habits? Whydoncha gimme tree a dem? Wouja like tree a doze? Er maybe tirteen a dem dare tings? Joododat? Meechatanite? Joologe? Jawin? Ya jerk. Didn't anybody ever teach you how to talk? Are you so stupid that you can't pronounce your th's?" Then Dave put an index finger to his mouth and worked it up and down between his lips so that he made a dribbling sound.

Phil looked like a raving maniac. I thought his head was going to explode, and I went for my rain gear because I didn't want to get blood on my clothes.

"Don't give me this holier-than-thou crap!" he shouted, suddenly losing the lazy speech habits. "You think you're so much better than everyone else? You think you've got to set an example? Trying to make the rest of us look bad? Spare me, freaks."

"So you *can* talk," Dave shot back. "That's good because I want them to be able to understand you in the nuthouse. Because that's where you belong—in the damn, stinking nuthouse. I'll bet you'd really go nuts if we did something really horrible like help an old lady across the street or went to the store for medicine for a sick person. Huh?"

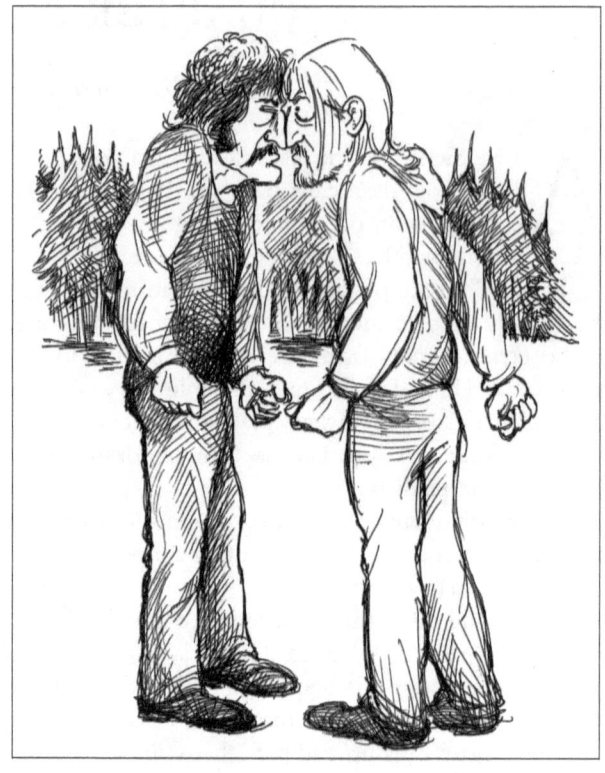

"Screw you."

"No, screw you. Get out of here, jerk."

Phil stayed put. After he calmed down, he explained that he was tired of people looking down on him because of the way he sometimes talked and because he was from a working-class neighborhood and because his dad was Italian and worked in a factory and his ma was Polish and often did other people's laundry to bring in money. He figured that because we were picking up our trash we were the types who would look down on him. He had graduated from college and then studied to be a paralegal. But even though he had completed the course near the top of his class, he couldn't get a job. He was told more than once by lawyers that his lazy speech habits embarrassed them. Law firms didn't need a "deez 'n doze" paralegal.

Phil, as we had learned in Arkansas, was from Chicago and was our age. He was shorter and heavier than both of us, a fact which made me feel superior. Even as a kid, any chance I got to tower over a shorter person I took because it made me feel good. He had even worked for the same grocery store chain that I was at, but at a different store. Phil had been on vacation from the job in

Chicago when we saw him in Arkansas. He started working at the Arkansas store because he needed money for a new car. He had wrecked his car one night by driving it into a fire hydrant after drinking a dozen beers and some whiskey. He nearly drowned in all the water that rushed into the car. Phil too had been looking for adventure, but he was too tied to his car, bars and grocery stores to really bust loose. We and our bikes had inspired him, and so he worked at the store for a few months, saved money and bought a motorcycle. Then he hit the road and went looking for us.

"You figured you would just come and find us?" Dave asked. "That's crazy. We could have been anywhere. This is impossible. No one will believe this."

"So what? Who cares?" Phil said. "It doesn't matter. I'm here. Let's drink." He walked across the road and got a half-pint of whiskey and a 12-pack of beer from the bags on his bike. I was itching real bad to drink some more, but Dave said we shouldn't. There was a national forest campground three miles up the road. It was already mid-afternoon, and the sensible thing was to drive three miles and set up our tents before drinking.

"Besides," Dave said. "it ain't right to get drunk and then drive. It's only three miles—ten minutes at the most—down the road. Let's go."

Phil would have none of it. "We're gonna drink here on the side of this road right now. Don't give me none of this holier-than-thou crap."

"What if we crash, you idiot?" Dave said. "Think about it."

"I have. It's not like we're in cars. What are we going to ruin? Crashing on a motorcycle is nothing."

Even I knew then that Phil was an idiot. He had no idea that crashing on a motorcycle was much more dangerous than crashing in a car; that crashing on a bike means having large sections of your skin scraped off and holes scraped into your skull.

"We either drink here or we don't drink. We drink now, here!" Phil demanded.

"Fine, drink by yourself," Dave said. "We're going."

Dave and I got on the bikes and drove to the campground. Phil pulled in five minutes later. After dinner, beer and burps, we sat around the campfire and drank some more. I wondered what Phil had done about his job. He had been on vacation, and it had now been several months since we had seen him in Arkansas.

"I just never went back," he said when I asked. "Screw 'em. I hated the job anyway. All these customers came in and you had to be nice to them. You had to be nice to jerks. That ain't for me."

Phil wanted to ride with us. Dave said it was okay as long as he didn't act too much like a jerk and demand that we litter or drink and drive. Although I had liked Phil when we met him in Arkansas, I didn't want him along. I felt he was intruding on the trip that was supposed to be mine and Dave's. I worried that he was smarter than me, would start making decisions, and that I'd be third down the ladder.

Once, when Phil got up to take a leak, I told Dave how I felt.

"It's not worth it for you to worry whether anybody is smarter than you," he said.

"Why's that?"

"Because *everybody* is smarter than you."

Like almost every night in the woods, this one was beautiful. The sky was clear. It was cool enough for a light jacket, but not cold. The air was different from that in the city. It was fresh and crisp and cool and clean and it inspired me and made me feel so good and special and proud and sexy and so confident—feelings that made me wish that Shirley could see me right then—that I wanted to breathe in as much of it as I could so that I might feel even better about myself. So I tried. I walked away from the smoke of the campfire and started inhaling as deeply as I could, trying with each breath to stretch my lungs so as to increase their capacity. I inhaled and exhaled deeper and faster with every breath. Soon my chest was stretching so much that it hurt. But I didn't care. I couldn't get enough of that air. Faster and deeper and faster and deeper I breathed until I was like a steam locomotive at full throttle with a hundred miles of flat, straight track ahead. I remembered the story that Walter had told us about Pancreatic Pete, the nursing home guy who nearly sucked all the air out of the building through a straw. I thought I might inhale all the air in the world and leave billions to suffocate. But I didn't care. I needed more and more of this gaseous elixir that was making me feel so good. I huffed and puffed and inhaled deeper and deeper, and huffed and puffed and inhaled some more, and—

Next thing I knew, Dave and Phil were pouring beer on my face to help me regain consciousness. I had made myself so dizzy that I had passed out.

"Jeez, you've been out ten minutes," I could vaguely hear Dave say.

"Trow water on him," Phil said, resorting back to his lazy speech habits. "Why are we wasting good beer on *him?*"

"We didn't know what happened to you," Dave said as he knelt down and lifted me into a sitting position. "You got up and left and you didn't come back, and we were wondering where you were and were hoping you weren't lost, and then we hear this noise like a tornado, and we get up and look around and walk in the direction of the noise, and then we shine our flashlights at the noise, and my god! It's you huffing and puffing away like a madman, and we figure you're having a fit, I mean a really bad one, 'cause we called out your name and you just kept huffing and puffing, and we called again and you huffed and puffed even harder, and then you started wheezing and making all kinds of noises, and then all of a sudden, kaboom. You're flat on your back and out. Ten minutes is a long time to be out. You okay?"

I wasn't. I was still dizzy, had a pounding headache and was soaked with beer. But as I wobbled to my feet that air got to me again, and there was one and only one thing in the world that I wished for: that Shirley could have seen me right then.

Huffing and Puffing Away

CHAPTER 30

Breakfast With Phil

N ow that Phil was along, we had to figure out what to do with him. His presence was like having a stranger barge in on a family gathering. Not only was his behavior an affront to good manners and class, but it was uncomfortable because we didn't know anything about him. Like family members who know each other's personalities, habits, political beliefs and oddities, Dave and I knew each other well. We had been friends since seventh grade. But Phil was a stranger, and we were going to have to learn who and what he was.

The next morning, Phil began showing us who he was, both by action and word. Dave and I were sitting on a log next to a smoldering campfire enjoying our usual breakfast of chili, onions and white bread in our small aluminum camping pots, when Phil walked up, stood next to me and held out his arm to offer me something.

"Put some of this on that chili; it'll make it taste good," he said.

I reached for the item in his hand and was stunned. It was a big bottle of whiskey.

"What am I supposed to do with this?" I asked sheepishly.

"Put some on your chili," he repeated. "It'll make it taste good."

"But, but, I don't want any," I said in a tone that said I knew that putting whiskey in chili, let alone doing it in the morning, was idiotic.

"Put some in your chili!" Phil barked as he waved the bottle in my face. "And soak your bread in it. And then take a couple of spoonfuls of chili and then wash them down with some swigs of this. That's what real men do. Are you a man or are you a wimp? Besides, we're on vacation. And when you're on vacation you drink."

"But I don't want to," I protested.

"I don't care what you *want* to do. It's what you're *supposed* to do. Now dammit, don't give me any of this holier-than-thou shit. Just pour this in your chili."

"No!"

"I said put it in!"

Phil didn't wait for another refusal. He unscrewed the bottle's top and tried pouring whiskey into my breakfast. Startled, I jumped away. Phil followed, intent on making me drink whiskey at seven in the morning. Dave jumped between us.

"Hold on there booze man," Dave said, making it clear that he too was annoyed by Phil's behavior. "If you want to drink whiskey for breakfast that's your business. But don't make anyone else do it."

"Don't give me any of your holier-than-thou crap. You're supposed to put whiskey in your chili."

"Says who?"

"Says me."

"You're crazy."

Phil was as angry as he was the day before when he had charged across the road at us. "Don't you ever say that again," he snarled as he pointed a finger in Dave's face. "Don't you ever criticize my old man like that again. I'll kill you."

"What does your old man got to do with this?"

"I said I'll kill you. Now stop it. Leave him out of this."

"You brought him into it. You're crazy."

Phil dropped the bottle and jumped at Dave. But Dave stepped to one side and Phil landed in the dirt on his chest. He got up, started swearing, and denounced Dave for denouncing his father. He went on for fifteen minutes before he calmed down and finally told us that his dad and his dad's buddies and their entire families drank whiskey for breakfast on vacations. It was a tradition, Phil said, that was started by his father.

"What my dad does, I do. You mess with me and you mess with him. You criticize what I do and you're criticizing him, and I don't stand for it. No one messes with my family. Now, I'm telling youse one more time, you put whiskey in your breakfast. If you don't, you insult my old man and you insult me, and I won't put up with anyone attacking my father."

It was the first time I'd ever heard that refusing to pour whiskey on your breakfast was a direct attack on someone's father. I refused Phil's idiotic demand to spike my chili, but I sensed that having him along would be an adventure.

CHAPTER 31

A Good Deed Gone Wrong

Seeing that he'd never convince us to spike our chili with whiskey—especially at breakfast—Phil backed off, and in a dramatic change of mood, suggested that we hurry up and finish our food. When we asked why, he answered, "So we can start drinking. We'll just sit here and drink all day. It'll be a blast. That's what you do when you're on vacation."

"Says who? You or your dad?" Dave asked sarcastically.

Phil blew up again and threw a fit and screamed and swore until he was tired. He continued to insist that drinking all day was what his dad and his dad's buddies did while on vacation, and that by questioning him we were attacking his dad. When he calmed down, Dave was disgusted and angry. He lectured Phil:

"We are adventurers! Bold men! We're the boldest of the bold! We have adventures every day. Sitting around a campground all day and drinking and getting drunk isn't an adventure. You might think it's fun, and your dad might think so, but it's stupid. I don't mind booze, but not all day. We go out and do things. If you can't do that, then leave. There's a town a few miles down the road. Maybe there's something going on there. You can sit here and drink, or come with us. But we ain't coming back."

Phil packed up and drove into town with us.

It started raining hard just after we got to town, and so, at Dave's insistence, we ducked into a tavern and drank while waiting for the rain to stop. The sky cleared several hours later. But it had been a heavy downpour, and the streets, especially the areas close to the curbs, were flooded because trash and leaves had clogged the sewer grates into which the water was supposed to drain. We hopped on the bikes and rode around town looking for adventure. Dave said there could be gold and money in the streets—valuables that had been washed out of basements by the high water.

From what we could see, though, no gold or other riches had been washed out of basements, and we didn't see any skeletons—as I had hoped—that had been washed out of cemeteries. All we found in the semi-flooded streets were branches, leaves, garbage and other debris. Lacking any real excitement, because it wasn't a real flood, we were bored. Then Dave had an idea. It wasn't the most exciting thing to do, and it wasn't dangerous, but it was damn good fun. Like kids do after a rainstorm, Dave and I made little boats of whatever suitable garbage we could find—sticks, paper cups, foil wrappers, whatever—and floated them down the large puddles that had formed along the curbs.

We raced our boats, assembled fleets and did battle with each other, sunk cruise ships and depth-charged submarines, and had a good time of it, especially when the rain started up again because it meant more water for our fleets.

Phil refused to join us. He complained constantly that what we were doing was childish and dumb.

"Youse are acting like kids. Dumb little kids. Oh my, let's race our boats and pretend we're kids and having fun," he said in disgust. "Damn, we should be doing something real fun, guy-type fun, man fun, not this piddly-ass baby crap. This stuff went out of style in the 1920s. Grow up."

Phil kept complaining, and Dave, tired of the whining, said that if he had a better idea he should pursue it, and that we'd join in if it was real adventure.

It wasn't long before Phil started having his kind of fun. He saw an old man on the curb on one of those flooded streets. The oldster had white hair and he walked slowly and was hunched over, and from across the street where we had stopped the bikes and were watching him, he looked like he was in his seventies. He was using a hoe to try to unclog one of the sewer grates. That particular sewer was at the end of a block, and the puddle it created on account of being clogged was huge. In length it stretched all the way down the block, and in width it came almost to the middle of the street. Dave was thinking of talking to the guy, because he thought he might be interesting, when Phil elbowed us and said, "You want adventure? None of this juvenile, nineteenth century crap. Watch this."

He put his bike into gear and drove off down the block. Then he turned around, revved the engine and raced toward the old man. When he got near the guy, Phil steered the bike into the puddle and raced past and splashed him. When Phil was halfway down the block he turned the bike around and did the same thing from the opposite direction. The old man raised the hoe up to his chest as if to protect himself from the water, but it didn't help. He got drenched. Before we knew it, Phil had raced past the guy a third time. As he prepared for a fourth run at the guy, who by this time was walking very slowly away from the curb, Phil started laughing. He completed his fourth assault and laughed even harder. Dave and I were disgusted. We motioned for Phil to come by us, and when he did, we screamed at him and demanded he stop.

Phil was stunned and hurt.

"The guy's a jerk," he said. "A big, old, ugly jerk. If he doesn't want to get splashed, why is he out on the curb? It's his fault. And it's his fault for being old. I'm sick of old people. What the hell is he doing out there? Jerk."

Dave and I parked and shut off our bikes and ran after the old guy, intending to apologize to him. But he saw us, and probably figuring that we too were out to get him, started running. At least he tried to run. His old legs couldn't run, let alone walk real fast. He shuffled along the best he could. It was one of the saddest things I'd ever seen. He was scared. We wanted to be nice to him, but he didn't know it. I wondered how terrified, helpless, sad and angry he must have felt; sad that a young punk would lack so much respect for age and for life itself, and angry that his body was so old that he had to try to run from a punk who in his prime he probably could have easily destroyed. From a distance we shouted that we were sorry, but he didn't respond. At one point he turned around and raised his arm and made a bony fist and shook it at us. We yelled again that we were sorry, but he kept moving.

He made it to his house and into his backyard before we could catch up to him. Dave said we should let the matter drop, but I couldn't. Phil had acted like an incredible ass, and I felt that we had to apologize for his jerkism. I was embarrassed for the human race, and I wasn't going to let it drop. I was determined to set things straight, to right a wrong and to stand up to evil. Dave advised me against doing anything, but my sense of justice and desire to do something right was so strong that not even an admonition from the Almighty could have stopped me. I was going to apologize for Phil's despicable behavior.

I walked up the front stairs to the guy's house and rang the doorbell, confident in knowing that what I was doing was righteous and good. There was no immediate answer, but I had expected that because of how slowly the guy moved. I figured it would take him a while to shuffle to the door. But three minutes seemed like too long a time, and so I rang again. This time I waited two minutes before ringing again. There was no answer, and so I rang again, and waited, this time a minute. The result was the same: no answer. So I rang again and got no answer, and then I rang again, each time halving the time between rings. I rang again and again and again, and pretty soon, I was ringing the bell every two seconds, and still, no matter how often I rang, there was no answer. I started banging on the wooden front door. That got no response, and so I started banging on the front windows. Still, he didn't come out. I started shouting for the guy and banging on the door at the same time, and pretty soon, I was screaming and demanding that he come out so I could apologize. I started stomping my feet on the wooden front porch and—bang! There was a loud explosion and one of the front windows shattered! Then there was a second explosion and another window was gone! And then there was a shotgun barrel sticking out one of the broken windows, and I knew it was time to leave and I stumbled down those steps and ran to the bikes. Phil was laughing and Dave was shaking his head, and pretty soon we heard sirens and decided that it was time to leave.

We drove off, but didn't go far because a block away we found an old, abandoned garage in an alley. We drove the bikes in, pulled the door down behind us, slumped to the dirt floor and talked. We figured that the sirens were from cop cars that had been called by the old man. Dave decided that since he hadn't been involved in the incidents, he would go down the street to try and mingle with the crowd that was sure to form, see if the sirens had been for us, and try to get information. He left, and I calmed my nerves with some of Phil's whiskey and kept as quiet as possible, lest somebody hear us and

A Good Deed's Reward

snitch us off to the cops. About forty-five minutes, or most of the whiskey bottle later, Dave returned and explained the situation:

"It was the cops, and an ambulance, and jeeze, don't you ever try to do any more good. The guy was shooting at you. He figured you were trying to break in and kill him. And then after he shot at you and the cops came, the commotion got to him and he had a heart attack, and now the cops are after us. You two are jerks. Turns out that the old guy is a former mayor of the town and a retired judge, and damn, somebody really important. And now that everybody thinks that we were trying to bust into his house and kill him, the heat is on us. There's cops out everywhere, and the state police, too. They've got the roads blocked, and there's an All Points Bulletin out for us, and goofballs, we're in big trouble."

"Is the old guy going to be okay?" I asked.

"Don't know. They took him out on a stretcher and were banging on his chest pretty hard trying to get him started back up. Just don't know. Now, with everybody looking for us, we've got to figure out an escape plan."

While Dave and Phil schemed about how to escape, I went off to a corner to brood. I told myself that the world was a sick place, that right was now wrong and wrong was now right, and that it was so corrupted that it made no sense to even try to do good. I decided right there that it would never be worth it to apologize to anyone, and that I never would, no matter how badly I had hurt them.

CHAPTER 32

Ideas For Escape

As hard and as long as we tried, we couldn't think of any creative, outrageous and adventurous escape plans. Aside from Phil, who suggested that we create a diversion by setting fire to a large section of the town and then riding off while the cops and firefighters were tending to the fires, we were mired in conventional thinking. Dave rejected Phil's suggestion. It had been raining most of the day with no signs of a letup, and with all that rain it would have been difficult, if not impossible, to start fires.

Phil disagreed, but did concede that we would have needed an enormous amount of gasoline to do the job, and that it would have aroused suspicion in a small town if three strangers bought up all the red metal and plastic gas cans from the hardware stores and went to gas stations to fill them.

Several hours of scheming got us nothing but the idea that we either make our escape in a heavy rainstorm when the cops wouldn't be so inclined to look for us or to chase us, or at three in the morning in the dark when there would be only a skeleton force of cops on patrol, and when we could ride with our lights off and not be seen.

But finally, after several cigars and the rest of Phil's whiskey, our minds started to loosen up. Dave suggested that we dismantle our bikes and smuggle them out of town piece by piece and then reassemble them at a remote location. Not only would that have taken weeks, but I explained that I was mechanically inept and would never be able to put my bike back together, and that that would be the end of the trip for me.

"Not really," Dave said in pushing for his plan, "if you can't put the thing back together you can throw all the parts into a huge wheelbarrow and push it around. That way you'll still be on the trip. Think of the benefit of it. Pushing six hundred pounds of motorcycle parts around the country will get you into incredible shape. You'll have more muscles than the muscleiest of the muscle-men. And babes like muscles. Women will be dying to meet you. You won't even have to talk to them. They'll just be interested in the muscles."

I told myself that a body knotted up with muscles on top of muscles would be a winner with women, especially Shirley, and was something that I wanted. I also figured that people would laugh if they saw a guy pushing a wheelbarrow filled with a dismantled motorcycle around the country. As much as I wanted the muscles, I wasn't willing to pay the price of the ridicule.

Phil didn't like the idea of dismantling and rebuilding the bikes because he didn't want to get his hands dirty.

"I'll tell you what," he told Dave, "you take apart my bike and put it back together and I'll go along with it. And get me some beer while you're out there."

That idea was junked, and so was one of Phil's that we race out of town during the day and we tell any cops who stopped us that we were modern day Pony Express riders.

"Everybody loves the Pony Express—everybody! We just tell them we're using motorcycles instead of horses. People are stupid; they'll believe anything."

"Yeah, but what do we do when they see we ain't got no mail?" I asked.

"How are they gonna know? We'll put big sacks on the bikes and fill them with flour. And if the cops ask to see the mail, we just say that no one sees the U.S. mail, that the mail is none of their damn business."

That idea also went nowhere. Then I thought of one.

A Babe Magnet

"Since the streets are already flooded because the sewers are clogged, why don't we flood the whole town out by clogging up all the sewers?" I said after one satisfying drag on a cigar. "If the place is flooded, everybody will have to leave, and then we could build rafts for the bikes and float them and us out of town when everybody is gone."

Dave liked the idea, but Phil didn't because it involved work. He eventually bought into it, though, and we spent several hours that night running around trying to clog up all the sewers. We must have stuffed paper and garbage into thirty or forty sewers before we realized there were hundreds of sewers in the town and that we'd never get to them all. Besides, by early that next morning the stars in the sky told us that the weather had cleared and that the chance for rain, and thus a huge flood, was unlikely.

No, it looked like we'd have to do something as dull and as ordinary as a mad dash out of town in the dark of night. It was about four or five in the morning when, exhausted from drinking and from clogging up dozens of sewers, we decided to sleep. Before we passed out, Dave announced that he had a bold plan and that he'd share it with us when he woke up. That said, we unrolled our sleeping bags and went to sleep.

CHAPTER 33

Another Brilliant Plan

"Up you lazy good for nothings! Up! Bold men don't sleep when there's a caper to pull! Up!"

Phil and I would have stayed in our sleeping bags had Dave not been kicking us so hard. We were dead tired, but even exhaustion gives way to kicks to the ribs from steel-toed boots.

Dave was pacing around the garage like a nut, while Phil and I cleared our eyes and heads. He was impatient and excited, and already had been up and out on a shopping spree.

After a few minutes, Dave dug into his jacket pockets, pulled out several small bottles and handed them to us while gushing:

"With this we're going to be able to drive away in broad daylight, damn the cops, damn the townspeople, damn the old man, damn the state police, damn the FBI, damn the KGB, damn everybody. They'll stop us, but they'll never be able to take us. Smear this stuff all over yourselves. Put it everywhere—on your clothes, in your hair, in your ears, on your skin. Undress and pour it all over your bodies."

"Dave, or should I call you Mister Bold Man, are we going out on dates or what?" Phil demanded.

"No, not at all."

"Then why are you ordering us to drench ourselves in cologne? If you're saying that I stink, I ain't having it. I don't take crap like that from nobody. And if I do stink, I'll find a place to take a shower. I'll find a stream. Covering up body stink with perfume is what they did in the Middle Ages. Them people were sick. I read all about them in history, and I ain't going to do that."

"I know, it's not what your dad would do, right? Fact is, both of youse stink. You stink worse than stink itself. But you don't stink worse than this cologne does. This is the cheapest stuff I could find. Figure it out. What's one of the awfulest smells there is?"

"The smell of money burning," I blurted out.

"You got a point there. But even worse than that is a guy or gal who puts on too much cologne or perfume. You've smelled them. They stink. And I don't care how good or expensive the stuff is, if you wear too much of it you stink. And you've also smelled that real cheap stuff; it stinks worse. You can smell this stuff a mile away. What could smell worse than drenching ourselves in really cheap cologne?"

"Your feet," I said with a laugh. "Why don't we use your feet to get us out of this mess? You're not going to let that powerful weapon go to waste, are you?"

"They're too powerful. I don't want to kill anybody or drive them crazy. I just want to escape. Smear ourselves up with this cheap cologne and we'll smell like pimply-faced teenagers on their first dates, or pathetic, middle-aged men and women who are trying to cheat on their spouses and who can't tell that they've overdone the cologne or perfume. No one will want to come near us. When the cops stop us, they'll be overwhelmed by this sweet, sickly cologne smell. Now pour it on."

We emptied twelve bottles between us—four bottles each—and we stunk so bad that we couldn't stand ourselves. We fled the garage as soon as possible because the odor in the confined space was unbearable, and headed straight to the main road and out of town. We weren't on the road more than three minutes when the cops spotted us and turned on their squad cars' sirens and flashing lights. After we were pulled over and stopped, Dave told us to stick close together so as to concentrate the cologne smell. We did, but I figured we were headed straight to a jail cell, what with such a totally asinine idea of becoming arrest proof by wearing too much cologne.

"Don't say nothing," Dave said as the first cop approached. "Just take your cues from me and do what I do."

"Gentlemen," said the first cop as he approached at about twenty-five feet away with his right hand near his holster and gun, a loud, angry, vengeful tone, and a mean look on his face. "You boys like to intimidate old men?"

He moved toward us with slow, measured steps, all the while talking and sounding angrier. "You punks like to give old men heart attacks?" he said at about twenty feet. He advanced a few more steps, unsheathed his billy club and started slamming it into his open hand. "Well maybe you scumbags would like to see what it feels like to have a heart attack. Maybe you boys are going to be happy spending twenty years in prison for attempted murder. Maybe you boys are going to like being gang raped in the shithouse. Maybe yo—Whoah. Whew! Something stinks. What goes on here?"

He had gotten to within fifteen feet of us when the intense odor hit him. He started rubbing his eyes and holding his temples as if suffering from a terrible headache. "Whoah. Man. What is going on here? What stinks?" he repeated over and over.

"Can we be of any assistance, officer?" Dave asked as he took two steps toward the cop.

"Stand where you are! Don't come any closer!" the cop screamed as he ripped his gun from his holster and sank to one knee in intense pain. Five other cruisers had pulled up by then. The other cops had seen what had happened to their colleague and they rushed toward us with their guns drawn. But when they reached their fallen colleague they too were hit by the concentrated odor of cheap cologne.

The Stench Of Cheap Cologne

"Good god!" one exclaimed as he dropped his service revolver on the ground. "Wow! What stinks so bad? This smells as bad as my wife and her friends. It smells as bad as the chief and his wife when they go out to a function. This is bad news." He too dropped to his knees and rubbed his temples. A third cop hit the wall of smell and turned back toward the squad cars. The others who came forward never got closer than twelve feet before they staggered backwards, overwhelmed by the stench.

"Is there anything we can help youse with officers?" Dave asked again. "Can we help you up and walk youse to your cars? Would you like us to sit in the back of your squads so youse can question us? We can come down to the station and spend a couple of hours while you fill out police reports? We want to cooperate."

"There's only one way to cooperate," the first cop, who by now was crawling through the mud on his belly back to his car, shouted at us. "Get on those bikes, leave and never come back. Get the hell out of here!"

We drove off all smiles and with an even greater appreciation for cheap cologne than we had had in high school.

CHAPTER 34

A Dumb Bet

T he cologne was a huge success. As Dave had predicted, it repelled state police officers, FBI agents and even a couple of people we figured were foreign spies. But there was negative aspect to this brilliant plan: We stunk so bad that no matter how often we washed ourselves and laundered our clothes, the smell wouldn't go away. Everyone who got within ten feet of us came down with headaches and sick stomachs. They couldn't stand to be near us. This caused big problems. Waiters and waitresses in restaurants wouldn't serve us. Neither would bartenders. For a while we thought we would starve, and worse, remain sober for lengthy periods of time. No one would talk to us, not even bums. But then we discovered the positive side of the plan. Grocery stores emptied when we walked in. The workers and store managers fled, and we had the places to ourselves. And since there was no one to accept our money for the stuff we tried to buy, we got food, beer, cigars, whiskey and motor oil for free. Even banks emptied out when we arrived, and we had all the money we didn't need. What good is money when you can get everything for free? It was a huge discovery, and one that we noted and appreciated. But after two weeks we grew tired of it. We were lonely and sick of talking only to each other. We discussed the situation and agreed with Dave that the thing to do was to drive to Iowa and Wisconsin and hope that the smell of pig and dairy farms would permeate our clothes and skin and overpower the stench of cheap cologne.

Riding through Wisconsin in the late summer was a special thrill for me. The state was loaded with eighty and one-hundred-twenty-acre family-owned dairy farms that assured all that if you were willing to work hard and weren't afraid of physical labor you could still make it in life as a farmer. As kids, my brothers and I had gone every summer to our aunt and uncle's dairy farm in Wisconsin where we spent the long, hot July days helping bring in the hay, marveling at how much waste Guernsey cows expelled, and playing in the hayloft. Until I take my last breath, and probably even beyond, I will remember those most pleasant days of my childhood when my brother and I would walk for hours through pastures while lobbing rocks into cowpies to see who could splatter the manure the farthest.

Our crossing the Wisconsin state line was a momentous event, so significant in fact, that we got off the bikes, inhaled the manure-scented air and gave thanks that we would finally be free of the smell of cheap cologne. Dave and I were familiar with dairy farms, but not Phil. Prior to this trip he had been out of Chicago only once in his twenty years, and that was to cross the street to the suburb of Cicero to look for hookers.

It was a huge shock to me and Dave one day when we were sitting on the side of a gravel country road munching on salami and stale rye bread, and watching the cows in a field rest while chewing their cuds, when Phil bolted up, raced to a barbed-wire fence and started shouting at the cows:

"Get up you lazy bastards and move around! Get up and do something! Just move around! Don't just lie there!" He threw sticks and rocks at the brown-eyed bovines, which upset me and Dave more than it did the lumbering beasts. The cows just lay in the sun and moved their jaws from side to side while chewing their cuds, and they blinked their eyes slowly while Phil's face turned red as a ripe tomato. Dave and I jumped up and tackled Phil to prevent him from throwing more sticks and rocks.

"I can't take it anymore," Phil said when we had finally settled him down by giving him a few swigs of whiskey. "We've been riding through this state for a week now and all I ever see are cows lying around in the fields. Don't they do any work? Why are they so damn lazy? No wonder there's no steel mills or factories or foundries and no other signs of progress up here. The whole state is lazy. These people must take after their cows. Don't the cows ever move? Why do they just lay there all day? Damn. It's driving me crazy."

Phil was incredulous when we told him that cows made milk.

"How?" He demanded. "With what? I don't see no pots or pans or factories or nothing. They're not running machines or lathes or nothing; they just lay there. They're even lazier than me, and that's pretty bad."

We explained once to Phil the biological process of how cows turned grass and water into milk with their four stomachs. We were willing to repeat the explanation as many times as it took to enlighten poor Phil, but once was enough because we might as well have been speaking a foreign language to him.

The days flew by and we smelled less and less like cologne, and we were eating sausages and cheese and whole milk and butter and eggs and bacon and ham and biscuits, and it wasn't long before I was having dizzy spells and chest pains. We rode around the state, and, as we were in America's Dairy Land, I renewed my childhood love affair with milk.

As a kid there was nothing I had loved more than cold milk right out of the refrigerator. I drank two or three glasses of it at a time, four, five, maybe six times a day. Not only did I love milk for the taste of it, but because of what I thought it could do for me medically. Milk, I knew, was loaded with calcium, and calcium was necessary for strong teeth and bones. I had both. Never had I had a cavity, and my head, my brothers told me, was hard as steel because I had been dropped several times on it with no discernable negative effects. I was thrilled that I had perfect teeth. It was the only thing, I thought at the time, that

I had going for me. If I could keep my teeth strong, I might someday impress a woman into dating me.

So I drank milk like a fiend, consuming at least a gallon a day. In the seventh grade I thought I learned about milk's curative powers. I had chipped a front tooth and was in a deep depression over it. So, in a desperate act of self-medication, I tried to grow the chipped part of the tooth back. How? By consuming huge quantities of milk with its bone-growing calcium. I put myself on a milk diet. I drank gallons of the stuff every day and gave my chipped tooth milk baths. That is, I filled my mouth with milk and swished it around for several minutes at a time. This undoubtedly defies medical science, but after six months, the chipped portion of the tooth had grown back. At least I thought it had. When I boasted to my dentist that I had grown back part of an adult tooth, he laughed and suggested that maybe the rest of the tooth had worn down and become even with the chipped part. I never went to him again.

Remembering that tooth-growing episode and how my teeth had ground into powder during the freezing, shivering ride from Chicago to Carbondale, I figured that if massive milk consumption and milk baths could grow back that chipped tooth, it could grow back a whole mouth full of teeth.

So I started drinking milk, not just an eight-ounce carton or two at a time, but half-gallons. I drank milk for breakfast, lunch, supper and snacks. I substituted milk for beer and drank each half-gallon as fast as I could. Soon I was boasting of my milk consumption, saying that no one loved milk more than I did.

"How much milk do you think you could drink in an hour?" Dave asked one morning after I had guzzled a half-gallon. It was something I had never thought about, but being immensely proud of my milk-drinking abilities, I answered that I could probably drink two gallons in an hour.

"That's it? I thought it would be at least three. Anybody could do two. Even I could, and I don't even like milk."

Stung, and not wanting to concede that somebody could drink more milk than I could, I answered that I could easily drink three gallons in an hour.

"How about four? Someone who drinks as much as you, a milk lover like yourself, must be able to drink four gallons in an hour."

"No problem. I can do it easy."

"That I figured, but how about five? Do you think you could do five? 'Cause I don't think you could. No one can drink that much milk."

"I can!"

"Naah! You want to bet on that?"

"Damn straight I do."

"That's too easy a bet. Anybody could do that. I'll bet though that you can't drink five gallons in a half hour. No one loves milk that much."

"I do, and I'll do it!"

"Naah! You drink that much milk in a half hour and you'll get milk skin."

"What's that?"

"Where your skin turns white from drinking too much milk."

"Bull!"

"Well, you'll get it if you drink six gallons in a half hour."

"You're a liar, and I'll show you you're a liar."

"So you can drink six gallons in a half hour?"

"Easy!"

"Actually, I think you can do that. But I'll bet you can't drink seven gallons in fifteen minutes?"

"Yes I can!"

By the time I realized that Dave had been goading me and that I was making a fool out of myself, I had insisted that I could drink ten gallons of milk in fifteen minutes. Dave and Phil bought the milk in eight-ounce cartons and stacked them in front of me. When I saw them and realized that I had to drink one thousand two hundred and eighty ounces, or one hundred and sixty, eight-ounce cartons of milk in fifteen minutes, I felt sick and knew that I had exaggerated my milk-drinking prowess. But so eager was I to prove that I could do something worthwhile, and so unwilling was I to admit that I was wrong, that I ripped into those milk cartons and guzzled milk as fast as I could for as long as I could. I tore open carton after carton and raised their wax coated cardboard spouts to my mouth. Milk splashed on my face, poured down my chin, under my shirt and down my chest, and I drank and drank and drank, and Dave and Phil laughed, and I drank more in a frenzied effort to show them that I could do what I said I could, and to stop those laughs and prove that I was no fool. Milk filled my stomach and backed up into my windpipe. I feared that milk was going to start shooting out of my ears. I cursed cows and wished they had never been created. But I didn't dare stop. I had something to prove. The more I drank the harder they laughed. And the harder they laughed the more I drank. And finally, they laughed hysterically when I threw up.

I might have drunk a gallon and a half, certainly no more than that. I was humiliated, and it was a costly lesson, but I was learning. I vowed right then that I would never again bet that I could drink ten gallons of milk in fifteen minutes.

No. I'd give myself an hour.

CHAPTER 35

We Meet Another Nut

"Come to me in the morning and we will have some fun in the afternoon! Come to me in the morning and we will have some fun in the afternoon! Come to me in the morning and we will have some fun in the afternoon!"

It wasn't fun that either of the two people we were watching outside a zoo in a small Wisconsin town were having.

The guy shouting those words was having a rough time. He was being kicked and beaten with a purse, getting his face and arms scratched, and was being screamed at.

"Freak! Weirdo! Misfit! Assho—"

They were words that would have perfectly characterized Phil, but they were being shouted by a woman who was fighting to free herself from the arms of the guy who kept screaming that line at her:

"Come to me in the morning and we will have some fun in the afternoon!"

She eventually—and rather easily—won, gaining victory, not by physical strength, but by something more powerful than the bulkiest and strongest muscle: unrelenting criticism.

"You're a jerk! You're not funny! You scare me! You're weird!" she screamed at him.

The guy, crushed by the barrage of insults, slumped to the ground and released the woman. Not satisfied with her verbal and mental victory, she kicked dirt and spit on him before rushing off. He sobbed loudly. Dave said we should talk to him to see what had happened. Phil wanted to talk to him too, but for another reason:

"He's just been dumped. He's hurting real bad. He's dying for some friendship right now. If we pretend to be his friends, he'll buy us beer and gas and stuff. You know what I say, when people are at their weakest is when you've got the best chance of taking advantage of them. You heard the broad. He's a jerk. And I'll tell you right now, there's something about him I don't like."

On Dave's order we approached the guy cautiously and from three sides, just in case he was armed and so upset that he might start shooting. That was an unnecessary precaution, though, because even if he had a gun it would have been waterlogged. He was sitting in the dirt with his legs crossed Indian-style and crying like crazy. Tears seemed to spray out of his eyes. The button-down white, short-sleeved dress shirt he was wearing was soaked. So was his striped polyester tie, plaid dress pants and white socks. There was a puddle at his feet, and the heels of his maroon penny loafers were muddy.

I had never seen anybody cry that much, not even myself after Shirley dumped me. We tried four or five times to talk to the guy and to get him to calm down and talk to us, but he kept sobbing. Phil finally got him to stop by pouring a can of beer on his head.

"Now shut up and talk crybaby," Phil growled, "and tell us who you are and what's going on. Because if you don't you're gonna get it! And I'm gonna give it to you!"

After a few false starts in which he got his convulsions under control, the guy told us his story. His name was Ed Browning, and he was older than us by ten years, although the crew-cut hairstyle he wore and his baby face made him look younger. And he, crazily enough, had been a store manager for the grocery chain that Phil and I had worked for, although we had never run across him. He loved his job, the grocery company, the stores he worked in— even their floors. He was especially proud that he would always have the floors, even the back-room floors that got caked with dirt and grime, "super-cleaned."

A Super-Cleaning Dude

"Super-clean the floors, super-clean the windows, super-clean the toilets, super-clean everything. Super-clean is what I stand for," he told us in a squeaky, irritating voice. "And always remember this: Let's do it over because we didn't do it right the first time. That's my motto: Let's do it over because we didn't do it right the first time."

While managing one store Ed had gazed upon the woman of his dreams. Her name was Judy. She was beautiful and vivacious, but unfortunately for Ed, he wasn't the man of her dreams. Oh, they dated for a few months, and at first she thought him kind of cute, but she began to lose interest—slowly and reluctantly in Ed's mind—when for a date he took her to the grocery store and watched as the stock boys super-cleaned the floor. She didn't share his excitement over how a can of lye, bucket of hot water, a mop and somebody else's muscles could remove week's worth of caked-on grime from a concrete floor. She grew decidedly cool toward Ed when he really started opening up to her by showering her with gifts of cleaning products. Ed believed he was giving of himself when he gave her a mop and a case of lye. She thought otherwise. But it was when Ed announced proudly to her that he had changed his name to "Ed Browning, Jewel Junior," Jewel being the name of the grocery store chain, that she left him for another and another and another and another, and maybe even another. Although devastated, Ed rallied and launched a campaign to win her back. It failed. Judy didn't think that his gifts of light bulbs and used cardboard boxes from the store were particularly romantic. Ed tried again, this time pouring out his heart and soul to her in a love poem.

"I've got it right here in my wallet," he told us as he started to cry. Would you like to hear it?" We said we would, and he pulled a black wallet from his pants pocket, opened it, took out a piece of paper and carefully unfolded it.

He did more than carefully unfold it. He *lovingly* unfolded it, and handled it with the gentleness and care with which a mother handles a newborn. He looked at it as if it were a prized possession so valuable as to be priceless. I knew from my experience with Shirley that it *was* his prized possession, that it was the one thing—the piece of loving magic—that linked him to her.

"It's called," he said, "Love Never Dies." Then he trembled as he held the handwritten paper between his fingers, cleared his throat and read:

Love Never Dies

I love you my darling.
I love you my dear.
I love you at the beginning
And end of the year.

I know you don't love me,
But like me a lot,
So by the time you read this
I'll pro-bly be shot.

My brains 'll be splattered
All over the wall,
And someone, I know,
Will give you a call.

When you first see me
Please try not to cry;
Just remember, my darling,
It's for you that I died.

I know you will come
And visit my grave,
And I hope when I'm gone
You'll fine-ly behave.

When you visit at the beginning
And end of the year,
Just remember, my darling,
I love you my dear.

Love poem! It sounded more like a suicide note to me. If we hadn't been sure about Ed before, we certainly weren't sure about him now.

Judy had turned white, cried and then fainted when Ed read the poem aloud to her one Saturday afternoon in the grocery store's small break room while other employees listened. She hit her head on the hard tile floor and went into a coma for several days. When she awoke, the doctors refused to let Ed see her. He figured that it was because she had been overwhelmed by his outpouring of love and was so unused to being loved that she simply couldn't take it. It was as if she was allergic to love.

So Ed saw himself as the unfortunate lover whose love was so intense, pure and abundant that it overwhelmed the sacred object of his affections. It was like giving a two-pound steak to a starving person. The food is delicious and nutritious, but because the person hasn't eaten for so long, the food shocks their system and causes death. And, as hearty, delicious food can be harmful to a starving person, so too can love be harmful to someone who has been deprived of it. Ed *knew* that Judy loved him and that it was his poem that had won her. But because his love was too pure for her right then, he decided to buy a motorcycle and travel around the country while she recovered and worked herself into shape to be able to accept full doses of his undiluted love. He was helping her recover by occasionally sending her small doses of his love—short notes and love poems—and was looking forward to the day when she would be strong enough so that he could return to Chicago, read his masterpiece to her again and sweep her away to the altar.

Even in his short notes to Judy, Ed kept to his theme of endless love.

"Dearest Love," said one note he showed us, "I could gaze all day at a pool of mud full of flies and bugs and never stop thinking of you. Love Never Dies! Ed."

Another read: "'Till all the clouds fall from the sky. 'Till all the birds get sick and die, baby I'm yours! Love Never Dies!"

And a third said: "Although most people are repulsed by your warts, to me they are just warts. Your warts make you unique. I don't think they're that ugly. Love Never Dies!"

Ed loved Judy and was always thinking of new ways to express his affection to her in doses small enough so as to not put her into a coma again. When he thought of romantic lines he tried them out on other women to test their effect. He had determined from the behavior of the woman who had just beaten him that his, "Come to me in the morning and we will have some fun in the afternoon" line was a bit too strong and in need of dilution. He said that in the coming weeks he was going to refine the line. But in the meantime, seeing that we too were on motorcycles, he wanted to ride with us and share our quest for adventures.

"Adventure is in my blood and my blood is in adventure," he said in that annoying voice of his. "We'll have a dandy time. A Class-A time, a superior time. We can tour grocery stores and see which ones are superiorly stocked. We'll examine the displays and grade them, and then we can compile a list, or write a book on the best looking and best stocked grocery stores in the country. And the cleanest, too. Oh, this will be dandy. It'll be just like a restaurant guide. It will also be an invaluable service to the grocery shopping public. We'll tell them where to shop when in Montana or Colorado or Illinois or California or anywhere. If stores are dirty or ill-stocked, we'll offer advice on how to improve them. We can even hire ourselves out as the super-cleaners. We'll be the super-cleaning team! We can go into stores and tell the stock boys and the produce clerks and the managers and assistant managers to do jobs over again because they didn't do them right the first time. And please, don't call me Ed. That's a one-dimensional name that doesn't fully describe me. Call me Jewel Junior. That's the true me."

Dave called him a lot more than Jewel Junior—and it wasn't pleasant—and said firmly that Ed could not ride with us. Phil said Ed could come along so long as he bought us oil, gas, beer and cigars, and as long as he rode at least a hundred yards behind us and camped the same distance away when we stopped. So with the vote tied, the decision was mine. I was torn. I was uncomfortable when Phil showed up because I felt he had intruded on mine and Dave's trip. I felt the same way about Ed. I didn't like strangers. Yet I wanted him along. My intense dislike of strangers and fear of change was being challenged by one of life's most powerful desires, and in Ed I saw a great opportunity for myself to fulfill that desire. With Ed around I would be able to—finally—dominate someone else.

I could tell that Ed was more naive and less sure of himself than I was. With him along I would no longer be the lowest man on the ladder, the one who was the butt of all the jokes and who took all orders. After having been bossed around and teased all my life, I wanted to do some bossing. It was one of life's great opportunities. I could get revenge for having been picked on and abused by picking on and abusing someone weaker than me. I could dish out ten times more abuse than had been inflicted on me. That, I thought to myself, would really be living.

"He can ride with us," I said.

Chapter 36

A Scary Story

It was late August, and the crowds of vacationers whose vehicles had filled the roads were gone. The weather was changing, and we could feel and smell fall, and to me it was beautiful. The nights and days were cool, and much of the time it was cloudy, windy and rainy. Dave figured one day that it was time for us to stay somewhere for a while so we could work on the bikes, clean up, rest, reorganize and plot our next moves. He wanted a spot that was isolated and where we wouldn't be bothered. A ranger in a National Forest Service office listened one day to Dave's request for help in finding such a place.

"I'm not saying we're on a secret mission, but I can't tell you exactly what it is we're doing," Dave said gravely. "And I'm not saying we've killed people and are running from the law, but we need an out-of-the-way place. It's massively important. I can tell you that we are four bold men, and that bold spelled backwards is dlob. Please, for the sake of the planet, ask no questions."

The ranger couldn't ask any questions because he was trying to keep himself from busting out laughing. But eventually he pulled out a map and showed us a campground that he said was almost never used.

"It's so far out of the way, so isolated, so lonely that no one really goes there," he said. "If something happens there's no way to get help. You could scream for hours out there and no one would hear you. Forty years ago it was a very popular place, but then, something happened, and it was as if people got scared to go there. People from around here who are old enough to remember having gone there a lot, and who remember it being suddenly abandoned, don't talk about it at all. I've asked around, but when I do, people shudder and shake their heads and walk away. You can understand the locals not using it anymore, but the real strange thing is that everyone else stopped using it too. It makes no sense. Why would people from Illinois or Michigan who know nothing about the area stop using it? How would they know that something might have happened there? Is it instinct? Or some crazy form of subconscious communication? I'm not the superstitious type, but it's odd.

"Anyway, if it's solitude you want, there's where you'll find it," he continued as he pointed to a spot on the map that he had spread out on the office's wooden counter. "It'll be a tough ride."

Had we known how difficult it was to reach the place when we started out we would not have gone. What should have been an hour's ride took nearly three. The road that led to the campground was really a dirt path so narrow and overgrown with weeds and walled in by a dense, hardwood forest that it was nearly impassable. A few times we thought we had lost the road, and were set on turning back, figuring the ranger had given us bad information, but we always managed to find it. It was a dark, cloudy day, and riding on a narrow, lonely path through such a dense, dark forest was scary. Along the way we saw evidence that at one time the path had been a road: a few rusted pickup trucks, their windshields long ago shattered and rubber tires rotted, that were overgrown with weeds. Dave said they were from the 1930s and 1940s. We stopped to look at each of them. Dave wondered who had owned them and speculated about how they had gotten there. In each case he figured the drivers had met horrible deaths at night in violent thunderstorms. We searched for skeletons, but found none.

There were also a few abandoned wooden sheds. At least I thought they were sheds. Dave said that in the olden days whole families lived in what looked to us like sheds, but had actually been houses. They were all leaning and twisting and the spines of their roofs were bowed. Their floors were dirt, there was no glass left in the window frames, and they creaked when we went inside. They would not have made good shelters from the rain because they were full of gaping cracks and holes where the walls and roofs had rotted or caved in. Most were one-room, single-story structures. We looked for evidence that they had been inhabited. At one place we found rusted tin cans. We also found an old, creaky outhouse and some rusty, wooden-handled steel tools lying on the dirt floor. There was nothing else to tell us anything about the place or about who might have lived there other than a door that led to a second room. The wooden door had no doorknob and it was nearly off its hinges. I was about to kick it down to see what was in the room when Dave shouted, "Don't! Don't do it!"

"Why not?" I asked.

"Because you don't want to see what's back there, and we'll be cursed if you do! I've got a bad, bad feeling about this place. I can sense it! I can feel it! I can see it! There was a family here. There were nine of them, you know, a husband, wife and seven kids, and they were trying to scratch out a living by raising cows and vegetables, and they were terrorized by a demented, lonely man who had fled to the woods after killing a bunch of farmers by sneaking up on them from behind on dark, rainy nights and smashing their heads in with rocks.

"Imagine it! They're sitting here eating supper night after night around a big wooden table in this room that was lit only by candles, and all they can hear is rustling in the bushes, rocks being tossed onto their roof and crazy, spooky howling. Their dogs are barking, and the husband loads up his shotgun and goes out the door and, man, there's nothing he can see to shoot at, and then he comes back in and they go to bed scared, huddling in the same room together thinking there's a madman out there who wants to kill them.

"The next morning they go about their farm work and milk the cows and work the fields and then, when the mother calls 'lunch!' they gather around the table in here and then—holy smokes—the five-year-old boy is missing! They shout for him and start racing around the house and through the fields looking for him, and they check the outhouse to see if he was taking a dump, and he's not there, and they get sick and nervous and they search all afternoon and into the evening and they can't find him, and they're scared as hell. And this is before they've got telephones out here, so there's no way the people can call the cops. They all go to bed crying that night and without supper because they've been too preoccupied with the search for the little one. The mother sobs as she remembers his sweet, innocent smile.

"After what seems like an endless night, the father gets up in the morning and vows to go into town, which is who knows how many dozens of miles away, to get the sheriff, and he gets in his pickup truck and he tells the wife and kids to load their guns and to be careful. They're scared, but they get hysterical when he drives off. Then, twenty miles down this road, where we saw that first truck, the damn machine runs out of gas. The guy is angry and nervous and he starts walking back to the house so he can get gasoline he has stored in fifty-five-gallon drums for the tractors and stuff.

"By noon he ain't back, and by mid-afternoon he ain't back, and by early evening he ain't back, and by now the wife and kids are scared witless and they've turned the house into a fortress, and two of the older boys decide to go out looking for the old man. They cut across their fields and find a dead cow with its head bashed in and they get scared, and one runs back to the house while the other continues on.

"Finally, around ten o'clock at night, the father comes stumbling up to the house, exhausted from his twenty-mile walk. The wife lets him in and the kids cheer and cry and—oh my! The kid who was left out in the field ain't home. A search party goes out, but it starts storming—lightning, wind, rain and thunder—and there's nothing they can do except go back to the house and wait until morning. The mother is devastated. The fourteen-year-old who is missing now was the joy of her life. He helped her bake and wash dishes and clean house, and he was so gentle and kind.

"Next morning, the father and the rest of the boys—three of them, ages sixteen, eleven and seven—go out armed with guns looking for the missing kid. In the field not far from the dead cow they find his bloody hat. The seven-year-old shrieks. They hunt for the fourteen-year-old, but can't find him. Now they know that he has come to a bad end, too. The father sobs. They go back to the house, where the father issues orders that no one is to leave the house alone.

"But it's too late, one of his daughters has already left to go to the outhouse. She took the family's collie with her, but still the father is beside himself. The father races out the house and flings open the outhouse door and his heart nearly bursts right there. She's not there. But the dog is, and he's dead. His head has been bashed in by a rock. The wail that the husband lets out tells those inside the house the sorry news. The father returns. The family huddles in *that* room behind *that* door. A rock comes through *that* window over there. The wife screams. The kids cry. The father goes out and fires his shotgun in frustration several times into the black night. He hears a taunting laugh and goes back inside. Rocks bang off the roof all night preventing that weary, terrorized family from getting any sleep.

"Dawn comes and finds them passed out on the floor. The madman presses his face through the broken window and sees the same thing. He quietly opens a back door and steals off with another child, this time the three-year-old girl.

"Oh, the cows and the wolves and the bears and the birds in the forest cry too when they hear that family's shrieks when they discover that the little girl is missing. The father is almost insane with grief and terror. The mother wants to leave with her three remaining children and husband and go to town for help. The husband can't. He can't leave his two daughters and two sons behind while knowing there's a chance they are still alive and in need of his help and protection.

"He's insane. All he can think about is how, when the kids were young, they adored him and smiled at him and trusted him and looked to him—their father, their king—for food, shelter and protection. And now those four souls who had so depended on him were in danger, and he is helpless to do anything about it. He thinks about how they must have screamed for help in their time of most desperate need and how he wasn't there to help them. It goes through his mind over and over again and he is crazy with rage over a parent's biggest fear and worst nightmare, and he throws himself into walls and onto the floor, and he bangs his fists on the wooden table and he cries and cries and cries.

"He outfits the remaining three boys and his wife with shotguns, rifles and a large can of gasoline and sends them off down the road to the truck. As she says goodbye to her husband and protector of those so many years, the woman regains her sanity, but she loses it again when she looks into his eyes as he sinks to his knees. She sees in those eyes that he believes he has failed to do the single most important thing that parenthood is about. He has failed to protect his children. Her heart and mind break when she sees how shattered he is, and she wails as she stumbles off down the dirt road with her arms around the three boys' shoulders.

"No matter how lost the situation was now, the farmer knows that he has to do one thing before he dies: He has to find his four kids so he can at least kiss them one last time goodbye and rub his cheek on theirs' and caress their hair with his beefy, calloused hands, and see that they at least are buried next to each other and not left lost and alone in the deep, dark forest.

"He searches and searches and looks everywhere—in the barn, in the fields in the hayloft in the machine shed—but he can't find his darling children. By nightfall he is in a panic, as if that were still possible what with how emotionally drained he is. The wife and three boys have not returned from their quest for help. Is there such a thing as going insane when you're already insane?

"Is there such a thing as going madder than mad? There is for this poor man. That he retains some shred of awareness about his situation is a tribute to his absolute love for his family. But that he does sends him into the realm of torment beyond comprehension. Four children and a cow already lost; the rest of his family—the only thing in life that he lives for—unaccounted for and stalked by a madman. Not even this noble and stout man can bear it. It is too much to think about, and so his brain shuts down and he goes into a deep sleep.

"Evil is evil, and sometimes there is no explaining it. As if this man needs more pain. When he wakes up he sees the most sickening site: Locks of his wife's brown hair and the shoes of his three sons are laid out on the dirt floor in front of him. The madman has struck again! Oh, that poor man! He races around his farm for hours and hours searching for his family, oblivious to the lightening and thunder and rain and nightfall and the next day's sun and wind.

"He hunts that whole day and the next, and the next as well. At night he hears no taunts and hears no rocks on the roof. That is an even greater torture because now he is all alone in his torment and insanity, and there is nothing like silence to make you dwell on the negative. At least the rocks on the roof and the taunting laughs would have taken his mind off his dead children. Was he going to be left alone to die in his insanity?

"That next morning he hears that maniacal laugh again, this time from the direction of the outhouse. He grabs his shotgun and races toward the building. The door is open. He looks inside and his mind all but explodes. Stuffed into the slop pit through the wooden hole in the seat, are his wife and two kids. The other family members are piled tight in the small building.

"Somehow he stumbles back into the house. Waiting for him in *that* room, behind *that* door, is the madman! The farmer is too broken to do anything. He can't even move to attack the man who has murdered his family. He stands there numb, useless and totally devoid of anything human at all. The man-devil laughs as he ties the farmer to a wooden chair. He laughs day after day as he brings out from drawers in the house articles of the farmer's wife's and children's clothing and makes the poor man smell them.

"After several days of this, and when the farmer is near death, the madman brings him back to life, so to say, by whispering manically into his ear, 'I've got kids, too. They're just like me. And they're out there. Haaaaaaaaaaaaaaa!'

"The farmer struggles to break free of the chair and ropes. He wants to destroy the madman, and he wants to hunt down the monster's kids and destroy them too. Even though he hasn't had food in days, that brave man breaks free and lunges at the maniac. His finger's grip the man's skinny, slippery neck. His fingernails gouge into his moist, pale skin. His grip grows tighter. The madman gasps. His face turns blue. His eyes bulge out. He gasps again. The farmer, his hatred for evil fueling the attack, summons his last bit of strength and further tightens his grip. The lunatic gurgles. His body stiffens, and—crunch! A rock slams into the back of the farmer's head. He falls to the floor and is hit again and again and again. The madman recovers, gets slowly off the table and smiles at the person who crushed the farmer's skull.

"'Thank you, son,' he says.

"So," Dave said, while shuddering, "*don't* open that door! Evil lurks behind that door! And *don't* go into that outhouse!"

I didn't need orders to keep me from opening the door. Neither did Phil or Ed, or for that matter, Dave. We raced out of the house, hopped on the bikes and drove off fast.

Stuffed

191

CHAPTER 37

A Spooky Campground

I t was late afternoon when we pulled into the campground. The approaching dusk made a gloomy forest even gloomier. I don't think we could have found a more isolated spot. We were deep in the woods, more than thirty miles from the nearest town. The campground, as the ranger had said, was a forgotten place. What was supposed to be the road running through and around it was a weed patch. The campsites were so overgrown with weeds and bushes that only a trained eye could tell that they were campsites. If you walked back far enough into them you could find rotting wooden picnic tables. In one place, after hacking our way through a field of weeds, we found one of those old, rusty hand water pumps. Surprisingly, the thing worked, but the water came out rusty and smelled like rotten eggs. In a couple of places we saw what were once sturdy, galvanized steel garbage cans chained to wooden posts. They were so rusted that the slightest touch caused them to crumble. The sky was a deep, solid gray, and we were tired and still scared. That was the crazy thing. Phil, Ed and I knew that Dave had made up the story about the farmer and the madman, but we were still scared. We thought there might still be a madman lurking in those woods! Even Dave was scared!

We stomped down some weeds and made a little clearing for ourselves. After a quick meal we were in better spirits. We managed a few nervous jokes about how many skeletons we would find if we dug up the campground's old outhouse, and we joked that the madman's kids were still around.

It was getting late and darker, so instead of unpacking the bikes and setting up our tents, we started looking for firewood. The desolate area was loaded with downed trees and dead wood, so it didn't take long to gather up a huge pile. Dave piled up wood for a huge blaze, and we were about to unpack our gear when Phil said he heard a voice off in the distance. Even Dave was irritated at what he thought was a lame attempt to scare us. Phil insisted that he had heard a voice, or, as he put it, "something real weird, real spooky," and he motioned for us to keep still and to listen. We stood silently, staring at each other while straining our ears for a voice, or for Phil's "something." I heard plenty of "somethings," mostly the howling wind and the tops of trees banging together. I was about to yell at Phil when Dave spoke up and nervously said that he heard a moan that sounded like it came from "somebody who's dying."

My arms broke out in goose bumps. We were in the middle of nowhere in a dark forest with no help around for dozens of miles. If there was something out there and somebody was dying, we had nowhere to go. If it was just Dave pulling one of his dumb jokes, well, I didn't need that.

"Do you smell that?" Dave asked as he punched me in on the shoulder. "It's smoke! We're not alone!"

Ed squeaked that maybe somebody was being burned alive, and suggested that we leave.

"Where we going to go, dummy?" Dave asked. "It's almost dark, and we're thirty miles away from anywhere. Now, who knows if we've been spotted. Hopefully we haven't. No loud talking. Let's whisper."

We listened and sniffed the air for a few minutes. We all smelled smoke.

"Follow me," Dave whispered as he set off in the direction he thought the smoke was coming from. We carefully headed down the old, weed-choked road, stopping occasionally to listen and to sniff the air. After going about a quarter mile, we saw in the rapidly darkening sky ahead of us a site that made us stop and shudder: a column of smoke rising above the trees fifty or sixty yards ahead.

Moments like that are strange. For all we knew we had not been spotted. There was no reason for us to go forward and investigate. We could have huddled near the bikes until early morning and then gotten out of there. Investigating meant that we might be discovered and killed. Human beings hate danger and fear, and yet we are fascinated by and attracted to them. Even though we hate being scared, we constantly put ourselves in situations where we will be scared.

We paused to look at the smoke. Each of us must have been desperate to go back. I know I was, but a part of me also wanted to go forward. So we stood there as a group, letting our fear and apprehension do battle with our curiosity and thirst for adventure. Before we could decide, we were met with a hideous moan that drifted out through the woods. I wanted to go back. So did Ed and Phil. But we were shamed out of the idea by Dave, who called us "sissies, unadventurerers, nonexplorerers and boldless, pathetic wimps."

"Besides," he whispered, "you never know what we'll find. Maybe there's a murder taking place. This could be exciting. Maybe Russian soldiers have parachuted into the country and are setting up a base of operations which they will use to prepare for a massive invasion by launching hit-and-run attacks on our roads and electric lines and bridges and power stations. We could keep track of their every move and alert the authorities. And who knows, you know how backwards that country is. They can barely feed themselves. Maybe these guys are here to dig up our potato and cabbage crops and smuggle them back to starving Mother Russia. Maybe they've come loaded with vodka and with the intention of getting us all hooked on the stuff so that when the main invasion force lands we'll all be drunk and unable to defend ourselves, and boom, they'll take America just like that! We could be in the middle of something big here. Imagine what heroes we'll be when we capture them and reveal to the world that they were trying to steal our potatoes!

"You know, maybe, just maybe, there are still wild Indians around here. Not the ones on the reservations, but you know, some unknown tribe that was never subdued and who are just as wild and savage as they were three hundred years ago. And maybe they've got one of their enemies staked to the ground and are torturing him with hot coals, ripping out his intestines or cutting off his toes or biting off his ears. Maybe they've got twenty or thirty beautiful—and I mean, really, really beautiful—naked women tied to trees just waiting to have their way with them. Oh god, there's probably a whole tribe of savages dancing and hollering and screaming around those poor gals. Do you know how scared those women are? You think *you're* scared. Damn. And can you imagine how grateful those poor, beautiful, naked babes will be when we rescue them? They'll be so grateful to us that they'll just stay naked while in our company. We'll be out here in the woods with thirty beautiful, naked, incredibly grateful women who will want to thank us and thank us and thank us and thank us for saving their lives! Can you imagine that?"

That we could imagine, and we got off the road, and as cautiously and as silently as possible, started picking our way through the forest toward the smoke and the moans. Damn the fear, damn the terror and damn everything else, there were thirty beautiful, naked women who needed to be rescued, and we were on our way!

Chapter 38

Preparing To Attack!

The climb through the forest and thick underbrush to the top of a ridge from where we could look down and see the smoke more clearly, as well as the glow of a fire, took some time. We were trying to not make noise, and in the dark, which it now was, that was difficult.

We paused again at the top, where Dave lectured us about the importance of the situation: "The key thing here is to get down this ridge far enough and close enough to the Indians so that we can jump out and start screaming and be on top of them before they know what's happening. It's called the element of surprise. It works every time. The most important thing is for us to scare the hell out of them so badly that they'll be terrified and afraid to fight back. For that we need a slogan that we can scream. It's got to be something so terrible and scary and powerful that just hearing it will make them crap in their pants; that just hearing it once will make them drop dead. Any ideas?"

"Chicago!" I whispered excitedly. "It'll scare anybody."

"Naah. Since they're wild savages who don't even know about civilization, they won't know about the greatest city on the planet, and they won't be scared. Won't work."

"Let's just swear at 'em," Phil said. "I mean, we just charge out screaming 'Assholes!' at the top of our lungs, and they'll run like the cowardly savages they are."

"Naah. Too vulgar. When, in future generations, people read about what we did here—and they will because this is history in the making, this is big stuff— they might not want to read vulgarities. We need something else."

"Jeeze. Let's shout 'Super-clean the backroom!' at them. It has scared the living heck out of everyone else I've said it to," Ed offered. "Everyone runs away when they hear it."

"Not bad," Dave said, "but it's not quite what we need. These Indians need to know that we are not afraid of anything, that we are fearless."

"How about we read them Ed's love poem?" Phil asked. "The damn thing put his girlfriend into a coma."

Dave considered it: "That would probably work, but we can't deal with probabilities out here. We need certainties."

"So what can we scream that will make them drop dead?" I asked.

Dave motioned for us to huddle into a tight circle, looked us one by one in the eyes, shuddered, cleared his throat and said, "'Four Bold Men!' That's what we scream at them, 'Four Bold Men!' Just picture it. We come charging out of the woods screaming 'Four Bold Men! Four Bold Men!' and they're going to think we're so demented that they will be absolutely terrified. Their brains will explode and their hearts will stop. Because who but demons and evil spirits would be crazy enough to charge an entire Indian camp armed with nothing but the words, 'Four Bold Men?' That is boldness to the millionth power. Pure boldness. And there is nothing that scares people more than absolute boldness.

"But if they're Indians who've never been discovered, they ain't gonna know English," I said. "And since they don't know English, they ain't gonna know what 'Four Bold Men!' means. And since they don't know what it means, they ain't gonna be scared."

"Wrong you are. The letters B-o-l-d strung together are universally understood. Everyone who has ever lived, and everyone who ever will live, understands and will understand the word 'Bold.' It is the only universal word. It instills fear and respect in all. It is the one great word. Never doubt the power of boldness. Now it's time for us to be bold. You guys follow my lead. Once I start screaming, youse do the same. Let's go."

We crawled, slid, rolled and walked down the ridge as quietly as possible. At times we lost sight of the fire, but we were guided to it by the constant moans that drifted through the woods. As we got closer I grew more excited. Deep down, I knew that Dave's idea was stupid; that it was ridiculous to think that a camp of Indians would be scared by four guys shouting "Four Bold Men!" I also knew that in twentieth century America there weren't any wild Indians roaming the woods. But I also knew that anything was possible in life, and that it *was* possible that there were lost tribes, and that shouting "Four Bold Men!" just might scare off an entire Indian camp. All my life I had lived safely, followed the rules and refused to take risks. But deep down, I knew that those who didn't know they couldn't or weren't supposed to do things always wound up doing them because they didn't know they couldn't. I was tired of living safely. I was thrilled that I was on the verge of trying to do the impossible. If logic and conventional wisdom said that four bold men couldn't scare off a tribe of Indians who probably didn't exist, I didn't care. This trip was turning me into a different person; a man who believed that the impossible is never impossible; who was proud to charge out from behind a tree while shouting "Four Bold Men!" in an attempt to scare off Indians. As I crouched behind a tree waiting for Dave's signal I was flush with pride. And I wished with all my might that Shirley could see me right then and see how far I had come in life.

Chapter 39

An Incredibly Strange Sight

It was the greatest feeling I had ever had when we charged out from behind the trees and rushed the fire while screaming "Four Bold Men!" There was no fear, just an indefinable thrill of unimaginable intensity. I rushed the fire like a madman, heedless of trees, bushes, boulders and the dark, hoping to be jumped by Indians. I ran faster and faster toward that fire, and I ran and screamed and ran and screamed and ran and screamed some more, and by the time I reached the fire I was a raving lunatic who believed four hundred and seventy-three percent that I was scaring away Indians and rescuing naked women who were tied to trees awaiting torture! And my, was I ready for those women to be grateful!

But that wasn't the case. There were no Indians and no naked women. We were winded and disappointed. But the disappointment wasn't complete because before us was a sight that was more than just a little strange.

There was a circular clearing, maybe twenty feet in diameter, which had been hacked out of the woods. The fire was big and bright enough that we could see wood chips, sawdust and recently cut tree stumps all over. A small tent had been set up near the back edge of the clearing, and in the middle of the circle burned the campfire. To either side of the fire were huge piles of firewood. Directly behind the fire was a four-foot-high stump, which was also surrounded by large piles of firewood. Sitting on top of the stump was a man.

He was hunched over with his face buried in his hands and he was crying and letting out long, loud, pathetic moans. He apparently hadn't heard our screaming, or if he had, he didn't care, and we stood around in a silent daze, not sure what to make of the scene. We watched with amazement as the guy, without lifting his face, picked up pieces of wood from the piles to his side and threw them onto the fire. After a few minutes, Dave spoke up to try to get his attention:

"How's it going, crybaby? Having a bad day?"

The guy lifted his head slowly, squinted his eyes as if to focus on us, and then dropped it back into his hands and continued crying. We shrugged at each other and stood there without a clue about what to do. Dave gave the guy another "How's it going?" But instead of answering, the guy blindly picked up another piece of wood and threw it onto the fire. After a while he lifted his head from his hands and stared at us. Big tears rolled down his face, which had one of the most sorrowful expressions I had ever seen. At one point he tried to speak, and just when it seemed he was going to, his head dropped back into his hands. Phil asked what he was doing there, but he too got no response.

Crybaby

It was a little too much for me, and I started thinking that the guy was crazy. I told the others how I felt, and we decided to get back to the bikes. As we turned to leave, Dave, as a parting gesture, offered the guy a cigar.

"No," came back a tear-choked answer. "No thanks."

Wasting no time, Dave asked the guy what he was doing there.

"Sitting here crying," was the answer.

We had had a hard ride over a crummy road that afternoon and were in no mood for stupid jokes. We told the guy so, clenched our fists and walked toward him like we meant business. Phil was the angriest.

"What's the matter, crybaby?" he snarled. "You got problems? Well, maybe we can fix them for you. And dammit, when we're done with you you'll really have something to cry about."

"No, no. I'm sorry," the guy said. "I didn't mean it. I'm sorry."

He seemed sincere, so we backed off. But our curiosity was up and we wanted more than ever to find out why he was there. I still thought he was crazy, and asked if he had escaped from a mental hospital.

"No, no," he answered, "You don't have to worry about that or anything. I'm not that bad."

"Well, what are you doing here?" Phil asked. "Why are you sitting in the middle of nowhere crying?"

The guy listlessly threw more wood on the fire, shook his head from side to side, let out a big sigh, and said in a slow, deliberate voice of undiluted sadness:

"It's, it's just a long, stupid story. I don't think I should bother you with the details."

We told him that he should bother us with the details because we were curious to see how messed up his life was, and we ordered him to tell us. Besides, it was dark, and we always enjoyed a good story around a campfire at night. The guy said his name was Mike. We introduced ourselves. Phil pulled a whiskey bottle out of a small backpack and offered him a drink. Mike took a decent swallow, told us that after all he could use an ear—even eight of them— and said he would tell us his story.

We pulled a couple of logs close to the fire, sat down, passed the bottle around and settled in for a long tale.

Mike had stopped crying by now and told us that he had parked his car on an abandoned road about five miles away, loaded three weeks worth of food in a backpack and hiked to the spot. He had been there a week, had cut all the wood, and spent most of his time daydreaming, thinking about the past and crying. He was twenty-eight years old and was from Milwaukee. He was wearing blue jeans, hiking boots, a red flannel shirt and a light jacket.

"I'm here," he began, "because I just don't know what to do anymore. I had to get away to think. It involves a girl. I loved her—still do—but she left me. I've never forgotten her. I was crushed when she left, and ever since then I've been thinking about her and hoping that someday we'll get back together. It hasn't been the same since she left. Oh, I've been reasonably successful at my work and get by from day to day, but since she's been gone something has been missing. I function, but I don't really live. I still laugh and joke around, but the laughs come, not because I'm happy, but to cover up the tears I cry every day. The thrill of female companionship is one that I don't feel. The happiness and contentment that comes with knowing that someone wants you, that someone needs you, that someone cares about you, is something I don't have. I don't think I'll ever feel love again. I was once the happiest man alive, now I'm the most miserable. Sometimes I just can't take the pain and sorrow, and I feel like killing myself."

I interrupted and asked Mike how long it had been since the girl had left him.

"Ten years," he answered.

"How long did you go out with her?"

"Seven months."

I couldn't help but laugh. Ten years is a long time to mourn a lost love. The situation was ridiculous. Here was this heartbroken guy sitting alone in the wilderness crying over a woman who had left him more than three thousand days before. I had no doubt that she had forgotten him long ago. He had only gone out with her for about two hundred days. I figured he was either goofy, or that those had been an incredible two hundred days. I glanced at Dave and the others and saw that they were laughing too. Mike continued:

"Her name is Carol. She lived near my neighborhood. We met while attending junior college. She was nineteen and I was eighteen. I guess you could say that we formally met on March second. We were freshmen and in our second semester. During my breaks between classes I hung around with my brother and his friends in the cafeteria where we used to sit around and play cards. One day, after my swimming class, I walked into the cafeteria and went to my brother's table. Carol was sitting there with some of her friends. From the instant I saw her I couldn't take my eyes off her. I just stared at her. I sat down a few seats from her and joined in the card game. I had always been real shy, was uncomfortable in crowds and rarely spoke. I was afraid of girls and had never gone out with any before. I felt ugly and worthless. But on that day something came over me. I was the loudest and most talkative person at the table. I was telling jokes and making witty remarks and winning all the card games. And all the time I kept glancing at Carol. One second I'd turn my eyes away from her, and the next I'd be staring at her again. And when I glanced at her I saw that she was looking at me!

"Whenever our eyes met we turned them away and pretended we didn't notice each other. I couldn't believe it. She was actually looking at me! I was so happy, and oh, she was so pretty. She had the most beautiful smile I had ever seen, and she was laughing and joking around all through the card games, and it seemed to me that she was the friendliest, most beautiful girl in the world!

"The group broke up after an hour because we all had to go to classes. I didn't try to talk to Carol. I walked out and pretended that I hadn't even noticed her. I felt like a jerk. All I wanted to do, the thing I wanted most in life, was to talk to her, but I didn't. But even so, oh, how my heart was pounding! The next day I was sitting in the hall by my locker reading when Carol came walking towards me. My heart started pounding and I thought for sure I was having a heart attack. We saw each other, but when our eyes met I glanced down at my book and pretended I didn't see her. Then, just as she was passing by, I looked up at her. She flashed a huge smile. I did the same and we said 'hi' to each other. She kept walking, but, oh, I was in heaven. She had smiled at me!"

Mike paused here and threw another armful of wood onto the little inferno he had been building. The fire was much larger and hotter than when we arrived, and we pulled the logs we were sitting on farther away in order to escape the intense heat.

"Well," he continued, "it went like that for a few days. We sat with the group in the cafeteria, always apart, but always smiling and staring at each other.

I was too shy and afraid to say anything to her in front of the others—I thought they would laugh and think I was stupid. Finally, on the second of March, we were sitting around with the group when they suddenly got up and went to class and left us alone. I was so scared and just didn't know what to say. My heart was pounding and I just sat there and stared at her. She did the same. It was a sunny day, and it was pretty warm for March, and it was a great relief from the winter weather we had been having. Finally, I looked out the window, and then turned to Carol and told her that she reminded me of a sunny day. You should have seen her face! Her smile was the brightest, happiest thing I had ever seen! I'll never forget it. From then on I called her Sunshine."

Mike broke into a huge smile. His eyes twinkled and he stared off into the distance. But there was sadness in his face. It and the melancholy tone of his voice told me that he was looking beyond us and into the past. When he spoke of her smile, good looks and lovely voice, I knew that he could see her. He could see her smile, her bright eyes, and he could hear that laugh and voice that was so dear to him. He seemed so hurt. I wasn't laughing anymore, and neither were the others. He kept talking:

"Then I asked for her telephone number. She wrote it and her address in one of my books." Mike pulled a paperback book about the American Civil War out of his jacket pocket and opened the cover and stared at it. "I still carry it around," he said. "Look at the penmanship. Isn't it beautiful? Look how confident and full of energy her writing is." Then he got off the stump and walked around and handed me the book. On the first page was Carol's name, address and telephone number. I passed it around to the others and then returned it to Mike. He had started crying again, and I suddenly felt very sorry for him. Ten years is a long time to keep a hope and a memory going, and his case now seemed special. And it reminded me of my situation with Shirley. She had dumped me, and here I was riding a motorcycle around the country trying to develop confidence so that I might someday return to Chicago and impress her. There was nothing funny or stupid about Mike's case now. His body was wracked by an infinite sadness. He threw more wood on the fire and continued:

"One day I finally worked up the courage to kiss her. When I did, her smile and face outshone her earlier ones, which I had thought were the brightest there could ever be! After that we were hand-in-hand wherever we went. We met each other before and after our classes, held hands and walked down the halls and talked and laughed and stared into each other's eyes.

"Everyone who saw us commented on what a romantic and perfect couple we were. One day Carol took me to the store where she worked and showed me off to her friends and co-workers. I think she was even happier than I was. As I said, I had been shy before and had never gone out with girls. All of my friends had, and they bragged about it all the time and teased me for being so shy. I felt left out and so alone—thought I was weird and that maybe something was wrong with me. But now all that was changed. I had a girl—somebody actually liked me! I wasn't weird or strange. If you could condense all of the happiness the world has ever known into one human being, that was me. In the mornings before classes I'd sit on a bench in front of the building and wait for Carol. She would see me from a distance and smile and wave and call out my name in the most excited and loving voice there was. And when her words floated over and touched my ears, I was in heaven! All the doubts and worries of the past were erased. All there was for me was the present and the future—the future with Carol!

"I would ride my bike, a ten-speed racer, to her house in the spring and summer and we would sit on her front porch and talk and laugh and kiss. Nothing mattered to me but her. I was confident and sure of myself, and just knew that everything would work out. I felt that whatever I wanted to do or be, all I had to do was make the decision and it would happen. I started doing well in school and participating in classes like I had never done before. I joined in every class discussion and answered questions. I also started doing better on my job—started talking to people without being afraid or shy. I would ride my bike home from her house on those nights, filled with a contentment and joy that can't be described. There was a small ridge just past her house, and when I'd reach it I'd ride with no hands and lean back on the seat and coast down, going faster and faster, the warm breeze in my face and the smell of Carol's perfume on my clothes. Sometimes on a summer night, when the breezes and smells are just right, I'm taken back to those nights on her porch, and I feel as I did then. It's funny what a breeze can do."

Mike paused and stared blankly off into the distance. After a while, Dave interrupted and asked him if the breezes were right just then.

"Yes," he said, shaking his head and smiling. "Yes."

Mike stared while longer and then continued:

"On the second of each month Carol would send me a card marking our anniversary. How I cherished them. No one had ever sent me cards before. I read and reread them every day and carried them around, and there wasn't an hour that went by where I didn't pull one out and think of her. I still have them."

Mike took a bundle of cards out of his pocket and passed them to us. They were torn and dirty from the constant handling. The one Carol had sent him in August read: "A sunny hello from someone who shares the warmth of friendship with you. Love, Carol."

I was having a good time except for the fact that Mike threw more wood on the fire and we had to move farther away from it. We had finished Phil's bottle, and Dave had opened a second. He offered Mike another swig, which he took. Then Mike took back his cards, sat back on the stump and told us more:

"After she finished her two years of college in the city, Carol was going to go to a school in downstate Illinois. It wasn't all that far away, and we talked often about how I would go down and visit her on weekends and attend the same school after finishing up at the junior college. Everything seemed perfect ,except for the fact that Carol's father didn't like me. He had told her that he didn't want her to go out with me, but she ignored him, and we kept seeing each other.

"Late that summer I took a vacation and went hitchhiking and camping in Montana. Before I left, Carol gave me a picture of herself. I still have it."

He started crying again, took an envelope out of his pocket, and carefully and gently pulled out a photograph, being sure to not let tears drop onto it. He looked at the photo and let out a moan and began sobbing so hard that I almost started crying.

"That was the best vacation ever," he said through the tears. "It didn't matter where I went or what happened to me, or whether I got a ride or got rained on. All that mattered was that I had Carol to go back to. When I hiked in the mountains I didn't see people for seven days, but I wasn't alone. No, I had Carol. I thought of her every second. I carved our names into trees and wrote them on boulders and on old buildings. Every time I sat down I took her picture out and stared at it. Every minute I felt like jumping up and shouting out her name. I felt like telling everyone I met that I was in love with her. It was the first time that I had someone to write to and to think about. It was the first time that I could take the thoughts and memories of someone with me on a trip and not be alone. Here she is," he said as he handed me the photograph.

The woman in the photograph was beautiful. She was sitting on a boulder in front of a mountain. Mike said it was taken when Carol had gone to Colorado with her parents. I passed it around to the others and we all agreed that she was one of the prettiest women we had ever seen.

The Love Of His Life

CHAPTER 40

Buck Up, Pal

We handled the picture with care and gave it back to Mike. He looked at it again and moaned.

"Well, what happened?" Ed asked. "How did you two break up?"

Mike threw another armful of wood on the fire and sat down:

"It all began after I got back. All during the trip I thought of nothing but Carol. I couldn't wait to get back and see her. But when I did get back I acted kind of dumb. I didn't call her for a couple of days. I was scared and was trying to act cool. My buddies made fun of me for wanting to call her so quickly. Funny thing, they're all married now and I'm not. Well, I didn't see her until two days later when I went to the college to register for the fall semester. She was helping out during registration and was sitting at a table helping some people. I stopped to say 'hi,' and then walked right by her, trying to act cool and tough. She got up and ran after me and we talked, but that's when she started getting annoyed with my shyness. You have to understand that even though I felt like a million dollars when I was with her, and even though I was much more confident than ever, and even though I loved her with every piece of my being, I was still shy and scared. Those things which I have wanted most in life I have been the most afraid of going after. Oh, my friends and enemies, let me tell you what a curse it is to be scared, to lack self-confidence, to be paralyzed by fear, to be driven to avoid the very thing in life that you love and want to embrace. I wanted to hug her and to kiss her and to laugh with her and to talk and to hold her hand and tell her about the trip and about how desperately I had missed her and how happy and absolutely thrilled I was to see her. But I couldn't. Ever since then all I've ever wanted to tell her was that that scared guy wasn't really me. I've wanted to tell her that the reason I acted that way was because I was scared of just about everything in life and that she was the one thing I loved. But I'll never get to do it. Fear and a lack of confidence lost the one thing in life, the only thing that I have ever loved. And because of fear, every day is misery for me and I hate everything and everybody. And I mean *hate*, especially myself. You don't know what poison fear is. Friends, if I can accomplish only one thing in life, let it be to tell people who are as scared of things as I am that it doesn't have to be. Push yourself and bust out of it, otherwise you will lose the things that you love. Otherwise all of the love and goodness and kindness inside of you will be killed by hatred, and you will wind up miserable. Fight the fear and beat it. Destroy it.

"The fall semester started and we took up where we left off, which now that I think of it, wasn't that good. We had a funny thing going. You see, we only saw each other at school. We hardly went out on weekends. I was afraid to ask her out. Anyway, the semester started and we saw each other at school and she started cooling off towards me.

"Carol was pretty, and a lot of guys started asking her out. I didn't know what to do or how to cope with it. Whenever a guy came up and talked to her in the hall, I clammed up and stood around feeling like an idiot. In October she entered the Homecoming Queen contest. When her picture went up on the bulletin board more guys started asking her out. She turned them down at first, but after a while she just got tired of my shyness and started accepting the offers.

"She started seeing this one guy, Frank. They met at school, and that was it for me. Finally, one morning in October, she handed me an envelope with a letter that said we'd have to break up."

Mike pulled the envelope out of his jacket pocket, took a letter out and began reading:

"'Michael, you and I are going to have to call it quits. Not goodbye, but cool it. I smashed the rose you sent me today and I feel like I also smashed someone. Remember, I do *love* you, and if ever a day comes, I'm going to get hold of you... Just remember, I *do* love you. Be good and friendly and kind and never ever change. Don't *ever* forget me. Love, Sunshine.'

"I was crushed and didn't want to lose her. I sat down and wrote her a letter and told her of my despair and how I loved her. She read it and cried and we made up. But the letter only delayed the final outcome. Finally, Carol told me to my face that we'd have to break up. The next few days were the worst in my life. How can things turn around so suddenly? One day we were holding hands and kissing, and the next we weren't talking to each other. I didn't want to accept it, but finally I forced myself to and decided to bow out with class. I saw Carol outside of one of her classes and told her that of all the times in my life, the moments with her were the best. Then I thanked her for all the good times and kissed her and walked away crying."

"That was the best thing you could have done," Dave said. "That had class. Broads like stuff like that. That's something she'll always remember. After that she probably felt worse than you did."

"I know, I know. But I goofed up after that. I got confused and thought I had to try to win her back. I tried and made a fool out of myself. Well, she finally went away to school. Her new boyfriend Frank went with her, and I haven't seen her since. But since then I have done as she asked me to in her letter. I've never forgotten her. I think about her constantly, go back to the college often and walk down the halls and think about how we used to be— think back to what beautiful times we had, daydream about her and hope and pray and wish that one day I'll come home and see her sitting on my front porch smiling and looking happy to see me. I can just see it. When I walk up to her she jumps up and runs to me and hugs me and kisses me and tells me that she's missed me and that she loves me and that she never ever again wants to be apart from me. Then I hug and kiss her and we hold hands and go for a walk and talk and laugh and vow to never be separated again, and we live happily ever after together. Why can't it come true? Why? Why can't I just see her one more time to tell her how I feel?

"I dream about her all the time. Once I dreamed that I was at a picnic with friends in a park, and she was there too, and we saw each other and talked and got back together. Another time I dreamed that I was riding my bike in the rain to her house, and another time I dreamed that I met her on the street and that she gave me her phone number and that I called her and that we went out and were happy again.

"I dreamed that I was at a commuter train station waiting for a train, when one pulled into the station. Carol was sitting in a seat by the window. She looked out and saw me and smiled and waved and motioned for me to get on. I wasn't fast enough, so I shouted for her to get off at the next stop and that we'd meet there. She shook her head like she understood, and the train pulled out. I caught the next train going in that direction. Well, I got off at the stop, but Carol wasn't there. I figured that she had gone back to where we saw each other, so I got on a train back to that station. When I got off, I saw a train pulling out towards the station I had just come from, and Carol was on it. We saw each other again and waved, and I motioned for her to stay at *that* station. I got on the next train going there, got off and saw Carol on a train going back to the first station. It was crazy. I hopped on the next train back there and got off, but she wasn't there. I got back to the second station as fast as possible, but Carol wasn't there either. I went back to the first station, and she wasn't there, and it went on like that for two hours. We never did meet. That's the saddest dream I've ever had.

"I think of her wherever I go. In crowds I scan the faces to see if hers is there; on buses too. I think the only thing that sustains me is the hope that someday we will get together again.

"I know you guys think I'm crazy, but you just don't understand. I don't know how often real love comes into a person's life. I *loved* Carol. Who knows, I might even find someone and get married, but I tell you this, Carol was, and will always be, my first choice, regardless of what happens.

"I know what you guys are probably thinking: I'm living in the past. That's true. But the past was the best. The future won't be as good, unless, of course, I'm with Carol. And you have to understand why I cling so much to the past and to her. It's because she never did get a chance to see the real me—the me that can laugh and have a good time and not be afraid. I just know that if I hadn't been so scared things would have worked out differently. In the letter that Carol gave me when we broke up she said, 'Don't ever forget me.' I never have and never will. That's my story."

It was a sad story, and I felt sick after hearing it. I so wanted him to be able to meet her again. Mike got up and threw more wood on the fire and sat down again. Then Phil spoke up:

"Jesus, pal. Did you ever think that you're lucky? That she was wrong for you? Maybe the reason you were afraid to talk to her is because subconsciously you thought she was a flake, a loser and a crackpot. Maybe your mind was secretly preventing you from making a bad decision. And has she ever called you or tried to look you up? No! She forgot about you the second she dumped you and hasn't thought about you since, not even to laugh at you. Here you are spending all this time—all these years—thinking about her and crying, and she hasn't thought about you one stinking, lousy time. Get over it and buck up. Here's how you get over this broad real fast. Imagine what she is now. She's probably a deadbeat loser who wasn't good enough for you and who would have dragged you into the slime with her. That's why you couldn't talk to her. Your mind was revolting and trying to save you. She's probably a drug dealer with dried puke all over herself passed out in an alley, or a thief who steals old peoples' medicine, or in prison for beheading boyfriends, cooking their brains and feeding them to her cats, or worse—"

"She's in Congress or she became a poet!" Ed blurted out. "Shame, Phillip. I think this was a super love. Michael, time is a great healer. It changes many things, especially peoples' attitudes. Maybe it has changed Carol's. It's clear that you love her. And it's clear that she loved you. Your immense love for her would not have let itself out unless it had received similar affection in return. If Carol's love for you is just a fraction of what yours is for her, it is a love that will rank among the greatest in history, a super love! And Michael, love never dies! But time is running out. You should look her up and try to talk to her."

"I know I should. But you just don't understand. I acted so stupid."

"But Michael, if the love is there the foolish action will have been long forgotten. She won't care."

"But you just don't understand. I acted so stupid I—"

"Well, have you ever tried writing her?"

"Once," Mike said as he took a letter out of his pocket and showed it to us. I read it to the others:

"Carol, this is a voice from your past; the voice of someone who loved you and who still loves you. In fact, you are all I have ever loved. You wrote in your goodbye note that I didn't know everything about you. True. But you didn't know everything about me. You don't know how scared I was of everything in life, and how I was frightened to go after that which I loved and wanted the most, which was you. I wish you could have seen the person that is really inside of me. When I told you that the times with you were the best in my life, I meant it.

"You inspired me to be more than I was or had ever thought I could be. You made me see how beautiful, wonderful, loving, exciting and fun life can be. When we were together, oh, I smiled so much. But it wasn't just my face or my lips that were smiling; it was my whole body. My bones smiled, my skin smiled, my insides smiled and my spleen smiled! I long for the day when my body will again convulse into smiles and quake with laughter! I wish we could get together and talk. Mike."

We agreed that it was an okay letter. Phil asked Mike when he had written it.

"Three years ago," he answered.

"You never sent it?"

"No—was afraid to—afraid she'd laugh, and besides, I just acted so stupid."

"What did you do that was so dumb?" Ed asked. "It can't be worse than anything I've done."

"I felt I had to try and win her back. I tried, and made a fool out of myself. After a couple of weeks I went up to her and told her that she would have good times with other guys, but that I was the only guy she'd ever be able to have a great time with."

"Bold line," Dave said. "That was a good thing to say. It could have been better. You could have told her you were a bold man studying boldness under David P. Nadolski, but it wasn't so bad."

"Yeah, I know, but she didn't believe it, and she walked away frowning. After that I started following her around the building while pretty much begging her to come back to me. A couple of times I demanded that she see me. She got mad and told me to stay away."

Ed pitched in here and told Mike that that wasn't so bad and that a lot of men act that way when women leave them. He said it was normal behavior. But those kind words didn't cheer Mike. He continued to insist that he had acted foolishly and was too embarrassed to face the woman he loved.

Mike threw more wood on the fire, which was now four or five times its original size. It wasn't a campfire anymore, but a bonfire that I feared would get out of control. Mike piled a few more pieces of wood onto the inferno and paced back and forth behind it. We had to stand up and move even farther away from the intense heat. Mike babbled on:

"I started following her home from school every day trying to talk to her. I drove by her house all the time, and a few times parked my car in front of her house and jumped out and tried to talk to her. She never wanted to listen to me. A couple of times I got drunk and rang her doorbell late at night. Her dad came out and chased me away. God, I acted so stupid."

We didn't doubt that those were dumb things, but we agreed that he could have done a lot worse, and we urged him to look her up. But again, he said that he had acted too stupidly, and he went on telling us how.

"Carol finished second in the Homecoming Queen contest. By that time she had been seeing Frank for a few weeks, but I was still trying to win her back. I was proud of her and knew she was happy for having finished so high in the contest. Yet I didn't have the chance to share that happiness with her. During the Homecoming football game she sat with a group of people who were strangers to me—her new friends. Frank was there too. I sat by myself a little ways from them and watched them laugh and joke with each other. I felt so cheated. I had been with her when she had entered the contest—helped her pick out the picture she used—and had shared her excitement and her hopes of winning. I felt that no one, absolutely no one, cared about me. Carol wouldn't even look at me anymore. The person she had smothered with kisses, the person she had gazed at with loving eyes, the person she had shown off to her friends just a few months before didn't mean anything to her anymore. It was the worst I've ever felt. During the game I drank a pint of cheap wine and started shouting obscenities at the players, hoping that she would hear them. I was trying to be cool and tough. I went down to a few rows in front of where she was sitting so she could see me, and I started swearing and talking real loud, hoping that she would fall back in love with me. I made a fool out of myself."

"Almost a great move," Dave said. "Almost. You blew it by not starting a fight with the jerk she was with. You should have acted like a badass. Then she would have loved you."

"He's right. You should have kicked his ass from here to kingdom come. But this first love stuff is stupid," Phil said. "There are a million babes out there. How can you say that the first and only one you met is the one you're supposed to spend the rest of your life with? That's insane. You don't think back to the first quart of beer you drank at age thirteen and say that's the brand for the rest of your life, do you? No. You try thousands of other brands before you find one you stick with. You gotta go out with other babes. Do that and you'll find dozens that you like better. Now, just to get this over with, I'll look Carol up for you and you can call her and set her straight."

"No! No! No!" Mike said excitedly, "You just can't do that. I acted so dumb. You just can't do that!"

"Those things weren't that bad," Ed said. "People forgive and forget. They change their minds. They see things differently after a while. We're often too hard on ourselves. All the things that you consider stupid and degrading, Carol might have considered valiant, noble efforts on your part. Look her up."

"I can't, just can't."

We were impatient with Mike. He was wallowing in misery. I enjoyed self-pity as much as anyone, but even I knew there was a limit to it. Mike hadn't done anything that could be termed a major disaster. We again urged him to look her up.

"I can't. You just don't understand. I—"

"We *do* understand, pal," Dave butted in. "We understand perfectly well. You just want to feel sorry for yourself. Believe me, if that's your game I'll give you something to really feel sorry about."

"No, no, please. I don't want to get you guys mad. I just feel so embarrassed, so stupid."

"Well, what the hell," Phil said. "You're acting just as stupid by refusing to look her up. She might be hoping that you *do* call her. Time ain't on your side. Do it now."

Mike had gathered another armful of wood and was standing near the blaze, ready to throw it in.

"I just can't," he said. "I acted so stupid."

"Be bold," Dave said. "Have confidence in yourself. Remember what you told us about why she dumped you? You were too shy. You were afraid to ask her out. Learn from your mistakes. Don't you see that by refusing to look her up you're being the same scared person that you were before? Don't be like that. Change, and change this instant! Be bold and things will work out. You remember her parents' phone number? We'll drive you to a phone booth in the morning."

"I'd love to you guys, but I just can't. I acted so stupid."

"Come on!" Dave shouted, "What could you have possibly done that was that stupid?"

"You just don't understand," Mike said, shaking his bowed head in shame, "I acted so stupid. After that I went and I—" He paused here, flung the armful of wood onto the fire and blurted out:

"I went and I, I went and I—I burned her house down and I fire-bombed her car!"

"You what?" we asked at once. "You burned her house down? Why?"

"I just wanted her to love me!"

"Love you? For that? Is she a pyromaniac?"

"No, she's Catholic."

"Did you torture her parents too?"

"No. What do you guys think I am, sick? Hey, you guys want to help me burn this forest down? Come on, it'll burn!"

That did it, the guy was nuts. Dave yelled for us to get out of there. Even though it was dark, we ran up the ridge and through the forest toward our bikes. Mike followed while constantly shouting things like, "Come on, you guys, let's burn this place down! I've got lots of matches!"

We made it to the road and struck out for the bikes as fast as we could. Luckily, the sky had cleared and a full moon provided some light. Mike kept gaining on us and I could hear him shouting, "Come on, it's only wood. I hate trees! They'll grow back. Let's burn this joint down! Got a problem with fire?"

As he ran, Mike lit stick matches and threw them to the ground, leaving a flaming trail behind. As he gained on us he started throwing lit matches at us.

"What did these trees ever do for you?" he shouted. "Let's burn the hell out of them!"

We got to the bikes, started them up and roared out of the place. I looked back and saw that Mike was still lighting matches and chasing us. But we were leaving him and his twinkling little trail behind. I heard his voice trailing off. "You guys! Come baaack! Fiiiirrre!"

Let's Burn This Place Down!

Chapter 41

Saturated!

Racing through the night on motorcycles over a mostly non-existent road in a dense forest is stupid and dangerous. But fear knows no logic, and Crazy Mike had scared us badly. My fear came from knowing that he *would* burn down the forest, and that if we were anywhere nearby when that happened we would be blamed for it. I was no tree hugger, and I did like fires, but I was not an arsonist, and I didn't want that on my record.

That we actually made it back to a real road that night has to be considered a miracle. When we hit pavement we opened the throttles wide and didn't stop until we were at least a hundred and fifty miles away from Crazy Mike.

Finally, we pulled into a wayside and fell off the bikes exhausted. It was sometime in the early morning, and being too tired to set up tents, we slept where we fell. We would have slept most of the day had we not been forced awake by a violent, drenching thunderstorm a couple of hours later.

The rain was heavy and steady and soaked us, and although it would have been wise to put up the tents, we were too tired to try. A restroom building promised us shelter, but it was locked. We were so thoroughly drenched that it didn't matter anyway. All we could do was stand around in the wind and rain and get wetter.

To say that we swore a lot that morning is an understatement. We—Ed included—swore at the rain, the sky, the clouds, our bikes, the sun, the moon, weathermen, each other, Bolsheviks, children, doctors, artists, plumbers, God and just about everything else. To express the full extent of our displeasure, we shook our fists at the sky and pounded them on the wooden picnic tables, against trees and on Ed's arms, back and ribs. Our display of anger, although impressive, didn't change anything. The rain kept pouring down.

The storm had started around six in the morning, about two hours after we had rolled in. At eight o'clock it was raining as hard as ever. By nine, roadside drainage ditches had turned into streams, and by eleven, as the downpour continued, I think our brains started getting soggy. We were past the point of being angry and were feeling goofy and silly. We started singing, splashing around in puddles and throwing mudballs at each other. To relieve the boredom, Phil suggested that we play a joke on Ed, a plan Dave and I agreed to immediately.

To start the gag, Phil gathered the four of us in a circle, stood in the middle and said in the gravest, most serious voice he could manage:

"I want to warn you guys. We're in big trouble. Real big trouble. And we'll be in even bigger trouble if this stinking, stupid rain keeps falling down. If it keeps raining for another thirty minutes or so, and if we don't find shelter, we will die."

"What do you mean?" Dave asked in mock terror while shaking Phil's shoulders. "What do you mean? And don't mess with us. We're too young to die!"

"What I mean," Phil said in the same serious tone, "is that we're in danger of becoming saturated."

"Saturated?" I demanded, "What the hell is that?"

"That, goofballs, is the process by which our skin's defenses against the water breaks down. When that happens our bodies will begin to absorb all this water, and, we'll—" Phil lowered his head here for effect, shook it from side to side, shuddered, stammered as if the next words were too terrible to speak, and finally blurted out: "We'll drown! We'll drown as we stand here, as God is my witness! This ain't no bull."

Dave and I feigned shock and terror started wildly wiping water off our arms and faces. Phil ran to the bikes and tried to crawl underneath a large sheet of clear plastic we had draped over them, and I picked up a leafy tree branch from the ground and held it over my head as if it were an umbrella. Ed fell to his knees, clasped his hands, looked to the sky and started to pray and cry at the same time.

"Jerk!" Phil shouted at him. "You're going to drown faster if you start crying. That's like someone who's drowning in the ocean asking for a glass of water! Don't do that!"

Ed stopped crying, stood up, and to our surprise, challenged Phil's theory.

"That can't happen," he said with a weak defiance. "We can't drown. I never heard of anything like that. You guys are playing a joke on me, aren't you? I've taken hundreds of baths and I've never gotten saturated. You guys are joking, right? Game's over. Ha, ha."

At that point it seemed like the game just might be over. Ed wasn't being his usual dumb self. But Phil gave it another try.

"Ed," he said solemnly while placing a hand on our colleague's shoulder, "have you ever taken a bath for sixteen hours straight?"

Ed's face paled and he squeaked out a terrified, "No!"

"That's a lot different from sitting in a bathtub for fifteen or twenty minutes, ain't it?"

"Sure it is. I—but wait a minute, you fellows are just crazy. Why is it that people who swim the English Channel never get saturated and drown? They're in the water for days at a time and not a one of them has ever drowned from saturation. Superior try at duping me, but you've failed."

This was brilliant thinking for Ed, but Phil wasn't worried. He was confident that Ed couldn't come up with three logical thoughts in a row, and said:

"Ed, why do you think they smear grease all over themselves before they start swimming?"

"I don't know. To—"

"To prevent the water from leaking into their bodies and saturating them. That's why, you big jerk."

That did it. Ed was terrified and trembling, and stood in the rain paralyzed with fear. I feared he would go berserk, and I asked Phil to calm him down, which he did with assurances that the situation wasn't yet lost and that we would somehow pull through. Then Phil called us together again and explained our options.

"We've got two choices," he said with a mock urgency. "Either we build a shelter or try to set up our tents, or we find a shelter that's already made and get into it." Pretending to be in deep thought, he shot us desperate

Deliver Us From Saturation

glances and said gravely that our tents would be ripped to shreds by the wind. Then, pointing to the dozen or more cars that were parked in the wayside's parking lot, he continued:

"There lies our salvation. If we can get into one of those cars we'll be out of the rain and saved. If we can't, we'll drown by saturation. Dennis, you, me and Dave will try to build a lean-to out of branches. Ed, you go to those cars and knock on every door. Explain our situation—that we're on the verge of being saturated—and convince someone to trade places with us for a couple of hours. Don't take 'no' for an answer. If they slam the door on you, open it up. If they roll up their windows, pound on them until they break, but get some shelter. Ed, our lives are at stake! We're depending on you!"

We couldn't stop laughing as Ed ran up to car after car, pounded on windows, pulled open doors, kicked tires, jumped on hoods and shouted and screamed and begged in an effort to explain that we were in danger of being saturated. We laughed even harder when people in the cars threw bottles and cans at him. The hilarity reached its peak when several motorists started their engines and tried to run Ed down.

We were laughing our heads off when Ed came back looking exhausted, discouraged and angry. He saw that we couldn't stop laughing, and after a minute or so realized that he had been tricked. His face took on one of the sorriest looks I had ever seen, and he started crying and walked off and stood by himself for fifteen minutes.

As far as we could tell, Ed was genuinely hurt. We agreed that the joke might have been carried too far, and I suggested that we apologize to him. But even though we felt bad about abusing him, we junked that idea.

"It's only Ed," Phil said. "He's just a jerk. He's not worth an apology."

Ed eventually walked back and joined us. "You fellows make me sick," he said through tears. "As soon as it stops raining I'm leaving, and I hope I never see any of you again. When I first met you guys I was real happy, super-happy. I didn't want to drive around by myself. But because of the way I am, I probably would have if I hadn't met you fellows. When we first started out I hoped that we could ride together and have fun and adventures. I thought we could see part of the world and the strange things it offers as friends and comrades. I wanted to travel with you because I figured you could teach me something. But it hasn't happened. You think you're better and smarter than me. You know you are. So what do you do? You've teased me and tricked me and taken advantage of me every chance you've had. You made me buy whiskey and cigars and food and gas, all because you knew that I was too weak and gullible and in need of friends to say no. You took advantage of someone who was weaker than you. And if that wasn't bad enough, you couldn't even be a little humane or decent about it."

He went on like that a while longer, and by the time he had finished, I felt ashamed. He was right. We *had* taken advantage of him. Phil and Dave stared at the ground and refused to make eye contact with him. While we were standing there feeling guilty, Ed spoke again:

"I think the least you gentlemen can do—I shouldn't call you gentlemen— but I think the least you can do is apologize."

There was a long period of silence before Dave finally spoke up:

"Ed, we're going to make this up to you. Believe me. We are bold men, the boldest of the bold, as bold as brass and even bolder than that. And bold men do not run away from accusations of sleaziness. We confront issues head-on."

With that, Dave motioned to me and Phil, and we picked Ed up and began carrying him around in the rain on our shoulders while singing "For He's a Jolly Good Fellow."

Ed was pleased—probably super-pleased. He had a sickening smile on his face—the kind a mama's boy flashes when he's been kissed by his grandmother and told that he's been a very nice boy. We carried him past the cars he had tried to talk himself into, and then, just as Dave said we would, we made it up to him. We walked him to the edge of a mud puddle and dropped him in.

We Made It Up To Him

Chapter 42

An Unsympathetic Cop

B y mid-afternoon the winds had died down, the rain had stopped, the skies had cleared, the sun had come out and we had managed to get a campfire going. We set up the tents and changed clothes—Ed had washed off in a nearby stream—and were ready to cook and then get some sleep, when a black police car pulled up. A state trooper in a black uniform got out, walked over and told us that camping was prohibited at waysides and that we would have to leave.

The nearest state park was seventy miles away, and we were in no condition to make a drive like that. Dave explained that we weren't really camping, but were merely resting from an exhausting couple of days. He explained about Crazy Mike and how we resisted his call to burn down the forest, and how tired we were and how dangerous it would be to drive any further in our condition. He asked the trooper if he could bend the rules and let us stay that one night.

A stern "No" was the response.

"Well could we just sleep here for a few hours until we feel good enough to ride again?" Dave asked.

"No," the trooper answered again.

"Why not? All the people in those cars over there in the parking lot, some of them have been here all night. They've slept here. How come they get to sleep here and we can't?"

"Because they're sleeping in their cars. You are in tents. The rules say there is no camping at waysides. Your tents signify to me that you are attempting to camp at a wayside, and camping is prohibited. You can sleep here in a car, but not in a tent. Do you understand?"

"That's unfair. Sleeping is sleeping. Why does it matter whether you sleep in a car or in a tent?"

"It just does," the trooper said in a tone that said he was losing his patience.

"But we're exhausted and we need to sleep."

"Fine. You are welcome to sleep on your bikes in the parking lot. You are not welcome to sleep in tents on the grass here. The rules forbid it."

"But if we sleep on the bikes and it starts raining again we'll get wet."

"So what. I have tried to be pleasant and patient here, sir, but you are now arguing with an officer; you are disobeying a direct order from a police officer, and if you gentlemen do not pack up and leave, I will cite you, not only for unlawful camping at a wayside, but for refusing to obey a police officer, disorderly conduct, resisting arrest, causing a public disturbance, damage to state property, interfering with the work of a police officer, and overwhelming stupidity for arguing with someone who can arrest you on the spot."

"But what happens if we fall asleep while driving and crash and slide all over the highway?"

Sweet Dreams

"You die," the trooper said with a grin. "Look, why don't you guys get a motel room for the night? If you're as tired as you say, you could use one. There's a couple of cheap motels down the road."

"But we can't build campfires in motel rooms, and we love campfires."

"You have fifteen minutes to get out of here. If you're not gone in fifteen minutes you're going to the shithouse. And I'm not giving you one second over fifteen minutes."

We were packed and on the road with seventeen seconds to spare, heading to the state park seventy miles away.

There are a lot of dangerous things in life: Holding on too long to a hand grenade, being too close when an atomic bomb explodes and sticking your head into an airplane's propellers. Riding a motorcycle on the highway when you're exhausted is just as dangerous. Although it might seem unbelievable, you can actually fall asleep while riding a motorcycle. I know because it almost happened to me. While we were riding to the state park, I dozed off for an instant and the bike veered onto the road's gravel shoulder. The jolt woke me up, and I steered back onto the road just before I would have driven down a steep embankment and crashed and died.

Dave said that he once had fallen asleep for two hours while driving his bike at high speeds on the highway. He said he would have crashed were it not for the fact that while he was sleeping he was dreaming about the *very* drive he was making and that that enabled him to make all of the correct turns and lane changes. In fact, he said that he really didn't mind falling asleep on the bike because it meant that he was able to drive and rest at the same time.

We made it to the park without incident, put up the tents, ate and fell fast asleep.

Chapter 43

Helping Ed

After breakfast the next morning, Dave told us that we were on our own for the day because he was sick of us and was going to drive around by himself.

That was fine with Phil and Ed, but it wasn't with me. I didn't want to be stuck with them, and I said so by shooting a desperate, pleading look at Dave that asked him to take me with. But he would have none of it.

"It's time for Mister Big Stuff, meaning me, to get away for a while. You silly little ninnies can find adventures on your own. I need some peace and quiet. I'll be back tonight."

"Go, you jerk. We don't need you. Oh, and on your way back, stop at the store and buy me some smokes and beer," Phil yelled.

Dave laughed, slammed his bike into gear, and drove off.

Seeing that I was depressed over Dave's departure, Phil tried to cheer me up. "Ah, forget him. He's a jerk," he said. "Nobody needs him. We'll have fun by ourselves. I'll show you. Watch."

He picked up a rock and threw it at Ed, who was sitting on a log about twenty feet away. After the rock whizzed by his head with a few inches to spare, Ed turned around and protested that it wasn't nice to throw rocks at people.

"Screw you!" Phil yelled. "Stop being a jerk and maybe we'll treat you better. Why don't you go to some of the other campsites down there and get us some beer and smokes?"

"I refuse to. I absolutely refuse."

"I'll give you refusing a direct order from me," Phil snarled. He picked up another rock and flung it at Ed, hitting him in the ribs. Ed winced and shouted, "Not fair! Not fair!"

"Yes fair! Yes fair! Maybe if you stop being a jerk we'll stop throwing rocks at you. Now go get some beer and prove that you're not an idiot!"

Ed refused to move from the log, an act of disobedience that sent another rock his way. This one found his back. He jumped up and started running.

"Now don't come back until you get beer and smokes!" Phil screamed.

I was upset and protested that it was wrong to treat Ed so poorly.

"Why do you have to throw rocks at him?" I demanded. "The guy's a human being who deserves better. Can't we just scream at him instead?"

"Don't give me none of your holier-than-thou crap. This guy's a jerk. We can throw rocks at him all day. It'll be fun."

"That's not fun; that's wrong. You're mistreating him."

"You're wrong, and you're mixed up," Phil explained as we walked down a dirt road while following Ed. "Is the guy a jerk? Yes or no?"

"Yeah, he's a jerk."

"Of course he is. Do you think he wants to be one all his life?"

"No."

"Why?"

"I—I don't know. Because?"

"Because jerks like him get taken advantage of. That's why. He doesn't want to go the rest of his life having to buy beer and smokes for people."

"Of course he doesn't."

"No, he doesn't. But what's always the first step in changing and reforming yourself and making yourself better?"

"I don't know."

"The first step is *always* admitting that you've got a problem. Now, do you think Ed can figure it out by himself that he's a jerk?"

"I don't think so."

"You're right. He can't. But if he never knows he's a jerk he'll never be able to change and better himself, right?"

"Right."

"So by throwing rocks at him and making him buy beer and gas, what are we doing?"

"Taking advantage of him?"

"No. We're helping him become a better person."

"How?"

"Because we're letting him know he's a jerk and how badly he can get taken advantage of by being one. If we don't treat him this way he'd never know that he has to change. Don't feel sorry for him. We're doing him a favor, a bigger favor than he'd ever do for us. The more rocks we throw at him the better off he'll be. So come on and have some fun."

Chapter 44

Ed And The Professors

Even though I knew that Phil's logic was ridiculous and insulting, I convinced myself that in abusing Ed we were actually helping him. It's always easier to convince yourself that what you're doing is right, no matter how wrong it is, than actually trying to do what's right.

The next few hours were a blast. Phil and I played "hand grenade," a game in which we lobbed rocks and clumps of dirt at Ed as he ran down the roads, through the woods and up and down the park's small hills. After a few hours, Ed's face and arms were black-and-blue and he was exhausted and barely able to stand. But that didn't stop us from trying to do him even more good through the infliction of abuse. Phil decided that Ed's bruises were in need of healing, and that handfuls of fresh mud were the best medicine. We made mud near a small steam and set out to practice medicine. The patient wasn't too happy with the proposed treatment, and he ran away before we could treat him.

We laughed as we chased Ed down a dirt road. We laughed harder after passing a sign that told us we were in a portion of a state forest that had been designated a primitive area. And we laughed even harder when Ed turned off the road and plunged into a dense stand of trees and underbrush. We chased him, thinking ourselves human hounds on the trail of prey. We would have laughed even harder when Ed collapsed to the ground had we not been scared to death by what we saw just in front of him.

There, in the middle of a state forest, were two guys who were dressed like they were going to a wedding. They both wore shinny leather shoes, pressed khaki dress pants, shirts and ties and tweed sports coats with suede patches on the elbows. They had managed to get a huge, white motor home off the road, next to which was a tent as big as a small house. Attached to the tent was a large sitting area enclosed with mosquito netting. A wooden table, on which about a dozen books were strewn, filled the middle of the sitting area.

Phil and I stared at the two, and as Ed got up off the ground, one of the guys greeted us with a "good day" and asked what he could do for us on this "fine, extraordinary occasion."

Phil said we had run out of beer and matches and asked if they had any.

"Matches we do have, and you are welcome to as many as you need, but I regret to inform you that we have no fermented malt beverages. We have some very fine wines, though, excellent wines I might add. Please, please, step into our humble abode."

We accepted the invite as well as an offer of a cup of coffee. After some small talk, the two asked about Ed's appearance, which Phil told them was none of their business. The guy who had greeted us introduced himself as "Doctor Theodore Deakin," and his colleague as "Doctor Douglas Lane Cantor."

I saw an opportunity to do some good for Ed without interference from Phil and blurted out: "If you guys are doctors why don't you get out your bags and medicine and bandage Ed up? He's bruised pretty bad."

Doctor Deakin rolled his eyes, shot an embarrassed glance at Doctor Cantor and cleared his throat. "We are not medical doctors," he said. "We are doctors of philosophy. We have doctorate degrees. We are Ph.Ds."

"P-h-ds? That spells 'fid.' That ain't no word," Phil said.

"No, we are not fids. We are doctors of philosophy. We are professors of philosophy. We teach philosophy," Doctor Deakin said.

Feeling a little embarrassed, I introduced myself. And before Phil and Ed could do the same, Ted asked if we wanted to stay for lunch. Phil declined for us, saying that he never ate at a place that didn't serve beer. But Ted insisted that we stay, saying that we'd have a "super time with good food, good wine, good cheer and superior conversation."

Except for the good cheer and superior conversation, it sounded like a pretty good deal, and I was about to accept for myself, when Phil asked, "How much wine you got?"

"An ample supply, my good friend. An ample supply."

"Sounds good. We'll stay."

Over glasses of wine we learned more about the two.

Ted and Doug were in their late forties and both taught philosophy at a prestigious East Coast university. They were close friends, and they and their families usually vacationed together. However, the men had left their wives and children at home this year because they wanted a respite from the aggravations of family life, and were looking for some peace and quiet. Both felt that the intensity and responsibilities of family life were tugging them away from books and from philosophy, and they were on an extended vacation, or a sabbatical, as they called it, from both family and work for the fall semester. The two were looking forward to spending the fall, and maybe some of the winter, in Wisconsin's North Woods. They had been at the park for nearly a month and had gotten permission from a sympathetic ranger to bring their motor home into the primitive area. Their days were spent reading, talking and thinking. Noticing how sloppily dressed and rugged we looked, they apologized for dressing so formally. Ted explained that they really weren't campers or outdoor types, but nevertheless enjoyed the fresh air and the solitude the woods offered.

Lunch was simple and delicious: Bowls of steaming clam chowder, French bread, wine and hunks of sharp cheddar cheese. After lunch, the professors lit pipes, and we poured ourselves glasses of wine and had pleasant conversation, touching on national defense, the economy, race relations, politics, sports, education, the environment and several other subjects.

I feared that Ed would be overwhelmed by the professors' intelligence and would start acting like his regular self and embarrass me and Phil. It's not that we couldn't have embarrassed ourselves, but Ed was special—Special Ed, Phil sometimes derisively called him—in that he was way too eager to please people. I had no idea why he was still riding with us, considering how badly we had treated him. But Ed conducted himself with dignity, and my fears were unfounded.

Eventually the conversation got around to philosophy, and Doug asked if we had a personal philosophy by which we lived. I had come a long way since the first days of the trip when Dave and I had met Walter and Floyd, and was beyond having "never fart in a closed room" as my motto. I knew now from travel and experience that you should fart any time you have to, because holding in a fart was unhealthy. But I kept the thought to myself and answered a quick "no" to the question.

Phil had several personal philosophies: "Screw others before they screw you. Kick people when they're down. Don't ever do anything nice for anybody. Don't ever take a bath while you're sleeping," and, "Whenever you can, drink someone else's liquor."

Ted and Doug cringed and tried to hide their obvious discomfort. Then Ed blurted out that he had a personal philosophy.

"But it's not personal in the sense that I thought of it myself," he told the two. "It's borrowed from Socrates." He then explained how he loved Socrates' idea that it was those who know that they don't know everything who are smarter than those who think they know everything, and he quoted the great philosopher:

"I am better off than he is—for he knows nothing and thinks he knows; I neither know nor think that I know. He, oh men, is the wisest, who like Socrates, knows that his wisdom is in truth worth nothing."

Ed ended by saying, "That's my philosophy, gentlemen. I neither know nor think that I know."

"Excellent, excellent," the professors said at once through clouds of pipe smoke.

"Socrates is a hero of mine," Doug said, looking as serious as if his mother had just died. "It is so wonderful these days, these days in which all are so eager to trash knowledge, to see someone embrace Socrates. You are truly a wise man, as wise as any person who adopts so noble an idea to guide him through this often shallow and pretentious world. And how incredible it is, too. Here we are, thousands of years later, and Socratic philosophy is still viable, still the guiding light to which men who seek true knowledge turn. I must tell you that the words of Socrates are nourishment for my mind. Let me say that it is refreshing and inspiring to see someone choose to walk the path of inquiry and knowledge, rather than that of ignorance. To hear a man admit that he doesn't know, that is beautiful. I'm impressed."

Ted said that Ed was a hero, and that his decision to live Socratically was doubly impressive because, as a lay person, the pressures of ignorance were much greater on him than they were on scholars like himself and Doug.

"Socratic philosophy, Doug's philosophy, your philosophy, is also my philosophy," Ted said. "It's easy for us to try to live by those words because we are scholars. Our mission is to study, learn and advance knowledge. We live in the rarefied atmosphere of knowledge. But for you to live those words, you—and I don't mean to be derogatory here—someone whom I suspect is out there in the everyday world where the air is heavy with ignorance, is truly a great thing.

I Too Had Studied Socrates

"It's as remarkable as it would be if someone who was raised from birth on a diet of mud developed a strong, sound, muscular body. Think of all the factory workers and truck drivers and office workers and coal miners, most of them have never heard of Socrates. And here you are, an everyday man, embracing his philosophy. That is remarkable."

"Really, what you are doing," Doug said, "is battling ignorance, and might I add, battling it almost single-handedly. By battling ignorance, you are fighting for freedom and intellectual integrity. To grow, those must be fertilized with intelligence and truth. Oppression thrives on ignorance. You are doing a great thing."

It seemed like the professors were getting carried away. I had read a little Socrates in college and agreed that he was a great man. I was stunned that Ed even knew about the guy and that he had decided to live by his words, but I didn't think Ed was a hero.

Doug and Ted compared Ed to all kinds of famous, intelligent people and began asking his views on world affairs and things. I was worried that the praise and attention would go to his head and cause him to do something stupid. An indication that that wasn't going to happen came when Doug asked him what kind of safety features he would like to see built into nuclear power plants.

"Oh, that's way out of my league," Ed said sheepishly. "I have no idea. I'm not familiar with the issue at all. I'm not an engineer."

"Well, how do you feel we should dispose of the spent nuclear fuel rods from these power plants?" Ted asked.

"As I said, I don't know anything about the subject. All I can say is that we should be disposing of them in a safe manner."

The professors asked Ed's opinion about a new technique in brain surgery, and he answered that he wasn't a doctor, let alone a brain surgeon, and that he didn't know anything about the subject and didn't have an opinion.

They asked if he thought a certain author's style was better than that of another author's, and he answered that he hadn't read either and couldn't answer. They asked how he would treat the nation's armed forces if he were president. Would he cut back on defense spending? Increase it? And if so, what weapons systems did he favor?

Ed said he knew hardly anything about the military, and that unless he was president and knew all the secret details about such stuff he couldn't say.

They wanted to know what cows he thought were best for a dairy farm, Holsteins or Guernseys, but Ed said he knew nothing about dairy farming or cows.

I was getting annoyed. I knew the professors were asking questions that Ed couldn't answer, but I thought he was adhering a little too strictly to Socrates' philosophy. He at least could have pretended to know a little about the subjects. The professors would not have objected. I sat back and listened as the conversation continued:

"Do you think the vehicles we're using for space exploration are adequate? Are they durable enough?"

"I'm not an astronaut. I don't know."

"Which team do you think is going to win the World Series this year?"

"I don't know. I don't follow baseball."

"Do you think the federal government has opened up too much of our national forest land to logging?"

"I just don't know."

The professors were getting agitated over the non-answers. Doug got up from his webbed nylon lawn chair and started pacing back and forth across the tent. Ted was starting to raise his voice. They continued the barrage of questions:

"Do you think that asphalt or concrete makes a better road surface?"

"I don't know."

"Do you think there is a better wood than Osage Orange from which to make policemen's billy clubs?"

"I don't know."

"Is there life on Mars?"

"I don't know."

"How often should you change the oil in your motorcycle?"

"I don't know."

Boom! That answer shook me. If Ed knew one thing, it was how often to change his bike's oil. Dave preached timely oil changes to us nonstop, and Ed had become an oil change fanatic. When that answer came out of his mouth, I realized what was going on: He was purposely distorting Socrates' philosophy and carrying it to an idiotic extreme. The professors' praise had gone to his head, and he probably thought that by feigning ignorance about everything, they would think he was smart. The professors kept spouting questions. Soon, they were getting only a three-word response.

"How often to you have to tune up the bike?"

"I don't know."

"How many miles have you driven so far on this trip?"

"I don't know."

"Do you think we should strengthen our immigration laws?"

"I don't know."

By now the professors were in a frenzy. Doug paced a lot faster, began slamming his fist into his hand and kept shaking his head while exclaiming, "Jesus, I can't believe this!"

Ted had gotten out of his chair. His face was red and he kept muttering louder and louder, "No one will ever believe this!"

Despite their fury, they kept up the interrogation:

"What's the square root of two million and forty-two?"

"I don't know."

"Is this your first bike?"

"I don't know."

"Do you like chocolate pudding?"

"I don't know."

"Who is the president of the United States?"

"I don't know?"

"What size shoe do you wear?"

"I don't know."

Doug dropped to his knees, raised his arms, looked to the ceiling and screamed, "Christ Almighty! Do you believe this?"

"I don't know," Ed answered.

That made Ted crazier. He started pacing around the tent, grinding his teeth and kicking furniture.

I didn't know what to do. The two were getting nuttier with every "I don't know" that came from Ed's mouth. I figured they would kill him, and I was torn between watching them do it, helping them, and getting Ed out of there and saving his life. I couldn't make up my mind, and so I listened as they continued:

"Are you married?"

"I don't know."

"How old are you?"

"I don't know."

"What's your name?"

"I don't know."

The professors were hysterical. They were running around the tent holding their heads with their hands as if to comfort bad headaches, while screaming that they couldn't believe what they were hearing. I figured they'd snap with one more "I don't know," and that that would be the end of Ed, and so I decided to save his life, and was about to hustle him out of the tent, when Doug, in a screaming, almost pleading voice, asked:

Do You Know Anything At All?

"Do you know anything at all?"

Ed hesitated, scratched his head, made a face that looked like he was thinking deeply, and calmly answered:

"I don't know."

Doug grabbed Ed's neck with both hands. Ted grabbed his shoulder, and they started shaking him. Their faces were red, eyes were squinted into tiny slits, their lips were trembling and their bodies were shaking. I thought they would explode before they got to kill Ed.

Doug took one of his hands off Ed's neck, pointed a finger in his face and screamed, "You! You!"

Ted's head shook wildly from side to side. He was trying to scream, but no words came out. They shook Ed even harder. His face turned blue, and then white. Then Doug, who was foaming at the mouth, stammered out:

"You! You! You're the—the smartest person in the world! You know absolutely nothing, and you're not even sure about that! You deserve a fellow-ship, a scholarship!"

Then Ted screamed: "Please come to our university! We need deep thinkers like you! We'll give you a chair! We'll give you a department! We'll make you president!"

Phil was as horrified as I was. We bolted out of the tent and sprinted to the bikes. In less than ten minutes were packed and on the road.

Chapter 45

The Greatest Meal Ever

We got to the highway, opened the throttles wide, had no idea where we were going, and didn't care. All that mattered was that we were going fast. The bikes nearly flew up and down hills, around curves, through hamlets and small towns, and generally all over the countryside. At one point I pulled even with Phil, and over the roar of the engines and of the wind ripping through our helmets, shouted to ask him when we were going to stop.

"Never!" he screamed. "Those guys scare the hell out of me."

We had to stop at some point, though, because the bikes were burning gas at an extraordinary rate. We screeched to a halt at one gas station, popped open the gas tanks, filled them quickly and threw money at the attendant as we roared off.

It went like that the rest of the day. We zigzagged all over a huge portion of Wisconsin in an effort to distance ourselves from Ed and the professors. We stopped often to get gas, and at one point loaded up with beer, whiskey and canned oysters. We didn't know whether they were following, but it didn't matter. I prayed again, asking the Almighty to hide us from Ed and the professors. I vowed that if my prayer was answered I would pray again in the future.

Shortly after sunset we pulled off the road and into a thick grove of trees on a hill overlooking a small, run-down town. Like many Wisconsin towns, it was nothing but a handful of decrepit buildings, including a one-story combination bar/restaurant made out of machined red logs, and an old, barn-like feed store with broken windows and grey, weather-beaten wood at the intersection of two rarely traveled back roads. From our nest on the hill we had a good vantage point of the surrounding area and could see all traffic.

We dared not start a campfire or light the small camp stove I had for fear that Ed would spot the light. A fire would have been nice, though, as it was late in the year and starting to get cold at night. We cracked open a few cans of oysters, soaked pieces of stale rye bread in their oil, washed it down with whiskey and beer, put on some extra layers of clothes and fell asleep.

If you are hungry in the morning—and you would be if you were camping and the previous evening's supper was canned oysters and stale rye bread—

nothing would make you hungrier—make that insanely hungry—than the smell of frying bacon wafting through the air.

We were up at six in the morning, or however early it was that the people who ran the restaurant in town got up and started frying bacon. The smell was irresistible.

"Damn," Phil exclaimed as he hurriedly rolled up his sleeping bag. "We're gonna have the biggest breakfast anyone has ever had. Eggs sunny-side up so we can sop up all the yoke with toast, thick-cut bacon, hash browns with slices of onions in 'em, coffee, tomato juice, sausage, steak, pancakes, French Toast, waffles, a couple of shots of whiskey—damn, let's get the hell out of here and fill up."

We made a cautious reconnaissance of the area to make sure that Ed hadn't followed, and then hopped on the bikes and raced down the road about a hundred yards to the restaurant.

I had never smelled anything as good, and I know I never will smell anything as great as that place smelled when we pushed open the door that frosty morning and were blasted with the odor of wood smoke, stale beer, whiskey, grease and cooking food.

"Four shots of your best whiskey, three for me and one for him," Phil ordered of the apparent owner, a guy in his fifties with thinning white hair who was wearing a food-stained white apron and who greeted us with a pot of coffee after we had taken off our coats and sat at a table next to the fireplace.

The place was like the taverns in Wisconsin I had known as a kid when we had vacationed at a small country cottage the family owned, or gone up to my aunt's dairy farm in the far northern part of the state. It was dimly lit, but not dark. Simple, clean, white curtains adorned the windows. The floor was wood. The tables and chairs were wood. There was a long, wooden bar, and hanging on the walls were at least a dozen preserved fish and stuffed deer heads. The kitchen looked like one in someone's house. It had a white refrigerator, a four-burner gas stove, a white porcelain kitchen sink and a wooden table on which all of the chopping and mixing for the cooking was done. The menus were hand-written on simple, lined white paper. Signs announcing daily specials were hand-lettered with black felt markers on white poster board. In the kitchen were two things that made me want to stay there forever: Two huge hams sitting in wire ham holders.

"What can I get you, fellas? It's all good, and we got the best food in the state. No skimping on food here," the owner said as he returned with our whiskey.

"Those hams are incredible!" I gushed. "I feel like ordering a whole ham!"

"Well, young man, they *are* incredible, but there's no need to order a whole one. A couple of half-inch thick slices with your eggs should do just about anyone fine. Of course, them hams and all that bacon is from hogs we raise ourselves. We feed 'em corn and potatoes and barley, and they just love it. We do quite a good business in selling them at market and, of course, we always hold some back for the restaurant. Same thing with our steaks and roasts and ground beef—the best around. Raise the cattle and cows on the farm down the road. Eggs are from our own chickens. Raise our own turkeys too. We make all our breads and cakes and pies and just about everything from scratch. We grow our own apples and berries. The whiskey we have to buy. Neither me nor the law is much into moonshining. Doesn't look like much of a place here, but we get good business from truckers who detour off the main highway 'cause they know we're here. They keep comin' back because we give 'em good, honest, fillin' food, and lots of it, and we don't empty their bank accounts feedin' 'em either. Now what are you fellas gonna have?"

Phil went first: "Four eggs sunny-side up with three extra-thick slices of ham, buttered white toast, a plate of hash browns with onions mixed in and some sharp cheddar cheese sprinkled on top, one of your breakfast steaks smothered in grilled onions, a short stack of pancakes, two side orders of that bacon, a side of pork sausage, two of the best beers you got on tap, and for desert, two pieces of apple pie topped with vanilla ice cream."

My order was similar: "Four eggs sunny-side up, two slices of ham, two Salisbury steaks smothered in onions and brown gravy with mushrooms, double order of bacon, sausage, hash browns with raw onion, short stack of pancakes topped with strawberries and whipped cream, two orders of toast, a large tomato juice, two beers, and for desert, heated blueberry pie with two scoops of butter pecan ice cream."

"You fellas sure are hungry. Sure you'll be able to fit it all in?" the owner asked.

"No problem," Phil answered. "We've been riding them damn motorcycles like crazy and not eating because we've been trying to ditch this goof. And last night all we ate were canned oysters and stale bread, and damn, I could eat them fish off the walls right now. This place is great. We're gonna keep coming back here. We'll triple your business."

"Well, it sure is a pleasure to feed a young appetite. I wished I could still eat like you two," the owner said as he shook his head in admiration.

Our orders weren't exaggerations. We had consumed even more food in the few times that we had actually sat down to a real meal. Eating chili and onions and hunks of salami was romantic and in fitting with our roles as adventurous he-men, but 21-year-old guys who are traveling on motorcycles and camping out need more than that.

We quaffed the beers down in single gulps and immediately ordered another round. The potatoes for our hash browns were peeled and shredded in the kitchen. The bacon and sausages started sizzling in cast-iron frying pans. The smell of the onions in the potatoes wafted to our noses and made us even hungrier. It was cloudy outside and had started to drizzle. When we heard a clap of thunder, the situation was complete and perfect. There was no need to go anywhere. We could sit out the gloomy weather eating rich food and drinking deliciously cold beer in this isolated restaurant, and when the day was done we could ride the short distance to the hilltop, throw up a tent and pass out. With the second clap of thunder I ordered a round of whiskey and settled in for a day of absolute and perfect laziness.

In due time, after our appetites had been honed by the smell of sizzling ba-con and ham, the owner started plopping down plate after plate of steaming food on our table. When it was all before us, the owner asked if we wanted anything else. Phil ordered us each a shot. The whiskey came promptly. Phil leaned forward across the table and raised his glass to toast. I did the same.

"Salud," he said. "To the greatest breakfast of all time. No, the greatest damn meal of all time. *This* is living!"

We downed the shots, banged the glasses down on the table and grabbed our forks and knives. I sliced away at the eggs, breaking the yokes and letting the rich yellow centers spread over the plate. I threw half a plate of hash browns on top of the eggs and mixed it together. Then I took a Salisbury steak, a hunk of ham, a few slices of bacon and four links of sausage and piled them on top of the potatoes and eggs. I topped it off with brown gravy and sliced up the whole concoction so that with each forkful I would get potato, egg, onion, bacon, sausage, ham, steak and gravy.

Phil was doing the same. In a few minutes his plate was a mountain of hash browns mixed with steak, bacon, ham, sausage, onion and cheese, all of it coated with glistening yellow egg yoke. There was one more step to his melding of flavors and textures: a dash of salt and a liberal sprinkling of black pepper on top of the whole beautiful mess. That done, we buried our forks almost in unison into the mountains of food. We twirled the forks around in the heaps to mix the food around one last time, and then, with shovel-like motions, dug the forks into the piles.

Gobs of eggs, potato, ham, bacon sausage and steak fell off the sides of the forks as we lifted them to our mouths. The steam from the food drifted into our nostrils. It was glorious. We opened our mouths and were about to shovel in the delicious mixture, when a voice shouted at us: "Yo-ho, gents. Let's do it over again because we didn't do it right the first time! Bravooooo!"

It was Ed! The forks and their loads of steaming food fell from our hands. Phil's eyes bulged. I started trembling. Phil bolted out of his chair. I did the same. We grabbed our coats and ran. I grabbed a wad of bills from a pocket and threw them at the startled owner as we flew toward the door.

"That's gotta be some damn good food. See ya next time," Phil said as we raced out the door.

We fired up the bikes and slammed them into gear, and as we skidded in the rain out of the muddy parking lot, the owner stood in the restaurant's doorway almost pleading with us: "My cooking can't be *that* bad!"

Chapter 46

Trouble!

We raced up and down the wet roads for an hour or so until we came to a small town, this time a real one with a small main street lined with two dozen well-kept buildings. Phil and I were starving and were intent on eating breakfast whether Ed showed up or not. We stopped in front of a restaurant and were about to shut off the bikes when a motorcycle came roaring off the highway onto the main street at the other end of town. The speed limit in town was much lower than on the highway, but the bike didn't slow down. I knew it couldn't have been Ed because he obeyed traffic laws and never would have speeded.

The bike zoomed right buy us, screeched to a stop at the other end of town, spun around and raced right at us. I clenched my fist and prepared to shake it angrily at the ass as he drove by. Phil picked up a rock and cocked his arm to throw it. The bike got closer and then skidded to a stop in front of us. The driver, appearing frantic, tore off his helmet and started shouting. It was Dave!

"Let's get out of here! Come on! Get on your bikes and move! Let's go! Move! We've got to get out of here!"

We obeyed and roared out of town behind Dave. We tore across the countryside for more than an hour in the rain before Dave turned onto a gravel road and stopped behind an abandoned barn.

"Whiskey! Whiskey now and plenty of it!" he demanded as he shut off his bike, tore off his helmet and threw himself on the ground and against a wall inside the barn.

"Whiskey will not solve your problems. Hard work, perseverance and a 'can do' attitude will," a voice squeaked from behind us. It was Ed!

"How the hell did you find us you freak, you weirdo, you no good piece of human misery?" Phil shouted. "Go away! Leave us alone! Nobody likes you! And no one ever did!"

"Well, maybe you gents could get somewhere if you stopped riding in circles all the time. We're not twenty-five miles from where we stayed yesterday. I can't believe how much gas you have wasted. Now, what do we have to do over again because we didn't do it right the first time?"

"Freak!" Phil screamed as he lunged at Ed and began choking him. "What kind of crap is that, 'We didn't do it right the first time?' Bullcrap! Get your whining, stinking, pompous, holier-than-thou ass out of here before I kill you!"

"You little sissified wusses. If youse don't give me whiskey and sit down and shut up you're going to be in a shitload of trouble! Real trouble, big trouble and even bigger trouble than that!" Dave shouted. "Give me some whiskey!"

Phil stopped choking Ed and got a quart bottle of hooch from his bike. Dave took several gulps and then closed his eyes and leaned against the wall.

"Look, this ain't no joke. We've got to lay low, really low. We've got to get out of this state fast. We're in big trouble," he said as he took another swig. There was no twinkle in his eyes, and he was sweating and trembling.

"I've done something real bad. We've got to get out of here."

"What did you do?" I asked.

"Something really bad. Look. I'm scared, man. Real scared. We've got to get out of this state tonight—maybe out of the country."

"Come on, pal. What did you do?" Phil asked.

"I, I, I just can't tell you."

"Bullcrap! You got to tell us. What did you do? We ain't going anywhere unless you tell us what you did."

Dave took another drink, shook his head from side to side, and stared at the ground in silence.

"What did you do that we must do over again?" Ed squeaked.

"All I can tell you is that it's bad and that we've got to get out of here. I just can't believe I did it. You guys will never believe it."

"Hey, come on, you big goof," Phil said. "You're acting just like

Dave Was Scared

that goofy arsonist. Tell us. What did you do? What happened?"

Dave took another drink and stared at us. His face had a combined look of fear, worry, sorrow, bewilderment, shock and helplessness. Finally, without looking up, he said unemotionally in a soft voice:

"I murdered a guy."

"Yeah right. And I'm Jesus H. Christ. What, did you cut him up in little pieces and feed him to the cows? Look, I'm starving. This is all fine, but unless you've got a funnier joke to pull on us, I'm going to ride back into town and get some breakfast," Phil said.

"Me too," I added. "I'm starving."

"I'm not. In fact I had two sumptuous breakfasts at that tavern back there," Ed said. "Didn't even have to pay for it."

236

Phil lunged at Ed again and tackled him. I pulled him off and yelled that something serious was wrong with Dave and that we needed to figure out what.

"Look," I told Dave, "I don't mind a joke, but sometimes you get carried away. You're a good actor and you've done a good job here. You had us scared for a minute, and now it's over."

Phil and I started telling dead-man jokes, but they didn't cheer Dave up. He just sat there with his back against the wall and looked depressed. Finally, he spoke again, but only to give us instructions on how we were going to get out of the state and avoid the cops.

"Until we get three our four states away we've got to travel only at night, say between ten o'clock and five in the morning. We'll ride two abreast so that in the dark our headlights will make it look like we're cars. We'll stay off the interstates and major highways, and until we get out of this state we'll use only back roads. Only one of us will go into stores for food, and it'll be a different one each time. We'll get some American flag decals and put them on our helmets so we'll look wholesome. We'll—"

"Wait a minute," Phil barked, "if you're the one who killed a guy, how come *we've* got to travel at night? We weren't even around when you murdered this guy, and we didn't take part in the killing, so why do *we* have to hide?"

"I need someone to ride with," Dave said in a humble and pleading voice. "I don't want to be alone out there. I figured youse are my friends and that youse would help me out and get through this thing, that's all. I wasn't trying to get you guys involved."

Phil wasn't appeased.

"Wait a minute," he continued. "This whole thing is going to stop here or it ain't. All I want is the truth. This is serious stuff, and I ain't playing anymore games. If we ride around with someone who's wanted by the law we'll have to watch ourselves and take it easy when we drink and stuff. That ain't going to be any fun. All I want is the truth. If I don't get it I'm getting out of here, and I'm going drinking and leaving you to the law and to your strange imagination. Now tell me the truth. Are you just farting with us, or did you really kill somebody?"

There was no sign of joy or laughter in Dave's face. He looked as depressed and dejected as a banker who has made only a one hundred percent profit on a deal. Speaking slowly, he answered:

"I really killed the guy. That's the truth. It was an accident."

"Jesus Christ," I said, "You actually murdered a guy? Do you realize what this means? We're talking prison. We're talking gas chambers, firing squads, lethal injections, electric chairs, bad food and showers with other guys. I'm your friend and I'll stick by you until we get a few states away from here, but then I'm taking off by myself. How about you guys?"

Phil and Ed agreed to help out, but said they'd go on their own after we got a few states away.

"Well, Mister Big Stuff," Phil said. "Before we officially become fugitives, tell us what happened. I'd like to know what I'm running from."

Chapter 47

Dave's Story

"Well, first off, it was an accident. I wasn't planning to kill him."

"That's great. You'd really be in trouble of you were *planning* to kill him," Phil butted in. "That makes a big difference, you know."

"Well, it just happened that way, ass. It happened this morning. I was at a campsite not too far from the town I just saw you guys in. I stayed there last night and had gotten up this morning and started cooking breakfast—bacon and scrambled eggs and cheese and onions and corned beef hash and bread and coffee and a baked potato. Well, before everything was finished cooking, this big fat guy, and I mean he was big and fat—he must have weighed four hundred pounds—came up and said that animals had eaten his food and that he was hungry. He asked if I could please cook some breakfast for him too. He offered to pay me, but like an idiot I was nice and said he didn't have to. I made myself four eggs, and figured that if a slim, muscular guy like me could eat that much, a fat guy like him could eat a little more, so I made him six eggs, threw in a few extra slices of bread and baked him two potatoes.

"It must have taken him fifteen seconds to eat all of that stuff. I swear he just inhaled it. After he finished he smacked his lips and smiled and thanked me and sat around and talked about nutrition and stuff. Then he said, and I'm quoting him here, 'You know, you're kind of skinny, aren't you?'

"I said, 'Yeah, so what? You gotta problem with it?' He said he didn't mean anything by it other than he was once as thin as I was.

"Then he asked me how much I weighed, and I told him a hundred and fifty pounds, and then he said, and get this, he said, 'That's what I figured. I was once that weight, and I know that skinny guys like you don't need half as much food as you've got in front of you. You've eaten enough. Give me the rest of your food.'

"I told him he was crazy, that I was a bold man and that he should leave. He started laughing and said he wasn't going to leave until he got more food. I was furious, but didn't think I'd be able to drag a four hundred pound slob away, so I calmly finished my food, and then started packing my gear, because I was going to leave. While I was doing that he started making fun of me for being skinny and for not being able to eat a lot. 'You skinny people make me sick,' he said. 'None of you have any stomachs. You runts can't eat. You people have no appetites. Two eggs, a piece of toast, a few hash browns, a cup of coffee and a couple of sausages, and you skinny people are full. What babies.'

"There was no doubt in my mind that he was crazy. He got up, stumbled to my bike and started going through my bags, looking for food. He found a potato and ate it raw, just like an apple.

"I ran over and punched him in the stomach, but it didn't have an effect. My fist got lost in his blubber. I think it tickled him because he laughed. I backed off and threw rocks at his head, and that got him away from the bike, but then he ran over to the picnic table and started eating the food I had there. I threw more rocks and drove him away, but he lumbered back to the bike and started digging in my bags again. I pulled him away a little, maybe ten feet or so, but I couldn't keep it up, and he just walked back to the bike with me holding on. He was laughing like a retard. Then he shouted, 'When I need food, I get it!'

"I had had enough. He was rude and arrogant. I was determined that he wasn't going to get all my food, so I took off one of my shoes, put it on a stick, and shoved it in fatso's face. You should have seen tubbo stagger away! He couldn't take the stink! I rubbed the shoe on the ground in a circle around the bike and then dared him to come and try to get some food. He came, and when he hit that circle he staggered backwards and nearly collapsed.

"Next, I made a protective circle of stink around the table. When he tried getting to the food there, the same thing happened. He staggered backwards, as if he had been hit in the head with a brick. Was it ever funny. He started screaming, 'You're skinny! You got no appetite! You're no eater!' I think he thought he was insulting me. Anyway, after a few minutes he started running around in a circle, holding his head with his hands and shouting, 'I need food! I need food! I haven't eaten in ten minutes!'

"After a few minutes he calmed down and laughed and said, 'Screw you, skinny man. You can't hurt me. When I'm hungry I'll eat anything.' Then he walked over to a tree inside the stink circle and chewed a piece of bark off it.

"I rubbed my shoe all over the tree and all over the other trees and plants in the area. I wasn't going to let him eat anything. I wanted to punish him, and if contaminating all of his food with stink would keep him from eating, I was going to do it. But you know what? Even that didn't stop him. He dropped down on his hands and knees and started scooping up handfuls of dirt and shoving them into his mouth. 'I got to have food! I got to have food!' he kept shouting.

"To me it was a joke. I thought it was funny, you know, seeing a fat man suffer and all. Anyway, I rubbed my shoe on the ground in smaller and smaller circles around the guy. Then I rubbed it on all of the dirt around him so he couldn't eat it. That made him crazy. He kept screaming, 'I need food! I need food!' and I kept laughing. I wasn't laughing for long, though. He stopped screaming long enough to say, 'I'll get food no matter what, skinny!' Then he laughed like a maniac, I mean like a real maniac, and he bit off one of his fingers and ate it. Imagine that! Then he started taking bites out of his arm. I didn't want him to hurt himself more than he already had, so I rubbed my shoe all over his clothes and skin so he couldn't eat himself. A few minutes after that he collapsed and fell on his back. I didn't think that much of it. I figured he was weak. Anyway, I took advantage of the situation to get some exercise. I climbed a tree and jumped on his stomach and used it as a trampoline. After a while, the guy stopped breathing and died. When I saw he was dead I went through his pockets, packed up and got out of there. I didn't want to get pinned with a murder."

"What did he die of?" I asked.

"Well, he was fat, and he hadn't eaten any real food for about twenty minutes, so I figured it had to be starvation. He starved to death in twenty minutes. Can you believe that?"

We couldn't believe it, and we told Dave so. We also told him how angry we were for being put through such a dumb joke and lousy story.

I told Phil and Ed about Dave's belief in the stink power of his feet, and even recited a couple of stanzas of his poem. We laughed and drank whiskey and had a good time. It would have been a better time if Dave had laughed too. But he was dead serious. When he announced in

Exercise

a grave tone that he had found a fat peoples' poem in the guy's pocket and would to read to us, I began to worry about his mental health.

Chapter 48

The Poem

Phil had opened a second bottle and we were in a good mood, and so when Dave stood up and pulled some papers out of his pocket and began to read the Fat Peoples' Poem, we sat back and enjoyed the show. Here's the poem as he read it that day:

Fat Peoples' Poem

I am always happy,
And in a cheerful mood,
When I look up and see my plate
Filled with lots of food.

I pick my teeth in public,
And I am very rude.
There's stretch marks on my elbows
'Cause I eat lots of food.

My friends are laughing at me;
They say that I'm so crude;
They say I'll have a heart attack
If I keep eating food.

They scorn and ridicule me,
But I ain't gonna brood;
'Cause they don't seem to understand
That I'm in love with food!

I eat food when I'm sleeping,
And when I'm wide awake;
Even when I'm on the pot
I've got to have my steak.

Mashed potatoes and gravy,
Salad and things to chew,
Soup and bread and beans and fruit
And cheese that stinks—pee-you.

Mostaciolli, pizza pie,
Tuna fish and pickles,
When that food goes down my throat
It just slides and tickles.

Cornish hens and hot beef stew,
A smelly seafood plate,
Liver sausage sandwiches—
There ain't a food I hate!

My stomach hurts. I've got the cramps.
I need some food right now.
Although I ate an hour ago
I still need lots more chow.

Good man, kind sir,
Dear lady never wooed,
Have some pity on my soul
And pass that tray of food.

Pass it if it's hot or cold,
Even if it's stale.
'Cause even though my belly's full,
I could eat a whale.

Pass it if it's cooked or raw,
I don't give a damn.
Food is food is what I say,
Let's have that case of Spam.

Polish sausage, Quiche Lorraine,
Chicken Cacciatore,
If you don't give me lots more food
Things may get kind of gory.

Apple pies and chocolate malts,
Some pudding and whipped cream.
Gimme me lots more food to eat
Or I'll turn very mean.

I'll sit on youse, you silly fools,
So don't push me too hard.
If you don't want to suffocate
You'll pass that tub of lard.

Now pass those plates and pass them now.
Don't bother saying grace.
Just keep that food a comin' in
And watch me stuff my face.

Chomp, chomp, chomp; chew, chew, chew,
To eat is so much fun.
If I keep going on this way
I'll weigh at least a ton.

I'll sit on chairs and break them all.
I'll cave in great big floors.
I'll break down lots of walls my friends,
I won't fit through the doors.

Some will laugh, but I don't care;
I don't give a damn.
While they're off telling stupid jokes
I'll be eating ham.

Skinny people laugh at me;
They think it's really funny
That all I do is eat all day
And have a big fat tummy.

They say that I should exercise,
That I should jog and run.
They think that 'cause they're thin and lean
That they're the handsome ones.

They say that if I exercise
That I'll lose lots of weight,
And that will make it easier
To find a sexy mate.

Won't Fit Through The Door

What they don't seem to understand
Is that don't interest me.
I just want food and lots of it,
It's this that they don't see.

Slobber, slobber, slobber,
Jesus ain't it fun,
To stuff your mouth with food all day
And be a big fat bum.

It's so much fun to eat all day,
To eat and eat and eat.
How thrilled I am when I look down
And I can't see my feet.

See, I don't care, I don't care,
Who gives a damn right now.
I don't want health. I don't want looks.
I just want lots more chow.

So youse can do your exercise.
That ain't stuff for me.
I'll just sit at home all day
And eat and watch TV.

Go jog you fools, you skinny things,
Go out and jog and run,
'Cause I'll be eating food all day,
To me that's lots more fun.

And go have sex you skinny twigs,
I ain't gonna brood.
'Cause while you're scuzzing up the sheets,
I'll be eating food.

I think I've said enough by now,
Goodbye you skinny dude.
Chomp, chomp, chomp; chew, chew, chew,
I'm in love with food!

We spent two hours trying to convince Dave that the only thing he had to fear was literary critics, that it was safe to ride during the day, and that he wouldn't be arrested for murder. He conceded our point only after we told him that because the guy had starved to death, the cops would never suspect murder. And even if they did, there'd be no way they could ever trace it to stinky feet. If they ever were to do the impossible and trace the death to stinky feet, and then to *his* stinky feet, he'd just have to smear the stink all over his body. No cop would ever get close enough to arrest him.

Chapter 49

A Disgusting Social Club

S atisfied that he would never have to stand trial for murder, Dave calmed down. The rain had stopped, so we went outside, ripped some boards from the barn's wall, started a fire and cooked the rest of Dave's bacon and eggs. Phil and I ate like maniacs.

The next week was dull, but that changed quickly one Saturday morning when we stopped at a state park outside a small town.

Dave had been to the park before on some of his earlier travels. He liked it because it wasn't very busy, offered solitude, and because he was always in danger of losing his life whenever he camped there.

"It's such a thrill to know that at any minute I could die here," he told us while we sat at a picnic table looking at maps. "It's exciting to know that at any minute I might have to jump on the bike and speed away as fast as I can in order to outrace death. That's what I call living."

When we asked why his, and of course *our* lives were in danger, he answered:

"A few miles up the road there's a concrete dam that holds back billions, maybe even trillions of gallons of water. It was built to form a reservoir to hold the area's drinking water. If this thing ever were to break, this entire area would be flooded under thirty feet of water. I camp here every chance I get, and hope it breaks."

"Why do you hope that?" Ed asked.

"Because it would be an adventure. Can you imagine how exciting it would be to try to outrace a flood?"

"Pretty bold talk for a bold man who a week ago was shitting in his pants because he thought the cops *might* be after him," Phil said with more than a little sarcasm. "But what's the story? Is this a hundred-year-old dam that's ready to fall apart, or what?"

"No. It's only five years old."

"Then why are we in danger?"

"Because you never know when a catastrophe is going to happen. You just never know—especially the way they build things nowadays. Some politician's brother-in-law or uncle or cousin or brother who never built a dam in his life probably got the contract, and his company probably used substandard materials. It could break tomorrow for all we know."

Realizing that we weren't in any danger, Phil, Ed and I dropped the subject, started a campfire and were about to cook breakfast when a middle-aged guy walked up and invited us to an all-day picnic that a community group he belonged to was holding. The guy looked clean-cut and decent, but he picked his nose a lot, and Phil, Ed and I said we didn't feel like going. Dave proclaimed that it was a sin to turn down a free meal, and so we accepted the invitation.

Our Host

The guy was happy that we did and gave us baseball caps embroidered with the initials "NPSA." We followed him to a large open field between two groves of trees, where about three hundred people had gathered for the picnic. Everybody was talking and laughing. They all wore NPSA hats. There were twenty large grills set up in a place that had been designated as the cooking area. Strung between two large trees was a huge yellow banner that read: "NPSA Welcomes All. Everyone Is One Of Us."

The guy's name was Jim. He showed us around and introduced us to his friends, and, as is usual at a picnic, we talked with them about the weather, sports, politics, business, religion and other things.

After a half-hour or so of conversation, we asked Jim what NPSA stood for.

"Well, I'm glad you asked that," he said. "As a matter of fact, in just a few minutes we're going to unveil our new flag. You gentlemen should watch. And you know what? We're always looking for new members. And even though you gentlemen aren't from the area, we'd be glad to have you. It's good to be part of a community. There is nothing like community spirit and people working together for a common cause.

"As I said, we're always looking for new members. I think that after seeing what our group is about, you gentlemen will be eager to join up. Our dues are reasonable, and—"

"That might be so, but what's your name? What do you do?" Dave asked.

"Shhh, shhh. Just wait a minute, here it comes," Jim replied as a voice began talking over a loudspeaker:

"Ladies and gentlemen, can I have your attention, please. This is very important. Please, please. May we have some quiet. Thank you. Thank you. Today we are thrilled to be able to unveil our new symbol and flag. It took a lot of hard work and dedication to get here, but we've done it. It would take too long to thank everybody personally for helping make this a great and memorable day, so, on behalf of all of you, the *Nose Pickers Society of America* proudly presents its new flag!"

With that, a huge flag with a picture of a nose with a finger in it was raised on a wooden flagpole to a thunderous and frenzied ovation.

As the flag went up, a chant of "Pick! Pick! Pick!" arose from the crowd. When it reached the top of the pole, everybody started picking their noses. Some stuck a finger in each nostril. Others were trying to stick two or three fingers in a nostril. We could see that the real experts and connoisseurs were trying to pick their noses with their thumbs. We were at a nose pickers club picnic!

"This is the sickest, single most disgusting thing ever in the history of ever," Dave said. "Let's get out of here."

We started walking away fast, but Jim shouted to the club members, and in an instant we were surrounded by a mob, all of whom were constantly and joyously picking their noses.

"Where are you gentlemen going so fast?" Jim asked. "Why don't you stay for a while and have some fun? We're going to have games and contests and food and drinks later on. It'll be fun.

"Now," he said, turning to us, "what do you gentlemen think of our group? We are the Nose Pickers Society of America! We pick and we're proud! Are you ready to join up? Why don't you pick your noses? Everybody does it!"

"This is sick and disgusting," Dave shouted. "We ain't ever going to pick our noses. Never! You people are sick."

"Now hold on there a minute, fella," Jim said with great offense. "Give us a chance. Don't be rash. I'll tell you what, I'll tell you about the organization, show you around, and we'll show you the different chapters we have, and you can decide which ones you fit into.

"First, about the organization. We're millions strong. Our people come from every walk of life. Let's face it, everybody picks their nose. You can safely say that every human being who has ever lived has picked his or her nose at least once. Nose picking transcends racial, ethnic and nationalistic bounds. Everybody picks! Russians pick. Americans pick. Mexicans pick. Canadians and British do. So do the Muslims and Catholics and Protestants and Jews. It is the

LONG MAY OUR BANNER WAVE...

one thing that brings us all together as brothers and sisters and members of one big happy family. It is the common bond of mankind. It is where our differences end and we all come together.

"Watch people and you'll see that it's true. We've got every type of person there is in our groups: doctors, lawyers, nurses, judges, cops, firefighters, politicians, teachers, garbage men, machinists, truck drivers, nuns, priests, children, drunks, bankers, athletes, butchers, mothers, daughters—everybody! So, knowing that, ask yourselves this: If everybody does it, how can it be wrong?

"Now let me show you around."

The crowd parted with a wave of Jim's arm and we began the tour.

"Now here we have a beginners section," he said, proudly pointing to a cluster of about fifteen tents. "You don't see people out and about here because they're inside the tents picking their noses. These are people who don't pick in public, only in private. They're ashamed. But hey, that's okay. At least they're picking. In a few weeks they'll overcome their shyness and embarrassment, and they'll pick in public and join another chapter of the Society.

"Over here we have people who pick and then flick their boogers. We call them flickers."

The flickers section consisted of thirty people standing around picking their noses and flicking the snots on the ground and at each other. Walking us to another group, Jim said:

"Here we have people who pick and eat. Rather than flicking their boogers, they eat them. You've seen it on the street."

Jim called for a member of the group to come over and meet us: "Judge. Judge Gravy! Over here judge. Come over here!"

The judge came by, and Jim introduced him to us: "Judge Milton Gravy, I'd like you to meet these fellas. They're going to join up a little later on. Fellas, the judge has been with us for fifteen years now."

"Oh, pleased to meet you," the judge said as he came over, stuck a finger in his nostril, yanked out a long, slimy snot and stuck it in his mouth. "I'm sure you'll join. I've been with the group for fifteen years now. I pick all the time—when I'm in chambers or at home, or when I'm playing golf or anywhere. I've picked my nose in law school and—and I'm proud to say this—I pick my nose on the bench while I'm holding court. As a matter of fact, I've written a little poem about it. Let me recite it for you:

> I pick my nose on the bench my friend
> In court so all can see,
> That justice is tempered by snots these days
> By nose-picking judges like me.
>
> One booger, two,
> Two boogers, three,
> A booger for you
> And a booger for me!

The judge beamed with satisfaction and dug another snot out of his nose and stuck it into his mouth. Jim walked us to another group:

"Back over there, we've got a group who wipe their snots in their clothes. They don't like flicking or eating, so they wipe. Next to them are people who put their nasal mucus on furniture. They don't like to get their clothes dirty, so they soil the nearest chair or sofa. Back there we have a group that rolls snots up into little balls and drops them on the ground. We have every type of nose picker there is.

Everybody Picks

"Over here we have the ultimate in nose picking—a lovers' section. These are lovers who pick each other's noses. Isn't it beautiful?"

Pointing to another group, Jim continued:

"Next we have people who pick only when driving vehicles. They feel comfortable in their vehicles—like they're alone and that no one can see them, and so they pick.

"It's great, isn't it? Our people pick their noses anywhere and everywhere and at any time. They pick while they're working or playing or whatever

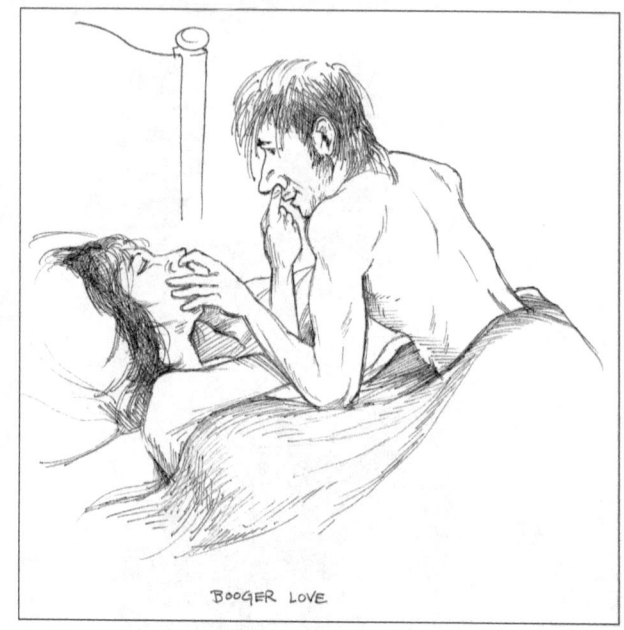

BOOGER LOVE

they're doing. It's the most incredible thing there is. At any given second on any given day there are hundreds of millions of people around the world who are picking their noses—hundreds of millions! God made noses to be picked!

"Over here we have people who pick only while reading. It's something they don't even think about. They don't normally pick their noses, but the minute they sit down with a book their fingers shoot straight up into their noses. I see someone you should meet." Jim shouted for a "Professor Mike" to come over. A thin man with black-rimmed glasses and a thick, black beard soon joined us.

"Professor, I'd like you to meet these fellas. They'll be joining up a little later on. Fellas, this is Professor Mike Wright. He's one who picks his nose only when he reads. Isn't that right, professor?"

"Sure is, Jim," the professor said, looking sheepish, proud and embarrassed. "It's hard to explain. I don't usually pick my nose, but put a book in front of me and—boogers! I just start picking away. I've picked my nose while studying Kant and Shakespeare and Tolstoy and Cicero and all of the great ones. How about a little demonstration? Now I've been talking to you fellows for a couple of minutes, right? And I haven't picked my nose during that time, have I? Well, then, watch this."

Mike dashed away and was back a moment later with a book and a wooden chair. He sat down, opened the book, and to our disgust, started picking his nose.

"See," he said. "Isn't it incredible? I started picking the minute I started reading."

After the demonstration, Professor Mike explained to us what he usually did with the snots he dug out of his nose.

"You know," he said, pulling us aside and looking indignant. "*I'm* not like the others. I mean, *I've* got class. *I'm* not a slob. I'm university trained. I don't go around flicking snot on the ground or smearing it on clothes, or heaven and thinking people forbid, eating it. That's vulgar and that's not me. I may pick, but at least I've got the decency not to spread my germs. Do you know what I do with my snots? I put them in the back of my books. That way I'm not a slob about it. Look."

Mike turned to the back of the book. It was caked with a layer of dried snot.

"Well, if you're so sanitary and better than the others, how come you cake snot all over a book that belongs to the public library? How is that being responsible?" Dave demanded after noticing that the book was stamped as belonging to a public library system.

"You're sick," the professor said angrily. "Can you do something else other than find fault with others? Why are you so damn judgmental? That's demented," he added as he stomped away.

After that it was time for lunch. We lost our appetites when we saw that all the cooks constantly picked while handling the food. Some even flicked snots into the burgers, hot dogs and potato salad.

"My god! I thought only screwed up teenagers put snots in other peoples' food. This is the most disgusting thing I've ever seen," Dave said.

After lunch the nose pickers broke up into groups for games and contests. The first contest was to see who could pick their nose the fastest. The second was to crown the slob who could produce the most snots in an hour. One was held to find the person who could stick the most fingers in one nostril, and another was held to see who could flick snots the farthest. The top prize in each contest was a jar of dried snots which could be reconstituted with water. As is the case with all properly organized athletic competitions, medical personnel were standing by to treat the competitors for nose bleeds and other injuries they sustained while picking.

When the games were finished, Jim took us aside and asked us which section of the Society we would join:

"Okay, now I'll let you talk it over amongst yourselves. You decide which chapters you belong to and which ones you want to join. I'll be back in a while to officially swear you in as members of the Nose Pickers Society of America!"

When Jim left, Dave warned us that he wouldn't tolerate nose picking from us. "Anyone who picks their nose and joins this club will never ride with me again," he said. "These people are sick. I've never picked my nose in my life, and I ain't going to start doing it now. That's the filthiest, most disgusting and unsanitary thing a person can do. It's wronger than wrong, sicker than sick and dirtier than dirt. Nose pickers should be executed. You guys with me?"

We were, and the four of us vowed that we would never pick our noses or join the club. We wanted to leave, but couldn't because Jim had posted twenty guards around us with orders to break our legs and noses if we tried to escape. Jim returned a while later and asked which chapter we wanted to join.

"Let's make a choice and let the picking begin!" he said as the crowd roared in approval. "Time's a wasting and snots are going unpicked. Gentlemen, which are the lucky chapters that get new members today?"

Dave wasted no time in stating our position with bold defiance: "We ain't going to join this disgusting, sick and unsanitary club. We will *never* pick our noses because it is filthy and wrong! Only slobs and the unsanitariest of the unsanitary pick their noses. It is the most disgusting thing a human being can do. We hate you and the uncleanliness your group stands for. You people all belong in nut houses or in graves, and we four bold men are going to put youse there."

Chapter 50

Held Captive, Threats And Escape

The speech was a hit with us, but a flop with the three hundred nose pickers, all of whom started shouting that they wanted to break our bones and stuff our nostrils full of fast-drying concrete. And they would have done it had Jim not calmed them down.

"Just hold on," he said. "Let's give reason a chance to prevail here. There's no sense in getting violent until we have to. Let me try to reason with our misguided friends.

"Look, fellas," he said, turning to us, "why don't you pick? Why do you have to be different? Why don't you go along with the crowd? It's easier that way. You don't want to feel like oddballs, do you? If you're the only ones here who don't pick, all of these people are going to think you're crazy. The hell with this individuality stuff. If you don't join, people will think you're different, and you'll be miserable. But if you join, you'll be happy. Independent thinking only creates outcasts. Go along with the crowd."

"Yeah, don't be different," a guy in the crowd shouted. "Be like the rest of the world. Pick your noses!" With that the crowd cheered and began chanting again for us to pick. When they stopped several minutes later, a guy told us how he overcame his initial aversion to picking.

"I understand how you feel," he said. "I used to think it was disgusting. I hated it. But after running with this crowed and being threatened by them for a few weeks, I changed my attitude. It's no fun resisting and being different. Forget about being individuals. You heard what the judge said. If a *judge* picks his nose it can't be wrong."

He stepped back into the crowd and a woman about our age with short brown hair and a bloody nose stepped up and gave us her pitch on behalf of picking:

"I've been through the same thing you guys are going through. I never used to pick. I thought it was wrong. I shouldn't say I never used to pick; I did, but I was ashamed. When that finger would shoot up to that nostril I'd catch myself and pull out a handkerchief. I carried tissues and rags with me. But not anymore. I pick all the time now. It's fun, and it's so satisfying, too, when you hook into a big booger. There's a sense of achievement and accomplishment in nose picking.

You pick your nose, and the next thing you know your self-esteem is shooting through the roof. Don't be different. Pick."

When she finished, a short bald guy in his mid-thirties tried to convince us to pick:

"You've really got to look at the entire situation, the big picture. Everybody in the world picks their nose. How can it be wrong if everybody does it? It's natural. Just watch people. They pick their noses in grocery stores, on their jobs, in church, in restaurants, in washrooms, while they're playing—everywhere. It's automatic. Most people don't even think about it. Walk down a busy street and pick out ten people at random and watch them for ten or fifteen minutes and I guarantee that within that time each and everyone of them will have picked their noses. The highest class rich people and the poorest, smelliest bums pick their noses. I guarantee it. The president of this country picks his nose, and so does the Queen of England. The leader of every nation on earth has picked his or her nose, and that's fact. Every human who has ever lived has picked his or her nose. It's about time that we celebrate this natural and instinctive action, and that we stop denigrating something that is so natural a thing to do. We should look at nose picking, not as a bad habit, but has a virtue. I say a clean nostril is a good nostril!"

Jim spoke again: "Look at it this way, fellas. Most people pick their noses an average of twenty times a day. That comes out to one hundred and forty times a week, seven thousand, three hundred times a year—seven thousand three hundred and twenty in a leap year—and five hundred forty-seven thousand and eight hundred and seventy-four times in a seventy-five-year life span. Can you imagine that? How can that be wrong or unsanitary or disgusting?"

"Oh, come on, get real," another guy shouted. "If picking your nose is so wrong, how come cavemen did it? You can't answer that, can you? Well, I'll tell you why. They did it because *God* wanted them to. That's right. God wants everybody to pick their noses. That's why we're born with fingers and not handkerchiefs. And you know what? Snots are biodegradable. Picking is as natural as going to the washroom. You don't think that going to the washroom is bad, do you?"

"Not unless you're doing it on someone's front lawn or on their doors or books or furniture or clothes like you pigs do," Dave bellowed. "And remember this: I don't pick my rear-end with my fingers."

That remark infuriated the crowd, and they started flicking snots and throwing rocks at us.

Our decision to never join the club or pick our noses remained unchanged, even after an hour of arguments like those. Our continued resistance made the crowd angrier. At one point Jim said that if we didn't join and start picking, he'd have to take drastic action. When we again refused, Jim started the crowd chanting, "Pick! Pick! Pick!"

The pickers encircled us, and for two more hours they chanted, picked their noses and flicked boogers at us. We tried dodging the snots, and at first we were successful, but they tightened the circle, bettered their aim, and in no time we were caked with the stuff.

Snotted

Despite the abuse, though, we didn't submit. Jim was in a rage. His nose was raw and bloody from two hours of non-stop picking. He pointed a bloody, snot-caked finger at Dave and shouted:

"You, mister foolish ringleader, you and your friends are in big trouble! I can do more than just pick my nose. I have a special power, and I'm warning you fellas now: If by tomorrow morning you don't join and start picking your noses, I will, with the snap of my finger, turn you into the most disgusting, worthless and useless human beings that have ever existed. You will feel the shame, guilt, depression and absolute misery of knowing that you never did anything worthwhile and that you wasted your life. You will feel so wretched and like such an absolute waste to society that you will want to kill yourselves. That way I won't have to kill you."

Dave laughed and said:

"You talk big, bold stuff, but I think you're unbold. Go ahead, turn us into bums, turn us into cripples, newspaper editors, drug addicts, politicians, lawyers, social workers, folk singers or even snot miners like yourselves. We can take it."

"Fool!" Jim laughed while shaking his head in disbelief. "Being a drug addict or a lawyer or a folk singer or a newspaper editor would be a blessing compared to the fate that awaits you at the snap of my mucus-caked fingers. Do you realize what I'm saying? I'm going to turn you fellas into the most disgusting, wretched creatures the universe has ever seen or ever will see. Do you know what that means? Do you comprehend the seriousness of this? You're going to be more worthless than a piece of dried snot."

Fools!

"You unsanitary, vile pig you. I understand the seriousness of it all," Dave answered. "But I don't care. I'm the boldest of the bold and even bolder than that! I can take *anything*. Turn me into a drug addict and I'll kick the habit. Turn me into a lawyer and I'll sue my mother. Turn me into a duck and I'll quack the loudest. And know this, freak, these guys have been taking lessons from me, and they can take it too. There ain't anything you can turn us into that would be so terrible that we would want to commit suicide."

"Yes there is," Jim sneered.

"What? What in the universe can you turn us into that would make us feel so ashamed of ourselves that we'd want to slit our throats? What?"

With a smirk, and a confident, but mean voice, Jim pointed his finger at us and said triumphantly:

"I'm going to turn you all into restaurant critics!"

Holy smokes! I fell to the ground and recoiled in horror. Phil let out a terrified shriek and tried to escape through the crowd, but he was pushed back. Ed started crying hysterically. He sunk to the ground and started digging a grave with his hands. Dave's knees buckled. He stood there, facing Jim and the nose pickers, but he was quaking with fear.

"What do you think of *that?*" Jim sneered.

"I think you're lying. No one—not even God—has the power to be that mean and cruel to someone. And even if you did, I don't think you're bold enough to be that sick."

"Well, you just see how bold and sick I am. If by tomorrow morning you don't join and start picking, I'm going to turn you all into restaurant critics," Jim said. Then he ordered fifty nose pickers to stand guard around us for the night and stomped off.

Dave huddled us together and discussed the situation. We vowed again to resist Jim's demands:

"I'd kill a million babies, set old people's homes on fire, conspire against God, and I'd pick my nose a thousand times a day before I'd let myself be turned into a restaurant critic. And I'll say this, if it comes down to it, I'll pick. But personally, I think the guy's lying. I don't think he can do it. We may have to challenge him on it. And if we have to, Ed, we're going to let you go first. And if you suddenly start babbling useless stuff about how some sauce had one grain of salt too little, or how a piece of meat was cooked a tenth of a second too long, we're going to start picking our noses as fast as we can."

"But I don't want to be a restaurant critic. I'm worthless enough the way it is," Ed protested.

"Don't worry about it. If he's powerful enough to turn you into a restaurant critic, then he's got to have enough power to turn you back. We'll just tell him that you want to join the club, and you can see how badly they want members, so there's no doubt that he'd be thrilled to turn you back. But let's stop talking about that. As I said, I don't think he can do it. Even so, we've got to figure out how to escape. Now I've got a plan."

We were being held captive on a small hill with lots of trees and shrubs, and Dave ordered us to collect all of the wood we could. We worked through the night uprooting small trees and gathering other wood and bringing it all to Dave. I figured that he was building a fort or some sort of barricade. Then, just before dawn, we were told to dig up clumps of grass and dirt. We did, and a few minutes later we pushed Dave's creation into the middle of the field where the nose pickers had held their picnic. It was then that I realized that Dave had devised a brilliant plan. We were pushing a twelve-foot-tall wooden nose he had built! Noticing that our guards had fallen asleep, I suggested that we forget about the nose and run for the bikes and take off. That was too simple an idea for Dave, though, because it lacked imagination and a sense of adventure.

"Besides, if they go for this nose, it'll be one of the greatest stories ever told, one of the greatest stories in the history of the world, and people will remember our names forever," he said with the glee of a kid about to throw ants into a spider web.

When the nose was in position in the middle of the field, we, in an effort to make it look like it was full of snots, stuffed the nostrils full of dirt, grass and branches. Then we went back to the hilltop and waited.

Shortly after dawn broke a wild shriek arose from the nose pickers' camp. It was followed by a second, and then a third and a fourth, and in less than a minute there was a deafening roar. They had seen the nose! The roar continued as three hundred of those disgusting people charged the nose. In an instant they were swarming over it like ants on syrup.

We watched for a minute or two, laughed, and then sprinted for the bikes. When we were nearly to them, the nose pickers realized that they had been tricked. They gave chase, but we beat them to the bikes and sped away.

Dave screeched his bike to a stop in front of a hardware store in the town, raced in and came running out with four sledgehammers. He gave us each one and we drove a few more miles and then stopped at the dam that Dave had told us about. We jumped off the bikes, and, sledgehammers in hand, followed Dave as he ran out onto the top of the dam. At its midpoint, he let out a savage scream and shouted:

"Death and destruction to the

They Couldn't Resist It

criminal and unsanitary nose pickers!" Then we hammered away at the concrete like maniacs. After an hour the dam began to crack. We ran back, and as soon as we reached the bikes, it burst and the whole area below us, including the state park and the nose pickers, was flooded. We threw the sledgehammers into the water, stripped and dived in to cleanse our bodies of snot. Then we got out clean clothes, dressed, threw the snotty clothes into the water and got on the bikes and raced away.

Death To The Nose Pickers!

Chapter 51

Flood And Disaster

We didn't drive far. A campground just above the broken dam beckoned, and we stopped and nearly laughed ourselves crazy over how we had outsmarted the witless nose pickers. Although I laughed as hard as the others, I felt a little guilty. I asked Dave if we had been wrong in killing them, because although they were vile creeps, they *were* human beings. He calmed my fears with his soothing and unshakable logic:

"Earth is a pretty decent place. The only thing wrong with it is that there are many forms of human garbage living on it. We've got lazy people, communists, drug addicts, college professors and grandmothers messing up the planet for the rest of us. Of all human scum, nose pickers are the worst.

"When you're at home, what do you do with garbage? Do you keep it in the house forever? Do you put it in a bowl on the dining room table so it will grace your table at meal times? No. You throw it out. By killing the nose pickers we did nothing more than throw out the human garbage."

That cheered me up and I was happy until Ed squeaked:

"What about all the other people?"

"What other people?" Dave asked.

"The innocent farmers and others whose land we've flooded and whose lives we've ruined."

"I don't know. I didn't even think about them. Besides, who cares? It's their fault for living where the nose pickers were."

We agreed, then went to sleep, satisfied that in flooding the nose pickers we had done the world a big favor.

The next morning, we weren't so sure. We went into a town for breakfast and bought some newspapers. The bold headlines proclaimed news of a monumental disaster, and the stories told of the death and devastation the flood had caused.

A horrifying number of people had died and been injured. A majority of the valley's buildings had been destroyed, and with them, invaluable treasures, personal belongings and the necessities of life. Food was scarce. Shelter was even scarcer. Nearly every farm was under water. The crops, which had been ready for harvest, as it was late in the growing season, were a total loss. Countless head of livestock had drowned, and grain stocks and seeds for the next year's crops had been destroyed. Families had been wiped out, and lives had been ruined.

The stories quoted law enforcement officials as saying that the disaster was no accident, that it was believed the dam had been sabotaged and that witnesses had seen several men hammering away at it shortly before it burst. Authorities, the stories said, had launched a massive manhunt for those men.

After reading the stories, Phil and Ed suggested that we leave the area as soon as possible. I agreed, but Dave didn't. He said the flood was nothing to worry about.

"Youse are scardie cats. This isn't that big of a deal. Relax and calm down. This water is gonna evaporate. In a few days everybody will have forgotten the whole thing. And besides, look at it this way: Aside from the fact that we drowned nose pickers, we've actually helped these people out. The flood has made their land more fertile. The rich deposits of silt that will cover the land when the water recedes will be better than any fertilizer they can buy. They'll be able to grow twenty times more food than they did before, and that means several good things.

"First, there will be more food and fewer people going hungry. The farmers will make more money, and that'll make them happy. Because they're happy and making more money, they'll work harder and produce even more food so that even fewer people will go hungry. The ultimate effect of this will be that the farmers will be making so much money and working so hard and will be so happy and be producing so much food that starvation will be eliminated from the earth. There's nothing wrong with that, is there?"

There wasn't, we agreed, but only after ridiculing Dave for his hypocrisy. Just a few days earlier he had wanted to ride to another part of the nation, and ride at night, because he had killed a fat man. After reading all the disaster stories we drove back to the campsite and hid, fearing we would be arrested and hanged as murderers. One day of that was enough. We were restless and decided to explore the area and see for ourselves the damage we had caused. We left the bikes at the campsite, and, pretending to be damage control experts from the federal government, we walked to a farm just above the flooded valley.

We were met at the front door of the white, two-story frame farm house by a depressed looking kid of about sixteen who told us his name was Johnson. We identified ourselves as damage control experts from the government who were in search of information about the flood.

"You guys are either way too late, or you government people are incompetent," Johnson said, looking bewildered and annoyed.

"How's that?" Dave demanded.

"Look at all that damage down there. You guys didn't control a thing!"

Johnson invited us in and updated us on the horrible details. He said officials feared that the valley, known as the Valley of the Adversairs, might be permanently flooded, and that the flood was being described as the greatest single disaster in that area's history. The president had declared the valley a disaster area and was sending in federal troops to help with the cleanup.

However, Johnson said that while the rest of the nation was as glum and as sad as could be over the situation, the valley's residents were tough, resilient people who had successfully weathered several catastrophes in the past, and were a lot more optimistic about things than everyone else.

He gave directions on how to get into the valley, loaned us a canoe and paddles and wished us success in whatever it was we were supposed to be doing for the government. We walked to a point on the river to just above where the dam once was, put the canoes in the water and began paddling into the Valley of the Adversairs.

Chapter 52

Valley Of The Adversairs

Reading about and getting second-hand accounts of death and disaster is not the same thing as seeing it. Words can never fully convey the horror, wretchedness and the sense of despair that accompanies a flood. We had read and heard about the destruction, and knew that it existed and that it was awful, but we didn't really know how bad the situation was until we had seen and felt it.

The flood had turned the valley into a miles-long lake that was littered with the debris of a destroyed society. Everywhere we saw fragments of houses and farm buildings, bloated carcasses of dogs, cats, chickens and livestock, human corpses, furniture, clothes, farm machinery, tools, automobiles, bicycles and every conceivable household item floating by in sickening silence.

Children, adults, teenagers and old people were huddled together on patches of high ground, anything that could float, and on roofs of buildings that were not completely under water. We saw a screaming infant floating by on a wooden plank barely larger than it was. We paddled furiously toward the little thing, but when we were less than a hundred feet away, the plank tipped over and the child fell into the water. The baby screamed and we paddled even faster, and when it seemed as if we would get to it in time to pluck it out of the murky water, it let out a water-choked, gurgling scream and went under, never to surface again.

We saw a dog and a cow struggling to maintain their balance on the slippery peaked roof of a farm building that was floating by. The terrified yelps and the mooing the two made when they fell off and began thrashing in the water made us retch. Somehow the cow, her big head barely above the water, swam alongside us. We watched helplessly as the beast's nostrils flared as she gasped violently for air, stared at us with big brown eyes and let out a pathetic moan as if pleading with us to help. But help, the one thing we would have given our lives to be able to provide, was something we couldn't give her. We had no floatation collars to put around her neck, nor any piece of floating debris large enough to secure her to. She struggled alongside the canoes for a few minutes before the weight of her huge body began to drag her head under the water. As the first waves of water covered her eyes, she let out another sickening moan and gave us a sad, pleading, 'I'm your friend, please help me' look that made us cry. We sobbed and paddled away when she went down for good.

In The Valley Of The Adversairs

And in the people I noticed something I had read about. The disaster had been so sudden and great that it had apparently shocked many people into insanity. We came across one family—a middle-aged man and wife and two teenage sons—huddled with six cows, a dog, four chickens and a cat on a small, but dry, hilltop. They were sobbing about their misfortune, which, of course, was a normal reaction. But when we paddled up and questioned them, we found that they had been seized by insanity.

The man said that half his house had remained intact, that the family had shelter and a sizeable portion of their food stocks left, that the cows and chickens would provide the nucleus for a new herd of animals, and that when the water receded he and his family would be in excellent shape and living prosperously again in a few years.

When we told the man that he was lucky and appeared to be one of the most fortunate families in the valley, he shrieked, fell to his knees, gazed at the sky, shook a clenched fist and shouted:

"Why me? Why us? Why couldn't we have been totally ruined like everyone else? Why were we spared? Where is the justice?"

His wife said it was the saddest day in the family's history, and that she too wished the family had been totally ruined.

I had read that victims of disasters who have not suffered as much as their neighbors often feel guilty about it and wish that the same, or an even worse fate had befallen them. Now I was seeing that that really happened. We paddled away and noted the family's location in case we ran across someone who could provide them psychological help.

Off in the distance we heard laughter and singing coming from a barren hilltop. There we found a man and his wife, seemingly delirious with joy, singing over the bodies of three young children. It was a frightening scene, and I didn't want to investigate, but Dave did. We got out of the canoe and approached the couple. Dave said we were damage control experts from the government and asked how they were doing.

Another Happy Flood Victim

"We're doing just wonderful," the husband said, "and we'll keep doing that way as long as you people keep your noses out of the situation and don't try to control any damage. My wife and I are totally ruined. Our farm is under water, every building on it has been washed away, our crops are destroyed, our food is gone, every animal we own is dead, and so are our three children. This is the greatest day in our lives!"

The guy and his wife fell to their knees and began sobbing and thanking the Lord for their good fortune.

A little while later we passed an older guy in a rowboat who smiled, tipped his hat at us and said: "Nice flood, isn't it?"

An inquiry as to how he was doing brought the answer that he didn't know whether to be happy or sad. He was happy because of the flood, but sad because he knew the waters would eventually recede. We took down his name and added him to our list of people who would be in need of a shrink.

The attitudes of those few people were not unusual. It seemed like everyone was in a state of shock and seized by illogical reasoning. It was strange, scary and pathetic. Not only was the valley ruined financially, but it appeared that it was ruined emotionally as well.

A full day of viewing carcasses, corpses, ruined homes, ruined lives and ruined minds was all we could take. We had been told that although the town had been hit hard by the flood, a small hilly section of it remained dry and that law enforcement officials and town residents had gathered there to discuss the situation and coordinate relief efforts. We decided to go there in order to determine whether the police had any leads as to who had destroyed the dam.

The trip to town was as depressing as meeting with valley residents whose lives and minds had been shattered. As dusk set in, the haunting moans and hysterical laughs of the residents echoed across the valley. Each moan and laugh reminded us with sickening clarity that we had caused the tragedy. For once, I agreed with Ed when he said that we had "perpetrated a crime against human-ity."

Our dilemma was what to do about the fact that *we* were responsible for this evil. Ed argued that the only honorable thing would be to turn ourselves in and face punishment. Dave rejected the idea, arguing that surrendering wouldn't do the valley residents any good.

"What's the most important thing for these people to do right now? It's to rebuild their lives as soon as possible, isn't it?" Dave asked.

We agreed.

"Well, they should devote every ounce, every iota of their energy to that end, shouldn't they? That's the best and only thing for them to do right now, isn't it? Now if we go in there and turn ourselves in, they're going to be pretty mad at us. And you know what happens when people get mad? They want revenge. These people are going to want to get a lot of revenge. But if we allow them to do that we'll be diverting their attention and energy away from rebuilding their lives. Now do you think it's right to take people you've already committed crimes against humanity against and hurt them even more? Do you really want to go out and hurt these people again? I think only the sickest of the sick would do that, and I don't think that's us. Now how about it, do you want to go down in history as people who go around hurting people who've already been hurt? I don't, and I don't think you guys do either.

"And let me say this: I'm not against turning myself in. I'm bold enough to take anything. But I just don't think the time is now. If after eighty or ninety years you guys want to admit to this stuff, give me a call and I'll join you, but not until then."

It was a powerful argument that convinced us to keep our mouths shut about our involvement.

We reached the town just after dusk. Most of the place had been built on a plain that sloped gently upward before erupting into three big hills. The buildings on the high ground were the only ones that weren't under water.

After beaching the canoes at the foot of one hill, we began walking up toward a large, wooden, one-story building from which a great deal of commo-tion was coming. It turned out that the building was the Town Hall and that the commotion was being caused by several hundred wild-eyed people who were demanding in savage, hysterical voices to know who was responsible for the flood. I didn't think it was a good place for us to be, and I suggested to Dave that we leave.

"We can't leave yet," he said, "because we've got to find out what they know. If we find out that they have an idea who they're looking for, and that they've got suspects who fit our descriptions, then we know we have to leave real fast and never come back and keep our mouths shut about this for all time. On the other hand, if we learn that they don't have any suspects, and don't have any idea who they're looking for, we can stop worrying and relax and not waste time running. If we relax we'll live longer. Besides, if they don't have any suspects we can stick around and maybe make some money by helping people clean up their houses when the water recedes. And if it doesn't, we can dive into abandoned homes and steal money and valuables. Either way, we've got to know what the story is. Remember, the truth shall set you free."

The meeting was as depressing as everything else in the area. Person after person got up on a stage before the crowd and detailed their losses. Some sobbed uncontrollably. Others remained straight-faced, and others laughed as they told of the misery and hardship the flood had caused. Everyone who spoke had lost their home and at least one family member. Many had lost their entire families, while others had only half the mouths to feed than they did before. All said that they doubted that they would ever recover, and all agreed that it was the worst disaster to ever hit them.

One Of Our Victims

If all those stories weren't depressing enough, the final victim, an old lady, told the shocked crowd that she had lost everything she had worked for and loved in seventy years of life, including her farm and every building and animal on it, her pet cat, husband of fifty years, life savings that she had hidden in a wall of the house, and her six adult children who had lived in the area and who had drowned. On top of that, she had lost her eyeglasses, so that now she couldn't see; her eye drops, which had to be taken every day to prevent blindness; her heart medicine; kidney pills, without which she would die in a few days; and her arthritis medicine, which kept her joints loose and enabled her to walk.

She had also broken an arm and a leg, both of which would probably have to be amputated, and she had broken her hip, which, even with arthritis medicine, would prevent her from ever walking again. But the biggest loss of all

269

for that poor woman was that of her mind. It was evident that she had lost that by the cheerful manner in which she recited her losses to the crowd. Yet when she had finished detailing her misfortune, the cheerfulness vanished and she sobbed, asked God why she had not been killed and then begged that her life be ended.

After a few minutes, several men helped the old lady off the stage. Then another guy, who I figured was the mayor or the town president, addressed the crowd, which was growing louder and angrier by the minute. He got the people even more worked up by reciting another list of horrors that had hit the valley's residents. They passed over the edge of madness when he demanded that the person or persons responsible for the flood by "hunted until eternity" and brought back to the town to answer to valley residents.

"We can, we must and we will find the people responsible for this disaster!" the mayor said before his voice was drowned out by a savage, barbaric scream that came in unison from every throat in the building but ours.

The roar degenerated from an in-unison shout to a deafening cacophony of voices screaming every

Ed Confesses

imaginable variation of the mayor's call that we be found. People pounded on tables, stomped their feet, turned over furniture, punched each other and smashed windows.

What happened next was even scarier, and something that I thought I'd never live to tell about. As the noise was dying down, Ed pushed his way through the crowd, climbed up onto the stage, grabbed a microphone and shouted:

"We did it! We did it! Me and my friends over there, we did it! We're responsible for this disaster. We broke the dam. We've perpetrated this crime against humanity. We deserve to be hanged. We deserve to be beaten to death and torn apart limb by limb. We're guilty! Do with us what you will!"

The room fell silent and several hundred pairs of eyes stared at Ed.

"Say it again!" someone demanded.

"We're the ones, me and my friends over there," Ed said, pointing to us, "who are responsible for the flood—the greatest disaster you've ever known. We broke the dam with sledgehammers because we wanted to drown a group of nose pickers. Then we threw the hammers into the water and drove away on our motorcycles. We caused the flood. We, and we alone, are responsible for this disaster. We have brought all of these troubles upon you good people and your good community."

It was useless to try to run. The room was too crowded. So we stood there and watched—thinking that every second would be our last—as the crowd silently spread to form a circle around us. It was the most terrible moment of my life. I imagined a hundred different ways they were going to kill us. I figured they would beat us with sticks or stone us, or tie big boulders around our bodies and throw us into the water, or worse, that they would rush us all at once, smother us with their bodies and trample us until we were blobs of bloody mush.

I turned to Dave, figuring he could find a way out of this one, but for the first time since I had known him he was a man without a solution.

"I guess we just die. It's only a matter of how," he said as he shot a death look at Ed when he returned from the stage. By that time the mayor had gotten back on the stage and was addressing the crowd.

"These, these are the people who broke the dam and caused the flood and caused you all of this suffering! What do you want to do with them?" he shouted. Not waiting for an answer, he continued:

"These are the people who took their sledgehammers and broke the dam which had been built to hold back the river and prevent it from flooding us every year! What should we do with them? These are the people who destroyed your homes, killed your relatives and sons and daughters and ruined your lives! What should we do with them?"

The crowd was silent, but not inactive, as the mayor spoke. They tightened the circle around us, moving themselves—and for us, certain death—closer and closer. The maddening silence was broken only by the mayor's words:

"These are the people who have perpetrated this crime against humanity. Edwards, these are the people who are responsible for killing your wife of thirty-seven years. What should we do with them? Fred Phipps, these are the men who destroyed your barn and killed every animal in it; who killed your infant daughter and paralyzed your wife. What should we do with them? Martha Grobis, these are the men who killed your husband, your children, your mother, your father, your aunt, your uncle, your cousins, your brothers, your sisters and left you as alone as a person can be! What should we do with them?"

The mob was nearly on us as the mayor prepared to finish his remarks.

"These are the people," he said, nearly hysterical by now, "who have brought this complete and everlasting disaster upon you! What do you want to do with them? The choice is yours. Tell me, what should we do with them?"

Just as he finished, the crowd was on us. Those people, hysterical by now—crazy by now—grabbed and clawed and screamed at us. There was nowhere to hide and nothing we could do. I gasped for air as dozens of arms grabbed for me. I prayed, for what I thought was my final time:

"Dear God, please make it painless, and forgive me my sins. Lord, please give me a better life the next time around and let me come back as a stinkbug."

Suddenly, I had some air. So did the other guys. The mob lifted us into the air and carried us around the room to the chants of "Hail them! Hail them! These men are our heroes!"

It was crazy. The room had erupted into happiness. Men laughed, shook our hands and "hoorayed" us. Women blew us kisses. Teenagers asked for our autographs, and children looked at us with admiring eyes. We were deposited on the stage next to the mayor and saluted with a deafening ovation. The mayor shook our hands and hugged and kissed us. When the noise died down, he addressed the crowd again.

"We have here the greatest heroes in the history of the town of Adversity and in the history of the Valley of the Adversairs. We're steeled to adversity!" he shouted to another thunderous ovation.

"Gentlemen," he said, turning to us. "By bringing this disaster upon us you have helped us steel ourselves to adversity! You have helped us to be better able to cope with life's problems, and you've helped us stiffen our backbones and build character and become better people. We thrive on adversity. We're steeled to it. We welcome it. It makes us better citizens. Thank you! Bless You!"

It was the most amazing thing I had ever heard. We had ruined these peoples' lives, killed hundreds of their relatives, and were considered heroes!

"Why are we heroes?" Ed asked meekly.

"Because by bringing this disaster to us, you've helped us better ourselves," the mayor said. "You've given us the opportunity to improve ourselves. That's the greatest gift of all. Let me explain. This is the town of Adversity, the Valley of the Adversairs, and we are known as Adversairs. We welcome adversity, tragedy, disaster, commotion, politics, noise, religion, the clergy and just about everything else that will disrupt and ruin our lives. We believe that suffering though adversity and disaster builds character, makes you tough and makes you a better person. This flood will make us tougher and better able to cope with the next disaster.

"We'll apply the lessons we've learned in this tragedy to the next one that comes along. The more we suffer, the stronger and wiser and the better we'll be. If we never had disasters we'd be weak, spineless people who would never be able to cope with disaster, let alone minor setbacks like acne, bad haircuts and unseasoned food. We here in Adversity are so steeled to adversity, and are so tough and strong, and so able to cope, that the death of family members doesn't cause us grief anymore. As a matter of fact, we're so strong that we welcome the death of loved ones so we can prove that we can take adversity. More than that, we hope that more and more of our relatives die, because it'll make us that much stronger. It's a sad day in this town when a disaster strikes and no one dies.

"You gentlemen—I should say you heroes—were out in the boats. I'm sure you came across some of our fellow citizens who were angry and depressed because the flood didn't hit them hard enough and didn't kill enough of their family members. But just the opposite, one of my good friends lost his whole family, and he's now one of the happiest men in the valley. Conversely, Martha Grobis, the elderly woman who is going to lose her arm and leg, wishes that she had been killed because that would be the ultimate in character-building bad luck. Maybe next time she'll get lucky and die.

"We haven't had a disaster around here in a long time. We're forever grateful to you for having given us the opportunity to steel ourselves. Thanks to you, we're stronger than we were a few days ago."

Chapter 53

The Town Of Adversity

After thanking us for destroying the town and its residents' lives, the mayor told us the history of Adversity and how the town got its name.

The place had been founded seventy years earlier by a small group of people who had grown tired of their factory jobs in the city and wanted to either farm or start their own businesses in the tranquil valley. It was originally named Hawkinsville, after Joe Hawkins, whose idea it was to leave the city and the factory jobs behind.

About two weeks after the group had finished building the thirty log cabins in which they were to live, the river, which was a mere one hundred feet from the buildings, overflowed its banks and washed away the houses and most of the peoples' personal belongings. Although it was a terrible disaster, the people knew that they had no choice but to rebuild. So, even before the water had receded, they went into the surrounding forest and began felling trees for new dwellings.

Hawkins and his fellow citizens were smart. Figuring that another flood would wash away the cabins as had the first, they built the new structures on stilts of tree trunks which they embedded deep into the ground. The new building technique proved to be a wise choice, because shortly after the new homes were completed, the river overflowed and flooded the valley again. But this time the buildings remained put and the town survived.

When the water receded, the people of Hawkinsville celebrated and congratulated themselves for their ability to learn and for their ingenuity. During the celebration, Hawkins told the others that they had learned some-thing from the first flood and that the disaster had made them better, smarter and stronger. He told them that nothing was more destructive than a flood, and that people who could survive one would have the strength of character to survive any disaster. He said that something positive could come out of any disaster, and urged them to incorporate that lesson into their personal constitu-tions. The townspeople agreed, and intoxicated by their success at having survived the second flood, as well as by generous amounts of cheap whiskey, they became cocky and began boasting that they could survive any calamity. One resident suggested that if they suffered enough tragedies they would become the strongest willed and smartest people on the earth. In a drunken roar, everybody agreed, and right then they changed the town's name to Adversity and adopted its official motto: "Steeled to Adversity." They also adopted as official policy the idea that disasters were good, and they thought of themselves as tough people.

More whiskey was consumed, and, near the end of the day, drunken supplications were made to a higher authority for a fresh catastrophe. The prayers were answered just a few minutes later when a cabin caught fire after a drunken resident broke a bottle of whiskey inside it and knocked over a lantern. A strong wind whipped the flames, and pretty soon every one of the new buildings was burning. Because everybody was drunk and unable to put out the fires, the blazes raged unchecked and the cabins were destroyed.

Undaunted by the third disaster, and filled with the idea that they were learning and getting stronger, the people went into the forest in the following days and felled more trees. Hawkins, not wanting to be caught off guard by another flood or fire, came up with what he considered a brilliant plan to make the town fireproof: The new cabins would be built on stilts in the river!

It's not necessary to waste words in describing what a disaster that was. The cabins never got built because the logs, and with them several townspeople, floated away when they were put into the water. Although the remaining people were depressed, Hawkins urged them to cheer up because they had learned that a cabin couldn't be built in the middle of a rushing river.

Before more trees could be cut, a tornado struck. The roaring black funnel lifted everyone into the air and deposited them on the ground one hundred and fifty miles away. Hawkins and the others spent the next month hiking through the dense forest back to the town. They cut down more trees upon their return, but they were unable to fashion the logs into shelters because a blizzard, and then a deep freeze hit, making it impossible for them to build homes.

Thinking it was just an early storm, Hawkins expressed little concern and didn't push the people to build even the flimsiest of shelters. Unfortunately for them, the blizzard was the first of a series of unrelenting storms that ravaged the area the entire winter. Without shelter or a steady supply of food, many people died. Those who lived suffered severe frostbite, which led to later amputations, and two men died because their brains froze. Several people were killed by wild animals. By the time spring came, only half of the original one hundred and forty townspeople were alive.

An earthquake swallowed half of those, and most of the others died later of starvation. The four people who were still alive a month later—Hawkins included—proclaimed the expedition the greatest success in the history of civilization, and, to make it even better than that, began to kill themselves one-by-one. Hawkins went first, and then two others followed. The remaining citizen was about to slit his own throat when a group of settlers arrived on the scene, seized the knife from his hand and scolded him for giving up on life. He, in turn, said that it was not cowardice that led him to the act, but the desire to become an even stronger willed person. He then related the history of the town to the newcomers and they agreed that adversity was a good thing.

After completing the history the mayor went on to tell us that the flood we had caused was especially welcome because the area had not suffered a major natural disaster since the dam had been built by the federal government five years earlier. Before the dam, the valley suffered ruinous floods every year, a situation that caused most residents to think that they had found heaven on earth.

The people howled in protest when the government announced that it was going to build the dam as part of a flood control project. Citizens wrote letters to their congressmen, senators and the president, staged protest marches in town and in the state capital and vowed armed resistance, all in an unsuccessful attempt to block the project.

During construction the citizens voted to move and to relocate the town to an area where natural disasters—especially floods—occurred on a regular basis. The plans were made and the move was about to begin when a village youth suggested that the fact that they would no longer be the victims of regular floods would be a disaster in itself because they would be denied character-building catastrophes and the opportunity to steel themselves even further.

The boy was proclaimed a genius and the move was canceled. When, in the following spring, the flood didn't come as it had done every spring for the previous seventy years, the Adversairs were initially depressed. However, the fact that they were going through a monumental disaster by not being flooded out cheered them, and they survived that first floodless year.

The second year was harder to take, and the Adversairs went to church every day and prayed for trouble. The prayers went unanswered, and after living through two years without mayhem, the people became mighty uneasy.

After the third spring without a flood, the people were so upset that they decided to create their own misfortunes. They burned each other's homes, slaughtered one another's livestock, killed each other's relatives and tried to make life as unhappy and as unpleasant for each other as possible.

The self-inflicted tragedies satisfied them at first, but the Adversairs soon began to feel empty and dissatisfied over the artificial troubles. They realized that the man-made mayhem could not be as fulfilling as a natural disaster. By the fourth year the Adversairs were a dull, lifeless and directionless bunch whose enthusiasm for life had been drained and whose brains had been numbed and rotted by a trouble-free existence. They had stopped burning down one another's homes, had stopped praying for disasters, and had become resigned to the horrible reality that they might never deal with adversity again. Even the thought that their lives were now one big disaster could not cheer them up.

By the fifth year they were so dispirited, depressed, defeated and broken that they decided to leave the area and return to the city to see if the factory jobs the town's original founders left behind seventy years earlier were still open. They were beginning to move out on the day we smashed the dam. So, the mayor said, by breaking the dam, we had delivered the people from the painful, sad and humiliating trip back to the city and the miserable existence they would have led by working in the factories. And because we had saved them from that horrible life, we were honored as heroes and were made honorary Adversairs.

Dave told the mayor about the nose pickers and how it had come that we had destroyed the dam. The mayor replied that the nose pickers had once invaded Adversity in an attempt to draft townspeople into their association. The Adversairs thought the club was disgusting and they attacked the nose pickers and drove them from the town. That night, however, the nose pickers sneaked back in and smeared snots all over the streets, homes and shops.

The Adversairs were sickened when they awoke and saw what had been done, and they considered it a great disaster to have had their streets and homes made slimy with nose mucus. But, for the first time in their

The Battle Raged

history, the Adversairs did not welcome tragedy. They hated what the nose pickers had done, formed a militia and marched out to do battle with those enemies of good personal hygiene.

The nose pickers had no weapons, and fought by picking their noses and flicking boogers at the advancing Adversairs. The townspeople were shocked by the barbaric tactics, but fought back with clubs, spears, guns and rocks. Many an enemy were killed, and around noon, the nose pickers took refuge in the dense forest outside the town.

Fearing that they could not hold out forever and that they'd all be killed, the nose pickers proposed a treaty. The Adversairs, who felt they would be permanently contaminated if hit by more snots, agreed to the terms, which said that the nose pickers could use the state park once a year for their picnic, but that they could not step outside the park nor try to recruit members in the valley.

Thus, not only were we praised for having busted the dam, but we were cheered for having killed the nose pickers as well.

The day could not have turned out better for us. We were welcomed as heroes, given an impromptu parade in rowboats through the town's darkened and flooded streets, and honored with a meager but delicious meal back at the hall.

CHAPTER 54

Success In Adversity

The next few weeks were even better. The valley dried, the villagers were able to bring in food from the outside, and we were the guests at nightly banquets held in our honor. Our stay in the area, which lasted for many months, turned out to be profitable in other ways too.

Knowing that the Adversairs had to rebuild their homes, businesses, barns and sheds, we set up shop as building contractors and started erecting overpriced buildings for which we took only cash in advance as payment. Because we had no construction experience, everything we built fell down.

Toasted At Nightly Banquets

Our first barn collapsed in front of us, and the farmer who had paid us cash in advance for it, just a few minutes after completion. The farmer was a big, powerful man who seemed unhappy with life and who could have easily killed us with his bare hands. He stared at the rubble for a while and looked concerned. Then he stroked his chin as if pondering how to torture us, and just when I thought he would lunge at us, he erupted into roaring laughter and danced around like he was the happiest man on earth.

When he calmed down he told us that this new tragedy would make him an even stronger and better person, and that he was as happy as could be. We said there was no guarantee on the work, and that if he wanted the barn rebuilt he'd have to pay us cash up front, just like before.

He happily paid us again and we rebuilt the barn. But just as before, it fell apart. I thought the farmer would kill us for sure this time, but he didn't. In fact, he seemed happier. He looked at us with sparkling eyes that seemed to say that we were his only friends on the planet, and then muttered something about how his backbone was stiffening and how his character was growing.

The farmer cheerfully handed us another large sum of money for a third try at building a barn. We rebuilt it again, and because we were learning more and more about construction from our mistakes, the third barn stood for a half an hour before it collapsed. The farmer was now happier than the two previous times combined. He laughed and danced wildly for nearly an hour while mumbling that he could feel himself being steeled. When he had calmed down enough, he telephoned a friend to brag about his "great misfortune."

We kept rebuilding the barn under the same conditions—cash money in advance—and it kept falling down. With every collapse, the farmer got happier and happier, so that by the seventh one, he was delirious with joy. It was the craziest thing I had ever seen. He threw himself on the ground and began bouncing around while shouting, "I'm steeled! I'm steeled!" He was still acting like that several hours later, so we called an insane asylum and had him taken away.

The Poor Man Was Steeled

We pocketed enough cash from just that one farmer to support ourselves on the road for a couple of years. When you multiply that by the thousands of other buildings we put up under the same conditions—cash in advance and no guarantee for the slipshod work—you realize that we made a fortune in the construction business.

Being greedy types, we weren't satisfied with our success in the construction field, so we opened several other businesses, all of which, because we had no experience, expertise or talent in the area, were great successes.

Our auto repair shop was successful after word got around that the first car we repaired blew up as it was being driven out the door. We acted like real auto mechanics and overcharged for our work, did unnecessary, sloppy and incomplete jobs, and sabotaged vehicles so that they broke down after they left the shop. Every vehicle we "repaired" was back in the shop five or six times in the space of a few weeks.

A Successful Auto Repair Shop

The Adversairs thought our shop was the greatest thing that had ever happened to the town because it provided a fresh disaster every day. After a couple of months, every vehicle in the valley was ruined, and the Adversairs were blissfully happy.

Figuring that we could make them even happier, and ourselves richer, we opened a law office. Like real lawyers, we filed lawsuits for no reason other than to pad our wallets. Disputes that easily could have been settled with five minutes of conversation and handshakes between the parties wound up in court when they were brought to us. We encouraged people to sue their friends, neighbors and relatives, and we walked around town acting like we were the most important people on earth. Within a few weeks, every Adversair had filed a lawsuit against every other Adversair. Some even sued themselves. They all faced financial ruin from excessive court judgments, and were thrilled at the prospect.

Many of our clients won large monetary judgments from their friends, and the fact that we took ninety-eight percent of the money as fees, thrilled them even more. We practiced criminal law, and every person we defended wound up with a long prison term, a situation that made the Adversairs even happier.

After that we went into the insurance business and sold the unsuspecting Adversairs bank account-busting policies they would never need. Then, whenever anybody filed a claim to collect on the policy, we refused to pay up, a situation that sent the Adversairs into ecstasy.

We went into the financial consulting business, got everyone to give us their life's savings, pocketed hefty commissions and put the remaining money into bad investments. When we announced that everything had been lost, the people put on a carnival and praised our investment instincts and strategies.

We set up a private firefighting firm and charged expensive weekly rates for the service. Although we had no firefighting skills, no one ever found out because we never got to any fire before the building was destroyed. We always got out of the station quickly enough when the call came in, but we didn't know our way around the area, and thus got lost on every run. We didn't put out one fire or save a single building. The Adversairs said we were the best firefighters they had ever had.

We became police officers who never arrested one crook or prevented a single crime, and although we routinely kicked, clubbed and jailed innocent people, we were regarded as law enforcement visionaries.

Our fertilizer business pleased the Adversairs because our first batch, and every one thereafter, was a mixture of salt and poisonous chemicals that killed crops and ruined the land forever.

The University of Ignorance we opened was a huge hit. Rather than teaching the Adversairs the subjects they signed up and paid big money for, we acted like the professors we had had in school and spent class hours spouting our own political views and filling their heads with Marxist and anti-American philosophies. Students who disagreed with us flunked, while those pathetic losers who nodded their heads affirmatively at our every word, passed. Either way, no one learned a thing, and our degrees were worthless. But the Adversairs were happy.

Remembering our experience with Paulette, Ned and the others at the newspaper, we started a paper. Our stories were biased, and we libeled everyone in town. We practiced nepotism by hiring only our friends and their relatives, but we wrote editorials day after day blasting politicians and other public officials for doing the same. We railed against greed while charging our advertisers outrageously high prices, paying our employees low wages and keeping our profit margins at obscene, double-digit levels; championed in print the cause of free speech, but fired employees when they expressed views that differed from ours; boldly proclaimed the mistakes of others in big headlines and front-page stories, but never printed a retraction when we made a factual error; said we were the paper of the people, but wrote stories we thought would impress other journalists and win awards; tried to run politicians out of office, but cried oppression and censorship when they urged people not to buy our paper; denounced power politics by public officials, but schemed unceasingly against each other in the office; and generally acted like immature, insecure, spoiled brats. Our papers often consisted of blank pages, and yet the Adversairs bought them in record numbers and we made a fortune in that venture.

We opened a hospital in which no one ever got well, a restaurant that served rancid food, an extermination business that never killed a single bug, a taxi cab company whose drivers were permanently lost, an airline that never had any flights, and many other businesses. Throughout all of this, the Adversairs smiled and said they were fortunate, because each time they lost money and were victimized by one of our schemes, they were growing mentally and were becoming steeled, and they implored us to enter into new ventures.

Chapter 55

Botany Gone Mad

We were sitting around making poison in our fertilizer factory one day when Dave said he had noticed in the rival newspaper that four or five Adversairs were reported missing each day. He thought it was an unusually large number, and said he wanted to find out how and why so many people could be missing in such a small town, and why no one seemed to care. The paper never reported that any of the missing people had been found. In fact, no follow-up stories were ever done on the initial missing person reports.

"It seems a little goofy, but knowing these people, I suppose it's normal," he said. "Anyway, I want to find out where all these people are going. People who are missing are people who ain't putting money into our pockets."

Four people were reported missing in that day's edition. The column contained a brief biography of each. The items read:

"Joseph A. Pernicki, 33, of 1303 N. St. Louis Dr. A fine man, wonderful gentleman and model Adversair who, in his life, had been steeled a million times over. His prayers were answered last night when he was abducted while trying to make the roof of his house fall on his head. (MG)

"Mary B. Conroy, 27, of the Conroy Farm, Rural Route #3. She was spirited away last night while teaching her pre-school children to play with loaded guns, matches and gasoline. Her children regret that the lesson was never finished. (MG)

"Nelson "Ned" Baker Jr. III, 12, of his mother's house at 2514 N. Avers. He was kidnapped last night while attempting to choke his three-year-old brother by feeding the toddler chicken bones. (MG)

"Rev. George Z. Dackson, 52, of the Church of Eternal Agony, who disappeared last night while playing "Adam and Eve" with his wife and trying to remove several of her ribs. (MG)

"They were all steeled, and we pray that the abductions will temper them even further."

Dave figured that foul play was involved and vowed to unravel the mystery, even if it took "years, decades, centuries or millenniums."

We shut down the fertilizer factory for the day, an act that disappointed the farmers whose fields we hadn't yet poisoned, and raced off to the police station to get more background material on the victims in an effort to establish clues as to who had taken them.

We found the police chief and grilled him for several hours about the biographies and habits of the four. When he asked us why we wanted to know, Dave answered: "Because I'm the detectingest of the detectives and I'm going to find out who stole those people, even if it takes me a billion years. I want answers."

"I don't think it'll take you that long," the chief said. "I can tell you right now who took them if you want, or then again, I suppose I can wait several years if you prefer. I don't care. Either way is fine with me."

Dave was disappointed. "This would be a lot better story, a lot better caper, if it takes a billion years to figure out. I mean, who but the greatest, most persistent detective would follow a case that long?"

"True, I suppose. But then again, a detective who took that long to solve such an easy case might be regarded as an idiot. I mean, this ain't too difficult."

"Well then, just tell us now. Who took them?"

The chief grabbed the newspaper from Dave's hand and pointed to the "MG" at the end of each item in the Missing Persons column.

"That's who took them," he said. "It tells you right there in the paper. It don't take no investigation. The MG took them. That's the Mad Gardener. It's right here in the paper."

"Who or what is the Mad Gardener?"

"He's the one who kidnaps people. He kidnaps them, takes them to his farm and plants them. I think he got the idea from a science fiction book. Either that or he's crazy. Anyway, he takes them and plants them," the chief said, acting as if what he had just told us was an insignificant, normal, everyday occurrence.

The chief gave us directions to a remote part of the valley where the Mad Gardener's farm was located, and we set out for it. Heeding the chief's advice to be careful, lest we fall into the Mad Gardener's hands, we sneaked up to his farm through an adjoining patch of woods.

A sight that would make even Satan vomit greeted us at the edge of the Mad Gardener's small field. Sticking out of the ground were scores of bleached human and animal skeletons, as well as assorted bones and skulls, and human and animal bodies in various stages of life and decomposition. Near a small cabin, which we later learned was the Mad Gardener's home, were twenty live people buried up to their waists.

We rushed forward, shouted the names of the four who were reported missing in the paper, and received a response. Dave found a shovel and furiously began digging the twelve-year-old out of the ground.

The Mad Gardener's Place

"Whatever are you doing, kind sir?" the youth asked in a cheerful voice.

"I'm digging you out and saving your life."

"Oh, that's unfortunate. I thought you were going to dig a hole and join us."

The remark stunned us, and before we could recover our senses, several of the others who were buried, but still alive, shouted that rather than dig the boy out, we should dig holes and "plant" ourselves.

Then, an insane looking man slunk out of the cabin, made gurgling noises and rushed at us. But before he could grab us, Dave slammed him in the knees with the shovel and knocked him to the ground. As Dave put it, the guy was the "ugliest of the ugly and the despicablest of the despicable."

The guy smelled worse than a barnyard, had one tooth; six fingers—three on each hand; one foot, no eyebrows; shoulder length, black, greasy hair; and four big warts,—one each on his forehead, chin and both cheeks—which would have formed a diamond if connected with lines. He wore a dirty, red plaid flannel shirt with no buttons and one sleeve, and a pair of black pants which he said had been white several years ago. He was the Mad Gardener!

Dave held him in abeyance with the shovel, demanded to know his story, and got this reply:

"I'm the Mad Gardener, or the gardener who's mad, or the Mad Mad, or the Gardener Gardener, or whatever you want to call me. These are my plants. I kidnap people and plant them because I like to watch things grow. I'd like to watch you gentlemen grow, too. Would you like me to watch you grow? Growth is good. I got real good soil here—composted and everything. You'll grow real big here."

It was difficult for us, what with the smell and horror of the scene, but we listened as he ranted for more than an hour and told us his story.

As a youth he loved to garden, and he planted as many varieties of flowers and vegetables as possible on the tiny plot that his parents had set aside for him on their small farm. Although he had asked several times for permission to enlarge the plot so he could grow more vegetables, his parents refused, thinking that he would lose his zeal for botany with age, and that it was more important to grow cash crops such as corn and wheat, rather than flowers and hobby vegetables.

However, rather than decrease with age, the young man's zeal and love of botany increased exponentially. Although his high school offered no formal classes in the subject, he joined several gardening clubs and even organized his own botany club.

In college he studied the subject with such vigor and dedication that his professors were convinced that he would be the field's next genius and would provide stunning breakthroughs in plant research and develop so many super-productive varieties that hunger would be eliminated from the planet.

During his freshman year in college the gardener's small experimental tract at school, and the one on his parents' farm, were hailed as the most productive in the world. By the end of his sophomore year he had surpassed his professors in terms of knowledge of botany and agriculture, and by the end of his junior year, nations were offering him jobs as their agricultural ministers. By this time the word on him was not that he would someday become a genius, but of how many times over he had already become one.

During this time of his great accomplishments and worldwide acclaim, the young man, who had always been possessed of an unbreakable devotion and love of his parents and the farm, had repeatedly asked for permission to expand his small garden on the farm. But unfortunately for him—and eventually for them—the parents refused, citing the fact that cash crops, and not an experimental agricultural station, was what were needed to support the family and to pay for the remainder of the young man's college education.

Before the gardener had finished his senior year he had reached such a level of knowledge in the subject that the world had exhausted its supply of praise and awards to describe and honor his genius. The world's former hungry masses were growing fat and heavy thanks to the new plant varieties he developed, and all nations claimed him as a national hero. The gardener himself, flush with the satisfaction and knowledge that he had helped the human race as no other had helped it before, was as close to perfect happiness as any human being could possibly have been. The only speck of dissatisfaction, the only thing that prevented his spirit from shining blindingly and perfectly bright with bliss and satisfaction, was the fact that even after he had graduated and was considered the greatest botanist in the history of civilization, his parents still wouldn't let him expand his plot on the farm.

The gardener, although satisfied with himself for having eliminated hunger on earth, felt he was compelled and duty-bound to look beyond the planet and into the infinite vastness of space to try to solve the hunger problems for the billions and trillions that might someday be discovered in other worlds. He wanted to solve the hunger problem forever and for all time and for any place and anywhere that ever did or ever would exist. He went to work, and in just a few years had so improved his already super-productive varieties that it was feared the world could become so heavy with food that it might fall out of its orbit. Grain silos overflowed. New ones were built, and they too overflowed. Food was so cheap that even poor people were eating healthy diets. Riots ceased because the poor and underprivileged were full and satisfied. There was so much food that plans were drawn up for huge spaceships in which to rocket food surpluses off to other planets. Despite this incredible success, though, the gardener was still unhappy. Something else was bothering him. He wanted to teach at a university so that he could pass his knowledge on to others. He wanted every botanist to develop as many new, super-productive plant varieties as he had. But he knew from the words that had haunted him since the first time, when as a junior in college he had dreamed of teaching, that he never would and never could teach, unless, in the words of his college advisor, he had a master's degree.

The words bounced around in his head like a rubber ball on stimulants: "You ain't going anywhere without that degree, fella. If you want to teach, you've got to have a master's."

Thinking that his expertise, genius and reputation as the greatest botanist ever in the history of history, in other words, that his work experience might be accepted in lieu of a master's degree, the gardener sent his resume to thousands of universities and colleges in the hopes of landing a teaching job. The most prestigious universities and the smallest community colleges all replied, saying that although they appreciated that he had eliminated hunger on earth and was the greatest botanist of all time, he could not teach botany at the college level unless he had a master's degree.

Depressed, but not defeated, the gardener sent his resume to nurseries and plant stores, hoping that one would hire him to give talks about plants and gardening to customers on weekends. Every reply was the same: He couldn't teach or lecture without a master's degree.

Next he sent his resumes to public school districts, hoping to get a job teaching second-graders about plants and botany. The reply letters were even harsher: The teacher's unions wouldn't let anybody teach the second grade, not even the world's greatest botanist, unless he had a Ph.D. in education.

Determined to fulfill his dream of teaching, the gardener, the man whose work had put ample amounts of delicious and nutritious food into every human belly, went back to school to get a master's degree. To get the degree, though, he needed to conduct original research. To do that research and to properly impress his professors that he was indeed doing the required original research, the gardener felt that he needed the expanded plot on the family farm so that it would compliment the land he was given use of at the university.

But the young man's mother, perhaps not understanding the depth of her son's convictions, his insatiable desire to eliminate hunger for every life form, whether it was on earth or on some distant comet, and his dream of some day teaching botany, denied the request for the extra space. Times were bad, she said, and although research was a noble thing, it couldn't pay the bills, and cash crops were what the family needed just then. And if research was what the son wanted, she said, the dirt on which to conduct it would have to come from the university.

But all was not bad, for the gardener's mother also said that there was *one* circumstance under which she would grant the request for an expanded plot.

The gardener, his ears cocked and his heart beating with a joyous speed, listened for the one request that he was determined to instantly fulfill and win himself untainted happiness. The mother, who had always tried to do the right thing, turned to her son—her genius son, the man who had created the most productive crops on earth and who had helped eliminate hunger from the planet—and said calmly:

"Get a job. Bring in some money and help pay your tuition bill and you can grow as much as you want. Just get a job."

Those words devastated the gardener because he knew that no matter how much he tried, technically, he could never fulfill the requirement. A job, he thought, was something one did strictly for money, and not because one enjoyed it. It was implausible that he accept a position outside of his field, and thus, any position he got growing food couldn't be considered work, only joy. Technically, he could never get a job, and so he couldn't fulfill his mother's request.

The gardener argued. He pointed out that with an expanded plot he'd be able to grow more food than the family could ever need, with enough left over to sell at a hefty profit. The mother remained unconvinced, and the gardener returned to the university to conduct his research.

But he was a changed man. And although he continued to make astonishing breakthroughs in plant development and greater food production, he fell short of his goal of teaching botany. He had trouble with the master's degree course work and required papers and thesis. Well, sort of. The trouble wasn't really his, it was his professors' and advisors' trouble. In his papers and thesis, the gardener often quoted himself and his previous work. His professors and advisors were furious at that and they contemptuously accused him of plagiarizing the greatest botanist of all time. When he protested that he had plagiarized himself, the professors and advisors said that plagiarism in any form was against university rules, and so he was kicked out of the master's degree program.

Denied his dream of being able to teach, and steeped in a boundless unhappiness and an all-consuming bitterness, the gardener blamed his defeat on his never being allowed to expand his small garden on the family farm. He brooded and brooded and brooded some more, and one day he finally snapped, and in a moment of unmitigated rage, he stormed over to the farm, dragged his parents out of the house and planted the terrified couple shoulder deep in a section of the farm he had coveted for his expanded garden but had never received.

The gardener remained in that hateful state for several days, dancing around his parents while shouting bad jokes and Latin plant names at them, and taunting them for never having allowed him to expand his garden.

By the fifth day he had calmed down enough to speak to his exhausted, starving, dehydrated and hysterical parents. They told him that the five days in the ground had made them realize that they had erred in not letting him expand his garden, and they said they would turn the farm over to him, and they begged for forgiveness and mercy.

The gardener, now fully in control of himself, was engulfed by a sense of shame. He granted the forgiveness and mercy, asked the same for himself, apologized profusely and vowed to never again lose control. As he began

digging his parents out of the ground, the three, in an attempt to smooth over the misunderstanding, began joking with each other. The gardener told a few jokes, his mother told one, and finally, his father, trying to make light of the situation, said:

"Son, as a matter of fact, I think we ought to be grateful for what you did. We recognized we were wrong. Five days in the dirt did that to us. In a way, our brains expanded—they grew—our brains grew while we were in the dirt."

The gardener, intrigued and seized by a new spirit of investigation over the possibilities of growing human brains in dirt, quickly covered his parents back up with soil and watered them. They remained there for several weeks, during which time the gardener watered them daily and measured their heads.

After his parents died, the gardener's mental and physical state deteriorated, and he began to prey on the Adversairs, who, always being on the lookout for a decent tragedy, happily allowed themselves to be kidnapped, planted and killed.

The gardener, although mentally disturbed, had enough control over his mind to realize that none of the peoples' brains ever grew. In fact, he realized that they died, and he became even crazier, or as he put it, "seized" by the determination to grow some part of the human body. Thus he began chopping off peoples' arms and legs and planting the individual limbs.

Possessed by this new determination, he severed his foot, four of his fingers, one ear and half of the other, pulled out most of his teeth and ripped out his eyebrows hair by hair and planted them. After a while he became convinced that peoples' bodies drained energy away from their heads and prevented growth in the ground. His solution to that was to chop peoples' heads off and plant them.

We had been enraged by many of the things we had seen on the trip up to then, but nothing equaled the meanness we felt toward the Mad Gardener. Dave was nearly speechless with hate for the man, but he did manage to stammer out this question:

"Why, why, you piece of evil scum? Why didn't you put them in a big flower pot in the house or a greenhouse or something? Why did you have to kill them?"

The question went unanswered. The gardener did eventually acknowledge that planting his parents and the others was not a nice thing to have done.

Dave was about to beat him bloody with the shovel when Ed suggested to the gardener that he reform, pay his debt to society for the plantings, and eventually resume his research.

"It's not right to waste such a brilliant mind. Though you've done wrong, you can still do good. You can still help the human race. You can develop new plants and help eliminate hunger, even in animals and insects," Ed said.

The gardener's eyes sparkled at the suggestion.

"I would love to do it! I will pay my debt to society!" he said. "I will cleanse my mind, and then I will pay society interest on that debt by developing new and outstanding crops which will feed all of life everywhere forever and for all time, whether it be a Martian, snake, dog, bug or germ. I will make sure that even microbes get a balanced diet! I can and I will do it!

"I can do the research right here. My parents, unbeknownst to me at the time, had stockpiled several gold bars which they had obtained by melting down gold my father had mined on the farm. Their value is high enough to allow me to live a life of luxury for the rest of my days. Thank you, kind sir. You've given me the inspiration I have needed. I will reform and return to my field of brilliance and help feed the bugs, insects and microbes."

The seventeen "planted" Adversairs cheered the gardener and offered him their encouragement. Ed giggled uncontrollably. That would have settled the matter were it not for Dave, who suggested to the gardener that he immediately start fortifying his brain so it would be in shape by the time he resumed his research.

The gardener agreed that it was a sound idea and accepted Dave's suggestion that he purchase a bag of our Super Brain Food Fertilizer. Dave gave him the "Brain Food," which of course was the same poison we had been selling to everyone else in the valley, and he ate several handfuls of it and dropped dead on the spot. We took the gold bars from his house and had a good laugh.

We Had A Good Laugh

Chapter 56

A Strange Goodbye

The Adversairs protested when we started digging them out and told them that they would be returned home to their families. We were, they said, depriving them of character building tragedy they so desperately needed to experience. But we reminded them that it would be an even greater tragedy if they were denied—and they were being denied—the opportunity to suffer through the disaster of being planted and killed. They accepted that logic and walked away happier than they would have been than if they had died.

Growing Lazy In Adversity

Although we had always felt that we could have stayed in Adversity for the rest of our lives and devised new schemes to make money, after about eight months there we realized it was time to leave. Our schemes had made enough money so that each of us could live lavishly without ever having to work again. We had wanted to stay and make even more money, but the Adversair mentality was beginning to infect us, and we realized that if we stayed we might become exactly like them and lose our money.

We had become careless in our personal affairs and work habits, and had begun to suffer a growing number of injuries, though none of them serious. At first we were angry with ourselves for being careless, but as time went on we got a certain thrill out of being injured. As time passed we began hoping for more serious injuries. One day, as a joke, Dave set fire to one of our shops. We laughed and danced with joy as it burned to the ground, but when the last ember had finally stopped smoldering, we realized that the Adversairs' brand of insanity had infected us. Dave summed up the situation:

"You hang around with crazy people long enough, you go crazy yourself."

Going crazy and turning into Adversairs was something we didn't want, so the decision was made to leave while our brains were still normal and we were still good citizens. We considered not telling anyone about our decision and just driving away in the middle of the night, but Dave said the idea lacked class and that we deserved a big celebration and departure banquet.

The announcement that we were leaving stunned and saddened those people. Petition drives imploring us to stay were started, and the mayor and City Council passed an ordinance that declared us town treasures and barred us from leaving. The ordinance read:

"Whereas, the good citizens of Adversity and the Valley of the Adversairs desire to steel themselves and build character and stiffen their backbone, and,

"Whereas, to accomplish this wonderful and noble goal requires the suffering of tragedy and disasters by said citizens, and,

"Whereas the four motorcycle riders and organizers of bad and disastrous schemes, to wit: Dennis, Dave, Phil and Ed, have visited upon our Valley superb and wonderful disasters, to wit: floods, death, poisoned ground, ruined vehicles, unsound structures, unnecessary lawsuits, rampant crime, overpriced insurance policies, a college of ignorance and the death of the Mad Gardener, and,

"Whereas these monumental disasters have visited great pain and suffering and loss and extreme mental anguish on the good citizens of the Valley, and,

"Whereas, the pain and suffering and anguish has caused said citizens to become steeled to adversity,

"This august body correctly and forthwithly concludes that the Disastrous Four provide a constant source of mishap and disaster for the citizens, and,

"Whereas, the character building and steeling of the citizens is directly proportional to the mayhem and mischief provided by the Disastrous Four, and,

"Whereas, the departure of the Disastrous Four would mean a loss of tragedies and a corresponding loss of character building and steeling of said good citizens,

"This body concludes that the Disastrous Four constitute Town and Valley Treasures, and,

"Whereas, it would be foolish and unwise for a political subdivision to disregard its Treasures, this body declares the Disastrous Four to be Public Treasures of the Town of Adversity.

"This being so, it is hereby declared that no Public Treasure shall be allowed to leave the Valley, and,

"Whereas, the Disastrous Four are Treasures, they are not allowed to leave Adversity. Violation of this ordinance is punishable by death.

"It is thuswith, heretofore, so forth and maybe so, so ordered."

The second the ordinance was signed we filed a lawsuit challenging it on the grounds that it violated our civil rights. Being the shrewd, make-believe lawyers that we were, our damage request asked for the total assets and lives of every resident of Adversity.

We were granted an emergency hearing, and the judge said that our complaint had no basis in law. He was about to dismiss the lawsuit when Dave suggested that our request for damages, if granted, would constitute the greatest disaster in the Valley's history.

Being an Adversair, the judge's eyes sparkled, and he agreed to hold hearings on the case in the future. However, citing the fact that the court system had become bogged down by the thousands of frivolous lawsuits we had filed, the judge said he wouldn't be able to hold the hearing for at least twenty years.

That was too long for us to wait, so we took another course of action. Dave, in a public speech, convinced the Adversairs that our leaving would be a greater disaster than all of the small ones we could ever work up because it would mean no more disasters, and thus, no steeling and character building. That, Dave said, would be a disaster they would certainly want to suffer.

The Adversairs agreed and gave us permission to leave.

Our final day in town was one of the most memorable of our lives and one that brought tears to my eyes. Beginning at six in the morning, a celebration in our honor, including carnivals, food, games, speeches and every valley resident, began. We were the subjects of hundreds of speeches, and words of praise and adulation for us issued forth from every mouth.

The speeches were the only normal thing about the event. The games were, to put it mildly, unorthodox. Arson contests were held to see who could burn down the most buildings in a given period of time. Contestants went about the job with a joyous zeal, as the first-place prize was the right to have one's own home or business torched.

As smoke blackened the sky and blotted out the sun, amateur marksmen began shooting high-powered rifles at distant wooden targets that were surrounded by people who were hoping to get hit by stray bullets. The winner of that contest was the person who suffered the severest wound or who died. While people were collapsing from bullet wounds, a separate contest was held for ambulance drivers, the first-place prize going to the driver who arrived on the scene of the shooting last.

Youths armed with degrees in law enforcement from our college were given sledgehammers, generous amounts of whiskey and the order to keep the peace and not let anybody push them around. Many law-abiding citizens were hammered that day, making it a disaster to have poorly trained and drunken youths act as police officers.

At lunch time, the people ate quickly, hoping that their meal would be the one laced with poison. The first-place prize for that contest was instant death.

After lunch we were honored with more speeches and an act that left me stunned. Everyone who had been adversely affected by one of our money-making schemes brought forth evidence of the fact and laid it in front of our table as a "Thank You" offering.

Death certificates, preserved, amputated limbs, coffins, bankruptcy petitions, sections of collapsed houses and barns, ruined vehicles, certificates of ignorance, buckets of poisoned soil, ruined crops and numerous other pieces of evidence of the grief our schemes had caused were laid before us. By the afternoon's end, every valley resident had put something down. The Adversairs cheered us wildly.

Finally, in the early evening, the mayor gave a speech in which he said we were the greatest thing that had ever happened to Adversity and to the Valley of the Adversairs, and he thanked us for our services and contributions.

"Will you all—The Disastrous Four—" the mayor said, turning to

Strange Contests

us, "will you return someday and visit upon us great and unbearable disasters? Disasters that help us build strength and character! Disasters that steel us to adversity!"

We promised that and more. The federal government had already begun rebuilding the dam, a situation that deeply depressed the Adversairs. Dave said they could fully expect the rebuilt dam to be smashed to pieces in the future, and he promised that we would return someday to either burn the town and valley to the ground, or to actively pursue our lawsuit.

The crowd cheered wildly and then gathered for several blocks along both sides of the main street that were to take on our drive out of town. We stepped down from the stage that had been built in the town square for the celebration, packed our bikes, making especially sure to secure the numerous money bags we had, shook the mayor's hand, put on our helmets, started the bikes, and watched as the mayor stepped back onto the stage to make one final statement.

"We love you," he said in a trembling and tearful voice. "Although we want you to stay forever, we realize that we cannot make you do so. So the next best thing we can do is wish you what we would wish for ourselves, and try our best to make that wish come true. And that wish is—"

Anticipating the mayor's final words, we slammed the bikes into gear and began riding slowly forward through the throngs of people who had lined both sides of the street.

"And that wish is," the mayor continued, "have a lousy trip! May your journey be filled with disaster and tragedy! So long!"

As the mayor finished, we were met with a deafening chorus of "Have a lousy trip!" from the crowd, and we were bombarded with bricks, rocks, bottles, vegetables, hammers, and just about anything else the Adversairs could throw at us. Whenever we tried to speed up, the crowd surged and tried to knock us off our bikes, all the while shouting, "Have a lousy trip!"

Huge boulders and pieces of furniture were thrown into the street in front of us in an effort to block our path. People tried to smash our legs with crowbars, and children threw themselves in front of our bikes, hoping we would run them over. People beat our helmets with hammers and tried to smash our hands with rocks. Attack dogs were set after us. Ropes and wires were stretched neck level across the street. Sewers and manholes were left uncovered. Broken glass and sharp tacks were spilled in front of us, and cars were sent down the street at us in an effort to run us over. It was a touching outpouring of emotion. I never knew they liked us that much!

It took us nearly an hour to run that gauntlet. When we finally got through we were battered and bruised, but to the disappointment of the Adversairs, each still in one piece. At the town limits we turned around, waved goodbye, speeded up and left the mob and its missiles behind.

We stopped on a hill a half a mile from town and looked back on Adversity, which was still shrouded in a smoky haze from the work the arson contestants had done. The crowd had begun to dissipate, but many of the people were still waving at us. Some, their desire to do us a kindness and help us have a lousy trip apparently unspent, were still throwing things in our direction. And, as far away as they were, we could still hear their shouts and screams.

Dave took off his helmet, wiped the crud that had gotten through it off his face, grabbed a handful of twenty-dollar bills out of a money bag, smelled them, beamed with satisfaction and said:

"You know, I'm going to miss those people."

Phil, Ed and I said the same, and we all had a big laugh. Dave put his helmet back on and stuffed the money back into the bag. Then we slammed the bikes into gear and drove away.

End of Book Two

Back On The Road

It's still not over. Dennis and Dave a long way to go on this nutty adventure. Will Dennis *ever* realize that Shirley was a goof? Will Dave ever admit to a mistake? Will these two ever stop traveling and live normal lives? Find out in Volume Three of *I Got Stinky Feet*. Watch for it. In the meantime, you can contact Dennis at: f.brilliant@yahoo.com

Dennis Domrzalski is an author, reporter, and columnist. His best known talent is helping everyone he meets come to grips with their own glaring shortcomings. He lives in Albuquerque, New Mexico.